TALES OF KAIATAN

A SECONDARY WORLD FANTASY COLLECTION

UNEXPECTED HEROES
BOOK 5

MARTY C. LEE

Bookaholics Press

Books by Marty C. Lee

Unexpected Heroes series

Wind of Choice

Seed of War

Wave of Dreams

Spark of Intrigue

Tales of Kaiatan

Legends of Kaiatan

Nobody's Revenge (novella 0.9)

The Cat's Fortune (a Legends novella)

Unexpected Heroes: The Complete Series

Unexpected Tales: Four Short Stories of Kaiatan

(an excerpt of Tales of Kaiatan)

Return of the Fae series

The Coming of the Fae

The Peril of the Fae

The Academy of the Fae

The War of the Fae

The King of the Fae

The Heirs of the Fae

The Escape of the Fae (novella 0.5)

Spotting the Fae (novella 0.8)

As M. Cate Lee

Relatively Haunted series (2026)

Book design & publication by Bookaholics Press LLC, Provo, Utah
Edited by Martha Rasmussen
Front cover design by Lara Wynter
Maps by Michelle Allan and Naomi Rasmussen
Author photograph by Melissa C. Baxter

ISBN-13: 978-1-950230-18-1 (epub)
978-1-950230-19-8 (mobi)
978-1-950230-20-4 (paperback)
978-1-950230-21-1 (large print paperback)
978-1-950230-30-3 (hardback)
978-1-950230-64-8 (audiobook)

Published by Bookaholics Press LLC
Provo, Utah bookaholicspress@gmail.com

Contact the author at MCLeeBooks.com

For Joseph, because I'm okay being your second-favorite author, and for Dora, who needs to share.

CONTENTS

INTRODUCTION

Dear Reader,

If you've read the Unexpected Heroes series, welcome back to the world of Kaiatan! Here you will find stories connected to the series (prequels, sequels, and backstories), tales mentioned in the series, stories of minor characters, and tales of characters you didn't know existed. I arranged the stories chronologically, but they cross over sixty years and cover all four countries, so hold onto your hat and buckle your seatbelt for the ride.

If you are new, welcome! Some of the stories will make as much sense for you as for return readers. Some of them might be spoilers of minor or major degree. You don't *have* to read the series first, but you might *want* to... If you do, start with *Wind of Choice*. ☺

Have fun in Kaiatan, and come again soon,
    Marty C. Lee

Map of Kaiatan

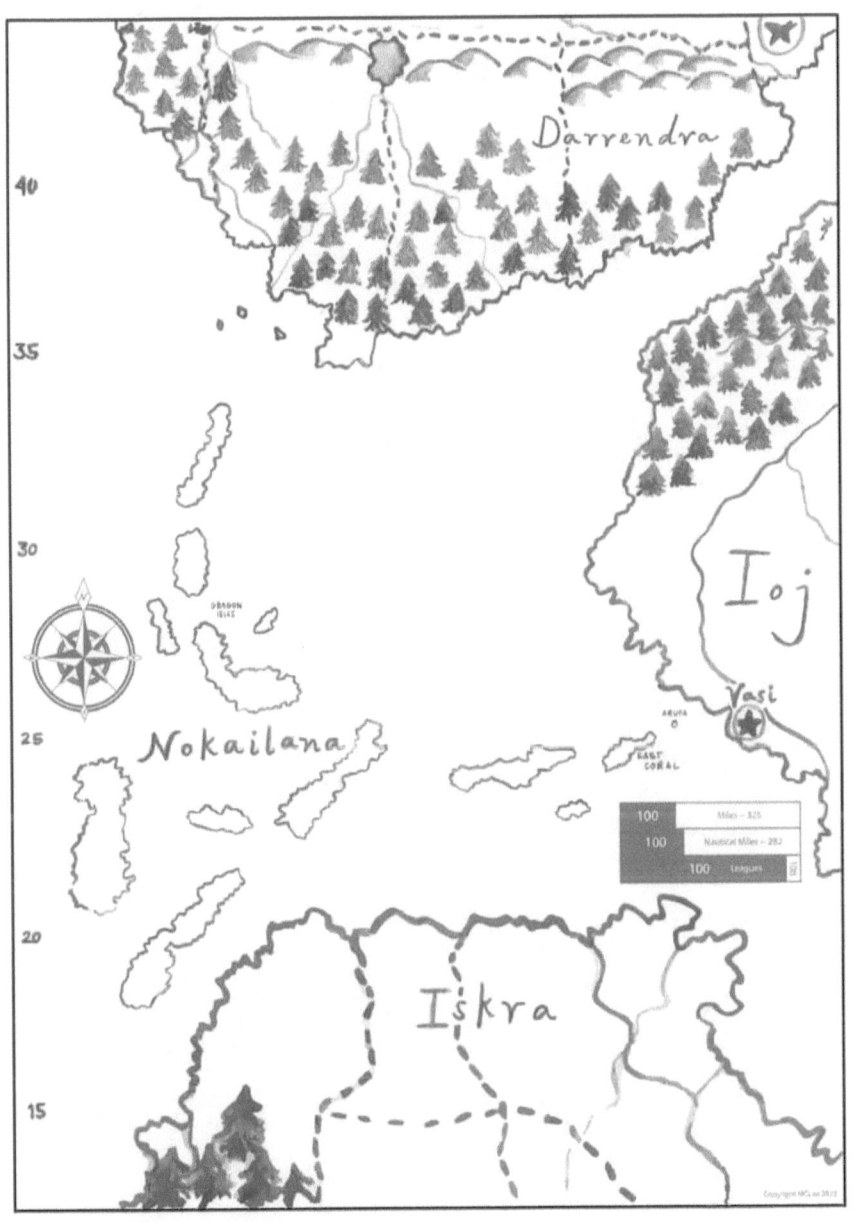

WINDS

(ALMOST 60 YEARS
BEFORE WIND OF CHOICE)

1. CHOSEN
(MURA, IOJ)

The initiation is the first time novice priests feel the focused touch of Irajahan's mind.
Handbook for Winds

Amrafel stood in front of the temple-hut, shivering with cold and nerves, wrapping his gray wings around himself for an extra layer of warmth. He shouldn't have let Mother talk him into wearing his nice coat instead of his warm one. Beside him, she coughed in the frosty air and wrapped her scarf higher around her face.

Behind Mother and Father, the rest of the villagers gawked. Winter was dull enough that everyone wanted to see what occupation he'd be assigned, despite the lack of options. He would probably be a farmer like his parents, or perhaps a woodcutter like his uncle. But it was up to the will of Irajahan the Omnipotent, as relayed by the priestly Wind in their village. And speaking of Sefu, their lowly Gust now exited the hut with his Breeze novice.

Sefu clasped Amrafel's hand. "Fair winds."

"Fair winds, Flurry Sefu." Amrafel used the formal term of address for the occasion.

The Breeze set out two stools, and Sefu took one and gestured for Amrafel to take the other.

Amrafel hurried to sit, nearly tripping over his own feet. This would be easier if there were another new adult to share the attention, but no one else in Mura had turned sixteen in months.

Sefu smiled. "Relax, this won't hurt. Since we don't have school records for you, we have to assess your education a little differently. We'll start with a simple test."

The priest pulled out a sheaf of parchment and read off arithmetic problems between Mother's coughs. Amrafel got halfway through the page before he started getting them all wrong.

The Gust turned the page and quizzed Amrafel on history. Then it was time for geography, politics, weather, and more. No one made a sound except for Mother's coughing. Amrafel's spirits sank with every question he got wrong.

The priest handed the next page to Amrafel. "Please read this aloud."

Amrafel took a deep breath and put his finger on the first word. "Ioj is the greetest—"

"Greatest," someone said.

Amrafel continued without looking to see who was prompting him. "Greatest county—"

"Country."

"Country in all of... Kaiatan." He winced, but it seemed a logical guess. What else could it be?

"You may stop now." Sefu took back the page and sighed.

"I'm sorry," Amrafel whispered.

"Don't be," the priest said. "I should have pushed harder to get a new teacher when the last one died. Six years is too long to leave you children without one."

"Nine," Amrafel whispered.

The Gust rubbed a hand across his face. "Nine."

"It doesn't matter for a farmer." Father gripped Amrafel's shoulder. "His mother and I can teach him enough to label his seeds and figure his yields."

Sefu sighed again. "I'm afraid it matters for a Wind."

Amrafel gaped at him. A Wind? Winds were the voice of Irajahan, honored everywhere in Ioj, and he was merely a farmer's son.

His father's hand tightened on his shoulder.

No one said anything for a long minute.

"Wind?" Mother finally asked between coughs.

"Your son has telepathy. He's slated for the priesthood."

Amrafel tried to protest that he didn't have telepathy, but his voice failed him. Wouldn't he know?

"How do you know?" Father asked.

"Irajahan prompted him with the reading test."

That led to another round of silent stares. Amrafel struggled with an awful mix of gratitude and embarrassment. Though he was thankful for the help, he'd rather his god didn't know he was nearly illiterate. How could it be worse?

"I don't mind you teaching me," Amrafel said. "I'll study hard."

The priest winced. "I already have a novice. They won't let me have two in such a tiny, remote village. I'm afraid you must go to Vasi for training and be assigned somewhere in Ioj later."

Amrafel jerked back until he almost fell off the stool. "But — Vasi is so far away. And my parents are here."

"I know. I'm sorry. We'll hold your initiation here tonight, and in the morning, we'll fly to Vasi." He glanced at Amrafel's parents and pressed his lips together. "Meet me back here after sundown."

Father tugged Amrafel out of the temple and led him back to their house.

Amrafel closed the rickety door and stood in the single room, blinking in the faint light of the small window as he tried to understand what had happened. *Wind. Vasi. Fly in the morning.*

His parents sank to their mattress on the dirt floor.

"Vasi," Father said.

Mother's lip quivered.

Amrafel noticed his parents as he hadn't in a long time. Father's wings were gray, like his own, and his black hair had faded to match. More importantly, one wing was crooked from a poorly healed break when the plow horse kicked him. Mother's pale green wings, beautiful and bright, worked perfectly, but she coughed all the time in winter.

Neither of them could make the trip with him.

Amrafel dropped on his knees in front of them and wrapped them in a hug. "I'll learn to read better," he promised. "I'll send you letters. Sefu can read them to you."

Mother pressed her sunny blonde head to his shoulder, and her tears soaked through his thin coat. Father wrapped his arms around them both.

Eventually, they pulled themselves to their feet and dished up the dinner porridge.

Amrafel helped Father feed the horse and chickens before they returned to the temple-hut in the faint light of the two small moons.

Flurry Sefu ushered him into the miniature temple, which was just big enough for them and the novice to kneel at the marble shrine.

"My Lord Omnipotent," the Gust prayed, "we come to present a new Doldrum to Thee. Bless him with Thy Almighty presence. Touch him with Thy mind. Bind him in everlasting service to Thee, Omnipotence."

Amrafel waited nervously, but nothing happened.

Sefu prayed again. "Irajahan the All-Powerful, great God of Air, we seek Thy presence and Thy blessing."

Still nothing happened.

The Gust sat back on his heels. "He's probably working his way through Vasi and the bigger cities. He'll reach us eventually. Relax for a few minutes." He chatted with Amrafel about departure times for the morning and how many days they would travel and what to expect at the temple in Vasi. "It will be fine, you know. You'll see. Oh, here he is."

Something touched Amrafel's mind. At first, it was a hint of a breeze, a whisper that could be mistaken for a random memory. Then the wind trickled through every corner of his mind, gathering his thoughts and twisting them into a tornado that led south.

As his thoughts pulled away, Amrafel grasped one tightly for a moment. "Thank you for helping me read." His mind went blank, filled only by a cool wind of awe and wonder.

When someone shook him from his trance, the stained glass window glowed blue from the first hint of dawn. The stone floor was frozen under his knees, and his joints creaked when he tried to move.

"You're welcome," someone whispered with a trace of amusement. The wind in his head vanished.

"Hurry," Sefu said. "Go eat with your parents. We need to leave soon."

He tugged Amrafel to his feet, holding him steady until his aching knees straightened, then dragged him gently to the door.

Amrafel limped home, unable to put two thoughts together. His previous nervousness was replaced with an eager anticipation. How fortunate he was to be chosen to serve his god. How lucky that fate had given him the ability to communicate directly with the source of all that was good in this world.

His steps slowed as he reached home. It meant leaving his parents, and he didn't know when he could visit. He'd never left home. Amrafel squared his shoulders and promised himself he would work hard and be worthy of the honor, whatever it took.

He and his parents ate a breakfast of hard boiled eggs and porridge with a rare dusting of sugar. They asked him about the initiation, but he merely smiled and said he would be fine. How could he explain to someone who had not experienced the wonder?

After breakfast, Amrafel folded his blankets lengthwise, and spread his nice coat and his spare outfit across them. He added another pair of socks and the scribble his older sister had drawn of the family before she died of a fever twelve years before. After rolling everything tightly and rigging rope to loop over his shoulders, he put on his warm coat and gloves and wrapped his scarf around his neck.

Father took his bedroll, and Mother held his hand while they walked back to the temple. Sefu was already outside, bundled in several layers and with a proper pack resting between his black wings. While he spoke to his novice, Amrafel turned to his parents.

"Good flight, Mother," Amrafel said. "Good flight, Father."

Both of them hugged him again. "Good flight, Amrafel."

Mother tightened his scarf. "Be safe."

Father helped him sling his bedroll between his wings. "Be good."

Amrafel nodded emphatically. "I will, and I'll tell you everything." He turned to the Gust and bowed. "I'm ready."

Flurry Sefu looked at his novice. "Remember what I told you. I'll be back as soon as I can."

He spread his wings and took off, and Amrafel followed. They circled higher in the apricot sky to gain altitude, then turned southwest. Below them, the village huts disappeared into the land between the branches of the river. The lake shimmered in the early morning sunlight, not far from the vast northern forest now falling behind them.

Even from this high, Vasi was too far away to see. Nine hundred miles lay before them, and the trip would take days. Though Amrafel was used to hard labor on the farm, it wasn't the same as flying all day. Poor Sefu would have to turn around to make the return flight almost immediately.

With his scarf wrapped around his ears to block the frigid wind, Amrafel couldn't hear much, but Sefu didn't talk. They flew in silence for an hour
before stopping for a rest and a drink.

Sefu used the break to instruct him on the priestly ranks and badges,
from Doldrums with the empty circle to the Typhoon with six wind curls.

"But you won't stay at Doldrums for long, I'm sure," he said. "You'll
make Breeze quickly."

They flew for another hour, and at the next rest break, Sefu quizzed
Amrafel on the ranks. When he recited them perfectly, the Gust taught
him how to address each rank. Amrafel already knew a Breeze was
addressed as Zephyr and his or her name, and Sefu, as a Gust, was
addressed as Flurry Sefu. In their small village, both the priest and his
novice were frequently addressed only by name, but Sefu emphasized that
the temple would be more formal.

The last three ranks used only special terms, without the personal
names, and it took two rest breaks before Amrafel recited everything
perfectly enough to satisfy Sefu.

Winter days were short, and they stopped at twilight in a small village,
where Sefu knocked on the door of the temple. A brief explanation led to a
hot dinner and room to spread their blankets on the fancy split-log floor of
a nearby house.

Despite Amrafel's loneliness and apprehension, exhaustion pulled him
into sleep within minutes.

In the morning, Amrafel and Sefu ate breakfast and stretched their
aching muscles before flying again. The Gust again taught Amrafel
during their rest breaks and the longer stop for lunch. Night found them in
a city with a temple big enough to have an actual bed for Sefu.

Every day, they flew and studied, sleeping in a different town each night.
After a week, Amrafel stopped aching so badly and began to enjoy the
constant flying.

At twilight of the tenth day, Amrafel expected Sefu to land again, but
the Gust kept flying. Not long after, lights came on in the distance like
stars reflected on a lake, brighter than the crescent of the big golden moon
that shone above them.

Sefu waved his arm at the glow, and Amrafel nodded vigorously.

More lights sprang up, and more, until the twinkle on the ground turned into a blaze stretching for miles. Amrafel gulped. How could so many people live in one place?

Sefu headed for the largest gleam. In less than an hour, they could see ordinary cobblestone roads made for the convenience of wagons and wingless visitors, and a black marble road from the market to an immense building with high arches and many towers. Stained-glass windows cast streaks of color across the courtyard and illuminated the gray-and-white marble traced with gold. A twinkle separated from the temple glow and moved to the center of the courtyard, waving.

Sefu landed next to the beacon, and Amrafel followed. He blinked as he landed, and the light settled into a lamp in the hand of a robed priest with gray and white wings.

Out of the cold upper sky, the air was warm enough to make Amrafel sweat in his coat. He unwrapped his scarf and removed his gloves.

"Fair winds, Sefu," the unfamiliar priest said. "We prepared beds for you and your Doldrum. Everything else will wait until morning. This way." He turned and hustled toward the temple.

Sefu pushed Amrafel gently. "I told them all about you while we flew." He winked. "You'll learn how to speak to the other priests with your mind, too. Don't worry; they'll explain everything. For now, sleep. In the morning, they'll get you settled and show you around."

Amrafel followed silently as Sefu was shown to a room shared with another priest. Feeling abandoned already, he followed the strange priest down many halls until they reached a long dormitory room filled with occupied beds.

"This is the male side," the priest whispered. He pointed to an empty bed at the far end of the row and closed the door behind Amrafel.

Amrafel slid his bedroll from his back and tiptoed through the room. He pulled off his ankle boots and coat and crawled under the blankets, which were warm and softer than anything he owned. City lights shone softly through the windows, and no crickets chirped. The sound of breathing echoed from the stone walls.

He squirmed on the soft, sagging mattress. After tossing and turning for a while, he gave up and spread his bedroll on the floor. In minutes, he was asleep with his sister's scribble under his hand.

2. DOLDRUMS

(VASI, IOJ)

Unless remedial classes are needed, novices spend their days learning priestly duties and ordinances.
Handbook for Winds

S omeone nudged Amrafel. "What do we have here?"
Amrafel mumbled and threw his arm over his eyes to block the light.

Laughter filled the room.

Amrafel opened his eyes and jerked to his feet.

Rows of young men in two shades of apricot robes stared at him. Some hid their chuckles behind their hands, but most howled openly.

"Couldn't you find your bed?" one asked, smirking.

Amrafel said nothing, unsure how to explain he didn't like their mattress without insulting their hospitality.

"Or your nightclothes?"

"No, those must be his nightclothes. They're too old and mended to be worn in public." They all snickered. "And wool! He'll bake himself."

But they were his only clothes. Wool could be spun at home, unlike fine cotton and linen and finer silk. Even his nicer outfit was a thin wool, better suited to the north than to this warmer climate.

"I see the problem," the first one said. "He's too dumb to understand anything."

They all laughed harder, wings shaking with amusement.

Amrafel ignored their rudeness and held out a hand to shake. As the newcomer, it was proper for him to be on his best behavior.

"Fair winds. My name is Amrafel. I'm from Mura, in the north."

"Listen to that accent," someone bellowed. "He can't even talk!"

The room erupted into a chaos of mirth and taunts.

And where was *their* best behavior? Amrafel clenched his fists and rolled up his blankets, face hot and wings folded so tightly all his sore muscles ached.

The door banged against the wall. "Doldrums! Breezes! Silence!"

The young men jerked to attention with their hands behind their backs.

A middle-aged priest entered with a pile of pale apricot robes in his arms. "Is this how we taught you? Shame!" He smacked his hands together. "Off to breakfast, unless you feel like washing dishes for the next month."

The novices scattered. When Amrafel started to follow, the priest touched his arm.

"Not you. Let's get you settled first. I'm sorry we didn't have time last night. Here, try this on."

He handed Amrafel one of the apricot robes with a blank-circle badge. When that proved to be too long, he gave him another, making notes on a sheet of parchment.

"Keep that on. Now that we know your size, I'll get more for you." He glanced at Amrafel's clothes and the spare outfit folded on the bed. "And nightclothes. You can keep what you're wearing for chores and your others for your day off." He wrinkled his nose a little.

Amrafel nodded, blinking back tears. His mother had made his clothes, and they were all he had from her.

"I already talked to Flurry Sefu," the priest continued. "Here's your class schedule and a map of the temple. We've assigned you a tutor. Report to Tempest Pillan every morning. In the afternoon, you'll attend telepathy class with everyone else and be allowed a flying break before chores. Once you've caught up, we'll reassign you."

Amrafel nodded.

"Do you have any questions?"

"When is Sefu leaving?"

The priest frowned, pinch-lipped. "I'm afraid *Flurry* Sefu already left this morning. He has to return to his post. And didn't he teach you how to address priests?"

Amrafel gulped and nodded. "I'm sorry. I'll remember from now on."

The priest sighed. "Well, hurry along. Get breakfast and go find Tempest Pillan."

Amrafel bolted for the door. In the hall, he pressed himself against the wall to study the map. If he went down this hall and turned left twice, he should reach the cafeteria. He folded the map and schedule into his pocket and tried to look like he knew where he was going.

Sefu was already gone? Without a chance to wish him good flight? Loneliness swept over him like storm winds, but he fought it down and hurried faster.

The cafeteria was not at the end of two left turns, but a temple servant took pity and showed him the way. By the time Amrafel arrived, breakfast was nearly over. He gulped down three of the most delicious muffins he'd ever eaten, along with a glass of juice, and wandered through the halls until he found the room that said Tempest Pillan next to the door.

He hovered near the open door until the orange-robed priest inside looked up and frowned. His wings were a pale gray, almost silver or white.

"Yes?" he snapped. "What do you want?"

"I'm Amrafel. I was told to report to you."

"What did you say?" The middle-aged priest raised an eyebrow.

Amrafel repeated it twice before the priest rolled his eyes. "I see we must add diction to our lessons. And address me as Your Turbulence. Didn't your village priest teach you anything? Come in, come in. Sit there." He pointed to a stool in front of the desk and pulled out a stack of parchment. "I have your evaluation here. I must say, it doesn't look good."

Amrafel sat awkwardly, trying to arrange his new robe without falling off the stool. "Our teacher died nine years ago." He had to repeat that, too.

"And why didn't the village hire a new one?" Pillan asked.

"No one wanted to move to Mura." Amrafel said it as slowly and clearly as he could.

Pillan shook his head. "I suppose I don't blame them. Let's start with arithmetic."

The next four hours were sheer misery. Amrafel couldn't seem to please the Tempest no matter how hard he tried. He didn't know enough. He didn't speak clearly enough. He didn't learn quickly enough. And Great God of Air, he didn't read better than a baby. Amrafel had covered his mouth in shock at the frustrated Tempest's language and earned himself another disgusted look.

Tempest Pillan — His Turbulence, Amrafel reminded himself — sent him to lunch with a stack of homework for the next day. Amrafel fingered his badge, feeling almost as empty as the circle that branded him the lowest level of novice.

After the most luxurious lunch Amrafel had ever had, he followed the other novices to telepathy class. Though the students were both male and female, they all wore the same Doldrum badge.

This teacher was also middle-aged, with russet brown wings and hair, and his badge had the three wind curls of a Gale, but he was laughing with one of the students. Amrafel fought the sudden pang of homesickness at the thought of Sefu's kind heart, despite his lower rank.

The priest shooed the student to his seat and sat casually on the front of his desk. "Fair winds, class."

"Fair winds, Jirish," the students chorused.

Amrafel gaped at the casual address. Jirish turned to Amrafel and raised an eyebrow.

"Fair winds, Squall Jirish," Amrafel said in a rush.

The young men and women in the class laughed.

Jirish stared at the class with his lips pressed together. To Amrafel's surprise, the students immediately stopped laughing.

Jirish turned back to Amrafel. "I take it you are our new student. Come sit. Would you like to tell the class something about yourself?"

Amrafel looked at the class and shook his head as he found a seat at the back.

Jirish raised his eyebrow again. "May I confirm what I've heard?"

Amrafel nodded.

"I believe your name is Amrafel? You come from Mura, near the northern forest?"

Amrafel nodded again.

"And you have better manners than most of my students, but it's not necessary to be formal in this class. Please call me Jirish."

Amrafel ducked his head.

Jirish sighed. "Some of you Doldrums have been in my class for several weeks already. Would someone please tell Amrafel what we learn here, and what he can expect when he moves to the advanced telepathy class?"

A young woman with blue-gray wings raised her hand. "In this class, we learn how to tell our own thoughts from those of Irajahan or our teachers. We learn to open and close the doors in our mind. We learn how to project clearly."

One of the rude young men from that morning raised his hand. "In the next class, we will learn to speak to one another, to limit our projection to only the person we want to reach, and to strengthen our power and increase our reach."

Jirish nodded. "And which of those is the most important skill?"

To Amrafel's surprise, the class immediately began an enthusiastic debate. Most voted for clear projection or strengthening power and reach, though a few thought speaking to another priest was more important, since Irajahan could make himself heard despite any weakness in a priest.

Squall Jirish folded his arms and listened with a pleasant smile. When the class wound to a stop, he said, "Excellent arguments. You're all wrong."

The class groaned.

Jirish shrugged. "In fact, you might hear other teachers advocating your viewpoints. They're wrong, too. The most important skill is the ability to close your mind to others and the willingness to open it."

Another young woman raised her hand. "But why? Isn't that as easy as closing our mouths? And if our job is to communicate with the Almighty, why would we ever want to close our minds?"

Amrafel agreed with her, but he didn't dare say so.

"Is it easy?" Jirish asked. "How many of you can shut out Irajahan?"

No one volunteered.

"I assume you all remember your initiation?"

A chorus of sighs circled the room from the students, Amrafel included, who wished he could feel the wonder again.

"How much work do you think you can get done when you're flooded like that?"

Amrafel blinked at him. He didn't even remember the night passing.

None of the students replied.

"How much thinking can you do like that?"

Still no one said anything.

"How much did you feel like yourself at that time?"

Amrafel frowned. He didn't like feeling like himself. He'd rather feel all-powerful.

None of the students spoke.

Jirish sighed. "We'll keep working on it. You need to be able to close your mind to keep your own voice separate from those of others. For our first exercise, let's divide into teams."

At the end of class, Amrafel ducked out while the other students swarmed the teacher. He ran to the courtyard and sprang into the air, spiraling around the temple until he was higher than the tallest tower. When he was as high as he could go and still breathe, he looked north. His home wasn't visible, not even the vast northern forest. He was alone.

The warm air didn't reach this high, and the icy wind froze his tears on his cheeks. He stayed in the sky until he couldn't feel his limbs anymore. As he finally staggered to a landing, he glanced at the big sundial in the courtyard. If he didn't hurry, he'd be late for chores.

He jogged through the hallways, making several wrong turns before finding his way to the kitchen. An assistant cook questioned him while she pulled out ingredients, then sent him to the gardens to dig vegetables for dinner.

"We're glad to have a farmer, since most of our students can't tell a turnip from a tomato," she said, rolling her eyes.

Amrafel spent an hour gardening, pleased to find something familiar in this odd place. At home, it was much too cold to garden now. Even here, it was cool, but the garden was in a sunny spot, protected from the wind, and the cold-weather vegetables were flourishing near fruit trees that had not yet bloomed.

After his chores, he had two hours to struggle with his homework. He only finished a quarter of the stack before it was time for dinner.

When he walked into the cafeteria, the students turned their backs and huddled in small groups, looking over their shoulders to mock him. Amrafel ate as quickly as possible and returned to his bed to study.

By curfew, hours later, he still wasn't finished. He stacked his parchment neatly under his bed and climbed under the covers. The other young men chattered and teased each other, but no one spoke to him.

After the lights went out, Amrafel tossed on his too-soft bed, listening to their breathing for a long time before he fell asleep.

I n the morning, Amrafel tried talking to the other young men. When they ignored him, he ate breakfast by himself and reported to Tempest Pillan with his half-finished stack of homework.

His Turbulence berated Amrafel for a quarter hour for laziness and spent the rest of the morning criticizing his handwriting, incorrect answers, and general stupidity. After assigning another pile of homework, he released Amrafel to lunch.

This time, Amrafel took his lunch to the courtyard and ate as quickly as possible, tracing the circle of his badge. He was not stupid. He wasn't. He just needed a little time.

He showed up to telepathy class early and tucked himself into the back corner. When Squall Jirish arrived, he smiled at Amrafel and started to approach, but another student grabbed his attention until class began.

Amrafel paid attention, and Jirish frequently smiled at him. Then again, Squall Jirish smiled at everyone, even when they gave wrong answers.

After class, Amrafel flew by himself before reporting to the kitchen. When he finished gardening, he tucked himself into a sunlit corner and fought through some of his homework. He begged a plate of dinner from the kind assistant cook and ate in a kitchen corner before returning to his assignments.

The next day was a holy day, and he attended morning temple services with everyone else. In the afternoon, he struggled through a short letter to his parents, but he didn't know how to send it. Finally, he tucked it under his pillow with his sister's drawing and went to dinner.

He spent the evening working on his homework and went to bed with most of it done.

W hen he proudly showed Tempest Pillan his work the next morning, the priest glowered.

"Most of your answers are wrong and the rest are unreadable. And you didn't finish."

Amrafel cleared his throat twice. "I'm trying, Your Turbulence."

"What? I can't understand you."

Amrafel shook his head and blinked back tears.

"This is hopeless. You're worthless." The priest threw Amrafel's homework into the fireplace and stood. "Follow me."

Amrafel mutely followed him to the kitchen, where Tempest Pillan introduced him to the head cook as a new kitchen worker.

Amrafel clutched his novice badge. It meant nothing. He was nothing.

The cook glanced at Amrafel's apricot robe but merely said, "As Your Turbulence commands."

After the priest swept grandly from the kitchen, the cook sat on a stool and picked up his cleaver. "Do you have any classes you'd still like to attend, boy?"

Amrafel shrugged. "I was only in one real class. Telepathy, right after lunch."

"Will that teacher let you continue?" The cook grabbed a handful of vegetables and diced them in seconds, faded rust-orange wings idly twitching as he worked.

"Probably."

"You should go. Who knows where the currents will blow you next week, hmm? Now, I need more carrots, please."

Amrafel grabbed a shovel and headed outside.

After chores and lunch, which he ate in the kitchen, he headed to Jirish's class. By keeping his mouth shut and never volunteering, he made it through unseen enough that none of the other students told the teacher he was no longer a real novice.

Dinner was again spent in the kitchen, and he snuck into bed before the other boys arrived. He pulled his blankets over his head and cried himself to sleep with his hand on his sister's drawing and the letter he still hadn't figured out how to send.

3. BREEZE
(VASI, IOJ)

Though not as large and impressive as the Great Library in Vasi, the Temple Library has the largest collection of religious works in the world.

Handbook for Winds

The next morning, Amrafel pretended to be asleep while the other male novices dressed and pounded out of the dormitory for their morning classes. Once the room was quiet, he slowly dressed.

Tempest Pillan thought he was useless, but the Almighty Irajahan had called him to the priesthood. Amrafel smoothed his blankets and tucked them under the mattress with rough jerks. He wasn't stupid, no matter what Pillan thought. If only he weren't so far behind. Because his parents needed him on the farm most of the year, he'd only gotten a few months of schooling each year until he was seven, when the teacher died. His parents practiced his numbers and letters with him a little, but they didn't own any books. Hardly anyone in Mura did.

Amrafel was sure he could learn, if he had a real chance. The Tempest hadn't told him to leave, only to stay in the kitchen. If he could study on his own, perhaps he could learn enough to convince Pillan to tutor him again. Or skip the tutoring and move to the regular classes.

The other young men didn't seem likely to help him, and he certainly couldn't ask one of the priests for help or His Turbulence might find out before Amrafel was ready. So who might know enough to help but be sympathetic to his plight?

The cook who had told him to keep attending Squall Jirish's class. Or Jirish himself? No, Jirish was a priest and thus couldn't be trusted. The cook, then.

Amrafel slunk through the hallways to the kitchen. After collecting his breakfast and washing dishes for an hour, he gathered his courage and approached the cook.

"Would you mind — Is it allowed — May I—" He stumbled to a stop.

The cook put down his bread dough. "What is it, boy?"

Amrafel took a breath and pushed it all out at once. "I want to learn on my own, but I need books and somewhere to study where the Tempest won't find me and I don't know any place in the city so where should I go?"

Heat rushed up his cheeks, but he stilled his twitching wings and held his ground.

The cook grinned. "Slow down and breathe, boy. The Great Library has the most books, but I think you'd get caught sneaking out. The temple library has enough books, but I can't risk helping you defy Pillan."

Amrafel slumped. "I understand. What chores do you want me to do today?"

The cook scratched his chin, leaving a trail of flour. "Grab that broom there. Now, I want you to sweep from *that* door, out the hallway, down the second hallway to the left, all the way to the end, and then the short hall on the right. That's a lot of sweeping, and I want you to do a good job, so I don't expect to see you back until luncheon. And you have more experience gardening than cleaning, so I will leave you on the sweeping assignment until I'm satisfied you're competent. Make sure you tell that to anyone who questions you in the hall, boy. Do you understand?" He raised his eyebrows and frowned at Amrafel.

"Yes, I'll sweep." Amrafel sighed and grabbed the broom.

The cook shook his head. "I want that hall spotless, boy. Don't come back before lunch."

Amrafel nodded and slipped out the door. The hall already looked clean, but he swept anyway. Hardly anything moved under his broom, and he traveled the halls quickly. Within minutes, he was at the end, staring at a plaque on the door. Lih...berry. No, library!

Don't come back until lunch, the cook had said. *Tell anyone who questions you that you have to sweep until you're competent.*

A slow grin crept across his face. The cook couldn't defy Pillan, but it wasn't defiance to make him sweep a hallway, even if it did end at the library. And if the door was open, the floor didn't end until the other side of the room.

He checked the hall behind him, then cracked open the door and looked inside. Bookshelves lined the walls from ceiling to floor, filled with rows of books in matching leather bindings. Some shelves turned to create reading nooks with tables and padded stools, with lanterns and ink pots bolted into place to avoid accidents. The scents of ink and parchment and dyed leather floated through the air. So much knowledge, if he could get his hands on it.

If this didn't work, if Pillan found out, would Amrafel be sent home entirely? Or did the temple have worse fates for disobedient novices? He gulped, then gathered his courage and slipped through the door.

At a desk in the front of the room sat a priest in an unadorned medium-orange robe that clashed horribly with his pink wings. He scowled at Amrafel, who smiled weakly and held up his broom until the priest rolled his eyes and beckoned him forward.

"I don't want to know what you did," he whispered fiercely. "Sweep until your detention is over, and then get out of my library."

Amrafel's heart sank, but he nodded quickly and swept toward the far end of the room. Once the priest seemed occupied with the parchment on his desk, he ducked into a reading nook and flattened himself against shelves.

After several minutes without the priest saying anything, Amrafel set his broom in the corner and puzzled through titles. Many of them used big words he had no hope of interpreting, but he put a few possibilities on the table. He was still searching when a young woman in an apricot robe walked in, nose in a book, and sat on a stool without looking at him. Amrafel froze, book in hand, holding his breath.

The girl's badge had one Wind curl, the mark of a Breeze, the second rank of novices, and she looked a few years older than him. Her wings were a pretty speckled-brown, and her curly brown hair was cropped short. She put her book on the table and turned a page. After pulling out a folded sheet of parchment, she dipped a pen into the ink pot and made a note, then turned the page.

"If you don't breathe soon, you'll explode," she murmured, turning another page.

Amrafel squeaked.

"Girls don't bite."

Amrafel put back the book and reached for his broom.

She looked up. "I won't report you for reading during detention."

Amrafel's cheeks burned. "I'm not—" He clamped his mouth shut.

She closed the book and turned to face him. "You're not reading? Or you're not in detention?" She wiggled her finger between the books and his broom.

Amrafel shook his head.

She squinted at him, then pointed to another stool. "I want to hear this story. Sit!"

He looked toward the door, but if he left now, the priest at the desk would wonder what he'd been doing for so long. Seeing no way out, he sank to the stool, clutching his broom.

"If you aren't in detention, what are you doing with the broom?" she whispered.

"Cook," Amrafel gulped.

Her eyes widened. "You're skipping chores?"

He shook his head harder. "Cook told me not to come back till lunch."

She tapped her fingertips together. "I love a good mystery. Not in detention, not skipping chores... You didn't steal that robe, did you?"

Amrafel nearly choked.

"No." She pinched her nose. "Are you skipping classes?"

"My tutor told me to work in the kitchen from now on, but I want to study. Cook says he can't defy my tutor, but he sent me to sweep the hall, which doesn't need it."

She winced. "Say that again, slowly."

He repeated it with as little accent as he could manage, and she listened intently.

"Who's your tutor?"

"Tempest Pillan."

"Oh, he's a — Never mind. Why did Pillan send you to the kitchen instead of tutoring you?"

He blushed again. "I can't even read, he says."

"And thus the 'not reading' part." She closed her book and stared at him. "Do you know any reading at all?"

"I know the letters. And the numbers."

She examined him from head to foot, and he tried not to blush harder.

"There's no point giving you history or philosophy before you can read. Hmm. Stay here." She left her book on the table and walked away.

Amrafel cautiously peeked around the shelves to watch as she approached the stern priest at the front desk. She smiled and waved her hands in some explanation as she chattered too quietly for Amrafel to hear. The priest pointed to an alcove on the other side of the library, and she hurried over. After picking two books from that area and one from another, she returned to her original seat.

"I told him I was doing research on teaching methods, in case I need them for my first post when I graduate next month. So, here's a reading primer."

She placed a book on the table. "Once you finish it, I'll get you the next one. Here's some parchment for writing practice. Use the pen and ink in the library."

She added another book. "This is a basic mathematics text. Counting, addition, subtraction."

And a third. "This is the Handbook for Winds. It will be a lot harder for you to read, but you deserve to know what it says. Hide them on the top shelf behind you when you leave, which should be as soon as Dragon-Breath out there leaves for his lunch. How often are you supposed to 'sweep the hall?'"

Amrafel blinked at her insult to the priest and the flood of words. "Every day."

She nodded. "Then I'll meet you here and review the lessons with you."

"Why?"

"Because I'd love to teach Pillan a different lesson." She gathered her books and stood.

"Wait," he whispered. "What's your name?"

She grinned crookedly. "You know how Cook doesn't want to get caught helping you?"

He nodded.

"I know how he feels. See you tomorrow." And she left, waving at the front desk priest.

Amrafel spent the next hour reading, then snuck out when 'Dragon-Breath' left. He returned to the kitchen, assured the cook that the halls were spotless, then ate lunch, washed dishes, and hurried to Squall Jirish's class.

He found his usual seat at the back and listened intently, wishing he wrote well enough to take notes. Well, thanks to the Breeze young lady, someday he would. In the meantime, he'd take advantage of the one class he was allowed.

After class, he hurried back to the kitchen to help prepare dinner. Washing those dishes took him longer, and by the time he finished, he had only a few minutes to study his old homework from Pillan before he had to run back to the dormitory for curfew.

His days fell into a pattern. Breakfast and quick chores in the kitchen. Sweeping the hall to the library, then hiding in the same alcove to study. The young woman, whom he was now calling Sparrow, would come halfway through and correct mistakes in his lessons, then she'd leave, and he'd read for a little longer before he snuck back to the kitchen for lunch before telepathy class.

He moved from the first primer to the second, and to the next arithmetic book, though his writing still looked like he'd dipped a chicken in ink and turned it loose on the parchment. Each time he thought he'd improved enough, he rewrote the letter to his parents on parchment Sparrow provided. He didn't share it with her for fear she'd laugh at his homesickness. Only babies cried about their parents, the other young men mocked.

Deciphering the Handbook was painful, but he dutifully read at least a verse every day. Sparrow answered his questions about that, too, though she had some odd opinions about some of the official decrees and refused to speak about others. She did encourage him to pass from Doldrums to Breeze as quickly as possible, though she refused to explain why, so he gave up working on Pillan's homework in the evenings in order to practice Jirish's telepathy lessons.

Jirish's class made more and more sense as time went on, and Amrafel occasionally volunteered an answer. Squall Jirish always praised him for his correct answers, as he did for all his students, and Amrafel gradually felt more confident in both his telepathy and his intelligence.

After a couple of weeks, he showed up for class and discovered it was time for a test. He huddled over the parchment and tried, but by the time class was done, he still hadn't finished. He handed his incomplete parchment to Jirish, wings curved around himself, and slunk toward the door.

"Please stay after class," the Gale murmured.

Amrafel nodded and sank into an empty chair as the other students left. Most of the students smirked at him, though a few young women cast him concerned glances.

Once the room was empty, Jirish pulled out Amrafel's test. He read the first question aloud. "And what is the answer?"

"I answered it," Amrafel protested wearily.

"I see that. Please expand on it for me." The Gale leaned against his desk.

Amrafel clenched his fingers together and explained in more detail.

Jirish nodded and read the second question.

"Oh." Amrafel had misread a word and answered it completely wrong.

"Go ahead," Jirish said.

Amrafel took a deep breath and answered it properly, according to the Handbook he'd been studying.

Jirish read the rest of the test, waiting for Amrafel's answers each time. At the end, he put down the parchment. "What does your tutor say about your reading?"

Amrafel blinked away more of the pesky tears he couldn't seem to avoid. "He — he said I'm worthless and should just work in the kitchen."

Jirish muttered what sounded like a rude word but must not be. Priests didn't swear like common woodsmen. "You still come to my class."

Amrafel clamped his trembling lips together. "I'm sorry. I'll stop."

Jirish swore again, very audibly this time. "If you skip class, I'll report you." He dropped the tests on his desk. "Run along. I'll talk to you later."

Amrafel dashed to the kitchen and grabbed the shovel. While he weeded and harvested, he let his tears water the plants. He'd been trying so hard and still couldn't do anything right. But Jirish hadn't reported him — yet — and he still wanted Amrafel in class for some reason, so he'd go and learn. Perhaps he could still learn enough before Jirish lost patience and expelled him.

The next day, he told Sparrow what happened. She stared at him for a long minute before suggesting he ask Jirish for help.

Amrafel shook his head and clutched his primer to his chest. "Jirish might tell Pillan. Or Irajahan."

Her mouth twisted crookedly. "Irajahan doesn't care about you."

Amrafel's mouth fell open. "My Lord Omnipotent cares about everyone."

She rolled her eyes. "Read me the next page."

☆🌱⚓◎

For the next two weeks, Amrafel studied even harder, squeezing book work into every spare moment in the morning, then practicing his math facts during his gardening. The cook said nothing when Amrafel propped a cookbook behind the sink to read while he washed dishes. The evening was devoted to reciting memorized passages from the Handbook until he fell into bed with a headache.

He didn't care how hard he worked. He would find a way to stay, to please Irajahan, to make his parents proud. Somehow.

He pulled his blanket over his face to hide his tears.

4. GALE

(VASI, IOJ)

Priests will be assigned to posts when they reach Gust, though some continue to progress through the ranks.
Handbook for Winds

Amrafel woke one morning and slipped out for a quick bath. When he returned to his bed, he found the boys reading the letter to his parents and passing around his sister's drawing with rude comments.

His heart thumped. What were they doing? "Those are mine."

The young men grinned. "What did you say?"

The one holding his letter laughed. "Look at this. He doesn't write any better than he talks. I knew he was stupid. He's too stupid to know we don't want him here. Go home, stupid."

Amrafel lunged for the letter, but the taller novice held it above his head. In desperation, Amrafel flapped his wings and jumped. He grabbed the letter, but the novice didn't let go. As Amrafel landed, the letter ripped, and his heart tore with it.

"No," he cried. "Look what you did."

The novice holding his sister's drawing said, "That's a good idea. This is worthless, too."

He tore it into several pieces before Amrafel could reach him. He dumped the scraps on the floor, and all the novices left, snickering.

Amrafel dropped to his knees and gathered the fragments of both the letter and the drawing. He wiped his tears before they could smear the ink, then tucked the pieces into his pocket. Once he stopped crying, he washed his face and crept to the kitchen to eat breakfast away from the other novices.

He studied in the library until lunch, then crept down the halls to telepathy class. A smug novice had taken Amrafel's usual seat in the corner, and the students had spread out, filling at least every other seat. Anywhere Amrafel could sit was surrounded by tormentors.

He stood in the doorway, hiding his trembling fists in his loose sleeves, and tried to decide the least painful place to sit.

"Oh, there you are." Squall Jirish glanced from him to the other students and narrowed his eyes. "Come on in. I need an assistant for today's test, and you'll be perfect." He smiled widely and held out a stack of parchment to Amrafel. "Give one of these to everyone, and then have a seat in my chair until it's time to pick them up."

Amrafel shook his head quickly. A test was bad enough without having everyone watching him take it.

"Oh, don't worry about me," Jirish said. "I intend to walk around today and look over everyone's shoulder as they take the test." His cheerful smile grew a little impish.

With no way to refuse, Amrafel passed out the parchments, keeping his wings away from pinching fingers as much as possible, and sat at the teacher's desk with his own copy. He ducked his head and curled his arm around his parchment to hide his ink-blotched mess.

At the end of class, Jirish took Amrafel's test first, then made him collect everyone else's before again asking him to stay. Once the other students were gone, Jirish moved Amrafel's test to the top of the stack and read the first question.

While Amrafel was answering, one of the rude novices peeked into the room, leered at Amrafel, and disappeared.

A few minutes later, Tempest Pillan marched through the door and yanked Amrafel to his feet. "What is going on? Why aren't you in the kitchen, boy? Get to work and stop wasting others' valuable time."

Amrafel looked to Squall Jirish for help, but the Gale dropped the tests and left the room. Amrafel bowed his head. It was no use. No matter how hard he tried, he was too stupid, too worthless.

Pillan dragged Amrafel to the kitchen, yelling the entire time. Then, still squeezing Amrafel's arm tightly, he shouted at the cook about keeping his helpers under control. The other kitchen workers either slipped out various doors or pressed themselves into corners.

Amrafel ducked his head and furled his wings tightly. He knew it was useless, but he had to try to stay. "Please, Your Turbulence, give me another chance. I've been studying, and I'm getting better. Let me show you how much I've improved. I can read for you, if you'll let me."

"Stop mumbling at me," Pillan shouted. "You're an idiot. If you won't stay in the kitchen, I'll send you home."

"Please," Amrafel whispered hopelessly.

Pillan's face turned purple. "I told you to be quiet."

He grabbed Amrafel with both hands and shook until the novice's teeth clattered.

The Tempest kept shouting, but Amrafel stopped listening. What difference did it make?

"Are you listening to me?" Pillan screamed, face crimson and veins bulging in his neck.

He raised his arm to strike, and Amrafel covered his head with his arms.

"There you are." Jirish stepped into the kitchen and found a place at the counter.

Behind him, a priest filled the doorway. His bright orange robe had a large badge on the breast, with five wind curls. This Storm was the high priest for Vasi, higher than anyone but other Storms, the Typhoon, and Irajahan himself.

"Your Storminess." Amrafel tried to bow, but Pillan's grip on his arm kept him from moving.

"Did you come for a snack?" the cook asked. "I can have something ready in a few minutes, if you'd like to wait outside?"

"No, thank you." His Storminess crossed his arms. "Pillan, let go of that novice immediately."

"He's no novice." Pillan shook Amrafel again. "He's a stupid boy who needs to give back that robe."

Someone touched Amrafel's mind. "Can you hear me?"

Amrafel glanced sideways at Pillan. He jerked his chin down once, trying his best to project his voice to the Storm. "I can hear you."

"I said, let go immediately," the Storm repeated.

Tempest Pillan let go and wiped his hands on his robe. "Your Stormi-ness, you don't understand."

"Oh, I hope I don't." His voice was soft. "I hope I don't understand you are terrorizing a novice and almost struck him. I hope I don't understand you told a telepath he wasn't needed in the priesthood. I hope I don't understand you are abusing your position in the Winds. Is there anything else I don't understand?"

Pillan gulped. "No, Your Storminess."

"You are dismissed. I will talk to you later."

Pillan fled. Amrafel stared wide-eyed at Jirish. Why had he brought a Storm to defend a worthless novice?

Jirish slowly approached Amrafel, who ducked his head again.

The Gale stopped. "Your Storminess, do I have your approval?"

"Yes, Squall Jirish. Please keep me informed." The Storm left the kitchen, to the audible sighs of the cook and his helpers.

Jirish pulled up a stool. "Amrafel, please look at me."

Did he dare trust Jirish as Sparrow suggested? Amrafel peeked sideways.

Jirish shrugged. "I suppose that will have to do."

Amrafel took a chance and threw himself on his knees in front of Jirish. "Please don't send me home. I've been working hard, I promise. I'll work even harder if you let me stay."

Jirish grimaced. "Get up. If you work any harder, you'll explode. It has come to the attention of the temple that your prior mentor has not been... adequate. I've offered to be his replacement. I'm afraid I'm not as highly ranked, but if you want me, His Storminess has already approved."

"Really?" Amrafel scrambled to his feet and searched Jirish's eyes for a lie.

"Really," Jirish said without a hint of a smile.

Amrafel covered his empty badge. "But he said I'm worthless. I've been trying, but I can't read well."

"Someone is worthless," Jirish said, "but it's not you. Please, let the rest of us make amends for your poor treatment."

Amrafel thought back to the breathtaking wind that permeated his mind the first night in Mura's temple. Perhaps the empty circle only meant waiting to be filled. He could do this.

Overflowing with joy, he threw his arms around the priest, then jerked backward. "Um, sorry. I mean, thank you. I mean, yes?"

Jirish laughed. "Yes. Let's go get your things."

"Why?" Amrafel asked.

"Due to the extra tutoring you'll need, and other circumstances, I've also been given permission to let you live in my house. I'll bring you in with me every morning."

Amrafel stopped, suddenly remembering horror stories about old men and young boys. Was this why the priest had been so friendly when everyone else hated Amrafel?

Jirish raised an eyebrow. "Stop that. I only have a small house, but my wife and I have a spare bedroom for you. You won't even have to share with the baby." He looked down the hall. "Or would you prefer to stay with the other novices?"

Amrafel shook his head.

Jirish escorted him to the dormitory and stood guard while Amrafel gathered his blanket, old clothes, and extra robe. "Get everything so we don't have to come back."

Amrafel clutched his pocket of precious scraps. "I have nothing else."

Jirish frowned. "Let's go. We can get you what you need later."

They walked through the temple and outside into the city. As Jirish had said, even on foot, it took only a few minutes to reach his house, which didn't look small to Amrafel. It even had real glass windows. The small garden to one side desperately needed care, and he promised himself that he would make it flourish to thank the older priest.

When Jirish walked in, a pretty lady put down her mending and jumped to her feet. "Why are you home early? Is there a problem?"

She saw Amrafel and stopped talking, eyes wide. Her golden brown hair was lighter than Jirish's, and her wings were a creamy yellow.

Jirish leaned for a kiss. "Darling, this is my new apprentice, Amrafel. He'll be staying in our extra room. Amrafel, this is my wife, Isaura."

Isaura gave him a squint-eyed look. "If you'd told me before, I could have already moved out my fabric."

Jirish gave her a crooked smile. "Sorry, I just found out. We'll help you, though. Amrafel, put your things on that chair for a minute."

He and his wife walked around the corner while Amrafel obeyed, and he caught up in time to hear Isaura whisper, "Is that all he has?"

It took the three of them an hour to clean the room and set up a cot, chair, and makeshift desk while Jirish explained the situation to Isaura. It might have taken less, but the baby, Surahava, woke and had to be fed.

"I'm sorry we don't have anything better," Isaura said, rocking the baby.

Amrafel gathered his courage and spoke for the first time, as clearly as he could. "I get a wood floor *and* a bed, in my own room? What could be better?"

He fidgeted for a minute, then pulled the torn letter and drawing from his pocket and laid them on his desk.

"Oh, no," Isaura said. "What happened to these?" She scooted the pieces of the drawing together.

Amrafel shrugged.

Isaura stared at the parchment. "May I borrow these? I'll give them back."

Amrafel shook his head. "They're mine."

Jirish put a hand on his shoulder. "I promise she'll return them. Here, darling, give me Surahava."

He took the baby in one arm and escorted Amrafel with the other. "Let's go outside in the sunshine."

He led the way to the garden and sat on a bench, bouncing Surahava while Amrafel pulled weeds.

"We'll study at home every morning," Jirish said, "and go to the temple for our afternoon class. You'll still have chores after that, but we'll come back home for more studying, including self-defense lessons. If the other students bully you again, I want you to be ready."

He cooed at the baby. "I know I told you I'd be your teacher, but I will also have my wife tutor you in some subjects, if that's acceptable?"

Amrafel tossed a handful of weeds into the compost. "Why? She's no priestess."

Jirish smiled. "No, but she's better at some things than I am, and I do have a few duties I can't skip."

Amrafel shrugged his wings. "What if she can't understand me, either?"

"She comes from the north, though not as far as you. I think she'll manage. In fact, I'm putting her in charge of your diction lessons, since she had to overcome an accent, too. Now, I know you've already been evaluated on your education, but since I don't trust Pillan's opinion on anything, I'd like to go over it again."

Amrafel hid a shudder but answered all the questions as best as he could. Unlike Pillan, Jirish didn't mock him for the wrong answers, or even comment on them besides noting additions to curriculum.

By the time Isaura called them in for dinner, half the garden was weeded and Jirish had promised to buy whatever seeds were wanted. Amrafel had relaxed enough to tell Jirish about his home and family without worrying about his accent. They washed their hands and sat at the table, and Amrafel froze.

His sister's drawing lay on the table, completely whole.

He burst into tears and covered his face with his hands, trying to smother his sobs. What would Jirish think of his childishness? He tried to say thank you but couldn't catch his breath.

"Oh, dear," Isaura said. "I thought he'd like it."

Jirish carefully embraced Amrafel. "Shh, shh. Come look."

Amrafel scrubbed his eyes with his sleeves and picked up the picture as Jirish sat back. Isaura had carefully glued the parchment to a thin board, matching the torn bits so expertly that he had to squint to see the damage. She'd added a frame and a sheet of actual glass to protect the drawing. He picked it up in shaking hands and pressed it to his chest.

"My letter?" He didn't try to hide his accent.

"I didn't mend that one," Isaura said. "You will rewrite it as one of your exercises." She glanced at Jirish, then Amrafel. "If you agree?"

"Once it's legible, I'll send it to your parents," Jirish said. "I'm sure they'll be pleased to see how well their son is doing. And once you reach Breeze, I'll arrange a visit home for you."

Amrafel looked from the priest's kind smile to his wife's anxious eyes. What a difference from Tempest Pillan. He beamed at Jirish and Isaura.

"I *am* doing well." He filled his next words with as much emotion and truth as he could. "Thank you."

As soon he could write well, he would tell his parents all about it, and when he was older, he would find a way to repay the priest. Perhaps he could mentor Surahava, if she became a priestess. No, Jirish would certainly do that. His grandchildren, then. In the meantime, Amrafel would give the priest the finest garden in Vasi.

He looked at his pale apricot robe with the empty circle badge. Yes, his badge was merely waiting to be filled. He would work hard, and someday his badge would show three wind curls, like Squall Jirish, or even four, like Tempest Pillan, if Almighty Irajahan found him worthy.

BROTHER

(ABOUT 23 YEARS BEFORE WIND OF CHOICE)

1. PRESENTATION
(SAVERIO, IOJ)

If sixteen-year-old youths are too far from Vasi to present themselves for adulthood at the main temple, they will go to their local temple.
Handbook for Winds

"Don't go," Aria Faron whispered, closing her older brother's door behind her so their parents wouldn't hear. "What if you don't make it back in time?"

She shuffled her wings nervously, and her feathers rustled in the quiet room. The morning sunlight shone through the window, casting shadows of the window grille.

"I've always made it to Vasi and back in half a day," Keelin reminded her, stuffing food and water into his pack. "It's my last chance to get a faster time to show the priests."

She leaned against the door. "You're already good enough. What's wrong with your other times?"

Keelin made a face and tugged on her hair. "There are three faster fliers this month alone, and who knows if the Winds will fill all the openings now or leave some empty for upcoming Presentations."

"It's not that bad," Aria said. "If the priests don't recruit you as a messenger, there will be some other job you like."

Keelin flopped on his bed, dark golden wings spread wide on the navy blanket. "It is that bad. You'll understand in a few years, when you're sixteen and suddenly facing the decision that will be your whole world for the rest of your life."

Aria bounced next to his feet. "You're my whole world."

She dropped onto his chest for an awkward hug. No matter what job he was assigned that night, her best friend would be gone except for occasional visits, and her life would never be the same.

He laughed and then sobered again. "I have to do this, Aria. I'll return before the Presentation starts, I promise. Wait for me at the temple."

Keelin sat up and stuffed the last of his food into his pack, then put on his jacket. Despite her worries, Aria smoothed the back panel of his jacket between his wings and helped him tie the sides shut. In moments, he was gone through the window, and she was alone.

After sitting on his bed until she could fake calm unconcern, she went to the kitchen to finish her chores. As long as she was working, Mother and Father were less likely to ask if she'd seen Keelin.

By late afternoon, she had cleaned the entire house, even Keelin's share, and still her brother wasn't back.

"It's time to go to the temple," Mother said. "Where's Keelin?"

Aria gulped. "Running an errand. He'll meet us there." She clasped her hands behind her back and tried not to wince.

Mother muttered something probably uncomplimentary. "Fine. What choice do we have?"

She grabbed her jacket and headed for the door, still grumbling. As soon as she exited the house, she jumped into the air and flew off, pale gold wings fading into the apricot sky.

With wry smiles at each other, Aria and Father followed her to the town's small temple. While Saverio was not a farming community, it was no big city, either, and the gold-veined marble temple was only the size of a two-bedroom house. They were lucky to have a third-level Gale as a priest instead of just a Gust.

Vasi, the country's capital a few hours to the north, was the closest big city and the home of Irajahan's majestic main temple. Despite the relatively short distance, Aria's family only occasionally made the flight over the mountains, finding the sheer cliffs just outside their town enough of an adventure.

They arrived and stood in line to present their new adult to the priests, and still Keelin wasn't back. While her parents watched the crowd, Aria looked northward. Dark clouds boiled over the mountains, reaching toward the ground with long fingers of rain.

How long had that been going on? Keelin had better be on the home side of the storm, or he'd be grounded for sure. And if he was late, he might miss his chance.

"Fair winds," a low voice said. "Where's Keelin?"

Aria looked up to the blue eyes of her brother's best friend, who would face his own Presentation in another month. Eyes wide, she tilted her head toward the storm and shrugged.

Jayan Machol followed her gaze, narrowed eyes suddenly widening. "What?" he blurted. When her parents looked at them, he smiled until they turned away again. "What did he do?" Jayan whispered fiercely.

Aria stood on her toes and whispered the story into his ear. When she finished, Jayan ran his fingers through his white curls and mumbled, "Idiot."

He waited with her and her parents while the other young men and women took their turns with the orange-robed Gale. Then it was Keelin's turn, and he still wasn't there. Father and Mother stalled until the sun sank to the horizon and the priest excused himself for other duties.

On their way home, a blur of golden wings shot past them.

"Keelin!" Aria called, swooping in a tight circle to follow him.

Her parents caught up, and from the corner of her eye, Aria saw the fierce, angry look on Mother's face. Father's mouth twisted into something between a worried smile and a frown. They all followed Keelin to the temple, arriving as he pounded on the door.

"I'm here, Squall," he called, using the priest's formal address. "Let me in."

The door stayed shut. Keelin shivered on the doorstep, soaked from head to wingtips. Wet, his normally bright blonde hair was as dark as his wings and even straighter than usual. He pounded again, but nobody answered.

After five minutes, Father grabbed Keelin's hand as he reached to knock again. "He said he had duties tonight. You'll have to come back tomorrow."

Keelin leaned his head against the door. "I would have made it except for the storm." He shivered again, and his plum eyes were suspiciously bright.

Mother tapped her fingers against her folded arms before she sighed and patted his dripping shoulder. "You need dry clothes and a good night's sleep."

"You idiot," Jayan added.

Aria took Keelin's hand. "Come home."

They flew silently until Jayan reached his street, then Mother and Father scolded Keelin for the last minute before home. After Keelin changed into his night clothes and toweled off his hair, Aria gave him a hug and went to bed.

Right after an early breakfast, Keelin flew to the temple with the family. The Wind ushered him inside, leaving the others pacing the grassy courtyard.

After a very long hour, Keelin emerged, frowning.

Aria grabbed his hand. "What did he say?"

"Not much. He looked at my school records and my flying times and said he'd get back to me at next month's Presentation."

"A whole month?" Father asked. "Why so long?"

"I don't know. He didn't seem very happy, even though I explained what happened, and he agreed the storm would slow anyone. In fact, he was surprised I made it through at all."

"That's good, isn't it?" Aria said. "You're obviously a good flier."

"Mmm. It should be good." But the furrow between his brows stayed.

The next month passed slowly. The siblings spent a lot of time flying with Jayan, and by Presentation Day, both young men were in top condition. Aria learned several tricks from them she wouldn't need when she became a teacher in a few years.

Everyone arrived at the temple half an hour early and waited with a thin veneer of patience. The Gale interviewed the regularly scheduled applicants, starting with Jayan. At the end, he nodded at Keelin but proceeded to unroll his list without speaking to him.

Aria squeezed her brother's hand tightly as the priest read slowly through the assignments. After each name, he paused to allow the families to cheer. Jayan was apprenticed to a small but popular aerobatic troupe, which was unsurprising for the three-time champion of the local cliff-diving competition.

Finally, the Gale read Keelin's name, then, "Sanitation: sewer."

Aria gasped, and Keelin staggered.

"No," he moaned.

Jayan grabbed Keelin's elbow to keep him upright. "You can appeal," he whispered.

The priest's mouth puckered as he rolled the scroll. "I'm sorry. Orders came from above." He raised his voice. "If any of you don't know where to report, please come talk to me. Congratulations, everyone."

Keelin wiggled through the crowd, with Aria close on his heels. "I appeal," he blurted.

The Gale's mouth puckered again. "Irajahan already rejected your appeal."

"I didn't even make one yet, Squall," Keelin protested.

"I know. And He still turned it down." The priest clasped Keelin's shoulder. "He doesn't like people being late. I'm so sorry."

"But, Squall—"

Aria tugged on Keelin's hand, and Father pulled him away from the Gale.

"There's nothing more you can do, son. Come home and pack."

Keelin whirled, a horrid grimace on his face, and shot into the air toward home.

Though Aria and Jayan tried to catch up, Keelin stayed ahead of them.

Finally, Jayan cupped his wings to slow his flight. "Give him some time alone, perhaps?" he shouted to her. "We'll talk to him later." Despite his frown, he waved at Aria and turned for his house.

Aria slowed her own speed and waited for her parents. Perhaps Keelin could switch to something else in a few months, when Irajahan stopped being so mad. And if not, then perhaps he could work hard and move up to supervisor, with better hours and duties.

When they reached home, they found Keelin's bedroom door shut, and it remained that way for hours. Despite her sorrow, Aria helped her parents prepare dinner and collect any of Keelin's things that had strayed around the house. Mother packed his clean laundry into a basket, and Father carefully set all his books into a box while Aria slipped in a family picture. The only thing she couldn't find was Keelin's favorite toy that he hadn't played with in years but still left in random places.

Dinner was quiet, and Keelin stirred his food around his plate without taking a single bite. Afterwards, the family loaded a wheelbarrow with half of his belongings, and carrying the other half in their arms, walked across town to take Keelin to his new quarters with the unmarried sanitation workers.

The building was brown brick with small windows and multiple locks on the door, and the yard was mostly dirt with a few scraggly patches of weeds. Even from their position on the doorstep, the place reeked, and Aria tried not to gag.

"Come visit each week," Mother said, teary eyes contradicting her forced smile.

Keelin nodded wordlessly.

"Work hard and make us proud." Father piled the last of the boxes and baskets by the door.

Keelin nodded with a grimace.

Aria threw her arms around Keelin. "I miss you already."

"Oh, fledgling," Keelin whispered. "I miss you, too."

They hugged in miserable silence until their parents separated them and dragged Aria toward home. Through her tears, she cast one last look over her shoulder at the blur of gold and brown in front of the low building. The door opened, and the golden figure entered, and as the door closed, Aria burst into noisy sobs.

☆✝♫◎

Not until two weeks later did Keelin get time off to visit his family, and Aria spent the day in a happy daze of anticipation. A little late to dinner, Keelin showed up at the door, so freshly washed that his feathers were too damp to fly, but still reeking so badly that Aria coughed and covered her nose.

Keelin's shoulders sagged. "I'm sorry. I bathed three times. I'll go."

He turned, and Aria grabbed his arm. "Don't you dare. We already waited for you, and I'm starving."

She dragged him into the kitchen and shoved him into a chair, then rapidly served food for both of them. As she thumped his plate onto the table, their parents took their seats, breathing shallowly through their mouths.

"How is work?" Father asked, taking a bite.

He gagged a little, and Keelin's shoulders sank again.

"Yes, tell us all about it." Mother put down her fork and folded her hands on the table, smiling brightly.

While Keelin talked about his supervisor and fellow workers, Aria choked down a few bites. Finally, she couldn't take any more of the horrible taste her nose transferred to her tongue. To keep her brother from feeling bad, she distracted him with questions. He answered some of them, but some he turned away with a few words and a grimace.

None of them managed to finish eating, and Mother eventually put away the food.

"Next time," Keelin said miserably, "I'll come between meals. I'd better go so I don't miss curfew."

"I'll fly — walk back with you," Aria offered. Before he could answer, she darted for her jacket, dancing to settle the back panel between her wings. "Come on."

She grabbed his hand and pulled him outside, shutting the door in their parents' faces before they had a chance to follow. They walked silently, hand in hand, for a while.

Finally, Aria gathered enough courage to ask the question she really wanted to know. "Will you be all right?"

Keelin laughed, but it was half a sob. His fingers tightened on hers. After a minute, she tugged on his hand.

He sighed. "Honestly, I don't know. I'm doing my best, but this all stinks."

Despite good intentions, Aria giggled.

Keelin snorted and then laughed. "That wasn't what I meant, silly."

Aria swung their linked hands. "It *wasn't*? Are you sure?"

When she giggled again, Keelin grabbed her shoulders and looked her intently in the eyes. "I'm sure about this. If you say that again, I'll have to take you to work with me. Then you'll stink, too."

She crammed her fists on her hips and stuck out her tongue.

He ruffled her hair, and for the rest of the trip, they talked about her school assignments and chores. When she left him on the doorstep, he gave her a long hug.

"Next time, fledgling."

"Next time, featherbrain."

K eelin visited the next week. Aria arranged for Jayan to be there, but it made no difference. Keelin still refused to talk about his job, and he was so surly that Jayan excused himself early.

The next week, Keelin spent only half an hour with the family and refused to talk about anything at all. The week after, he gave flimsy excuses why he couldn't come. Aria went to visit him and stood on the doorstep for an hour before she gave up and went home.

A month after Keelin started work, Aria's school class was given an assignment to learn more about Saverio. Her teacher clapped her hands in excitement. "You could study the historic buildings, or the farms, or the coal mines, even though they're a little outside town. Anything you want! Just let me know so I can write down your choice. At the end of the year, we can give your reports on location. Won't that be exciting?"

After class, Aria waited until the other students left, then edged up to her teacher's desk, books clasped tightly in her arms and wings curved around herself.

"I want to study the sewers," she whispered. "May I?"

Her teacher blinked. "Oh, I didn't mean — I don't think you'd like that, dear."

Aria nodded quickly. "Yes, I would."

"The sewer? Are you sure?"

"Yes, please."

The teacher picked up her pen and slowly started a note, then froze. "Um, I don't think the class would like to visit there." She spun the quill pen in her fingers. "Would you — mind giving your presentation in class, instead. Or, um, I would accept a written report?"

Aria nodded again. "Whatever you want."

"All right then. You're dismissed."

Aria flew home in the sunshine, already planning how to research. If Keelin didn't want to talk about his work, she would find out in other ways.

On Keelin's day off, she waited at his dull living quarters for two hours, flying around and around past the windows until he finally emerged.

"Go away," he muttered, reaching to close the door.

Aria landed so close the breeze of her backwinging ruffled his hair. "No."

Stench rose from him, and his usually dark-golden wings were a speckled brown. Aria swallowed hard and refused to speculate what caused the color.

"I'm not leaving," she said. "Talk to me."

Abruptly, he sank to the doorstep and buried his head against his knees. "I'd rather die than keep doing this," he mumbled.

"Oh, no." Aria sat beside him and put her arm across his stinking shoulders. "That's a very bad idea. Why, if you die, then the only person Jayan will have to bother is me."

She smiled and raised her eyebrows, but her brother didn't even raise his head. Aria sighed and patted his discolored hair as his shoulders shook.

They sat in silence, and then Aria leaned closer and whispered in his ear. "Why don't you run away?"

Keelin froze, and after a few seconds he raised his head enough to turn toward her. "What did you say?"

"Run away."

"What about Mother and Father?"

Aria shrugged. "You don't live with them anymore, and you can write."

He sat up. "What about you?"

"You can write to me, too, and in a while, when everyone gets over being mad, you can come visit. Or you can give me your new address, and I'll go visit you."

Keelin took a deep breath. "You're a genius, fledgling. And now, if you'll excuse me, I need to go plan." He gave her a quick hug and darted inside.

Aria flew home slowly. She would miss Keelin, of course, but visiting him in another city would be fine. It might even be fun. Yes, it would be fine.

Two weeks later, several members of the Saverio guard showed up at the house. Aria peered over her parents' shoulders, gasping when she saw who they held confined.

"Keelin!" She tried to push past her parents, but Father held her back.

"What is going on?" Father asked.

"We caught your son trying to run away. Did you know anything about this?"

"No," Father said.

Mother shook her head, and Aria ducked behind Father.

"I'm afraid we can't allow that," the guard said. "If he tries it again, he will be executed, according to the dictates of Irajahan the All-Powerful. So encourage your son in good behavior. Good flight."

He saluted, and all the guards departed, dragging Keelin behind them.

As her parents gasped, Aria collapsed on the doorstep.

2. PLAN
(SAVERIO, IOJ)

**Irajahan the Omnipotent is a strict god and does not tolerate
disobedience.**
Handbook for Winds

After that, Keelin was confined to his quarters. Aria turned
somersaults as she flew past his building every day on the way to and
from school, in hopes he might see her. Mother and Father still hadn't
discovered her part in the disaster, and Aria spent most of her time at
school or doing research in order to avoid them.

She'd found a helpful person in the Saverio city offices and had talked
him into letting her roam through the plans of the underground systems,
based on a note from her teacher. Every afternoon, she copied a new page
of blueprints into her notebook, then asked the city worker to explain it to
her. Her town was lucky, so she was told, to have the new ceramic pipes and
a formal sewage system. Twenty or thirty years ago, her brother would have
been carrying night soil buckets and sweeping unmentionable refuse off the
streets.

Finally, after a month of no contact, Aria saw Keelin as she flew over his
quarters. She swooped lower to land and talk to him, and someone jerked
him inside and shut the door. Tears ran down her face as she flew on, stopping at Jayan's house long enough to report she'd seen Keelin and to stop

crying before she went home. Jayan, out of school and busy in his new apprenticeship, promised to arrange a few flying practices within Keelin's range of sight.

After another month, Keelin was allowed to talk to Aria for a few minutes with a supervisor hovering at his elbow. Aria limited her conversation to "I love you" and "Are you well?"

Keelin merely nodded and shrugged and squeezed her in a hug that threatened to crack her ribs.

Aria and Jayan redoubled their efforts to be seen flying overhead, and Aria spent even longer hours on her school research project.

By the time she had to turn in her project, she had three times as many pages as the teacher had required, explaining the processes and history of the Saverio public sewage system. Though she could have explained the layout in extreme detail, she included only the most general features. She also excluded the typical life expectancy of a sewer worker, because she couldn't bear to write "twenty years from start."

Her teacher took the report with pinched nostrils, but a week later, she handed it back with a good mark written on the front page and a note that Aria would definitely *not* need to give an oral report.

Unwilling to end the connection to her brother, Aria continued to haunt the basement of the Saverio records building, poring over sewer blueprints until she had them nearly memorized.

After another couple of months, her family was allowed to visit with Keelin again, for no more than a few hours at a time. He no longer bothered to bathe three times before he came, and visits had to be held outdoors. Though Aria and their parents, and Jayan when he was available, tried to involve him in their conversations, he said little, sitting with sagging wings and downcast eyes. Keelin had lost weight, and his feathers had fallen out in scraggly clumps until he could no longer fly well.

As summer passed slowly, Aria feared the coming winter would be the last for her brother. Though twenty years was the average longevity, that included healthy workers in a cheerful mood. Neither of those described Keelin now. How much longer could he last before his health collapsed or despair and apathy led to a careless accident?

She tried to talk to her parents about Keelin, but they were sure he would eventually become reconciled to his situation. With nowhere else to go, Aria waylaid Jayan one afternoon, waving frantically until he landed to speak with her.

"You have to help Keelin," she said. "He can't keep doing this. If he doesn't starve himself, he'll be in some awful accident."

Jayan shrugged his wings. "If our god wants him in the sewers, what can I do about it?" He pulled on his white curls until they stood on end.

"Keelin can run away again," Aria said.

Jayan scoffed. "No, he can't. If they catch him, they'll execute him."

"If we do nothing, he'll still die." Aria cleared her throat and rubbed her eyes. "If they don't catch him, he'll be free. We just need a better plan."

Jayan rolled his blue eyes. "And you think we can create a plan to outwit Keelin's supervisor, fellow workers, the city guard, and our god himself."

Aria's face burned. "Sorry for bothering you. I'll do it myself."

She turned to leave, and Jayan grabbed her arm.

"I'm sorry." He sighed. "Look, I don't think we can do it, but let's talk. If we can think of a good plan, I'll help you. If not, I want you to agree to wait, and we'll try to keep Keelin's spirits up, instead. Deal?"

"Deal." Aria reached for a handshake. "I have a few ideas, but there are some things I haven't figured out yet. Let me show you my research."

She pulled her school report and extra diagrams from her bag and headed for a shady tree.

Aria and Jayan worked on the escape plan every day for at least a few minutes. Between planning sessions, Aria asked careful questions about the sewer system, either from Keelin or her helpful city worker, who was under the delusion she was still working on her report.

It was the realization that the sewer pipes also collected storm water that provided a key. After, their plan progressed rapidly, though it would take all three of them and a series of random lucky events to make it work. They kept perfecting every step without telling Keelin they had a way out for him, so they wouldn't raise his hopes before they knew for sure if they could succeed.

"And when everything calms down," Aria said, "he can come visit. Mother and Father will be so excited when we can finally tell them."

"He can't visit," Jayan said, "and we can't tell them."

"Not for a while," Aria said, "but eventually. In a year or two. Perhaps he can return by my Presentation Day. But if not, anytime will be fine. I can be patient."

Jayan put down the blueprint he was studying. "He can never come home again. I thought you understood. And you can never tell your parents or anyone else that he is alive somewhere else."

Aria stared at him, lip quivering. Never come home? How could she lose him forever?

"But he can write to me. He can use a different name or something."

Jayan rubbed his forehead. "And what if your parents found the letters and recognized the handwriting? Or asked you how you know someone from another country? In fact, you'd better get used to thinking of him as dead, in case Irajahan or one of his Winds can read your mind."

"Can they?" Aria asked.

"I don't know, but we can't take the chance. And there's another hole in our plan. There must be no reason to think Keelin escaped, which means everyone else must think he's dead. Since we obviously won't be providing a dead body as proof, that means we need witnesses to see everything."

Aria dropped her head onto the table. "You were right; we'll never figure this out."

Reaching across the table, Jayan patted her hand. "No, I think you were right. We're getting closer than I ever imagined. Now, what do you think about this pipe here?" He turned the blueprint and pointed.

Finalizing the plan took longer than they expected, and summer edged into autumn by the time they arranged for a chat with Keelin. He was skinnier than ever and had lost half his feathers. Aria blinked back her tears and tightened her lips to hide their quiver. Her brother needed her help, not her pity, and they didn't have time to waste.

Jayan looked stricken, but he helped Keelin to a seat under a tree and stood guard to make sure they were undisturbed while Aria talked to Keelin.

"You must get out of here," she said. "We have a plan for you to escape."

"I can't escape," Keelin muttered. "I'll never escape except in death, and the sooner that comes the better."

Aria punched his shoulder. "You can escape, if you listen to me."

Keelin shrugged. "If they catch me, I suppose I'll just die faster."

Aria rolled her eyes. "Yes, that's the perfect way to think about it. But you won't get caught if you follow our plan. You'll have to do some preparation, and so will Jayan, and then we have to wait for a nice, pouring rain in a few weeks." She smacked his shoulder. "Now, are you paying attention?"

She spread her diagram across his lap and pointed out the important pipes. "This is the main sewer and storm water line, and I'm sure you know it's big enough to travel through."

She thumped her finger on the blueprint. "This is where the overflow pipe connects. It's near the top of the main pipe, so the water only goes through when the main system is full. The connection is covered by a fine mesh to filter the water before it dumps through the cliff face and into the ocean."

"I know all this." Keelin leaned his chin on his fist and stared absently at the diagram. "How does this help me?"

"Somehow," she said, "you need to find an excuse to go there, alone, so you can cut, break, or detach the mesh. Rig it so it still looks right. Also, make a handhold for you. During the next big storm, you'll let yourself be swept away as if you're drowning, in front of the other workers. When you are out of sight, swim to the overflow pipe and grab your handhold. Get past the mesh, reattach it, and crawl through the storm pipe."

"At which point," Keelin murmured, "I will fall out of the cliffs and smash on the beach because the few feathers I have left will be soaked and flying will be out of the question. I'm not seeing the escape part."

Aria glared at him. "I'm afraid it will be a tight fit through the overflow, but you have to make it work. Once you tell us you have the pipe ready, Jayan will attach a rope at the mouth of the exit in the cliffs. You will catch yourself on that instead of falling, then climb down the rope ladder he will also leave for you. You will dress in the clothes I will leave for you, buried by the big rock we always picnic near. Remember where that is?"

Keelin sat up a little. "I remember. So, assuming I don't drown in the little overflow pipe, my fellow workers think I'm dead, and then what? I can't fly away, and I can't go home. Are you leaving me on the beach forever and throwing sandwiches down to me?"

From his sentry post nearby, Jayan chuckled.

"No, you idiot," Aria said. "You'll take a boat to Iskra or the Nokailana

Islands — and don't tell me which." She smoothed the blueprint. "And you can't come back. You can't write or send messages. If I know nothing, then I can't tell anyone anything, even by accident."

A tear plopped from her nose, and a spot of ink spread across the lines of the diagram. "Oh, now look what I've done." She rubbed at the spot, which only grew larger.

Keelin put his hand across hers. "Thank you."

Aria sniffed. "We haven't freed you yet."

"No, I mean, thank you for trying. I know how risky this is, and I'm not sure I want you involved."

Aria threw herself across the paper and hugged him. "You're my big brother. What else can I do?"

His bony shoulders shook under her arms, and she clutched him tighter until Jayan cleared his throat and greeted someone loudly. Under cover of Keelin's spread wings, Aria hurriedly stuffed the blueprint and notes into her bag.

"I'll see you next week, Keelin. I love you."

And then he was gone. When the passerby was out of sight, Aria cried on Jayan's shoulder.

☆❦🜊◎

Then they waited, for weeks and weeks, until Aria thought Keelin would never find a way to breach the mesh barrier between the pipes. In the meantime, she and Jayan created the rope ladder rather than buy one, then dyed it to match the cliffs. Jayan practiced his aerobatics by the ocean every day, until everyone in town merely waved when they saw him. Once he had become a common sight, he practiced diving with a pretend ladder, attaching it next to the downpour of the storm pipe, and escaping with dry wings.

For her part, Aria frequently nagged her parents about how miserable Keelin was and how she worried he would die one way or another. Since it was all true, it was an easy cover for the real plan, which still waited for her brother's word.

Finally, during one of Keelin's weekly visits, he hugged her very tightly at the end and whispered in her ear. "Ready."

"Good flight," she said, squeezing him hard enough that she feared for his ribs, but somehow keeping her voice level.

After he left, Aria flew to Jayan's house and told him it was time to hang the ladder when rain came.

But the weather stayed pleasant, and Keelin came back the next week. Aria spent his entire visit tucked under his arm as he talked of childhood memories with their parents. When he rose to leave, she suddenly remembered what she had found earlier that week.

"Wait a minute," she said, then dashed to her room to grab the raggedy stuffed dog from her pillow. She ran back, hugging the toy to her chest.

"I found Tucker in the cellar." She held the dog toward Keelin, clutching him hard enough that if he were a real dog, he would whine.

Keelin laughed. "That's right; he was looking for his lost bone. I forgot." He took the toy and fingered the ribbon that held his name tag on his neck. "What happened to his collar?"

Aria shrugged. "It wore out, and all I had was an old hair ribbon. I can make something better, if you want."

Her eyes widened. If the weather stayed pleasant long enough.

"Don't worry about it," Keelin said. "I like this fine."

One hand clenched around the little dog, he gave Aria another hug, then embraced their parents and left.

All week, Aria watched the sky, but it stayed a clear and untroubled apricot. At this rate, Keelin would have time for another visit with the family, though he'd be trapped longer in his misery. Her relief struggled with her guilt, and still the sky was clear.

One day before her brother's next scheduled visit, clouds boiled up in the sky over the mountains. If the storm stayed distant or small, they'd have to wait for the next one. Aria sat by the window and watched the clouds get bigger and darker and closer. By evening, the first raindrops fell, and within an hour, rain poured like a waterfall.

It was time. Her brother would leave tonight.

Aria swallowed hard and distracted her parents with dinner and homework and chores, trying to act normal. Jayan would handle the ladder, and Keelin had already fixed the rest of it. All Aria could do was wait. She couldn't even pray, because if Irajahan listened, he would send guards after Keelin.

At bedtime, Aria pulled a chair by the window. As the rain fell and the thunder pounded, tears dripped down her face. So many things could go wrong. Keelin could miss the tunnel connection. He could actually be swept away instead of faking it, or get stuck like a cork in the smaller overflow tunnel and drown or break his wings. He could shoot out the cliff exit too fast to catch the rope and splat on the beach below. And even if everything worked perfectly, she would never see her beloved brother again.

When she finally fell asleep, the rain was still pouring.

During breakfast, Aria leaned her head on her fist while her parents chatted about work and gardening and the neighbors. She rubbed her swollen, gritty eyes and shoved her cereal around her bowl.

When would they hear anything about Keelin? Would they hear anything? Had their plan worked? She bit her lip and smashed her cereal flat.

Someone knocked. Aria dashed from the table and yanked open the door before her parents even left the table.

"Are your parents here?" a sober guard asked her. At least half a dozen people stood behind him.

Aria took one shuddering breath and then another. Before she could gather enough air to call her parents, they were there, sweeping the door from her grasp to open it wider.

A man in wet, filthy clothes stepped forward, wings wrapped around himself. Through shivers, he explained, "I'm the sanitation supervisor. There's been a horrible accident. Your son was working the night shift last night. When the storm hit, the—" He glanced at the guard, who nodded. "The pipes flooded, and your son was swept away. We tossed him a rope, but it slipped from his hands."

Aria tried to take a breath but couldn't force her chest to expand. Mother smothered a cry with both hands, and Father grasped her shoulders from behind. The supervisor winced and looked at the guard again, who motioned for him to continue.

"We tried," the supervisor said, "but he was swept into the tunnels. I'm afraid there's no chance he survived."

Mother collapsed to the floor, and Father knelt with her. Aria leaned against the wall, too numb to feel her feet and too dizzy to stand alone. Had the escape plan worked or not? Either her brother was truly dead, or he was dead to her forever.

The supervisor took a deep breath. "We'll look for his body today, but sometimes casualties are buried in mud or swept too far to retrieve. Since he was a city employee, we'll pay for the funeral. We just have a few questions about your preferences." He looked at them and clasped his hands together. "Whenever you feel ready?"

The guard stepped inside and pulled Father to his feet, then reached for Mother. "Come sit, and we'll plan everything just the way you want it."

Mother choked down her tears and waved their guests inside.

How could Mother and Father stop crying as if Keelin didn't matter? As the last guard entered, Aria ran out the open door and flew for Jayan's house. Landing on his doorstep, she pounded on the door. He opened it a minute later, and she threw herself into his arms, wailing louder than the thunder that had signaled her brother's last night in her life.

Jayan folded his arms around her, and though he was silent, his tears dripped onto her shoulder.

The funeral was two days later. Aria entered the temple with her parents and walked up the aisle past relatives, friends, neighbors, and morbidly curious strangers. Keelin's death was the talk of the town, and everyone found an excuse to attend. Jayan jerked his chin almost imperceptibly as she passed him and took her place on the front row with her parents.

Keelin's body had not been found, and only a carved gravestone and a small wooden box with a few of his feathers sat in front of the altar.

The priest, dressed up in his full Gale uniform of sky-orange brocade, stood behind the altar. "We gather in sorrow today to remember a young man of our community who is now in a better place."

Aria closed her eyes, clamped her quaking lips together, and shut out the priest's droning words. She pictured Keelin flying free at last, one way or another. In her mind, his plum eyes beamed over his broad smile like they had before his Presentation.

In too short of a time, the funeral was over and it was time to move on with her empty life. On the way out the door, she dropped behind her parents and took Jayan's hand. Though they could never even speak of it, they were the only two with a hope that Keelin truly *was* in a better place.

NEGOTIATIONS

(ABOUT 22 YEARS BEFORE WIND OF CHOICE)

1. SHARA

(HOTARU DISTRICT, ISKRA)

The smallest Iskrin clan is the Hotaru, known mostly for their legendary map-makers.
Iskrin Culture and History, vol. 2

Today it would actually matter that she was now an adult.

"Hurry, Shara," her mother called.

Shara Kaniyar hurried to wrap her scarf around her hair, tucking in a black strand that had escaped from her coiled braids. Despite her mother's calm tone, she knew how important these trade negotiations were for the clan. More importantly for her personally, she now got to participate.

She had been perfectly happy studying cartography with her parents, and they had to nudge her at the advanced age of seventeen to make her adulthood trek before she had no time for a second try.

Fortunately, she had succeeded. In fact, she had quickly found a scattered patch of water-bearing cactus to camp amid, and her month-long ordeal had been nearly boring. Though she spent every day rotating between cacti and her snares, loneliness was the biggest problem she faced, and she was thrilled to return to her family. True, she came back last week rather thinner than usual, but better food would fix that.

She ducked out of the tent and hurried to where her parents waited with the Hotaru chieftain and the priest. Chieftain Prathap, elected when the old chieftain died a year ago, was young for the job, but so far he had done well.

Shara slid into her place beside and behind her parents and took a deep breath to calm her panting. To the south, a cloud of dust indicated some of their visitors were almost here.

"Calm, Shara," her father murmured. "Remember, look for someone unimportant."

"Yes, Father." Shara tugged her cream robe straight and tightened her turquoise and yellow belt.

Her parents had coached her for days on what the clan needed from this trade and what they could afford to offer. Now that she was an adult and their official apprentice instead of merely their student, they had finally told her some of the Hotaru secrets, which included not only trade routes and maps, but information gleaned over centuries about the other Iskrin clans' resources and preferences. This collection of knowledge made them preferred guides and negotiators between the clans, helping all sides get a more favorable trade than they could alone. As the smallest, poorest district in all Iskra, and one of the driest, the Hotaru depended on their cut of these negotiations, and the hiring fee of their guides, to feed their clan.

While her parents and Prathap led the official negotiations, it was her job to look for tidbits of dropped information they could use from the Achira. Her parents' older apprentice, almost ready to set out on his own, would do the same for the Rikatsu shipbuilders when they arrived. Normally, the Hotaru would have met the other two clans in either of their two districts, but in this case, they had requested neutral ground.

The dust cloud grew larger, and faster than she expected, a herd of horses pulled to a stop in front of her. Shara ignored their riders while she admired the beautiful mounts. Under the dust, their hides gleamed, and they tossed their heads as if the long journey from Achira were nothing but an afternoon's canter. The group had come north through Rikatsu, following the West River instead of daring Tarvati's long stretch of barren desert, but the trip still would have taken them weeks.

Prathap was talking to the visitors, but Shara kept admiring the horses. Such pretty animals, so full of energy and life.

"And this is Shara, our new apprentice." Father subtly elbowed her.

Shara quickly bowed, staying low a second longer than required to give her burning cheeks a chance to cool. When would she learn to pay attention?

Someone chuckled softly, and as Shara rose, she examined the delegation. There, in the back, holding the lead ropes of the spare horses, was a young man about her age. His clothing had no embroidery or ornamentation, so he was probably the groom rather than a leader. Though clan members could use either clan color, his scarf and belt were charcoal instead of the cornflower blue of the rest of his group, and perhaps that was on purpose.

Shara tapped her mother's back to let her know she had found her target. Young, male, and unimportant. He could not be any more perfect. She looked toward the groom and smiled a little before focusing her attention on the greetings among the leaders. When she glanced back at the young man, he was still watching her. Perfect. She lowered her eyes as if embarrassed, but kept her face turned slightly toward him.

Soon enough, the greetings ended. Tonight, the entire clan would greet the visitors with salt and bread around a fire, but now it was time to make their guests comfortable.

"Shara," Father said, "please show Hesketh where to care for the horses and then bring him back to the guest tents." Once facing away from the Achirans, he winked.

The visiting leaders gave their reins to the young groom, then followed Prathap.

Shara smiled warmly at Hesketh, holding out her hands. As he approached, reaching for her automatically despite all the reins and leads, she swept her arms to the side and pointed.

"This way, please." She turned, shooting him another smile over her shoulder as she walked away. "We made a rope corral, since we do not have enough wood. But we brought several clay troughs, so your horses will have plenty of water. They are beautiful."

Hesketh caught up to walk beside her. "Yes, they are." He cleared his throat and whispered, "And so are you."

She let herself blush, but changed the subject. "To keep the water fresh, we did not fill the troughs. I will help you draw water, if you wish."

"Thank you, I accept." He smiled, petting a horse that pressed close to him.

The makeshift corral was outside camp, far enough from the well to avoid contamination. Together, they filled the troughs in an hour.

Shara gently flirted, building Hesketh's trust and interest. If the negotiations went quickly, her work would be unnecessary, but if they dragged on, she needed to have the trail marked before it was time to travel. Besides, Hesketh was attractive and attentive, and she was having fun.

Before sunset, she walked Hesketh to the guest bath and left him while she dashed home for a quick clean-up herself.

They met again at the chieftain's fire and maneuvered to sit by each other while the priest passed the traditional bread and salt to the two visiting clans. Shara's parents nodded with the tiniest jerk of their chins, and she scooted a thumb-length closer to the handsome young man.

Shara reported to her parents at breakfast, which only took a minute since she had discovered nothing yet. They reminded her that past negotiations sometimes hinged on offers made for assets and needs the involved clans did not realize were pertinent. After promising to keep trying, she scampered to the corral, where she found Hesketh already drawing water. After they filled every trough, Hesketh showed her how to brush the horses.

While they worked, Shara chatted, casually fishing for information. At first, she limited herself to his daily life, and was disappointed to learn everyone did *not* have a horse.

Hesketh laughed. "Does every Hotaru knows how to draw a map? A good one, not a sketch in the dirt? Who weaves your clothes and gathers fuel and makes tools?"

Shara stuck out her tongue at him. "Fine, it was a stupid question. How many of you *do* work with horses?"

He stroked the horse's shiny back. "We are a much bigger clan than the Hotaru, and only about a third of us work with horses, one way or another. At least half do something related to horses, like make tack or grow hay." He puckered his lips. "Perhaps two-thirds. Somewhere around a fifth of the clan actually own a horse, but only a tenth own more than one. A dozen families own most of our herds."

Shara nodded casually, but his numbers were more exact than anything the Hotaru had learned before, and she tucked them away to tell her parents later. If only a dozen families were involved in the massive breeding programs, then those were the names she needed. For now, she changed the subject to something innocent to avert suspicion.

Spending time with Hesketh was easy, despite the constant water carrying, and more pleasurable than she expected. His sense of humor blended well with hers, and he was always kind and thoughtful, calling for a rest whenever she got tired, before she even asked to stop. He treated her like the adult she now was, without the little slip-ups common to her parents and neighbors who were used to her being a child. His constant attention was flattering, and his admiring glances made it much too easy to flirt with him.

As the days passed, Shara continued her subtle campaign. The horses were delightful, and she enjoyed learning their different personalities. When she and Hesketh were not working with the animals, they wandered the Hotaru camp, watching various craftsmen at their work. They spent hours each day talking to each other about every subject under Resef's sun.

After the first week, she sometimes reached the end of the day and realized she had forgotten to hunt for trading clues in their conversations. In fact, sometimes she had given him far too much information about the Hotaru and reminded herself to be more discreet. She did not report her slips to her parents, even when her conscience twinged. What could a mere stableboy do with anything she told him?

Hesketh taught her to ride on the dullest pack horse, who was still lively enough to make her heart race. As the negotiations dragged on between the Achira and Rikatsu, Shara nearly forgot about her task in her eagerness to spend more time with Hesketh and the horses. She had faith her parents could help Prathap satisfy both the bartering clans no matter how long it took, but the delay was a blessing for her, since she dreaded the day Hesketh would leave.

After three weeks, she could ride any horse in the herd except the two rowdiest, and she knew them all by name and temperament and preferred treat. The horses were almost the favorite part of her assignment, passed only by their distracting caretaker.

"You make an excellent horsewoman." Hesketh smiled at her from his seat on the liveliest horse before swinging down to unsaddle.

She wiggled her eyebrows at him and dismounted. "I have a good teacher."

Shara had been riding one of the taller horses, and as she pulled on the saddle, she could not quite lift it off without dragging it down the side of the horse. Long arms reached past her and lifted the saddle.

"I can do it," she protested, turning around.

He watched her with a slight smile, and she suddenly realized the horse was just behind her and Hesketh was so close she felt the heat of his body.

Her protest died in her mouth, and she stood motionless, reins in hand, her heart racing as fast as it did while riding. He stood equally still, searching her face for something, she did not know what. Neither moved until the horse whinnied for attention, nudging her against Hesketh.

"Oh." Shara stepped backward, feeling her cheeks burn. "We need to give them water."

Hesketh cleared his throat. "I will care for the tack."

They walked in opposite directions, and once the horses were fed and watered, Shara made an excuse to leave.

For the rest of the day, she lay in her tent and made a list of information she had gleaned from Hesketh. That, after all, was her task, not admiring his warm brown eyes and his muscular arms. *Focus on what must be done.* She wrote that at the bottom of the slate.

What was wrong with her? She had never let a young man distract her before.

The boys in her clan were boring, but Hesketh was different and fascinating. She groaned and buried her head in her blanket.

Ever since the war between Heresa and Tetsuya, no one was allowed to marry outside their clan if it meant they would take clan resources. In Shara's case, the resources were in her head, which she really needed to keep with her, so she could not leave Hotaru. Her clan's secrets were now hers to protect, like her parents before her.

This was never going in her reports. Her parents must not know she was infatuated with a mere stableboy.

Mere stableboy. Shara ripped the blanket off her head and stared at the sunlight filtering through the tent walls. Hesketh was only a stable hand. He could change clans if he wanted. Now, if he were somebody important, it would be different. But Hesketh was nobody, and Achira would never miss a few pieces of tack or a single horse.

True, he would bring little to their marriage, but what did that matter? They could make it work.

Their marriage. Shara snorted. Now who was buying horseshoes before owning a horse? All Hesketh had done was look in her eyes, not propose. What were the chances he wanted to marry her? Not much. Even if he found her attractive, it was a long, tangled route from that to marriage.

Focus on her task.

She sighed and rose, shaking wrinkles from her robe and rebraiding her hair. When she looked respectable again, she covered her hair with her scarf and went looking for Hesketh. Until a trade agreement was brokered, silly dreams had no place in her head.

As the days moved on, Shara frequently reminded herself to pay attention to her work instead of his captivating smile. She dropped her flirting, hoping to cool his interest, but that only made him talk to her more. Her reports to her parents became useless, and she found herself dreaming about him at night and in her spare moments.

☆❦♪◎

When her parents announced a successful close to negotiations two weeks later, she nearly cried at the thought of losing Hesketh. If he did not propose to her, did she have the courage to ask him to marry her and join the Hotaru?

She pondered that question late the night before both delegations would leave. Hesketh found her sitting cross-legged in the sand by the corral, listening to the horses whisk their tails in the darkness.

"So, tomorrow," he said.

"Yes." She sighed. Tomorrow was too soon.

"Achira is a long way from here."

"Indeed."

"Someone on horse could make the trip easily." His warm hand crept over her fingers.

She straightened, suddenly cheerful. "Yes, you could be back in no time."

He coughed. "I mean, we are close enough to visit. I mean—" He rubbed his hand on his knee, then took both her hands in his. "I mean, will you marry me? I love you."

Shara inhaled and blinked back happy tears. Now was not the time to waste energy on crying; now was time to say yes! She blinked again and opened her mouth, but he was still talking.

"I will give you ten horses of your own for a wedding gift."

"Ten!" Shara laughed. "And how will you do that, stableboy?" She leaned her head on his shoulder and chuckled. "But 'tis a nice dream."

Hesketh stiffened. "I am Hesketh Ashvakosha, son of the best horse breeder in Achira. I own a hundred horses, and if I want to give ten of them to my bride, no one will stop me."

Shara bolted upright. How had she never thought to ask his family name? The Ashvakosha family *was* the best in Achira, the best horse breeders in Iskra. Even before she learned more from Hesketh, she had known that. A hundred Ashvakosha horses were a fortune.

Her heart crumbled like dry sand. The Achirans would never let a hundred of the Ashvakosha breeding stock leave the clan.

"Will you marry me?" Hesketh repeated, leaning so close she saw his face even in the darkness. His warm breath on her cheek did not thaw the icy disappointment creeping around her heart. He slowly reached an arm around her. "I promise you a good home with many horses."

He expected her to leave her clan. Her parents had neglected to say her last name so she could gather information without suspicion, but now their plot had killed her hope.

"I have to tell you," Shara croaked.

"Tell me what?" Hesketh whispered, kissing her cheek.

She forced the words past the lump in her throat. "I am no mere apprentice. I am Shara Kaniyar, oldest daughter of the Hotaru's best historian-cartographers. I have been studying with my parents since I could walk, and I already know their secrets. Half of my clan's resources are inside my head."

His arm fell away, and Shara struggled to her feet.

"I love you," she said, "but I will never be allowed to leave my clan."

She waited, but he said nothing, and after a few minutes of silence, she dragged her broken heart back to her tent and cried herself to sleep.

2. HESKETH

(ACHIRA DISTRICT, ISKRA)

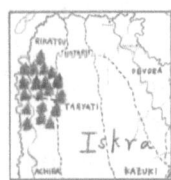

Danger and delight grow on one stalk.

Iskrin Proverb

S he could not marry him. Hesketh sat in the dark for a long time, until the night air cooled to the same temperature as his frozen heart. Eventually, he stumbled to his feet and staggered into the tent he shared with his father. As Father's snore droned on, Hesketh stared blankly toward the roof for a long time.

Shara was a Kaniyar, and not a distant cousin. She was one of *the* Kaniyar, one of the main assets of her clan. Her intelligence had attracted him from the beginning, but now he found himself wishing she were too stupid to learn her family's maps.

No, he did not. Hesketh loved her brain more than he loved her face. He would desperately miss both of them.

Then what could he wish for? In other circumstances, marriage. Marrying between clans was common, and most of the time, it did not matter who moved to which clan, or the partner with fewer clan assets relocated. But Shara could not leave the Hotaru. If he wanted her, and he certainly did, he must leave the Achira.

Hesketh rolled over and pounded his bedroll. He not only owned a hundred of the best Ashvakosha horses but had records of the bloodlines for hundreds of years. His family name meant "sound of the horse," implying they were so fast they could not be seen, only traced by the sound of their pounding footsteps. It was a family jest that stretched back generations, but the worth of their horses was no joke, and the clan could not afford to lose so many of them.

Even if he persuaded the clan leaders to let him leave, he must beggar himself and abandon the horses which were nearly his children. For all except a few of the oldest horses that Father had given him, he had raised his horses from foals, caring for them daily himself until the herd grew too large, and then still lavishing love on them. He knew them all by name and bloodline and training. How could he leave them behind? And with no assets, he could not support a wife, anyway. And what would he do instead? He had no other skills, no other riches.

Why would Resef allow Hesketh to fall madly in love with a girl he could not have? He finally fell asleep, only to be roused a few minutes later.

"Wake up, sleepy head," Father said. "Dawn is almost here, and we need to get ready to leave."

Hesketh groaned and rolled out of bed, eyes half-closed.

Father chuckled. "How late did you stay up courting your lady? Did she say yes? I imagine she is not ready to go with us today. We could pick her up when we drop off the trade goods to Rikatsu."

Hesketh closed his eyes and shook his head. He must tell Father, but not yet. Not until they were away from camp. Packing the accumulated mess of a month distracted him temporarily, and by the time his group was ready to leave, he had found enough calm to mask his distress.

Chieftain Prathap came to see them off, as did the Kaniyar cartographers who had been so vital to the new trade agreement. Their young apprentice did not come, and Hesketh found himself torn between relief and sorrow. She spared him the embarrassment of breaking into tears, but he could not see her one last time.

As dawn snaked blue tendrils from the horizon and the sky lightened to day's pale orange, he and his party rode west. Once they crossed into Rikatsu district and reached the river, they would follow it south to home, but he would leave his heart behind.

Father kept his horse at a walk and let the others pull ahead. "Why the frowns? I thought you would be happy today. I know 'tis difficult to leave her behind, but she will join you soon."

"Father," Hesketh started.

Father grinned. "Wait until I tell your mother. She thought you would never be interested in someone with only two legs, but I told her you would eventually find a girl more fascinating than a horse."

"Father."

"I'm only teasing. Your mother will love her."

"Father! She said no." Hesketh's voice cracked on the last word.

Father pulled the horse to a stop and stared at him. "What? Why? I thought she liked you."

Hesketh also stopped, pretending a great interest in his horse's mane. "She does." Two hearts were breaking instead of just his.

"Did you tell her you are rich? Perhaps she is worried about starting over in poverty. I could write a letter—"

"Stop!" Hesketh shouted, then patted his horse in apology for the noise. He took a deep breath, trying twice before he could speak. "She cannot marry me, Father. She's a Kaniyar."

"A—" Father stared. "A cousin? They said she's a new apprentice."

"The oldest daughter." Hesketh stroked his horse, unwilling to face Father until he could control the tears pricking his eyes.

Eventually, Father nudged his horse into motion again. "Oh. I'm sorry."

They rode in silence for a while, and Hesketh's traitorous mind paraded memories of Shara back and forth on the desert sand before him. Shara's face shining as she talked about maps in incomprehensible jargon. Shara's look of determination while she lugged heavy buckets of water for hours on end. Her brilliant eyes when she sat on a horse for the first time. Her smile as she pretended to flirt with him. Shara debating matters of trade and inter-clan affairs while grooming horses. Her laugh, her face.

Shara haunted him with every step.

Hesketh growled and kicked his horse into a gallop. Hoof beats sped up behind him, but not fast enough to catch him. Father was considerate, but there was no help for the real problem.

For days, Hesketh brooded as they traveled, taking care of the horses but ignoring the people. Father said something — he did not care what — that made the others leave him alone. Gradually, the barren sand of the Ho-taru district gave way to sparse grass, then to a thicker prairie before the northwest forest shadowed the horizon.

As they finally crossed into Rikatsu district and the dense forest that clan used for their ships, Father rode beside him again.

"Talk to me," Father suggested.

Hesketh shrugged. "Why? You cannot fix it."

"Perhaps not, but together we might think of something."

Before his better sense could prevail, his desperation spilled the whole story.

Father listened silently until Hesketh ran out of words, and then he rode silently for a while longer.

"Your lady's assets are in her head," Father finally said. "Where does our clan think yours are? Where are they really?"

"In my herd," Hesketh said.

"That answers my first question," Father said. "What about my second?"

Hesketh stared at him in confusion. The answers were the same, were they not?

"Hmm," Father said. "And while you are thinking about that, ponder what you want most and what kind of bargain could get it for you."

He patted Hesketh on the knee and rode ahead to chat with the others.

If Father knew the answer, why did he not tell him? While he thought, Hesketh let his horse walk.

Father would not tell him the answer because Father could not decide what Hesketh wanted most.

What did he want most? Achira or Hotaru? A hundred beloved horses or Shara? A herd or a wife?

He laughed, and the weight fell from his shoulders. Put that way, the dilemma did seem a little silly. He loved his horses, but they were just animals. Shara was his heart.

So, he knew what he wanted. Father's other question echoed. What kind of bargain could get her for him?

The problem was that his clan had too much to lose if Hesketh left. Some of his horses were bred for speed, some for strength or endurance or good temperament. Those were trade assets as well as handy at home. The best of the best had many desirable characteristics, and few of those left the clan. He could not leave Achira with so many assets, which were his herd, of course, whatever Father thought. But if he gave them up, the Achira would have no reason to keep him home.

A pang shot through his heart at the thought, and actually leaving his beloved horses would surely be more painful. Hesketh pressed a fist against his aching chest. Shara would be worth it. Shara would be worth anything.

Though the Hotaru would not let Shara leave, they would not care about him joining the clan, nor what assets he brought as long as he worked hard at something. Shara was interested in him when she thought he was a mere horse boy, so his poverty would not bother her, either. That solved the Shara half of the problem, but then what? What could he do then to support her and their future family?

Father seemed to have an idea. What had his questions been?

Where did the clan think his assets were? In his horses. Where were they really? In his horses! What else could Father mean? He was not like his darling, who carried her assets in her head and a few records. His riches ran on four legs and tossed their manes across glossy hides.

He patted the horse he rode. Poor beauties. Poor him; he would miss them so much. He had pored over their records until he had them memorized as much as anyone could. Ha, he did have records like Shara.

He stiffened, and his horse pranced. Excitement boiling over, he pulled beside Father.

"I figured it out," he said. "All I know is in my head, like Shara. I bred and raised my own horses, and even if I give the horses to our clan, I will still have my knowledge."

Father laughed and nodded, and Hesketh held up his hand before continuing.

"Achira sees my worth in my herd, the living riches of the clan. 'Tis expected, for what good does horsemanship do without horses? Knowledge does not pull a cart or lead a caravan or breed new foals. 'Tis not traded for metal and grain and tapestries. Since the Achira do not value what I know, they will not care if I leave with it."

"True," Father said.

"But the Hotaru see things differently. And if I lose everything but Shara, I will start over."

Father slapped him on the shoulder. "You built your herd from almost nothing, and you can do it again."

Hesketh nodded. "With Shara by my side, I can do anything."

H esketh spent the remaining weeks of travel planning tactics with Father until they had an ideal plan and a handful of backup plans, including his least favorite of leaving with nothing but the clothes on his back. He spent one night in his family's tent and an entire day with his beloved herd, saying farewell and weeping into their manes. Only for Shara could he bear to give them up.

The next day, he and Father went to the clan chieftain's tent. His belly churned with sorrow and excitement until he had to fight to keep his breakfast where it belonged. After a few preliminaries that took too much time, Hesketh got to the important part. First, he described Shara and their love, until Father nudged him. Then Hesketh coughed and explained why Shara could not leave her clan.

"Neither can you," the chieftain said wryly. "How can we deprive your father of an heir?"

Hesketh raised his eyebrows. "My brothers and sisters will be devastated to be so little esteemed."

Father half-bowed from his sitting position. "He has my permission to go."

The chieftain grunted. "But he does not have our permission to deprive the clan of so many good horses."

Hesketh rubbed his sweaty hands on his knees. "I am prepared to leave half my horses with either my father or the clan, as you see fit."

The chieftain narrowed his eyes and rubbed his chin. "All of them. What need have you of horses among the Hotaru?"

"Two-thirds," Hesketh countered, "and think how favorably the Hotaru will view you in future trades with one of their daughters married to a son of Achira."

"Hmm. But what if this Shara turns you down when you arrive? You may keep one horse to carry you home again." The chieftain nodded in satisfaction.

"Three-fourths," Hesketh said. "What good will I do you here when my heart is pining for Shara so far away? Absent minds make poor workers."

"I feel generous today," the chieftain said. "You may keep two mares of your choice as a reward for your years of service to Achira."

"I will give you nine of every ten," Hesketh said, "keeping a mix of stallions and mares. Ninety Ashvakosha horses is a generous ransom."

"Ransom!" The chieftain glared. "You are free to leave whenever you wish. But it saddens my heart to stand in the way of love. If you give us *all* your records, you may keep three mares and a stallion and praise my generosity to your beloved. And we will expect further collaborations in breeding and trades."

Hesketh took a deep breath before making one more offer. "Three mares and *two* stallions, and you keep the rest even if Shara decides she docs not want me. And if you want me to leave the Ashvakosha name behind, I will take Shara's name." He gulped, and Father pressed a comforting hand against his back.

His chieftain stared at him, then burst out laughing. "I think losing your records will be punishment enough. You may decide with your lady love whose name will pass to your family. Three mares and two stallions, and future breeding and trade. And if she turns you down, you may still return to us an Ashvakosha." He rose and bowed.

After bowing and promising delivery of the records by the end of the day, Hesketh and Father headed for their family tent.

"Could be worse," Father murmured.

Heart pounding, Hesketh nodded. Now he could rebuild his herd, and with no restrictions on his choices, he would take two mares that might be in foal but were too early to be confirmed. They had been corralled with other stallions, so his new herd would have more bloodline diversity than just the five horses could provide, though his chosen horses already carried a variety of favorable traits. The third mare he had chosen was Shara's favorite.

Back at home, his mother and six siblings gathered to hear the news.

Hesketh settled for, "I'm going," but Father made everyone sit for a recital of every haggle.

"Hesketh was brilliant," he finished.

"Oh, well done, and congratulations," Mother said over the cheers of the younger children.

"I will leave by the end of the week," Hesketh said, "and send word of the wedding date."

"No need," Mother said. "I think we should all go with you to meet your lady. We can have a nice long visit before the wedding."

His siblings cheered again and tumbled to their cots to pack.

"We are not leaving yet," Mother called, laughing.

Hesketh jumped to his feet. "But soon!" He dashed to his corner and started sorting his belongings.

The family was ready to go three days later, and they set off in a miniature herd. Hesketh rode one of his own horses and led the other four as packhorses. His siblings rode either their own mounts or more of the family herd, with a few extras for baggage and gifts. The rest of the herd was left behind with cousins and apprentices.

As agreed, Hesketh had left his breeding records with the chieftain. Since he had not been forbidden, he first memorized the bloodlines for each of his chosen five, all the way back to the original sires and dams. Once in the Hotaru district, he could write them down again. Every day while they rode, he recited each line until his head ached.

Once through the recitation, he talked to his family or brooded. Shara might say say no. What if she had only used their situation as an easy way to turn him down? Or she might not find him acceptable without his horses, or dread the years it would take him to rebuild his herd. What if she had already met someone else?

"Stop that," Mother said.

Hesketh glanced around. Had he gone too fast or hurt a horse?

"Stop fretting." Mother tapped his forehead. "Everything will be fine."

Hesketh grunted, but he relaxed his furrowed brows and pulled up next to his siblings to join their conversation. After his marriage, he would see them much less often, and he needed to soak in memories.

Weeks later, they crossed back into Hotaru district and had almost reached the site of the trade meeting, but the Hotaru camp was still not in sight.

"No worries," Father said. "You know the Hotaru are still the most nomadic of the clans. If we do not find them soon, we will split up and search for them." He pursed his lips and squinted at the family. "We can make four groups safely. One for each direction is perfect."

But within a few hours, they spied a turquoise and yellow banner on the horizon. It was too far to reach before sunset, so at the next well, they made camp, marking the correct direction in case the flag was gone by morning.

Hesketh spent a restless night and woke before dawn. By the time his family rose, he had already fed, groomed, and tacked every horse, and had packed his bags and tent. While the others ate, he rolled up the rest of the tents, and within an hour, they were back on the trail.

The flag still waved against the apricot sky, and the closer they got through the day, the harder Hesketh's heart beat.

Sha-ra, the horses' hooves beat into the sand. Sha-ra, his heart pounded. Shha-rra, the sun hissed. Shara, Shara, Shara. Finally, he could stand it no longer. He gave the leads to Father and goaded his horse into a canter. As soon as he saw dun tents on the white sand, he pushed into a gallop.

Someone in the camp called a warning. Within moments, guards collected in front of him, spears lowered. Hesketh slowed before he drove his horse into the spears, pulling to the side and raising his empty hands.

"Is Shara here?" he called.

After a brief chat among the guards, one of them walked toward the tents. Hesketh barely resisted the urge to yell at her to hurry. It felt like an eternity before the guard returned with a crowd of people.

And there was Shara. Hesketh slid from his horse and ran.

"Hesketh?" Shara said.

The guards parted to let him pass, though they did not lower their weapons. He slid between them, hands still in midair.

Stumbling to a halt in front of his beloved, he blurted his message. "Please will you marry me the clan let me trade in most of my horses but I still have a few and I will follow your rules and take your name if you want?"

As he gulped for air, Shara laughed.

A simple no would have been sufficient without humiliating him. His face burned, and he closed his eyes. Taking one last look at her, he bowed to knee height.

As he rose to leave, she threw her arms around his neck.

"Yes," she said.

Heart shattered, he reached up to pull himself free, then froze. "Yes?"

Shara nodded, lowering her gaze until her black eyelashes hid her warm brown eyes. "Yes, I will marry you."

Pink spread across her white cheeks, but her arms tightened around his neck.

"Yes?" he asked again, wrapping his arms around her. If only her clan were not watching, he would steal a kiss, but their current embrace was probably shocking enough.

She looked up, laughter in her eyes. "Yes, you silly, but I think we should keep your name. My parents already agreed to choose another apprentice if you came back. I still cannot leave, but I can keep your records instead of making maps."

"Yes!" Hesketh shouted, swinging her in a circle. As he whooped, the thunder of his family's horses drew up behind him. He reluctantly let go of Shara, twining his fingers with hers instead. "But we should start on those records soon, before my head explodes."

And when they got together to write down his records, they would have enough privacy for a kiss. Soon was not soon enough.

She laughed again, and they turned to greet his family.

FRIENDS

(ABOUT 20 YEARS BEFORE WIND OF CHOICE)

1. MEETINGS

(EAST CORAL ISLAND, NOKAILANA)

East Coral Island is the farthest-east occupied island in Nokailana.
Everything You Wanted to Know About the Nokailana Islands But Were Too Lazy to Ask

Alaneokawakani slumped on the bulwark as the pale orange sky darkened with blue streaks of sunset. "Why do we have to move again?" He stared longingly westward, toward their old home.

"I told you," his dad said, "I want to be closer to the shipping routes to the other countries."

He leaned on the tiller to aim their small trading ship around the coral reef to the small dock ahead of them.

"We've already moved five times," Alaneo complained.

"Well, we can't move any farther east than this," Dad said. "Look, there's East Coral Island. Isn't it beautiful?"

"What if you change your mind?" Alaneo said. "Why isn't it good enough to trade inside Nokailana?"

Dad sighed. "I told you; I'm looking for a more profitable route. Now, get ready with that sail. Let's make a good impression in our new home."

When the sail hid his face, Alaneo stuck out his tongue at Dad. He'd already combed and braided his pink hair and put on his brightest ocean suit. What else was he supposed to do? But he knew the answer. Compliment the babies, charm the girls, and make himself helpful to the adults until they trusted him. Memorize useful gossip to tell Dad so he could get the best trade deals. Everything was about finding an advantage and making use of it. He'd been helping Dad since he was only two thousand days old, and nothing had changed.

Nothing ever would change. He'd end up like Dad, drifting across the sea, thinking of nothing but profit. Was it wrong for Alaneo to want something more from life?

He furled the sail as Dad swung the tiller in perfect time to bump gently against the dock. After tying up the ship, they jumped onto the beach to survey their new domain. East Coral was much smaller than their last home, almost tiny. The gardens and orchards covered most of the island.

"Are you ready?" Dad turned toward the lavender ocean sparkling in the fading sunlight. "It's a festival day, so it should be easy to find everyone."

Alaneo turned with him. Beneath the water lay the village, safe from the storms and dangers of the upper world and freeing the limited land for food and surface-dwelling visitors. The underwater buildings sat next to artistic roads formed of colored rock.

In Alekona, Alaneo's favorite city, the roads formed a whale dancing with an octopus, accompanied by a singing fish, and to find the festival area, one merely had to find the eye of the whale. In this much smaller village, the streets made a picture of fish jumping through waves and coral. It always took a while to learn his way around a new place, but Alaneo memorized the picture for a head start. But for now, it didn't matter, since he'd be willing to bet a kiss on the prettiest girl in the village that the blinking atolla jellyfish marked the way to their festival.

In unison, he and Dad raised their arms overhead and dove into the water. The ocean was warmer than he expected, and it caressed his gills as they swam deeper, past the busy, colorful coral reef. The sun shimmered in ripples on the bottom of the lagoon. Though the noise from the upper world was muffled, the scraping of the beakfish feeding on the coral algae was loud enough to keep Dad and Alaneo from talking to each other, and the first explosive crack of thunder-shrimp made Alaneo flinch.

As they headed for the blinking lights, other Nokai swam past, waving and calling to each other on their way to the sixth-day festival, hair as colorful and varied as the fish that chased each other through the coral.

They passed the dome-roofed houses with their grated windows and jars of plankton light hanging in their sun-feeding stations. The little houses had the usual upper public rooms and the hatches to the private rooms on the bottom, though unlike in Alekona, these houses were only two levels high.

Until he and Dad arranged for their own house, they'd sleep in hammocks on their ship or merely float in the water with a tether. Unless Dad finally kept a promise, it wouldn't be worth the trouble of finding a house.

When they reached the theater, it was still empty, so they split up to browse the various market and entertainment stations and meet their new neighbors. Dad headed for the jewelry and more expensive goods while Alaneo swam toward some of the young people. If he made friends with them, Dad would have an advantage with their parents.

A pretty girl caught his eye. She had only braided half her long hair, and the rest swirled around her in a cloud of pale blue. That would be a mess to brush the next day, but it meant she was daring enough to make her own fashions. She was talking quietly to a young man with cardinal-red hair but frequently paused to greet other people. Alaneo liked her smile, and Dad didn't care who he talked to, as long as he made useful connections.

Alaneo slapped on the big smile Dad had taught him and swam up to her, shoulders squared. "Well met," he said. "I'm Alaneo."

"Well met, Alaneo. I'm Lani, and this is Manuai." She motioned to the redhead, who glared at Alaneo and grunted what might have been a greeting.

Alaneo dropped into his usual routine of complimenting the locale, adding plenty of personal compliments for Lani. He made sure to mention he'd lived in Alekona, the capital of Nokailana, and described the big city sights for the small-town girl's pleasure.

Lani smiled and asked questions despite Manuai's groans, and Alaneo kept talking. Even though her friends tried to interrupt their lovely conversation, he kept talking. The more their conversation was disrupted, the tighter her smile grew, and the more he smiled to assure her he couldn't be so easily scared off.

Eventually, he got to the point where he could mention his dad and their anticipated trading and how profitable it would be soon. He was just getting ready to ask her about opportunities when she looked to the distance and waved.

"I'm so sorry," Lani said, "but Mom is calling me. I must go. Do excuse me."

She swam away. Manuai glowered again and followed her.

Alaneo let his smile relax. After buying a snack, he found a hiding place behind a booth and took a break until he heard the call for the formal part of the festivities. Since the official announcements were a good clue to where to search for better gossip, he found a place in one of the hammocks around the theater.

The dolphins swam in a routine honoring Makanavailea, Goddess of Water, and then someone rattled off the birth announcements and other news. Alaneo noted a few items of interest, then, during the singing, searched for more likely people to meet. He had to stay for a few more hours, but Dad would probably stay until he fell asleep and drifted in the current.

In the morning, they would compare notes and make a plan. What choice did he have? Alaneo sighed, pulled his smile back on, and moved toward his next target.

2. CHORES

(EAST CORAL ISLAND, NOKAILANA)

Makanavailea the Omniscient gives each Nokai a birth gift from a wide variety of options.

Everything You Wanted to Know About the Nokailana Islands But Were Too Lazy to Ask

The day after the festival, Aolanikalia showed up for her community chores on land and groaned at the sight of hibiscus-pink hair next to Lelei. The only Nokai on the island with that exact shade was the new boy, the braggart. Why did he have to be scheduled in the gardens with her? Could she swap someone for gutting fish?

No, it was too late. Lelei had seen her and was beckoning. Lani smiled for Lelei's sake and walked over, standing as far from Alaneo as possible. The pink-haired pain was smiling at the middle-aged healer, too, with the same annoying grin as last night. He was about her age, not even an adult, so why did he think he was so great?

"Well met, Lani." Lelei kissed her cheeks warmly. Lani sometimes traded her friends for extra shifts in the gardens, and she loved to talk with the healer as they pulled weeds and fertilized. "Good news, my dear. We get help today from this handsome rogue." She patted her braids, which were a much paler pink than the boy's.

Alaneo waved, as if Lani couldn't see him standing right there. She hid a sigh. The new boy had ignored all her hints about ending the conversation the night before and kept boasting about his fabulous dad and the wonderful places he'd lived until she was ready to strangle him. And now she had to work with him? This would be the longest afternoon of her life.

Lelei didn't seem bothered by the pest and was already leading him toward the healers' garden. Did she intend to let an untested newcomer work in her precious herbs? Lani trailed behind, trying to figure out a way to warn Lelei that the boy didn't listen, without being rude to what's-his-name. She didn't get the chance. Lelei had Lani and Alaneo set up on adjacent rows before Lani could say anything.

While Lelei showed Alaneo which plants were herbs and which were unwanted intruders, Lani started weeding. It would take her twice as long to do her own work while she made sure Alaneo wasn't ripping out Lelei's herbs. Why couldn't *he* be assigned to gut fish? Fish guts didn't take precision.

Alaneo finally knelt in the next row and yanked plants with abandon. Lani kept her mouth shut for a few minutes, but the faster the stupid boy moved, the more her patience shrank. When he passed her and turned onto the next row, she exploded.

"Are you even looking at what you pull out? If you ruin the healers' garden, people might die, you idiot!"

Alaneo blinked and rocked from his knees to his heels, as if he might run. "I left everything she said she wanted. I thought anything else was a weed?"

"I've been working in this garden for a year," Lani retorted, "and I still have to *look* at the plants before I decide what's a weed."

Alaneo smirked at her. "If you want to check my work, go ahead." He waved at his pile of discards. "I'll get a drink while I wait."

Before she could yell at him, he rose and joined Lelei at the table where she was chopping herbs to make some kind of medicine. Lani was too far to hear what he said to the healer, but Lelei laughed and handed him a knife.

Lani scowled, then moved to the pile of weeds and started sorting them. If she moved quickly enough, maybe she could still rescue anything the jerk had mistakenly pulled out.

After a few minutes, she stopped and stared at Alaneo. who was carefully chopping herbs and laughing with Lelei, pink heads close together. There wasn't a single useful herb in the waste pile. Everything the boy had pulled was a weed. She dumped the pile into the compost and walked to the table.

"How did you do that?"

Alaneo glanced at the garden, then returned to his chopping. "You grab the plant near the root and pull. Most of them come right out."

"That's not what I meant. I heard Lelei explaining which plants to keep, so I know you weren't familiar with them. How did you identify them so quickly?"

He shrugged. "Just a knack."

Lelei chuckled. "Don't be silly, boy. Tell her the truth."

Alaneo shrugged again. "I can't take credit for it."

Lelei shook her head and dumped her chopped herbs in a bowl. "His birth gift is a perfect memory, Lani. After I showed him what to look for, he can recognize the plants in an instant. Help me convince him to train as a healer. With his memory, he'll never forget a treatment or a diagnosis."

Alaneo shuddered. "I don't like sick people or blood or any of that stuff. Yuck. I will be a trader, like Dad."

"So you said," Lani drawled. "Famous and rich."

The tips of Alaneo's ears turned almost as pink as his hair, and he stared at the herbs under his knife as if they would jump off the table.

"Lani," Lelei scolded gently.

"Excuse me," Lani said. "I need to keep weeding." She walked off without looking behind her.

Alaneo stayed with Lelei, and as she weeded, Lani couldn't decide if weeding alone was better or worse than having to put up with him.

She had half the herb garden weeded when an older man with jade green hair strutted straight for Lelei and Alaneo, who were now mashing herbs and adding other ingredients. The man stood across the table from the healer and talked loudly while he picked up herbs and jars to examine. When he crumbled an herb from one bowl into another, Lelei tried to make him leave them alone, but he kept touching and talking.

Even from the garden, Lani heard his boasts about his past trading and his future deals and his amazing son and how wonderful he would make the island.

East Coral Island was already wonderful and didn't need his help! She expected Alaneo to join with his dad, but the boy silently retrieved the medicines, subtly edging the older man away from the work area.

Lelei quickly started putting jars into a wooden crate. When Alaneo's dad picked up another jar, Lani jumped to her feet and hurried to help.

"Well met," she said, smiling prettily at Alaneo's obnoxious dad as she emptied bowls into jars as quickly as possible.

The smile was all the encouragement the jade-haired man needed to boast again. Lani kept her smile plastered on her face while she and Alaneo helped Lelei pack her precious medicines. Finally, the herbs were safe and Alaneo's dad showed signs of slowing his running tongue.

Alaneo pulled him aside and whispered something, then pointed and nodded energetically. The jade-haired man slapped him on the back and strode off like a conqueror.

Alaneo's shoulders slumped. He rubbed his hands over his face, then returned to the table. "Did you want to do more, Lelei?"

Lelei washed the table fiercely. "No, I think it's better to stop now. Thank you for your help. We got more done than I could have alone. If you won't be a healer, have you considered being an apothecary? You should make use of your gift."

"Dad says trading is the best use." Alaneo's tone was faintly bitter.

Lani stuck her fists on her hips. "Last time I checked, slavery was illegal. You can do what you want."

"Maybe next year, when I'm an adult." Alaneo picked up the crate. "Where does this go?"

Lelei grabbed a sack of dried herbs and led the way. Lani scooped up the knives and followed. As she washed the knives, she watched Alaneo's bright pink head bent next to Lelei's pale pink one, discussing the best way to put things away.

His dad was awful. Her parents laughed a bit at her obsession with sewing and weaving, but they never tried to stop her. In fact, all her friends got to do what they wanted. She'd never imagined a Nokai so intent pushing their child down a given path. And such atrocious manners. No wonder Alaneo had no idea how to behave.

Lani carefully dried the knives and took them to Lelei. Maybe her mom and dad would have ideas how to help.

3. MARKET

(SHARK ISLAND, NOKAILANA)

Many of the world's intercultural traders are Nokai.
Everything You Ever Wanted to Know about the Nokailana Islands but Were Too Lazy to Ask

A week later, Alaneo's assigned community chore was again weeding, this time in the vegetable garden. He traded with one of the local boys and headed for the healer's clearing. Lelei greeted him warmly and sent him to the herbs. Lani was already there, pale blue braids wrapped around her head to keep them out of the dirt as she knelt.

Alaneo picked a row two apart from her and weeded silently, rehearsing and discarding things to say. He hadn't made a good impression last time, and Dad had not been happy. More importantly, Alaneo regretted her low opinion of him, though he wasn't sure why. Dad never cared what people thought of him as long as his trades were profitable.

Lani cleared her throat roughly, then did it again. Alaneo retrieved the bucket and dipper and handed them silently to her.

"What's that for?" she asked.

"You sounded like you needed it."

"Oh. Thank you." She took a drink. "Actually, I wanted to invite you to come with me to the west market tomorrow." She winced a little and returned the dipper.

"Why?" Alaneo set the bucket and dipper aside and returned to his row.

"I want to pick up some fabric and dyes and other supplies. It will be too much for me to swim with, so Kaimana and I are taking a boat."

"I mean, why invite me?"

"You can help with the sailing and carrying the packages." She winced again. "And I thought you might like the chance to get away for a day."

Alaneo dropped a handful of weeds into his compost pile and tried again. "I got the impression you don't like me. Why not invite another of your friends?"

Lani sat back on her heels and rubbed the back of her dirty hand across her face. Alaneo hid a smile at the little streak of garden that still ended up on her cheek.

"I talked to my mom and dad about you." She returned to her weeding without looking at him. "They suggested the trip. They thought maybe you just need some friends here? But if you don't want to go, I understand."

Alaneo grunted. He'd never had any friends, only advantageous connections. He didn't know why anyone would want to be his friend. Nobody liked him any more than they liked Dad.

They weeded the rest of the rows in silence. When they gathered up the weeds, Alaneo said, "I'd like to go. Shall I meet you at the dock?"

"We're leaving at dawn." Lani beamed at him and darted away.

Her smile was gorgeous. Alaneo stood frozen for a moment, then shook himself.

In the morning, he waved farewell to Dad, ate breakfast on the way to the dock, and was ready by the time Lani and Kaimana arrived. After a brief introduction, they cast off to the accompaniment of Kaimana's girly chatter.

It took half the morning to sail to the next island west. Alaneo spent the trip reviewing Dad's advice. Dad might be happy with the way things were, but Alaneo wanted something better, and Dad's tips weren't helping.

As they left the boat and entered the market, Kaimana waved and turned left.

"The fabric is to the right, and dyes are straight ahead with the spices," Lani said. "Or you can go with Kaimana to pottery and seeds." She clutched her string bags until her knuckles turned white.

Alaneo smiled his best smile to calm her. "May I come with you? I believe you said something about carrying packages?"

Lani nodded, and as they walked, she pointed to different booths and explained the way the market was laid out. Alaneo ignored his dad's advice to always look like the smartest person, and instead of telling her he'd been here before, merely smiled and commented on the wide selection of goods.

As they walked and she bargained for her purchases, she talked and smiled more. The fabric merchants all knew her by name, and the dye seller turned her back on Lani to deal with other customers while she picked through the wares.

Alaneo and his dad never experienced such trust, and he watched open-mouthed as she rearranged jars for a solid half hour without being watched. Dad had a system for cozying up to the merchants, and Lani did none of the same things.

Finally, Lani waited for an opening and tapped the merchant on the arm. "I'll take these. And this jar is marked with the wrong color." She waved a bottle with a green label.

Alaneo gasped. What impertinence!

But the merchant thanked her, asked what it should say, and promptly relabeled it.

Alaneo waited until her dyes were packaged and they were out of hearing from the stall before he asked, "How could you tell?"

Lani pursed her lips and squinted at him. "Do you trade in dyes or anything with colors?"

He tore his stare from her pretty mouth and made himself focus on her equally pretty teal eyes. "Of course."

"And how do you select the coloring you want?"

"Sometimes by what looks nice; sometimes by matching it to something else."

Lani nodded. "I don't have to do that. My birth gift was a perfect memory for colors and the ability to tell them apart at a glance." She glanced at his hair. "I can tell your shade of pink apart from every other pink hair on the island, without having you next to each other. I've been working with these merchants for a couple of years, and they know what I can do."

Alaneo chuckled ruefully. "My perfect memory doesn't work on colors."

"But you can name a plant at a glance. I have to work through the identifying factors. This way." She led the way through the market.

Though his dad never revealed his secrets, he dared to ask Lani a question, which she answered openly. The more questions he asked about her specialties, the more she smiled, waving her hands as she explained. Her excitement lit her eyes and turned her pretty face beautiful.

Besides beautiful, she was smart and kind and friendly, and she asked for nothing in return. Around Dad, Alaneo felt inadequate. Around Lani, he could be anything. By the time his arms were full of packages, he never wanted to leave her. He was smart enough to not mention that to her.

At dusk, they returned to the ship and found Kaimana waiting. They loaded everything, and Alaneo shook his aching arms before he untied the boat.

Kaimana glanced at the sky. "We'd better hurry. A storm is coming in."

Alaneo looked up. Clear skies reached almost to the horizon before he saw a touch of cloud.

"Cast off," Lani said, and as soon as they were free, she swung the tiller.

Alaneo and Kaimana hauled up full sails, and they set off for home at full speed. They were only halfway when the sky suddenly churned with storm clouds.

"I told you," Kaimana said. The wind blew her violet hair in her face as the rain began.

"Yes, yes," Lani soothed. "You always know."

Her hands clenched on the tiller, and she leaned her whole body into keeping them on track.

"Would you like me to do that?" Alaneo asked. "I'm bigger."

Lani flashed a grin. "Indeed you are. Please, take over."

He stepped behind her and wrapped his arms on either side to grip the tiller with both hands. She shivered in her wet clothes, bumping against him. If he didn't have to keep the boat on track, he could think of a better use for his arms. He pushed away the thought of holding her. Few of the Nokai married, and maybe because of that, romance was strictly limited to adults rather than the children they still were.

"Ready?" As she turned her head to talk to him, her eyelashes brushed his cheek before she pulled away.

"Ready."

Lani let go and ducked under his arms, and he moved closer to the tiller. The cold rain pelted him, and the wind blew into his eyes. The girls scurried across the deck, bailing water and tying everything down more tightly.

As they adjusted the sail, a sudden gust of wind ripped it from their hands. It slammed into Lani and knocked her to the deck. Blood flowed from her head, and she didn't move or open her eyes.

Before Alaneo could pick her up, a wave swept over the boat and washed her into the ocean.

She was out of sight in an instant.

Kaimana furled the sail, cursing like a sailor. "Let the boat drift with the current until the storm ends." She tied back her hair and reached for a harpoon.

Alaneo grabbed the harpoon from her. "You know your way back better. I'll go after Lani."

He dove from the boat into the stormy ocean. At first, he saw nothing, so he swam lower, until the surface waves were out of his way.

Still nothing. No, there — a streak of red with a flash of blue at the end!

Alaneo followed the stream of blood to where Lani's still-unconscious body floated limply in the current. He grabbed her arm and looked for any kind of shelter. Eventually, he spotted a small trench behind a rock outcropping.

He dragged Lani to the trench and stuffed her mostly inside. With one eye on their surroundings, he pressed on her head wound. Fortunately, it wasn't as bad as it looked, and the bleeding stopped quickly.

The sharks, however, had already detected the blood in the water, and they arrived not long after. Two long shadows full of sharp teeth slithered through the waves toward the helpless girl.

Alaneo swam above the trench and raised the harpoon. No shark would steal Lani from him.

4. HOME

(EAST CORAL ISLAND, NOKAILANA)

Makanavailea's favorite number is six, so a Nokai child becomes an adult on their six-thousandth day. The occasion is usually marked by a large party.

Everything You Ever Wanted to Know about the Nokailana Islands but Were Too Lazy to Ask

Cool water swept across Lani's gills. Was it morning already? Why did her head hurt? She reached for the ache and discovered she couldn't move. Had her little brother tightened her hammock strap across her arms again, the rotten shark bait?

She opened her eyes and discovered she was in the middle of the ocean, stuffed into a crack in the seabed. Only moonlight trickled through the water, and she was certainly not at home. Someone's legs crossed the trench one way, and a harpoon ran the other direction. She blinked twice, trying to get her eyes to focus. The ocean suit next to her had blue puffer fish with yellow seaweed. That was familiar.

"Alaneo?" she croaked. "What happened?"

"You're awake." His head appeared in her view. "How do you feel?"

She reached for her head again and still couldn't move. "Terrible. Can I come out now?"

"Oh! Oh, yes." He stabbed the harpoon into the sea floor and helped her from the trench.

Lani reached for her head again, and Alaneo caught her hand.

"I stopped the bleeding," he said, "but if you touch the wound, it might start again."

"Where's Kaimana?"

Alaneo shrugged and reached for the harpoon. "On the boat. She'll meet us back at East Coral."

"Oh." Lani hugged herself and looked around. "What happened?"

"You were washed overboard."

Lani reached for her head again and stopped herself. If Kaimana had jumped after her, she wouldn't have been surprised, but she hadn't expected it of the pink-haired boy.

"Then what?" She tucked her hands under her arms to keep from touching her head. Even the gentle swirl of the water hurt her injury.

Alaneo tread water casually, but he watched her intently. "I found you, put you in the trench, and waited. Sorry about the cramped quarters, but it was the only shelter close enough." He waved his free hand in a circle, indicating the wide ocean. "At least it kept the sharks off you."

"Sharks?" Lani groaned. "What about you?"

He wiggled the harpoon. "I was fine. Do you feel able to swim home? I'll help you."

Lani shoved herself to an upright position, wavering in the water. "I can do it."

"If you say so." Alaneo looked around again. "Do you know which way to go?"

Lani squinted into the distance, turning to see all directions. "Maybe... that way? That big shadow might be the reef, do you think?"

"Whatever you say." Alaneo held his free hand toward her.

After a minute, she took it. His hand was strong, but he held her fingers gently as he swam. With him towing, travel took only half the effort. After a short time, she was doubly glad of his assistance, since she tired much too quickly.

At her injured pace, it took all night to swim home. Twice, the sharks returned, and both times Alaneo fended them off with the harpoon while she huddled on the seabed.

Lani tried to talk to Alaneo about why he'd come after her, but he ignored her questions, urging her to keep moving.

The shadow was indeed the reef, but by the time they arrived, she was too tired to move at all. Alaneo carried her in, her arm slung over his shoulders. The moons had set when he settled her at the door of her home and banged loudly.

By the time her mom and dad brought a light and opened the door, the boy was gone.

Lani was swept into the house and bandaged properly, after a promise to explain everything tomorrow. Kaimana was home safe, Mom assured her, and her goods had been unloaded by Dad.

That was enough for now. Lani closed her eyes and went to sleep, knowing Dad would tow her to her hammock like he used to when she was small.

In the morning, Lani swam to the dock to thank Alaneo for the rescue. As she climbed from the water, the boy pulled up the anchor and his dad let out the sail. She waved and smiled. Alaneo's smile became a frown, and he turned his back on her. And then the ship was gone.

Lani grunted.

"He's avoiding you," Kaimana called up from the water.

"No, he isn't. I'm sure he had to go with his dad."

"Yes, he is. I heard him asking his dad to go immediately."

"But why?" Lani flopped onto the dock and watched the sail shrink in the distance.

Kaimana shrugged. "He said something about trading for dyes."

Lani narrowed her eyes. Dyes? He wasn't interested in being friends after all. He'd only gone with her to learn her tactics, and now he didn't even care enough to maintain the pretense of friendship. She dove into the ocean and headed for the farthest edge of the coral reef so she could rage in private.

At the next sixth-day festival, Lani sought out Alaneo. She had told Mom and Dad what he'd done, but they still insisted she thank him. Now that he was back, she'd rather get it over as quickly as possible so she could start ignoring him.

He was treading water with his dad and a group of men and women who laughed loudly and slapped each other on the back. She preferred not to thank him in front of everyone, but she didn't want to be alone with him, either.

Lani faked a smile and approached the group. "Well met."

Everyone in Alaneo's group smiled back.

"Thank you for taking my son with you to the market," his dad said.

Lani somehow kept smiling at the conniving wretch. "My pleasure."

"He told me how much he learned from you. He's already put it to good use," he boasted.

The men and women laughed.

Lani glared before forcing the smile back on her face. Just one more minute, and then she could go back to her real friends.

"Really, Alaneo, I came to say thank y—"

"So, I wanted to talk to you about those dyes," Alaneo interrupted loudly, waving his hands. His golden skin turned pink. Blushing was not a good look with his hair.

Surprised by his reaction, she tried again. "After I—"

"Wait." Alaneo grabbed her hand and swam away, dragging her behind.

"But—"

"Wait." He swam faster until they were out of sight of the party, then stopped and dropped her hand. Behind them, the festival music pounded through the waves.

Lani glared at him. "I just wanted to say thank you."

"I know."

Lani shook her head. "Then what is the problem? You did save my life," she said between gritted teeth.

"I don't want Dad to know."

Lani blinked. "You didn't tell him? I'm sure he would be proud of you."

Alaneo grimaced, and his face turned red again. "Not really. He would use my 'heroism' for his advantage."

Lani crossed her arms. "I thought that's what you wanted. An advantage."

"That's what *he* wants. I've been thinking about what Lelei said, and maybe I'll use Dad's training for a route in herbs and medicines as well as the other things. But in less than a year, I'll be an adult, and then I can do what I want."

"So... you don't want to be like your dad?"

Alaneo shrugged. "In some things. I can be successful with my own style while I pursue what I want."

Lani uncrossed her arms and tread water. Why had he rescued her, if not for some advantage? What was his game now?

While she thought, Alaneo smiled at her and said nothing.

Finally, she gave up and asked. "And what is it you want, if it isn't to be rich and famous?"

Alaneo gave her a speculative look. "For now, just your friendship."

"For now? What does that mean?"

He smiled. "When is your six-thousandth day?"

"Does friendship expire? Do we suddenly become trade opponents when we're adults?"

"No. Mine is in one hundred and eighty-nine days." He raised an eyebrow and waited.

Lani threw her hands in the air. "Two hundred and thirty-five. What difference does it make?"

"None to a friend." Alaneo grinned again. "I'll explain in... two hundred and thirty-six days. Please, may we be friends?" He wiggled his eyebrows at her, then winked. "I'd do anything for you except battle sharks."

Lani laughed, and her feet twitched to the music still pounding from the festival. "Would you like to dance?"

Alaneo held out his hands. "Anything for a friend."

RESEF'S HAMMER

(TWO YEARS BEFORE WIND OF CHOICE)

1. TREK
(HOTARU DISTRICT, ISKRA)

You must do your own growing, no matter how tall your grandfather was.

Iskrin Proverb

Izo ran his blade down the whetstone again.

"You should take a different knife," Zefra nagged, sitting on the colorful mats that made the tent floor and combing fringe through her fingers. Her tilted, dark brown eyes were serious under her long black lashes, but she had always been too solemn, even as a small child.

Izo tugged his younger sister's hair. "Why?"

"You made that one. 'Tis not as sturdy as the blacksmith's work." Her stark white face turned pink at her bluntness, and she closed her inner eyelids as she glanced away.

"What a compliment." He cleaned his knife, sheathed it, and put away the whetstone. "I will be fine."

Zefra frowned at him. "Go over your plan with me again."

"Come here." He held out his arm until she snuggled against him. "You need not worry about me."

His thirteen-year-old sister tucked her head against his shoulder. "Why did you wait so long? If you fail, you only have one more chance next year. Why did you not go when you were fifteen? Or sixteen?"

"I only get two tries, anyway," Izo reminded her. "There is no hurry to waste the first one before I'm ready."

Zefra mumbled into his sleeve, "If you had gone last year, you could have practiced for two years before trying again."

Izo rumpled her hair. "I'm detecting a depressing lack of confidence in me."

"But if you come back early, you fail," Zefra muttered. "And some never return."

That was the unfortunate truth. The Iskrin survival rite threatened dehydration, wild animals, starvation, and bandits. Sometimes the candidates' bodies were found, but not always. Some came home early, but Izo refused to be a child forever — forbidden to marry, have children, or take any but the most menial jobs.

Izo hugged Zefra. "Listen, you skeptic. I can manage one month alone in the desert with nothing but my staff and my knife. And yes, I'm taking the one I made. I only have to go far enough to be alone. I must only survive. And I need bring back nothing but a decision about what I want to do with my life. I can do this. It will be an adventure."

Zefra twisted the hem of his sleeve around her finger. "You waited so long because you keep changing your mind about your profession. Why do you not know what you want? Are you waiting for Resef to tell you what to do?"

"Listen, impling, Resef does not care, and not everyone has plans for the rest of their life by the time they are twelve."

Zefra turned pink again. "He does care, and I like plans."

"I know you do. And when I return — not if — I'm happy to listen to them again." He tapped her nose. "Now, when are Mother and Father returning for dinner?"

Zefra tightened her boot laces and pushed herself to her feet. "They're bringing the little girls back in a couple of hours. I need to go to the market for supplies. Do you want to come with me?"

"Of course. 'Tis my last chance to buy food instead of chasing it."

Zefra snorted, and they both wrapped their scarves around their black hair and grabbed their staffs. Their tent was on the outskirts of the camp, near their father's horse corrals and not too far from the small market. While Zefra shopped, Izo wandered through the bustling market, collecting good wishes and advice for the morning from nearly everyone in their small clan.

He heard some large cities in other districts had shortened the rite, but the Hotaru still held to the old ways. What difference did it make in these modern times? Resef was undeniably real, but Izo had never once gotten an answer to any of his prayers. Like the rite, asking Resef's opinion was an obsolete custom.

Izo could choose for himself, and indeed, he had been investigating for years. Though he couldn't have a real profession until after his rite, he had informally apprenticed with many of the clan, testing what he liked best.

Working with Father and the horses had lasted almost a year when he was younger. After that, he had branched out to other relatives in the clan. The Hotaru was the smallest Iskrin clan, and many of them specialized in cartography, including his mother before she married Father and took over the breeding and sales records for his horses. Izo had lasted only a month in his grandparents' tent. He wanted something more active and exciting than maps.

For the past year, he had spent much of his time with the blacksmith. Making nails was boring, ever so boring, but he loved the sight of something new coming to life under his hammer and tongs and the feel of striking the hot iron while sparks flew. But was the good worth enduring the boredom? That was the question he intended to ponder before he took his decision to Resef the Omnificent, God of Fire, just in case He cared.

After waiting for his turn and bowing in greeting, Izo smiled at the butcher's pretty daughter and subtly flexed his muscles. "Will you miss me while I'm gone?"

She giggled and turned to hand someone their neatly wrapped package. When she turned back, she patted the black curls slipping from under her scarf. "I do not miss little boys." Her smile revealed her lie.

He grinned. "But when I return, I will not be a little boy."

Zefra tugged on his arm. "I'm ready to go now."

Izo shrugged one shoulder and winked at the butcher's daughter. "Sisters."

She grinned, and Zefra pulled Izo again. "Come on."

By the time they got home, their parents and little sisters had arrived. Everyone hung up their scarves and helped prepare the meal. As they worked, Izo memorized their faces, noticing again how different his sisters looked. Though they all had the nearly universal Iskrin black hair and brown eyes, they mixed their parents' features in different combinations.

Izo spent dinnertime soaking in their love. His heart ached at the thought he might never see them again. Despite telling Zefra she had nothing to worry about, he knew there was a chance he would not return. A small chance! Minuscule. His parents had trained him well, and he was strong from working with the blacksmith. He could handle whatever the desert threw at him. Failure was mounted on the slowest horse in the herd, and Izo would win the race.

He forced a smile for the rest of the meal, then chatted easily with Risa and Usri while the three of them washed dishes.

After helping put the three little girls into bed on their narrow cots — four times for little Haru, whose giggles fortunately betrayed the toddler every time she snuck out — he sat outside the tent with Zefra and their parents for another hour, watching the stars.

Mother and Father talked quietly about the horses and the girls and their plans for next year, though they sat close to Izo and touched him frequently. Zefra lectured him about navigating by the stars and reminded him how to set snares and where the caravan routes ran and which plants were poisonous.

Mother finally sent Zefra to bed before Izo strangled her, and he sat with his parents until the three moons set. All three embraced silently and went to bed, where Izo lay sleeplessly for hours.

As blue dawn crept across the sky, he rose, dressed, and grabbed his runes, knife, and staff without waking his sisters. The curtain to his parents' room twitched aside a handspan as he passed. According to tradition, they said nothing and did not show themselves.

"Bright day," Izo whispered despite the custom of silence, then ducked out of the tent. The turquoise and yellow firefly banner of the Hotaru flew above the camp, smaller and smaller behind him as he walked south.

Once past the camp, he adjusted his course to the southwest. Like most Hotaru candidates, he planned to head toward the closest caravan route, stopping before he actually reached it. He would have better access to water and edible plants, and hopefully fewer encounters with predators. As long as he stayed out of sight of any travelers and survived for a month, he would still be counted an adult.

He strolled all morning under the apricot sky, pausing only to harvest juicy cactus flesh when he got thirsty. At midday, he lay in the dubious shade of a scrubby bush and pulled the end of his scarf across his face for a little sleep. When the white sun moved enough to eliminate his shade, he walked again.

At nightfall, he slept for several hours, then kept walking. By morning, he was far enough from home that no one would run across him, but not yet close enough to the caravan route to be spotted. Good enough.

Izo picked a sand dune high enough to cast a large shadow and settled into the shade. First, a nap, for he had plenty of time in his adventure.

He slept until his shade disappeared, then scouted the location of the nearest cacti. There were actually three good ones within an hour's journey in different directions, so that met his next goal. One even grew near a thin patch of desert grass.

Third was food. His stomach growled in emphasis. Two days without food was no danger of starvation, but it was uncomfortable. He spent an hour gathering the sparse grass, then sat upwind of his tiny pile of bait with his knife in his hand, pretending he was a large, unmoving rock.

After three hours, he walked away. An hour later, he came back to try again, but the grass was already gone.

Izo screamed in frustration.

He cut himself more cactus and retreated to the shade to think. A snare might work better, but he needed a bit of hide first to make one. Or did he? A Resef's-needle shrub could be pounded into thread.

He searched the area without finding the spiky plant. By evening, he gave up and took his empty, aching stomach to bed. Perhaps Zefra was right, and he should have practiced last year.

In the middle of the night, he suddenly woke with an idea. He *had* thread. All he needed to do was unravel a bit of his scarf or the hem of his robe and twist it into string. Yes, he was brilliant. Zefra had nothing to worry about. He put his arms behind his head and whistled cheerfully until he fell asleep again.

In the morning, he carefully unpicked his hem and unraveled several cubits of tan thread, stopping while his robe still met his boots. It took him all day to get it to twist properly, but by evening, he had enough twine for a snare. He returned to the tunnel by the cactus and assembled his trap, then collected more juicy cactus and went to bed hungry.

Izo's belly woke him before dawn, and he crept to his trap with shaking hands. At the sight of his full snare, he fell to his knees. "Thank you, Resef!"

He skinned and gutted the dead hare, then realized he had no fire and no fuel. After staring at the raw meat for what felt like a long time, he took a bite. It was chewy but tasted better than he expected. Hunger forced him through the entire hare, and for the first time in four days, his stomach did not hurt.

He set aside the guts for bait and checked the snare for damage. It seemed fine, so he set it up again by the warren. Most of the day was spent twining a new string from more of his robe, and this snare he arranged farther into the sand with the rabbit guts as bait, hoping for a coyote or vulture.

Izo had a little time before sunset, so he spent the last of daylight searching for dry grass, withered shrubs, and a fire-starting flint. If — when — he caught more prey tomorrow, he wanted to be able to cook it.

But the next day brought one empty snare and one broken one. He twisted a new snare from string, in time to start drying the rabbit hide. Sunset came too quickly, and he once again went to bed hungry.

He woke the next morning to a howling wind and scrambled to his feet. In the distance, a cloud of sand rose toward the sky, coming his way. If he did not find shelter, his empty belly would not matter.

Izo grabbed his staff and ran to the biggest rock in the area. He unwrapped his scarf as quickly as possible and knelt on the leeward side, wedging his staff between his legs and the stone. After rewrapping his scarf to cover most of his face, he waited, heart pounding, watching the sandstorm until it was almost upon him. With his sleeves pulled down to cover his hands, he kept one hand on his staff and one holding his scarf across his face. At the last minute, he closed both sets of eyelids tightly, and bent until his head rested on his knees.

And then he prayed.

The wind howled, tugging on Izo's clothes and trying to shove him from the pitiful shelter. Despite covering himself, sand scratched under his collar and up his sleeves and under his scarf, until the itching, burning torture nearly convinced him that death would at least be less irritating. Nonetheless, he kept his eyes and mouth closed and leaned into the rock, determined to outlast the wind and sand.

To his surprise and delight, the storm was short-lived, and after less than an hour, he shook himself free of the piled sand and pulled himself to his feet. After removing his scarf and shaking out most of the sand, he leaned to retrieve his staff.

"That was not so bad," Izo said.

As he straightened, something pulled free of the sand, stuck on the end of his staff. He shook it loose, and it clattered as it fell. Dry bones. Some poor jackal, perhaps.

A hint of turquoise caught his eye, and he dug around the bones. The storm had nearly uncovered them, and it took only a minute to free the turquoise. It was a Hotaru belt, beaded with a compass.

He sat on the rock and stared at the belt, chills racing over his skin. No jackal, then. Iskrin bones, and from his clan. Someone had not made it home.

No one came to mind in the last few years, but he had no way to tell how old the bones were.

Izo rolled the belt and tucked it into his pouch, then carefully reburied the bones by the rock with a prayer to Resef. If anyone at home could identify the belt, he would tell them where to find the bones.

He put on his scarf and headed to the cactus to quench his thirst. At least the cactus would keep him alive a while longer, even without food. His stomach grumbled for his mother's cooking.

The next day, the sixth, he caught a small lizard, half-cooked it over his tiny fire, and gobbled it in three bites like the finest meal. He spent the remaining daylight hours working on the rabbit leather and went to bed with a sense of accomplishment. At this rate, he was sure to survive, because more practice would only improve his skills. Once he was eating regularly, this would be a real adventure worthy of a good tale.

With the lizard's innards as bait, he caught a stupid coyote pup the next day, which had no more meat than a large hare. The coyote destroyed the snare, too, and Izo regretfully unraveled another thumb-length of his hem. If he did not get some cured leather soon, his robe would end around his knees before he got home. And then Zefra would never let him forget it!

2. RETURN
(HOTARU DESERT, ISKRA)

Use runes wisely. Be warned that Resef listens personally to all prayers addressed to him.
How to Read Runes: Introduction

The next two weeks were depressingly the same. Sometimes he found a few edible plants besides the cactus, but mostly he did not. He spent all day, every day, searching for food and fuel. Every two or three days, he caught some kind of meat, though never enough to sate his growing hunger. His belt grew looser and looser until he had to cinch it in.

When he made a new snare of the rabbit hide, cut in a spiral to make a long strand, his prey snapped it the first time he used it. He tested it in his hands, and it snapped again. Ashes! Somehow, he had done something wrong, and the leather was too fragile to hold any weight. He threw the broken strap down the rabbit warren in a fit of anger.

Izo did have one thing to do besides live, so in his spare time, which meant while he wandered aimlessly looking for food, he thought about the jobs he had tried at home. Each had been fun, for a little while. Eventually, they were all boring. Which boredom could he tolerate for a lifetime? Would this month be his only adventure?

He prayed to Resef periodically, but when he laid his rune stones face down, none turned over in an answer. It seemed his god had no preference about his vocation. Or Izo was right and He was not listening.

Izo prayed for food, too, but still got hungrier and hungrier. Though his small clan was poor enough to suffer in times of drought, he had never been this close to starvation.

By the last week, Izo wondered if he would make it home or if his bones would lie forever in the desert, stripped of flesh by jackals and vultures. Perhaps Resef did not reply because Izo would not live long enough to have a profession.

He started for home slowly, leaning on his staff. To preserve his scant energy, he would spread the two-day journey across his last week. Each night, he prayed again, but still with no response. The city dwellers were right to discontinue this waste of time and energy.

Working with Father's horses let him do something different every day. It might be the least boring option. And he did like horses. Riding, training, and breeding, anyway. Feeding and brushing were tolerable. Cleaning up... He would have to make himself too valuable to be stuck on mucking duty.

Three days from the end, his musings were interrupted by a faceful of sand. He blinked his inner eyelids shut and yanked himself back to attention. Dirt blew into his face again. The sky was darkening, and the wind whistled. Izo cursed his inattention. Another sandstorm was beginning, and he had missed the early warning signs. How long did he have to find shelter?

The sand swirled around his knees.

Not much time at all.

What shelter did he have available?

No rocks, no cactus. Nothing.

What did that leave?

Do not get buried.

Izo raced up the hill. At the crest, he covered his face and knelt to cover his bare legs and make a smaller target. He placed his staff crosswise under his legs and held on with both hands, sleeves pinched in his fingers and face pressed against his knees.

He was barely in time. The wind howled, and the storm turned the air into a mass of stinging particles. Breathing was difficult and moving impossible. Izo held on and prayed. Daylight turned as dark as sunset, and the wind buffeted him, blowing hard enough to shift the dune under his body.

"Please, Resef, keep me at the top." If he slid too low, the blowing sand could bury him in minutes. He would be as lost as the owner of the compass belt in his pouch, and his bones might never be found. "Please, Most Holy Flame, end the storm and let me live."

But the storm continued.

Izo's knees cramped and his fingers ached, but he huddled despite the pain. If he died, which seemed more likely the longer the wind roared, it would not be because he surrendered.

And still the storm blew, battering him with sand and wind and sheer noise. The hilltop began to slide.

"Please, Luminosity," he prayed, "at least tell my family what happened to me."

The landslide continued, taking him over the crest and down the other side. The dune began to accumulate above him, burying his legs and creeping up his ribs.

Then miraculously, the landslide stopped. The wind lessened, and sand thinned enough for him to briefly sense the sun.

Perhaps he would live through his adventure. Izo had just begun a prayer of thanksgiving when a wind-borne rock slammed into his head and knocked him unconscious.

☆♀⚶◎

When he woke a few hours later and pulled his scarf from his face, he discovered a desert hare sniffing his boots. Izo scrambled to his feet and drew his knife. The hare bolted. Izo chased him up the dune, frantic for breakfast. The hare bounded down the other side, and Izo followed.

Halfway down, he tripped and rolled. He dropped his knife and staff for his own protection as he tried to stop, but he could not get a grip in the collapsing sand. The dune slid faster and faster under him as he tumbled, elbows and knees flying, and sand grinding across his skin.

After an eternity, he slid to a stop at the bottom, half buried.

The hare, safe under a scrubby bush, twitched its ears and vanished into a hole.

Izo brushed off his chest and struggled to sit, wincing as he pressed his hands against the rough ground. His dinner was gone. His knife and staff were at the top of the dune. Perhaps. They might be buried somewhere he would never find them.

And he was bleeding. During his fall, he'd peeled half his skin from his hands, and blood oozed across the white, higher than his elbows. He touched his face and winced. Ow. Yes, more blood on his fingers now. Izo took a deep breath and pushed sand away with his bleeding hands.

Once his legs were mostly free, he looked carefully at himself. His legs were also covered in blood, especially the bare section between his boots and his knees, but he did not see any bones showing. He tentatively moved one leg. Ow again, but it felt no worse than his hands and face. The other leg also seemed whole, though just as peeled. He carefully brushed off as much sand as possible, though without water, cleaning the wounds was impossible. With no mirror, his face was the hardest, and he finally gave up and hoped he had done enough.

Izo struggled to his feet and glanced between the hare's tunnel and the top of the dune. Food or tools? Limping with every step, he headed toward the bush, then stopped. What would he do, crawl inside the tiny hole to chase the rabbit? And how would he butcher it if he caught it?

He sighed and turned around to climb the hill. From the top to the bottom, a long streak of disturbed sand marked his path. The loosened sand gave under his feet, but he limped to the top, trying to bend his aching knees as little as possible as he followed the trail of his descent. Yes, descent sounded much nicer than fall. When he told the story to his family, he would have to use that word. He grinned ruefully.

Almost at the top, far above, metal gleamed. Why could it not be closer? He fluttered his robe away from his skinned knees and kept going. When he reached the gleam, it was the steel band around his staff. He painfully crouched and grabbed the unburied end. As he pulled it free, the sand shifted, revealing more metal. Oh, thank Resef, his knife.

Izo limped a few more steps and used his staff to support him as he crouched again. The knife was half-buried, and when he pulled it free, it ended halfway below the hilt.

Curse R— No, no that would be a very bad idea. He did not say it. He pretended he did not even think it and hoped it escaped the attention of the capricious god. Who was to say if Resef had not already punished him for his disdain of the rite?

Now there was no point to setting snares at night or chasing any more stupid hares. Even if he caught something, he had no way to skin or butcher it. Zefra would gloat about the knife being as bad as she said. Izo took a deep breath and turned downhill, shoving the broken knife in its sheath. It did not matter. He was on his way home. If he ate nothing for the next two and a half days, he would still survive.

As he limped northward, his skinned knees protested, and he amended his thought. He would survive if infection did not kill him. Or if the blood did not attract predators while he slept.

Two days. He could last two more days.

At the bottom of the hill, he shortened his robe again, tearing strips to bandage the worst-damaged skin. Though the robe covered most of his wounds, having the fabric continually brush against the abrasions was torture. A still bandage felt better, and his clothing was already ruined.

Izo limped steadily for the rest of the day, and after assessing his progress against the stars, he limped through half the night before collapsing in exhaustion. His last thought before he fell asleep was that a horse would be nice.

When pain woke him, he rewrapped his injuries, which fortunately showed no sign of infection yet, and struggled to his feet. That day, he stopped only to hide from the midday sun or hack bits of cactus with his broken knife. As he squeezed the cactus juice into his parched mouth, he changed his mind. A good knife would be better than a horse.

Izo fell asleep at night dreaming of knives. Long daggers, short eating knives, broken knives made whole. All night, the clang of imaginary hammers echoed as his dream-self made piles of sharp implements.

In the morning, he checked his wounds again. Some of them were turning a red that had nothing to do with blood. His face felt even worse. Today was his last day, and if he did not make it home soon, he predicted a raging infection and no way to treat it.

The answer was as obvious as the problem. He must get home.

Izo struggled to his feet and walked, leaning on his staff despite the pain in his skinned hands. The hours passed in a daze. Toward night, his pace slowed. If he could only rest for a while... Just a few minutes. He staggered to a stop and tried to sit. The pain in his knees woke him fully, and he forced one foot to move, then the other.

The Hotaru camp should be over the next hill, if he had not gotten lost. Another hour at this pace. If he kept going, he would soon have food, real water, and treatment for his infection. Izo chose not to think about how badly his face hurt or the blood that ran down his staff from his hands. He would get home. He must get home.

It took two hours, but as he climbed the hill and limped over the top, a scrawny rider saw him and pounded toward the camp on one of Father's horses, screeching at the top of her lungs. It did not surprise him when the entire camp poured from the tents to watch him arrive.

No one came to help him, though Mother covered her mouth, and Father clenched his fists. Zefra slid off the horse and pulled Heti, the clan healer, to the front of the crowd. As soon as Izo crossed the border of the camp, completing his journey, Heti and his parents ran to him.

Heti peered at Izo's face and hands and glanced at the makeshift bandages around his legs. "Bring him to my tent." He muttered a list of herbs and ran toward the well.

Mother carefully draped one of Izo's arms across her shoulders while Father took the other side.

"Zefra," Mother said, "watch the girls."

"But—" Zefra said.

"Now!"

Zefra stomped toward the family tent, and Izo hid a grin.

"I will answer your questions later," he called back to her.

No one asked him anything while the healer treated his injuries, but Mother chewed on her lip.

Once he was salved, bandaged, and full of medicinal teas, his parents took him back to their tent. The little girls were already asleep, but Zefra waited with her black hair in a simple nighttime plait, drumming her fingers impatiently. She handed him an entire jug of water and a bowl of soup. Her patience lasted only a few minutes before she rattled off questions. He ignored her until he had emptied the bowl and refilled it.

When his stomach finally stopped screaming at him, he answered most of her questions. He refused to tell her how he got injured, and he omitted some of his more embarrassing moments, doing his best to make it sound like an adventure instead of a disaster.

"And what did you decide for work?" Zefra asked.

Izo yawned. "I will tell you in the morning."

He was not sure if he wanted to admit it, but the antiquated custom had given him plenty of opportunities to consider his priorities.

"Leave him alone," Father said. "There will be time to talk later."

Zefra flipped her braid over her shoulder. "Blacksmith," she muttered as she left for bed. "What else?"

Izo watched her go with mixed affection and annoyance, wondering how many surprises she would find on her own trek. She was determined to stick to her plans, but did they match their god's? If Resef rolled Izo down a hill to direct his life as He chose, how would He hammer Zefra to make her a tool in His hands?

Father helped Izo into bed, and he fell asleep quickly, stomach full and skin nearly free of pain for the first time in days.

In the morning, Izo dressed in an un-shredded robe and reported to Is-vah, the Hotaru priest, who helped him sit on an extra-high stack of rugs to avoid bending his knees.

Izo reported on his entire trek, good and bad, sparing himself no embarrassment and avoiding no questions. He turned in the turquoise belt with a silent prayer of thanks that it was not his own.

When it came time to announce his choice of profession, he dropped his broken knife in front of Isvah. "I intend to make better weapons, better tools." He laughed. "I will make better nails, if I must."

Isvah nodded. "The blacksmith already told me he's willing to teach you more. He expects you tomorrow."

"Is no one surprised?" Izo asked. "Why ask us to ponder if everyone already knows the answer? Why send us away at all?" He showed his scraped hands before retrieving his broken knife. "Why did Resef answer my prayers like this when a few words would have been sufficient?"

Isvah laughed. "Why are young people always surprised their elders and family know them better than they know themselves? Let me ask you this: do you know yourself better now, and would you have listened to Resef if He merely told you what to do?"

Rather than wait for an answer, he helped Izo to his feet and escorted him from the tent. Zefra waited outside, scarf tidily covering her hair.

She folded her arms and squinted at him. "I have more questions."

Izo grinned. "Zefra, you will have to do better on your own trek."

She grabbed his arm and pulled him toward home. "I will. I already have plans. Let me tell you."

"If I listen, will you put more salve on my face?"

Zefra scowled at him. "Even if you do not listen."

She darted toward their tent, and Izo followed slowly. His sister might crave adventure, but he preferred an unremarkable life at home.

SPOILER WARNING

From this point on, most of the stories contain minor or major spoilers (Marathon excepted). You have been warned.

SAYAKA

(JUST AFTER WIND OF CHOICE)

SAYAKA
(HOTARU DISTRICT, ISKRA)

**Each god created his or her own people and maintained them with
private diligence. They spoke not to each other, neither meddled
in one another's affairs.**
A Comprehensive History of the Gods, vol. 3

As the wind puffed against the sails, Sayaka watched the lavender
waves run under the ship, one arm around her youngest daughter,
Keahi. Behind them was the new island of Arupa, created for the Mouth of
All the Gods, and home was only a few days ahead. Going home was the
best part of any job, and 'twas particularly welcome now.

Alas, even home had troubles, though fortunately milder ones.
According to her husband's letters, their son still had not shown an interest
or skill in any occupation. Which was better, having dreams disrupted, like
Ahjin, the new Mouth, or not knowing one's dreams? She could not help
Ahjin anymore, but she must find a way to help her son.

Her fellow warrior, Askari, joined them at the railing, leaning on his
good arm. "What an exciting adventure."

Sayaka raised an eyebrow. "A little too exciting, perhaps."

They had saved the four known gods from the deluded revenge of their
forgotten older brother, but the rescue had nearly cost them all their lives.

Kassian summoning her family and a ship to take her home was a small repayment toward a big debt, if she dared suggest a god owed her anything.

"How does your arm feel?" she asked.

He wiggled the fingers sticking out of his sling. "Much better than the last time I broke a bone. Ludik is a fine healer, whatever he thinks."

"Fortunately for us all," Sayaka drawled.

Her own wounds still ached, but they, too, were healing. The poisoned spider bite burned worse than the cuts and bruises, despite Kassian's antidote. Without the potion and repeated healings from Ludik, she would have died. As a warrior, the possibility of death was always present, but fighting caravan bandits never felt as dangerous as the monsters she had recently faced. She might never have returned to her family.

Keahi tugged on Sayaka's sleeve. "Are you leaving again?" Her cheeks, still round with childhood, sucked in with worry.

"I have to talk to your father and Chieftain Prathap," Sayaka said, "but I might stay home for a while." She squeezed Keahi closer. Though she intended to spend a lot of time with her son, she also welcomed time with her daughters. More than ever, she wanted to be a good mother, in case her next job went badly. "What about you, Askari?"

The lean man shrugged. "I had a guard job lined up with a caravan, but now I must delay until my arm heals." He ruffled Keahi's hair. "Lucky for you, since you will have time to hear all my stories about our adventure."

Keahi grinned and bounced on her toes.

Not all the stories, surely. If he mentioned their deaths, she would kill him. Sayaka scowled at him, and he winked.

Askari raised his voice so her other two children, seated on the deck with young Zefra and her siblings, could also hear. "Listen, and I will tell you how your mother is a hero."

An excited murmur ran through the crowd, and everyone hurried to get comfortable for a story. Sayaka took Keahi to sit with the family in a place with a good vantage point for glaring at Askari. She leaned contentedly against her husband's shoulder, and Vasu wrapped his arm around her.

Zefra's parents and older brother joined their girls. Isvah, the clan priest, claimed a seat on a barrel instead of the deck, and the sailors leaned against the bulwark or climbed the rigging.

Even the three Darrendrakar settled onto the wooden planks, brown faces dark in the sea of Iskrin white. Sayaka, somewhat to her own surprise, could tell Ludik apart from his identical brother even when he did not have his arm around Nemerra, but the brothers got frequent stares from the Iskrin sailors.

Askari waited until the tension climbed, then sank gracefully to a cross-legged position without disturbing his broken arm and began the story of their trek into the desert to find a clue left by their god. Sayaka let his one-armed gestures and somewhat imaginative version distract her from her worry over Razi for a while.

The story was compelling enough that when the Darrendrakar headed north, Ludik had to wrestle his brother to the other ship, and his complaints echoed across the ocean until they sailed out of sight.

O ver the next few days of travel, Askari told many stories. Fortunately for his continued health, he censored his tales a bit, leaving out the parts most likely to distress Sayaka's family. He spun Sayaka into more of a hero than she remembered being, and he heaped praise on Zefra and her absent friends until she turned as scarlet as her god-touched hair.

Though Sayaka's adventure to save the gods had lasted less than two months, she felt like she had been gone longer. All three of her children had grown while she was away, and she watched them with new eyes as they responded to the stories in different ways.

Keahi and her best friend, Zefra's younger sister Risa, loved the gods and the bits of magic in the stories and followed Zefra around the ship, begging her to call fire. Zefra distracted them with questions about her family's herd, and the two horse-mad young girls babbled for hours. In a few years, Keahi would likely seek a job with horses, which was safer than magic and meddling with gods.

Chitra, Sayaka's older daughter and already an accomplished archer, discussed vulnerable targets on the various monsters Sayaka had fought and the efficacy of different arrow points. Though she might follow her mother into the guard, 'twas more likely she would apprentice to the bowyer or the fletcher.

Those two, at least, knew what they wanted and were preparing for their future.

Sayaka's son, Razi, held widespread interests with no sign of preference yet. He solemnly asked many questions about the other lands and their cultures and traditions. Sayaka described her companions in detail and promised to let Razi write to them. She also recited Ahjin's account of his negotiations with the gods.

A pang of regret struck Sayaka so hard, she lied to her husband that a wound was paining her to excuse her wince. Her children would soon be grown and gone. Chitra was a little older than Zefra, though not as ambitious, and could leave on her adulthood trek whenever she liked. Razi would be right behind her, and even Keahi was eleven. If Sayaka took more traveling jobs instead of the lower-paying home guard, her last years with her children would speed by like sand in a whirlwind. She winced again.

Her husband scowled. "You need to see the healer the minute we get home." Vasu tried to escort her to a hammock, but she patted his arm.

"I'm fine, but we must talk."

After making sure their children were well occupied, they sat in a quiet corner of the deck and snuggled together for a chat. First, she gave Vasu the unedited version of the stories Askari had been telling, including just how close she came to death, several times. His arms tightened around her until her wounds protested, but he listened in silence.

"I'm not sorry I went," Sayaka said, "but I might stick closer to home for a while, if that is acceptable to you?"

He answered her with a long kiss, and a minute passed before she could get back to the conversation.

"I have been thinking about our children's futures," she said.

"I think Chitra will leave on her trek next year," Vasu said. "She hinted a bit, and she worked a lot with the bowyer while you were gone."

"I'm not surprised," Sayaka said. "'Twas one of my top guesses for her. Keahi, of course, will do something with horses."

Vasu laughed. "She is always with Risa and the herd. If the Ashvakoshas had a younger son, I would even predict a match in the future."

"Hmm. Perhaps she will leave us to marry into the Achira clan." A pang of loneliness hit Sayaka, even though the horse-breeders were only two districts away.

"Perhaps." Vasu sighed. "Perhaps we can help her find something closer."

"Fortunately, we have more time with her," Sayaka said. "But that leaves us with Razi."

"Ah, Razi. He has worked hard in his classes this year."

"He always works hard," Sayaka agreed.

They exchanged rueful glances. By thirteen years of age, most Iskrin children had at least some idea what they wanted to do as an adult, even if they spent another year or two narrowing it down.

"Has he given you any hints of what he wants to do?" Sayaka asked.

"Nothing with weapons," Vasu said, "though I want you to work on his self-defense skills before you leave again."

Sayaka nodded. Razi could shoot well enough to keep himself fed and follow instructions during fighting drills, but in any match, even with blunt weapons, he backed away and refused to fight. After he defended another child from a rabid coyote, it was obvious he was no coward, but he had no warrior's spirit. He was likely to be found in the middle of children's squabbles, but only to urge them to forgiveness, and anyone determined to quarrel would first make sure Razi was elsewhere. Those were good traits for a priest, perhaps, but Sayaka would never suggest her child be so involved with a god. All of them were trouble for a mortal.

"Did he develop an interest in any craft while I was gone?" she asked hopefully.

Her husband shook his head. "I made him visit every craftsman in the clan and all who visited. He loves watching and asking questions, but he likes people better than things. And he's a bit clumsy, I'm afraid." He caressed her back. "You should talk to him."

She rested her head on his shoulder. "I will."

Against her side, his chest rose and fell. The sun was warm, Vasu's arms were wrapped around her, and no one had tried to kill her for weeks.

"Mmm," she murmured. Razi could not escape her on the ship. She would talk to him in a few minutes.

Her husband leaned his head on hers, and she drifted into peaceful slumber.

When Sayaka woke an hour or two later, she hunted down her son, who was listening to Askari's stories. Before another began, she pulled him aside for a stroll around the deck. He took after his shorter father, which made him look younger, though his perpetually solemn expression added back years.

After chatting casually for a while, Sayaka brought up the topic worrying her. "I wondered if you have thought about an occupation yet. If you have something in mind, we can help you find more training before your adulthood trek."

Razi shrugged. "I like lots of things."

"You studied with Zefra's grandparents for a long time," Sayaka said.

For a while, with him pouring over maps and old stories, they thought he might end up a cartographer. 'Twas the longest he stayed with one interest, though instead of merely studying Iskra, he borrowed the maps of other countries and compared the versions, looking for what might be accurate instead of rumor.

Razi looked dubious. "I'm very bad at drawing. I like their stories better."

Sayaka sighed. "Storyteller," she suggested, determined to pin him down to something, anything.

"I want to see the world," Razi said.

"Traveling storyteller," Sayaka said.

Razi shrugged. "I want to help people."

"What about healing?" she asked. "Even without a gift, you can learn medicines and treatments."

Her son ducked his head and blushed. "I fainted at the blood."

Sayaka patted his shoulder. "Some people do. What about trader? You could specialize in helpful items rather than luxuries."

Razi turned even redder. "I tried that, too. My first customer was so poor, Mother, with a threadbare robe and such skinny arms. I gave her a good bargain, but when the vendor found out the price, he told me not to come back."

Pressing her lips together to hide a laugh, Sayaka squeezed him tighter. "You have a kind heart, Razi. You always have."

"Can I think about it longer?" He fidgeted with the hem of his sleeve. "Is there really a hurry? I have at least two years to decide."

To the young, two years sounded like forever, but Sayaka felt the sands of time slipping through her fingers.

"No, there is no hurry," she forced herself to say. She could wait until he felt the urgency himself. She hoped.

They finished their walk around the ship in companionable silence. Sayaka had no idea what Razi was thinking about, but she catalogued every occupation in the clan for when her son wanted to talk.

☆♀♆◎

They arrived at Iskra the next day, and after settling in at home, Sayaka signed up for camp patrol and hunting assignments instead of making herself available on the caravan list. Since Askari could not draw a bow until his arm healed, he kept watch, foraged for plants, and set snares.

In her spare time, Sayaka taught archery to the clan. Askari, who would normally help with the sword and dagger classes, assisted her, as did Chitra. Keahi was now old enough to draw a small bow, so Sayaka spent most of her time in the children's class. Despite being two years older, Razi was still in the same class until he learned to hit the easy target more than half the time.

Sayaka returned home after a particularly bad session and flopped next to Vasu on their cot. "He shot Keahi's target instead of his own. What will we do with that boy?"

Vasu chuckled. "He will figure it out."

Sayaka rolled over. "What about a teacher? Teachers help people, and he does well in his scholarly classes."

Her husband tugged off her scarf and leaned in to kiss her neck. "He wants to see the world," he murmured.

"Translator," Sayaka gasped as he pulled her closer and kissed her again.

"Worry..." Vasu dropped kisses along her collarbone. "Later." And then he distracted her entirely.

☆♀♆◎

Every night around the chieftain's fire, the returned heroes told stories of their adventure. Though Zefra's youth had created a closer friendship with the outdwellers, Sayaka and Askari's mature perspective was as valued. The clan endlessly discussed the new changes in the pantheon and the possible shifts in world politics and trade, trying to guess what Ahjin would do as Mouth of All the Gods.

After two weeks of the same conversation, Sayaka was tired of it. When could she focus on her own family's problems, especially Razi?

"Yes," Sayaka assured everyone, breathing on her dying ember of patience, though she preferred to toss the entire debate into the fire before them. "The gods really did say they would start working together."

"But can we trust the other gods?" Chieftain Prathap asked. "And will their peoples listen?"

Sayaka leaned in to reassure him, but Zefra spoke faster.

"Resef would weep to see your skepticism," Zefra said flatly. She turned to Isvah, the priest. "What did Resef say?"

Isvah grinned. "Ahjin is the Mouth of the Gods. Kassian has returned. A new day is warming Kaiatan with friendship and cooperation."

Sayaka grunted. Perhaps, though it would take time for changes to disperse.

Zefra spread her hands wide. "Let the words of the Holy Flame light our minds before He burns them into our souls. Excuse me, but I have to prepare to leave for Ludik's wedding."

Prathap stood. "When you go to Darrendra, see what the shapeshifters think of the changes. Watch Ahjin to see if you think he will be fair to Iskra and the other countries." He rubbed his chin. "Watch that Nokai, too."

Zefra stood, pulling herself to her unimpressive full height. "You want me to spy on my friends?" She tightened her grip on her staff.

Sayaka nudged Askari. She flicked a finger between herself and Zefra, then jerked her chin toward Prathap. Askari nodded, and both of them prepared to interfere if Zefra called flame.

"Not... spy," Prathap said. "Just see if they will continue being friendly when the world is not falling apart and the gods are back again."

"Spying." Zefra bowed to the crowd and stalked off, muttering to herself and stabbing her staff into the desert.

Sayaka raised her eyebrows and settled back cross-legged.

"Can we ask traders to collect more information?" Prathap asked.

"She's right, you know," Sayaka said. "I do not think spying will endear us to Ioj, Nokailana, or Darrendra. If the world is now to be one united family, then the countries should start acting like beloved siblings instead of leery rivals."

Zefra's grandmother leaned forward, hands clasped together. "But think how much we could finally learn about the other countries. The Hotaru have collected information about Iskra for centuries, even millennia. 'Tis time to move outward."

Askari winced. "And provoke them by spying? We should wait until we have permission."

"And we should think how best to deal with international affairs," Sayaka said. "Do we send cartographers or traders or someone else? From which clans? Who can best represent Iskra?"

Isvah scratched his head. "I will pray about our dilemma. Perhaps Resef has an answer. Go to bed."

And the crowd dispersed, still arguing.

Hand in hand with Vasu, Sayaka walked home, but instead of sleeping, she stared toward the dark ceiling. After spending weeks with Ahjin and Ludik and Nia, she knew the other races were people with the same concerns as Iskrins, but worldwide distrust was so deeply ingrained it was difficult to overcome.

In her opinion, Zefra had the experience to be an excellent choice for an ambassador, knowing all the trade routes in Iskra and how to read and draw maps, speak trade tongue and a few words of the three foreign languages, and bargain for supplies. She had even visited Ioj and had friends from each country, but Sayaka did not think the young woman would give up her own dreams. Even without her flame calling, she was remarkable, though. Of course, many of the Hotaru were nearly as remarkable.

Sayaka jerked upright. With few natural resources, the worth of their clan lay in their people and their knowledge. They had long been negotiators among the Iskrin clans, collecting information about everyone and using it for mutual advantage. Who else could represent Iskra so well to the rest of the world?

"What is wrong?" Vasu murmured, reaching for her.

She lay down. "Nothing. Go back to sleep." But she stayed awake for an hour, planning.

In the morning, she sat with the chieftain and the priest and went over the language, culture, and foreign geography classes the Hotaru would need to add to train future diplomats.

"I see you have given this a lot of thought," Prathap said.

"I agree with her," Isvah said. "It is time for the Hotaru to expand our endeavors to the world. We can probably turn out a few diplomats this year, if we rush the right adults through a few extra classes. It will take longer to produce a regular crop of more prepared youngsters, but that will also give us time to gather more information about the other countries."

"Hmm," Prathap said. "I think we need someone to oversee this. Hire teachers, track curriculum, coordinate with other clans and so forth." He glanced at the priest, who nodded. "How about you, Sayaka?" the chieftain asked.

"I suppose I could think about someone to recommend," she said.

"How about *you*, Sayaka?" Prathap repeated with emphasis.

"To be in charge of the training program?" Sayaka gaped at him. "I'm nothing but a simple soldier."

Isvah waved at the lists. "You seem to know what is needed."

Neither of them listened to her protests, and she left the tent with a new occupation and a stack of slates full of notes. Now her free time with her family would be even more rare. She carefully did not curse Resef's name.

Her family had mixed reactions to the news. Vasu was relieved she would be home more often. Keahi lost interest when she discovered no horses were involved. Chitra volunteered to help tutor the students in archery and self-defense. Razi asked many questions and eavesdropped on her planning meetings, but when she asked him if he was interested, he merely frowned.

Even with help from Askari, all the clan's teachers, and Zefra before she left, it took Sayaka a month to organize the program. Along with the teachers, Sayaka waited nervously to see if anyone would come.

The first three people to show up for class were adults who already spoke trade tongue and had learned at least a bit of a foreign language from their travels. For each of them, Sayaka compared the list of final requirements with their current knowledge, noting where they needed to fill in gaps. After class, she would help the teachers assign classes efficiently.

The fourth to come was Razi, who handed her a slate already listing his accomplishments and sat cross-legged in the front row without looking at her.

Sayaka clutched the stack of slates, feeling a smile creep across her face. Vasu was right; Razi had figured out what he wanted to do. In a few years, he would take his place among the best new diplomats in the world, representing Iskra to the other nations. What a perfect fit for him. He would do well. Her heart swelled with pride as she walked to the front of the tent to greet her new students. She could concentrate on her clan, now that her son was settled.

VISITORS

(ONE WEEK AFTER WIND OF CHOICE)

VISITORS
(ARUPA)

And established they The House of the Gods on Arupa, created for that glorious purpose. And lived there His Holiness, Ahjin the Great, first of the Mouths of the Gods.

A Comprehensive History of the Gods, vol. 7

Footsteps sounded on the bridge. Since all three current inhabitants of the small island were in the garden, Ahjin looked up to see what strangers had come to the isle of the gods. A break sounded wonderful, as heretical as it might sound to the gods. He left his baby sister, Maili, with Nia in the flowerbeds, then rubbed his aching back while he picked his way across the muddy ground to greet the first real visitors to his new home.

He hadn't wanted this job in the first place, and though he tried his best, the reality of the drudgery involved had not changed his opinion. When he wasn't working in the garden for the Goddess of Earth, he was mediating disputes between the gods, writing decrees, or reading every religious book in existence. And he wasn't a particularly fast reader. He would soon have several tutors to lecture him on rites from four religions and customs from each country, and until then, all five gods presented him with demands to fill his "free time."

He'd only been on Arupa for a week and was surprised anyone knew he was here, and yet, here were two visitors already. Unless they were volunteers.

He brushed some of the mud off his shirt and smiled to himself. Help would be nice. The garden certainly needed it, and if that wasn't to the taste of new workers, there were plenty of other tasks to do. According to the schedule in Darravani's book, it was time for fall cleanup and weeding. After two days of steady work, he had refused to look at the list for next week.

"Good morning." Ahjin squelched a few steps through the mud, stopping just before the visitors in desert robes and scarves. "How can I help you?"

He bowed to the Iskrins in a poor imitation of his friend Zefra. Learning a proper Iskrin bow needed to go on his very long task list.

The shorter man frowned and took half a step backward, hunching his already curved shoulders. Instead of the common Iskrin tan or cream, he wore dark green with a shocking pink belt and scarf.

The taller man sniffed. "You can direct us to The Mouth of All the Gods. We stopped by the temple, but it was empty." His hands flashed with rings on nearly every finger.

Nia giggled behind Ahjin. Her perpetually good spirits were unaffected by the hard work, although she had suggested he hire a gardener or six. His little sister, who was staying with him until his parents returned from an aerobatics tour, thought gardening was an excuse to play in the mud. Nia encouraged that idea to keep her from picking all the flowers.

"I am Ahjin." He held out his hand, then realized how dirty it was and pulled it back with another bow.

The taller man sneered as he examined Ahjin from muddy feet to uncombed head. "I do not care who you are, drudge," he said. "We want to meet with His Holiness."

Ahjin flushed. He shouldn't have allowed Nia to talk him into gardening in bare feet, threadbare pants, and a holey shirt. It was true he couldn't afford to ruin the few nice bits of his limited wardrobe, and they hadn't expected any visitors, but now he was very much at a disadvantage.

When the strangers wrinkled their noses at his shaggy wings, he clenched his fists behind his back. He'd lost all his feathers in a lightning storm while saving the gods, and it wasn't his fault new ones hadn't grown in yet.

"Certainly," Ahjin said. "What is your business here?"

The Iskrins sniffed. "That is none of your affair. Take us to His Holiness immediately."

Nia stepped to his side and tried to bow with Maili in her arms. "Well met."

His best friend was nearly as dirty as Ahjin, although the long, lavender braids bound around her head were somehow cleaner than his own curls. Her webbed feet were just as muddy. The mud-coated toddler on her hip squealed and reached toward the shiny pendants the visitors wore.

Both of the men gasped. The shorter man stepped backward again and put his hand on his knife. The taller one swatted at Maili's hands, and she cried.

"Don't touch her," Ahjin warned, stepping in front of the girls.

He narrowed his eyes and pulled himself as tall as possible. If they hurt his sister, they'd be sorry, no matter what the gods said about host manners. Guests were supposed to be polite, too.

"Nia, give me Maili, please. I'd like you to take these two... guests... on a short tour of the island while I find His Holiness. Give me at least half an hour before you bring them to the temple."

Since her flying was nearly nonexistent, he gathered his sister in his arms, then hurried toward the middle of town while he kissed her fingers.

To accommodate his new job as the Mouth of All the Gods — a fancy name for making them behave themselves, so far — the gods had enlarged Arupa from a mere pile of rocks to give him someplace to live that wasn't part of any country and thus wouldn't give an imaginary advantage to any one god. The entire island was only about a mile across, and "town" was centered around a small square in the middle. Two sides held empty buildings and market stalls for future use, while a miniature temple with elaborate architecture and marble columns towered over one corner.

Two roads crossed at right angles, one leading from the east dock to the garden in the west. The other street connected the four houses for permanent residents to the four guest houses built in traditional styles for each country. Currently, his family occupied two of the resident homes, while Nia lived in the Nokai guest house down the street.

He went to his parents' house first and quickly bathed Maili. When he put her down for a nap in her crib, he fastened the top netting to keep her from flying out. He didn't have time for a proper bath himself, but he washed off the worst mud and combed the dirt from his hair, then ran for the temple next door.

Eventually, he would host dignitaries or make official visits to foreign countries, but he'd thought he would have more time before then. At the very least, he thought the gods would wait until he learned more. After Ludik's wedding, perhaps, since Ahjin had to leave next week for Darrendra and would be gone for a couple of months.

If the visitors weren't volunteers, then he still needed to find out what they wanted. And please, let their request be within his capabilities. Telling someone he couldn't do something would be a lousy start to his new job.

Ahjin slipped in the back door to his inner sanctuary. Fortunately, he had practiced putting on all the ridiculous layers of his formal regalia. The gods were more concerned with their own claims to power than his sensibilities. His orange brocade robe clashed with a scarlet headband with three flames stamped in black, and neither coordinated with the lavender sash embroidered with purple waves and multi-colored dolphins, or with the bright green boots. The only bit of official insignia that was at all discreet was Kassian's silver star medallion around his neck.

Once dressed officially, he headed for the door to the outer temple, then paused to grab his bow and a plain cloak to cover his ragged wings. Soon, he heard Nia's cheerful prattling through one of the stained-glass windows casting rainbows across the floor.

She escorted the visitors through the front double doors. "Two noble Iskrins, Rada and Zerach." She pointed to each as she said their name. "They wish to see His Holiness, The Mouth of All the Gods."

With her back turned to the strangers, she made a face at Ahjin, then stepped into the shadows in the corner to keep watch.

The strangers hesitated in the middle of the room. The gods' five altars stood against three walls, but there was no priestly throne, no desk, no obvious place to present themselves. Ahjin watched them from his own doorway before he took a step forward, barely into the light.

Since they hadn't been impressed with him in the garden, he pitched his voice low, trying to sound older. "What brings you here?"

His voice echoed off the marble, and he barely avoided rolling his eyes. Irajahan liked the echo, of course.

"Your Holiness," the men said in unison.

They bowed so low Ahjin thought they might bang their heads on the marble floor. When they stood erect again, they examined his gaudy regalia, his white hair, and the apparent hunch of his back under his cloak.

Ahjin tried to look serious and impressive.

The shorter man, Zerach, stammered, "Your Holiness, I'm sure a mature, experienced priest like you will understand the importance of the gods having honorable and reliable priests. Yet Kassian, newly returned to this world, has no one. This is a situation we can alleviate. I would like to introduce us..."

Partway through the very long and improbable list of honorifics and accomplishments, Ahjin stopped listening. He still needed to compost the garden and divide perennials, gather seeds and cuttings, and collect herbs and flowers for drying. And his housekeeping chores. He counted how many days were left until his parents returned. Not soon enough. How long until Amrafel came for Ahjin's next lesson in telepathy and Iojif priestly protocol? He never thought he'd yearn for the lectures from Irajahan's high priest.

"Your Holiness?"

The question broke into his thoughts. "Yes?"

"Your Holiness, did you hear me? Will you give our petition to Kassian?"

Ahjin inhaled slowly, counting to ten. This was as tedious as weeding but less necessary.

He pointed to Kassian's star-etched block of glass. "If you would be so kind as to write your names and your question on a piece of paper from that altar. Do not list your qualifications. Put your note on the altar when you're finished."

As they headed for the altar, the excellent acoustics carried their whispers to his ears. "We could have done that without him," one said.

They grabbed a paper and started scribbling. "I thought he was supposed to help us communicate with the gods."

After a moment, they backed away. Ahjin gave the mental twist that sent the note directly to Kassian. When it vanished, the Iskrins gasped.

"Without me," Ahjin said, "your petition would have stayed there until Kassian happened to notice it. While you wait for your answer, please feel free to pray or wander the temple. I will return in a moment."

Ahjin slipped into his office and wrote a quick note to Kassian describing what happened in the garden and recommending against their request. He sent that one the same way, then returned to the main room of the temple.

The Iskrins were examining the altars to the other gods, twisted sneers turning their faces ugly. Ahjin watched them, silently unnoticed, until a scroll appeared on Kassian's glass block.

"There is your answer," he said.

They jumped and stared at him, then grabbed the scroll. As they read, faces turning purple and scarlet, Ahjin quietly read the copy that popped into his hand, then held it behind his back. Kassian had made a good decision, and now it was up to him to uphold it.

After a glance at him, the Iskrins smirked at each other.

"Your Holiness, our petition has been granted." Rada barely bowed. "Thank you for your service. We will tell everyone about your helpfulness."

And that confirmed Kassian's decision, if it were ever in doubt. Ahjin nodded to Nia, who grabbed her harpoon and came to stand beside him, no longer smiling.

"You lie." Ahjin held up his scroll and read aloud. "I need priests who are kind, intelligent, polite — and honest. You fail on all counts. Your offer is refused. Regards, Kassian."

Anyone who would hit a small child was unkind, dishonorable, and unworthy. Sadly, Ahjin could have used the men in any number of ways, and as the first to arrive, they could have chosen nearly any position if they had been willing to actually work.

"It does not say honest," Rada argued, storming toward him with his crony. "And—"

"It does now." Ahjin interrupted, turning his scroll so they could see the word added in crimson letters.

"We are intelligent," Zerach blustered. His face was red again, and to Ahjin's private amusement, he didn't dispute the other points.

Ahjin let the scroll roll up again with a snap and stepped forward into the light. "You don't seem smart enough to recognize me from an hour ago," he said in his normal tenor voice.

"The gardener?" Zerach asked.

"Why, you imposter," Rada started, drawing his sword halfway. He froze when Nia laid the point of her harpoon against his stomach.

Ahjin shrugged off his cloak and spread his scruffy wings from wall to wall. Whether planned or not, the room was just big enough for him to fill the space with his twenty-two foot wingspan without breaking any feathers. "I *am* the Mouth of the Gods."

The two men gaped at him.

"But — but you were gardening," Zerach stammered.

"Yes," Ahjin said, "among other things."

"But the Mouth of All the Gods does not dig in the mud," Rada said.

Ahjin rubbed his back again. "I assure you, he does. He also scrubs the temple floor, tends the candles, and answers all the letters."

The Iskrins exchanged glances again. "We want to talk to your overseer."

Enough. It was time to get these men off his island. "You already did." Ahjin nodded toward Kassian's altar and picked up his bow from against the wall. "I believe you are leaving now."

Nia lifted her harpoon enough for Rada to turn and exit. Zerach trailed him with frequent backward glances as they walked down the steps and along the eastern road.

Ahjin and Nia followed them silently, weapons raised, until the Iskrins reached the wharf and boarded their small ship. The sails went up and the anchor was raised while the two would-be priests leaned on the bulwark. They watched Nia and Ahjin intently, but the two friends merely smiled broadly until the ship pulled into the ocean.

"Warmth to you." Ahjin waved until the men were out of sight and had no chance to sneak back, then he let his smile fade. What pains. And how many more times would he have to deal with this sort of nonsense? It was bad enough dealing with the whims of the gods.

Nia rested her harpoon in the dirt and laughed. "Do you suppose we'll get a lot of visitors like those? Maybe you should hire some guards to go along with the gardeners."

Oh, no, not more to do. The gods *and* the garden *and* everything else. And if he wanted help, he first had to find it, sifting the chaff from the clean breeze.

Ahjin groaned. "Is it too late to tell the gods I've changed my mind about this job?"

TREFOIL

(BEFORE AND DURING SEED OF WAR)

1. SHANKHI

(KAIRRI, CANID TERRITORY, DARRENDRA)

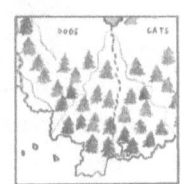

One meets his destiny often in the current he takes to avoid it.
Pinniped Proverb

S hankhi stared at the dead Darrendrakar at his feet. Regret fought with hate and lost.

He turned and searched for his next target, but all the Dogs around him were dead. Among the men lay women and children, and remorse tugged at his heart again.

Varin stepped beside him, walrus-tusk spear dripping with blood. "They deserved it. You know what they did."

Both of them looked toward the pile of sealskins on the beach. So many of their Seal kin had been slaughtered in their sleep like mere animals, and the evidence sickened Shankhi. Hate bubbled in his heart. The Dogs deserved worse than a clean death. The Seals had come in good faith and desperation, looking for a new home and a new life, but all they found was destruction.

Not long ago, the earth shook, again and again for weeks. The ocean waves rose higher than the trees. With no safety on land, the Pinnipeds retreated to the sea, hiding in terror. Most of them survived, but when the chaos ended, their little islands were very different. The trees and gardens had been wiped clean. The land itself had crumbled to a fraction of its size.

They tried to make do with the remaining land, but there was simply not enough. They must live somewhere else, and their little ones could not swim all the way north to their Walrus kin. No, Darrendra, the closest shore, was their only hope. All they needed was a small area, and they were willing to trade for it.

A few handfuls of scouts, including Shankhi and his brother, volunteered to search for territory. To reduce the demand on their home, they took their families with them. After swimming across the strait for days, they arrived last night near a small village and slept on the bare sand, exhausted and still in their seal forms.

In the first light of dawn, Shankhi turned away from the stack of seal-skins on the beach and nudged the dead Dog at his feet. They all deserved death.

The Dogs had come before dawn, spears in hand. They killed several Seals before the others woke, and they kept killing even as the Seals fled for the ocean. No time to shift or grab weapons or armor. No time to do anything but flee.

While the bulls guarded the cows and pups as they retreated for the safety of the ocean, Shankhi's brother approached the murderers, trying to persuade them to stop the slaughter. The Dogs ignored the traditional signals of peace and parley and cut him down. The cows and pups huddled in the ocean with the surviving bulls and watched the Darrendrakar skin their kindred and butcher them for meat. Their tears had blended with the salty waves.

His brother's familiar brown-spotted pelt was in the middle of the stack. Shankhi scanned the other bodies but couldn't see the bright red hair of his murderer. When the Seals buried the corpses, he would check until he was sure his revenge was complete.

Last night, when the sun set, the remaining bulls had crept from the water and shifted. Weapons in hand, they tiptoed through the village at the edge of the beach. When every Seal warrior stood on a doorstep, they burst into houses and destroyed the murderous Dogs. Few of them even managed to grab a weapon as they jolted from sleep.

The blood price was paid. Shankhi wiped his knife on a Dog's tunic.

"The village is now ours," Varin said. "We will be safe and can send for the rest of our kin."

Shankhi nodded. Without speaking, he dragged his last victim toward the pile for burial.

Varin beckoned a messenger, but before they could speak, Kaito rushed in. The young Seal had been sent to watch the village borders and warn of anyone approaching.

"They're escaping!" Kaito panted.

Varin grabbed his arm. "Where?"

Kaito waved a large arc. "North, east, west. Everywhere! They're running on four legs like the Dogs they are."

Varin bellowed, and warriors ran in from all over the village.

"We have runaways," Varin shouted. "We must track them down before they bring back help."

While Varin sent warriors after the fugitives, Kaito tugged on Shankhi's arm. "The one who killed your brother went east."

Shankhi whirled. "How do you know?"

Kaito tugged his own red-brown hair. "His hair was red as a snapper."

Shankhi gripped his knife. That did sound like his brother's murderer. He turned and interrupted Varin. "Let me go east. Please. Give me revenge for my brother."

Varin thought for a moment before nodding. "Here, take my spear. Teach them vengeance for us all."

"I will go with you," Kaito said.

"No," Varin said. "Stay home and be safe." He raised his voice and spoke to all the warriors. "Don't let them alert anyone else. Bring back proof of their deaths. Hurry!"

Kaito tugged on Shankhi again. "I will watch for your return," he whispered. "I will guard the way."

"Sure." Shankhi ruffled the young man's hair. He was barely older than a pup and certainly no guard. "You do that."

His wife handed him food and water in a pack taken from a Dog's house. "I added a sprig of birdsfoot trefoil," she said.

"Appropriate. Save my brother's burial until I return." He kissed her before running eastward.

Behind him, the other warriors ran north and west.

It took a few minutes to balance the spear without it tangling in his legs or wearing out his arms, but soon, he found a rhythm. He settled into the distance-devouring jog he could maintain for hours. On four legs, the Dogs were faster, but the ocean of hate flowing through his veins would let him chase until he caught his quarry.

No matter how long it took, the Dogs would not escape.

Once they were dead, he would bury his brother. Only then could he settle into his new home in peace.

2. KREVAN

(CANID TERRITORY, DARRENDRA)

Don't kick the tiger's tail before you have a plan to deal with his teeth.

Darrendran Proverb

Krevan lowered his head and ran harder through the night, despite the rough ground under his paws. Ahead of him, Madigan's longer legs carried him faster. At the next town, they could rally help, take back their village, and free their neighbors.

And who were their enemies? Had the Bears invaded? Kairri was close to the Ursid border, but they'd never had a problem before. The warriors on his doorstep had looked Darrendrakar, and he'd rather believe it was the Bears than that another village of Dogs had attacked.

They had been big enough for Bears. They knocked down doors as if brushing away flies, ducking to miss lintels and filling the doorways with their hulking shoulders.

What had Kairri done to offend the Bears?

Maybe they hadn't. Maybe the Bears were invading for a different reason. Would they stop at one village, or would they cut a swath into Canid territory, conquering more and more towns until they were glutted or Darravani finally noticed?

Now would be an excellent time for the goddess to send her Elephant priests to trample the Bears back into good behavior. But they lived on the other side of Darrendra, and even if they knew of the problem already, it would take them weeks or months to reach Kairri. They needed closer allies, and soon.

Krevan panted, wishing for water. How had he become so out of shape he couldn't handle a bit of a run?

Madigan turned his head. "Are you coming, Foxy?"

Krevan rolled his eyes. "Are you never serious? Now might be a good time to save your breath."

"I'm ahead of *you*," Madigan said. "It seems I have breath to spare." Despite his joking tone, the dingo's tail was tucked between his legs, and his ears were flattened.

"Then spend it on useful speech. What is our plan?"

"Durriel is a few hours away. Less, maybe, if we run fast enough." Madigan slowed a bit to pace beside Krevan. "We send a message to the temple priests, and we recruit help to free our village."

"Do you think they will help?"

"Why wouldn't they?" the dingo asked. "Stop worrying and just run." Despite his longer legs, Madigan stayed beside Krevan.

After an hour, they stopped for a break and a welcome drink from a stream.

Krevan dropped his head on his paws and panted. "How much farther?"

"It is eight leagues or so. We have traveled about half of it, I think." Madigan stretched and shook himself. "I'm going after a rabbit. Want to come?"

"Save me a bit." Krevan closed his eyes and listened to the younger Dog run off.

Years ago, he had that much energy. At some point, without noticing, he lost it somewhere. But he could ponder that after a nap.

He woke to the smell of raw meat under his nose and gobbled half a rabbit with his eyes half-closed. It was still night, and if he weren't so hungry, he would stay asleep.

"Hurry," Madigan murmured. "I think I smell someone on our trail." The dingo stared back toward Kairri, fur standing on end.

Krevan bolted to his feet. He stretched his tired muscles and took another drink. "I'm ready."

Madigan checked the stars and ran again.

Krevan forced himself to follow. Four more leagues? It already seemed they had run forever.

An hour passed, and another.

"Where is Durriel?" Krevan asked.

Madigan didn't answer.

Krevan forced a bigger breath and raised his voice. "Where is Durriel?"

"I heard you," Madigan said. "I — I think we passed the turn."

Krevan stumbled into a tree. "We missed it? How?"

"I only went once," Madigan protested. "And in daylight. I can't recognize anything in the dark."

Krevan staggered to a halt. "Should we turn around?"

Madigan stopped and hung his head. "And run straight into our pursuer?"

"We can't keep running forever."

"There are other towns."

"Do you know the way?"

Madigan shrugged. "No, but sooner or later, we should find one."

Krevan shook his head and forced his feet into motion again. "I hope you're right."

Now that they no longer knew how long they would have to run, they settled into a slower lope. Day arrived, but still they ran, hour after hour, stopping only briefly to eat and drink. When neither of them could run more, they hid in bushes and slept for a couple of hours before running again.

Madigan, with the enviable strength of youth, slept less than Krevan and kept checking their backtrail. Their pursuer kept following.

For three days, the Dogs ran. They never did find another town, though Krevan didn't know if they passed them at night or if they had somehow chosen a path between cities without ever crossing them.

Finally, Krevan collapsed under a bush. His blistered feet ached, and his muscles shook with fatigue.

"Just a short nap," he murmured, already half-asleep.

He woke to the sound of growls and shouts. Peeking around the bush, he saw Madigan fighting a huge Darrendrakar. The dingo's teeth were a poor match for the long spear wielded by his opponent.

Krevan staggered to his feet and growled. As a fox, he was smaller than Madigan, but two against one gave them at least a chance.

"Krevan!" Madigan dodged the spear. "Run!"

"I'm not leaving you!"

"I'll catch up once I don't have to worry about guarding you. Run!" Madigan slashed at the Darrendrakar's leg, and blood trickled down.

Krevan whined. If Madigan wouldn't run until Krevan was out of sight, then he needed to move fast. The younger dog was a good fighter, but he couldn't hold off his enemy for long.

Krevan whirled and ran, looking frequently over his shoulder, but no yellow dingo followed.

After a while, a tall shadow appeared, spear in hand.

Krevan whimpered and ran faster, no longer looking behind.

3. AGU

(FELID TERRITORY, DARRENDRA)

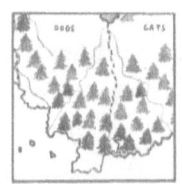

In a battle between elephants, the ants get squashed.

Darrendran Proverb

Agu crept through the underbrush, searching for game. In his leopard form, he was at home in the branches, but he couldn't smell as much up there. Sneaking along the ground would have to do.

Assuming Ludik's long-awaited friends arrived today, the wedding hunt would be tonight. Agu had promised to make it successful as his gift to the happy couple. True, Ludik was another hunter and capable of tracking his own game, but if Agu did it, the jaguar could stay with his friends and beautiful bride. The time, not the prey, was the true gift to his teammate.

All Agu needed was some dumb animal wandering through the forest. He'd follow it, either until Ludik and Nemerra arrived, or until he had a good idea of its habits and could report to the sweethearts.

He finally saw a trail of disturbed leaves and followed it between the trees. Just as he thought he neared the den, something bolted from the shrubs and bowled him over.

Out of reflex, he snapped at the animal. It bit back, and within seconds, they were fighting.

This was no prey, though. Agu backed up to get a better look between blows.

It was a fox! Was it rabid, to take on a leopard so much bigger? He inhaled and discovered the typical Darrendrakar tang under the foxy musk. His attacker was a Fox, a Canid from the neighboring territory.

"Stop it!" He clawed at the Fox, who kept biting despite the warning.

The smaller Darrendrakar panted, reeling cross-eyed with exhaustion as he fought.

Why was the Dog here? The border was ten leagues away, and the kindreds did not cross it casually. Darravani's children, normally allies, could be terrible enemies. The last interkindred war was two generations ago, when the hyenas temporarily conquered part of Felid territory. Were the Dogs now attacking? But Agu didn't see any others, and the Fox was older than the usual soldier. If he was a scout, why was he fighting instead of spying?

If the Cats were lucky, this was some misunderstanding instead of the start of a war.

"What is wrong?" Agu asked. "Are you lost?" He swatted the Dog again, trying to keep him away long enough to answer.

The Fox stared blankly and bit the leopard's ear. Agu yelped and tried to pull free, but the Fox held on. Agu shook his head desperately, and the weight of the Fox ripped off the ear. Blood ran from Agu's face as the Fox rammed into the leopard again.

Agu snarled and threw the Fox against a tree. He should have guessed the Fox wouldn't understand the Felid dialect. Unfortunately, Agu hadn't been a good student, and his trade tongue was nearly nonexistent. He had no way to speak to the frantic Dog.

The Fox struggled to his feet and jumped at Agu. His teeth closed around the leopard's throat and tightened. Agu frantically pawed at the smaller animal, desperate to get him loose. His claws ripped into the red fur over and over, but the Fox still clung, blocking Agu's air.

Another Darrendrakar moved between the trees, approaching the battle slowly. Was this the rest of the army, then? Agu clawed faster, trying to get free to defend himself against the new threat, but the huge newcomer merely watched, leaning on a tall spear and panting for breath.

Finally, the Fox let go and sagged to the ground. His red fur dripped blood onto the fallen leaves, red on orange and yellow.

Agu faced the newcomer, claws extended. "Who are you?"

The man said nothing.

After a minute, Agu gave up and turned to the Fox. As he slowly approached, he babbled in Felid, wishing again for competency in trade tongue.

"You will be fine," he promised. "I will get Ludik, our healer. When you are well, you can tell us what brought you here."

He reached toward the Fox, who whined without moving. Agu gently pressed on one wounded leg to stop the bleeding. When the Fox still didn't move, he reached for a more severe torso injury.

"If we can get you a little steadier," Agu encouraged, "I can carry you back to my village. Do not move, please."

When he pressed on the wound, the Fox whimpered, but the blood flow slowed a little.

"Oh, good, it is working," Agu said soothingly.

The man with the spear finally moved, and Agu smiled his thanks and pointed toward the Fox's next most severe injury.

"If you can deal with that one, please?" He knew the stranger wouldn't understand his Felid any better than the Fox did, but politeness never hurt.

The man lifted his spear. As calmly as if swatting a fly, he drove it into Agu's side.

The force of the blow threw the leopard backward. For a moment, Agu couldn't breathe, and then pain shot through his entire body. Black spots swam across his vision, and when he inhaled, his side turned to fire. He forced his eyes open.

His attacker watched the Fox bleed. Teeth bared uselessly and fear in his eyes, the smaller Darrendrakar stared at the man.

The man dropped an amputated yellow paw in front of the Fox, who whined pitifully as the man stripped off his tunic and shifted. Instead of the Dog that Agu expected, a seal appeared, very out of place in the middle of the forest.

Agu smothered his confused gasp. There were no Seals in the Darrendrakar kindreds.

The Fox squealed — a horrid, terrified sound — and clawed at the seal.

Despite the deep scratches now bleeding down his side, the seal merely wiggled backward until he was out of the Fox's reach. The Fox tried to roll away or crawl and failed at both.

Ignoring the pain in his side, Agu watched intently. Who was this stranger? Was this some sort of magic allowing him to imitate a Darrendra-kar? And what was he doing with the Fox?

Agu tried to move, but the spear pinned him to the ground. The seal glanced at him, and Agu instinctively closed his eyes nearly all the way. Playing dead seemed a good idea now. When the seal turned back to the Fox, Agu kept watching.

The wounded Fox had stopped trying to escape and simply lay there, eyes closed, bleeding to death. In less time than Agu expected, the last breath escaped and the bleeding stopped.

The seal shifted back and redressed, then approached the dead Fox with a drawn knife. He cut off the Fox's tail and dropped a bit of leaf on his chest.

When he turned toward Agu, the leopard held his breath and prayed for bravery.

Instead of torturing Agu, the man sheathed his knife and yanked his spear free, took the paw and tail, and left without another glance.

Agu watched through narrowed eyes until the stranger was out of sight. When it seemed safe, he tried to move. Nothing. The pain was fading, but his muscles refused to obey.

Death, then, was coming for him. He relaxed and waited. He and death were old friends, though they were usually in the same hunting party.

Time passed while birds sang and leaves fell. It was a beautiful day for a funeral.

After a while, Agu woke from an involuntary nap. Noises echoed through the trees, happy sounds of celebration. The wedding party was coming.

Agu tried to move again and failed. Never mind. If he could stay awake just a little longer, he could warn the village...

4. HOMEWARD

(CANID TERRITORY, DARRENDRA)

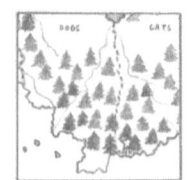

Revenge does not long remain unrevenged.

Pinniped Proverb

S hankhi tucked the fox tail under his belt and headed southwest, as directly toward his new home as he could figure. The Dogs had meandered a bit, and of necessity, he had followed. But now, he had no reason to avoid the straightest path back, at a more comfortable pace.

He pushed himself into a jog. Comfortable didn't mean lazy. It had taken him five days to track the fox this far, and he didn't want to take more than a week to return. He missed his wife and children, and when he got home, he planned to bury his brother and forget about this trip.

At least his mission was finished. He had caught both of his quarry and had the proof for Varin. He hadn't actually killed the fox, but dead was dead.

The birdsfoot trefoil from his wife marked his kill as a rightful vengeance. That should appease anyone who found the bodies. Would it soothe his own conscience?

He regretted the leopard, but he couldn't leave a witness to track him back to his family. Besides, the leopard had been trying to save the murderer. What was one more death after so many others?

He scrubbed his hands against his tunic, trying to wipe off the blood. Dead was dead, and merely watching didn't help his guilt after all.

With any luck, the other warriors were successful in their own hunts, and the Seals were now safe. Soon, Varin's messenger would return with the rest of their Pinniped kin, and then they would have enough guards to protect themselves from any danger. The deaths of a few enemies on his conscience were a small price to pay for the safety of his loved ones.

Shankhi shook his head and stepped up his pace until his pounding footsteps drowned out the memories of blood and fear.

He ran and walked and ran again, stopping to eat, drink, and sleep on piles of fallen leaves. Though he traveled during the day to find his way, most of the time, he saw no one at all. On the rare occasions he spotted a Dog in the distance, he hid or pushed himself faster until he was out of sight again.

The endless trees were nothing like his beloved sea and not much like the limited gardens and orchards they had on the islands. He missed his family and his people and hearing his own language. Even more, he wanted to swim in the ocean and bathe the feeling of blood from his heart. He had washed his skin and clothes in a stream, but it hadn't cleansed the invisible film clinging to his soul.

Perhaps nothing would remove it, not water nor fire nor his wife's sweet kisses. This taint might be his eternal punishment.

His family's protection was worth it.

Shankhi repeated that sentence every time doubt prodded him as sharply as Varin's spear, every time he scrubbed his hands in a stream to remove invisible blood from under his nails.

After five more long days battling guilt, he was almost home and anxious to end the trip. At a flash of color, he hid behind a tree, peeking out to find an escape route. The color ran toward him, and he ducked behind the tree again.

"Shankhi," someone hissed. Footsteps crackled toward him across fallen pine needles.

Shankhi peeked out again. To his surprise, his young friend, Kaito, was sneaking through the forest, waving his arms and unstrung bow.

Shankhi stepped out from behind the tree. "What are you doing?"

Kaito beamed at him. "Varin told me to scout out this town. I said I would watch for you." His smile dimmed. "But we need to hurry. I've been watching from the treetops, and people are following you."

Shankhi cracked a smile. "You climbed a tree?"

Kaito slugged his shoulder. "Aren't you listening? You're being tracked."

"I passed several Dogs out here," Shankhi said, "but none of them followed me."

"These are," Kaito insisted. "And they're catching up. Hurry!" He jogged away, looking over his shoulder and beckoning Shankhi.

"I'm coming." Shankhi forced his tired legs to move faster.

They ran through the trees until they reached the edge of a town. Before the residents spotted them, they ducked behind a stone wall abutting a barn.

"Look at all the people," Kaito complained.

"Where else would they be?" Shankhi asked.

Kaito grabbed Shankhi's arm. "That is not what I mean. They need to go. More of our people arrived, and we need more room than one village."

"No!" Shankhi rubbed his hands on his tunic. "There is no need to harm anyone else."

Kaito rolled his eyes. "I didn't mean that. Varin wants to scare them off. But first we have to get home. So if we set a fire here, they come to put it out, and we run around the town and disappear. But right now, they're all over, and they will spot us for sure without a distraction."

"Fires are dangerous, and I don't want blood on your hands."

Kaito pointed into the town square. "There is a well right there. They can put it out before it gets serious. And even if it burns a few houses, they can run away. Perhaps that will scare them off, too. Come on, Shankhi. Let's go home."

Shankhi shook his head.

Kaito crossed his arms. "Do you have a better idea?"

"Why don't we just sneak away?"

They crept on hands and knees for three steps before a Dog on the other side of the fence sniffed the air noisily. Kaito and Shankhi dropped flat on the ground and froze.

"Go ahead," Shankhi mouthed, "but be careful. And just a small distraction."

Kaito pulled handfuls of grass and layered them with dead leaves next to the barn wall. He nodded at Shankhi and drew his knife. When Shankhi nodded, Kaito scraped the back of his knife against a sharp stone and blew the sparks into his nest of tinder. The fire caught almost immediately. Kaito blew again and nestled small sticks against the flames.

Within minutes, the fire grew to a respectable size. Kaito dumped a handful of damp leaves on the blaze, and when it smoked, they crawled a few steps.

"Fire!" someone bellowed.

Shankhi climbed to his feet and ran, bent double behind the fence. Kaito stayed on his heels. By the time the villagers jumped the wall with buckets, the Seals were around the corner.

Kaito laughed. "It worked! I told you it would."

As they raced along the next wall, Shankhi glanced over his shoulder. The entire barn was burning, and sparks flew into the forest. A gust of wind blew the flames through the trees and the village, catching fire in a thousand places. The tiny sparks grew into greedy tongues, spreading from twig to branch and roof to wall.

At his gasp, Kaito whirled. "No! No, no, no. That is too much. We have to help."

The younger Seal lunged for the fence, and Shankhi grabbed him.

"We can't stay. We can't even talk to them, remember? You said it yourself, the well is right there. They'll put it out."

Tears crept down Kaito's face, but he followed Shankhi around the rest of the village and into the forest on the other side. Behind them, the fire grew larger, hotter, hungrier.

They had almost made their escape when a few villagers ran shouting in their direction.

Shankhi grabbed Kaito's bow and strung it, loosing arrows toward the villagers as fast as he could. The Dogs ran, and the Seals continued toward their new home.

A few minutes later, two more Dogs ran after them, armed and armored like soldiers. They shouted something in their awful Darrendrakar language, and one drew his knife.

Shankhi pushed Kaito behind him and speared the armed man, even as his heart winced. "Run, Kaito."

"No. I won't leave you." Kaito drew his knife.

The guard reached for his weapon.

To protect Kaito, Shankhi stabbed the second guard.

The man fell, bleeding into the dirt, and Shankhi dragged Kaito through the trees. As tears blinded him, he stumbled over roots and vines, but he kept running until the sounds of the village were inaudible.

Behind them, smoke rose to the sky, black and billowing thicker instead of dissipating.

Shankhi cursed. "How far did the fire spread?"

Kaito sobbed, "It's all my fault."

When the rain started a short time later, it blended with their tears. The sprinkle became a downpour and then a deluge. Right before it turned into a solid wall of water, they found a miserable bit of shelter and huddled together for warmth. Shankhi left the spear in the rain to wash off the blood.

"It's not your fault," Shankhi said. "And the rain will put out the fire." He sighed. "Varin will probably be happy. After this, the villagers might leave and rebuild somewhere else." His arguments sounded weak, even to his own ears.

Kaito buried his face in his hands and cried harder.

"It's not your fault," Shankhi whispered. He scrubbed his wet hands on his equally wet tunic and let his own tears fall.

They fell asleep while waiting for the rain to end.

In the morning, they plodded through the forest. Kaito said nothing, no matter how much Shanki tried to comfort him.

Eventually, they found a river leading to the sea. Shankhi shifted and let Kaito bind the spear and their clothing to his back, then Kaito shifted, and they swam home. Kaito still said nothing.

Varin met them on the coast, and Shankhi wordlessly showed the proofs of his hunt.

"Well done," the headman said, collecting the paw, the tail, and the spear. "The trefoil will testify of our blood price. You have avenged your brother and our other kin."

Kaito silently walked away, eyes reddened and shoulders shaking.

Shankhi joined his wife and washed his hands a dozen times. What price was vengeance worth?

HEALING

(JUST AFTER SEED OF WAR)

1. LEAVING

(DARRENDRA AND ISKRA)

Just as few strangers are welcome in Darrendra, few Darrendra-kar leave their home country.

A Brief Sketch of Mysterious Darrendra

L udik slung his pack over one shoulder, tucked a small wooden chest under his arm, and grabbed three bags with the other hand. "Is this everything?"

Maybe he should have helped Nemerra pack for their move, but she had insisted she could do it herself while he was hunting. His bride of two weeks was very determined, and he had selfishly let her take over so he could spend a little more time in his old job before they left and everything changed.

If they didn't hurry, they'd miss the ship to Iskra, where Ludik had an apprenticeship waiting for him. At least, he hoped he did. Shri Okechuku had offered months ago, but Ludik had only decided to accept in the last two weeks. If he was finally giving in to become a healer, he might as well get trained by the best healers in the world.

Though he sent a message with his friend, Zefra, when she left after his wedding, she wouldn't even be across the ocean yet. And he couldn't wait for a reply or they risked running into early winter storms. No, his only option was to leave now, hoping Zefra got the message to Okechuku. And that the esteemed healer still wanted him. He didn't know why an Iskrin wanted to train a Darrendrakar. His healing ointment might be good, but that didn't seem like enough of a reason.

Ludik sighed. If Okechuku had changed his mind... He didn't even know where they would live in Iskra before they made their way home in the spring.

"That's all yours," Nemerra called over her shoulder as she headed back to their bedroom. "My stuff is still in here."

One arm was still in the sling she'd been wearing for weeks to protect her wolf-torn shoulder and neck from strain.

"Don't you dare touch anything!" he yelled.

By the time he caught up, she was staring at a pile of two wooden crates, five bags, and a larger chest, her good arm on her hip.

"I don't know how you think you will do this yourself," she said. "You'll have to make at least four trips."

"No," he groaned before calling through the open window. "Haider, you were right. I need help."

"I told you so," his brother crowed, barging through the door with the rest of the family behind him.

Haider and Gurryon, his littermates, each picked up a box and a bag. Papa and Ludik's older brother lifted the large chest together. Mama and his older sister each took a bag in the arm that didn't hold a baby. Nemerra slung the smallest bag on her good shoulder, then took Hiranya's hand and led his little sister outside to where the spouses and sweethearts of Ludik's siblings waited with the rest of his young nieces and nephews and Nemerra's parents.

"This is so exciting." Hiranya bounced along the path. "I want to go with you." She reached the wagon first and jumped in to boss everyone through the loading.

Mama pulled her down and smoothed her dark hair. "I think you're a little young to go to another country. Ludik will send us letters, though." She paused for a threatening look at him. "And it will be almost as much fun as going to Iskra."

"I'll write, too," Nemerra promised. "I'll have plenty of time while Ludik is busy with his apprenticeship."

Ludik grimaced. He'd been quite happy with his original job of village hunter. The idea of being a healer was still peculiar, and having magic was odder yet. Life seemed determined to force him to embrace it, however, and his experiences in the past half year had resigned him to his fate. If helping his friends wasn't enough of a reason, then saving Nemerra was. He never wanted to feel as helpless as he had when she went down under the teeth of an angry wolf or her dress caught fire.

He tossed his pack on the top of the baggage, then worked his way through the line of family waiting for hugs. At least this was a more cheerful occasion than when he had left to chase a murderer. He helped Nemerra into the wagon seat, moving her skirt away from the half-healed burns above her boots. When he learned the magic for burns, fixing his beautiful bride would be the first item on his list. He swung up beside her and waited while Haider took the driver's seat.

Memories swamped him from the last time he'd made the trip, on foot, against his will, and with a couple of strangers.

He wrapped his fingers around Nemerra's and breathed in the crisp Darrendran air as if he could store it for retrieval when he reached the desert. Whatever happened, they'd be together, and he'd take care of her. They could do this, even if they were the only two shapeshifters in Iskra. Which they wouldn't be, but that didn't mean they would be near any of the Darrendrakar traders.

Nemerra laid her head on his shoulder and went to sleep. Ludik shifted his position to avoid strain on her healing neck. He wrapped his arms around her, partly to keep her upright, but mostly for the excuse to touch her. Marriage was even better than his high expectations.

During the hours it took to drive to the beach, Ludik split his time between his memories, worries, and talking to his brother. Haider and Gurryon would live in Ludik's new house until he returned or they married their sweethearts next year, whichever came first. Ludik lectured Haider on how to take care of it until his brother reached around Nemerra and thumped his head.

"We helped you build it. I think we can manage not to destroy it." Haider rolled his eyes and clucked to the horses again.

Ludik chuckled and rubbed his head. "Sorry."

It wasn't much longer before shorter trees announced the approach of the beach.

Ludik woke Nemerra with a kiss and a whisper. "We're almost there, sweetheart."

She mumbled and sat up, taking Ludik's hand again. "Can you see the ship yet?"

Ludik didn't answer, since the ship anchored at the dock was visible as they turned a corner. The small trading vessel was in bold Darrendran colors instead of the simpler themes of the Iskrin ship he had taken last time, with a white sail edged in black to indicate it was approved to trade with Iskra.

A line of sailors jumped down to help them load. "Move it, boys!" someone bellowed. "The tide's turning."

Ludik grabbed his pack from the top of the pile and helped Nemerra down. By the time they reached the ship, their luggage was already stowed. Haider hugged them both before the first mate guided them aboard and bellowed for the anchor to be loosed.

"I'll tell Mama and Papa you made it fine," Haider called, waving from the shore. "Remember to write. Keep well." He climbed back in the wagon and turned for home.

Ludik waved until the ship lurched and Nemerra gagged over the side.

"Honey, are you well?" He held back her hair until her stomach settled.

She accepted a cup of water from a sailor and waved off their concern. "I'm sure I'll get used to the motion of the ship in a few days. But now, if you'll forgive me, I think I'll go lie down."

"I'll help you." Ludik stroked her back and took back the cup.

"I'll be fine," she said. "Enjoy the view." And she disappeared below deck.

Ludik stayed at the railing and watched the Darrendran coast disappear along with his old life. When nothing was in sight but choppy waves, he gave up and went below to comfort Nemerra.

The trip took several days longer than usual, and the imminent winter caused miserably cold ocean spray and nauseating oscillation from high waves. Nemerra never overcame her seasickness. By the time they landed at the northern end of the Iskrin district of Devora three weeks later, Ludik was desperate to disembark and get Nemerra to solid ground.

His heart sank when he didn't recognize anyone on the dock. Logically, he knew it was unlikely any of his friends would be there. Not only was his arrival time uncertain, but they had probably only gotten home a couple of weeks earlier. Zefra lived one district to the west, and Nia couldn't have swum from Nokailana in the wintry sea. Ahjin, of course, was probably swamped on Arupa with his priestly duties as the new Mouth of All the Gods. Ludik hoped they would come visit, but if not, at least he would see them in the spring for Nia's party. That was one of the few advantages of being in Iskra; he was only days from the islands instead of weeks.

The sailors filed past him with his luggage. Nemerra vomited over the side of the gangplank as she followed them.

Ludik shoved aside his disappointment. "Come on, honey, let's get you to land so you can stop being sick." He took her uninjured arm and helped her ashore.

While Nemerra leaned against a piling and the local children stared at the foreigners, the sailors loaded their baggage into a wagon he hired using his adequate trade tongue. He helped Nemerra onto the small seat next to the driver, and before heading for his own seat in the back with the luggage, he asked for directions to the closest inn.

"You already have a reservation elsewhere," someone said behind him. "Okechuku arranged it three days ago. You're late."

Ludik whirled. A short, scrawny girl leaned on her staff and smiled at him. Her black eyebrows and dull tan robe made her look like a typical Iskrin, but a stray red curl had slipped from under her tan headscarf.

"You made it!" Ludik bowed awkwardly. "Good to see you."

Behind him, Nemerra echoed, "Good to see you, Zefra."

Zefra gave an elegant Iskrin bow, then clasped his arm in the Darrendran custom. "Bright day, Ludik, Nemerra. I promised I would come, did I not?"

Ludik shrugged. "I thought maybe you didn't have enough time to get here yet."

"We made it before the storms began. Are you ready to go?" Zefra vaulted into the wagon using her staff, landing neatly between the crates and taking a seat on a trunk.

He climbed up beside her, and after she rattled off instructions in Iskrit, the driver set the wagon into motion.

The trip took all day, and Nemerra spent the time practicing her trade tongue with him and Zefra. At evening, they finally reached a city made half of tents and half of stone and brick buildings.

The inn was a white brick one-story with a stable out back and a single tree next to the well. Their room was small but comfortable, and while Zefra helped Nemerra settle in, Ludik unloaded all their baggage and paid the driver.

It took him several trips to take everything to their room at the back of the inn, and when he finished, his stomach was rumbling. He dropped the last crate in the corner and flopped onto the bed.

Nemerra giggled. "Get up, dearheart, so Zefra can show us to the evening meal."

"Food?" Ludik shot to his feet and held out his arm for Nemerra. "Lead the way, Zefra."

They found a table in a corner of the busy dining hall and ordered a wide selection of Iskrin dishes. While they ate, or Ludik and Zefra ate and Nemerra picked at her food, they discussed their next steps.

"When is Okechuku arriving?" Ludik asked.

Zefra shook her head. "He's waiting for you in the Tukiko district. You will take a river ferry to him. I believe one leaves tomorrow."

Ludik made a face at the thought of moving all the luggage again so soon, but he grabbed another spicy pastry and kept his complaints to himself. At the sight of Nemerra's still mostly full plate, he refilled his plate with the mildest choices and traded plates with her without comment.

After Nemerra finished, they promised to meet Zefra early in the morning and fell into bed.

The trip up the river took over a week, and Nemerra's seasickness returned with a vengeance. By the time they arrived, Ludik was past ready to get his wife off the water. Zefra got them into another inn and sent a message to Okechuku, then she set off for home.

Ludik refrained from unpacking, since it seemed unlikely they would stay in an inn for his entire apprenticeship. It took two days for someone to come for them, and then it was Koray instead of Okechuku. Though he was from the Rikatsu clan instead of the Tukiko healers, and not even close to Shri rank, the animal healer had helped Ludik heal Ahjin last year. Bird bones weren't on the normal curriculum of most healers, even the Shri.

"Bright day." Koray said in trade tongue. He bowed to both of them and smiled at Nemerra, his stark white skin turning a faint pink.

"I was not expecting a lady with you," he murmured to Ludik. "Is this your sister, to cook for you? That is not necessary; the dormitories will provide everything you need."

Ludik held out his hand to Nemerra. "Nemerra, this is Koray, who helped me save Ahjin's life. Koray, this is my wife."

Koray's mouth dropped open. "Your *wife*? Apprentices do not have wives!"

Ludik would not have delayed his marriage again for any reason, not even to train as a healer. He wrapped his arm around Nemerra. "I do. And she is coming with me, or I will go home."

The slender young healer rubbed his hands over his face. "A wife. Oh, dear." He stared at Nemerra. "I did not think you are old enough to marry."

Ludik shrugged. "In Darrendra, we marry between our eighteenth and nineteenth years, after a year of betrothal. I actually married late, because I was here on my planned wedding day."

Koray picked up two bags and headed for the door. "Come on, grab your things. The wagon is ready to leave, and when we arrive, we need to find you different housing." He walked out, muttering, "Wife."

Nemerra took the smallest bag and followed, smiling serenely. How could she be so calm? What if they had said she couldn't come? Ludik grabbed a big crate. One battle down that he hadn't known he would have to fight. How many more would surprise him?

This time, the wagon ride was short, and they arrived before the midday meal. A complex of long stone buildings surrounded a square green center fed by a thin stream from the river. Farther from the river, the land gradually turned from earth to sand, and the plants dwindled into almost nothing.

Koray left them outside and disappeared into one building, reemerging with a brisk, middle-aged woman. She examined Ludik and Nemerra, fists on her hips, then raised her eyebrows and spoke to Koray in Iskrit, pointing toward one end of another building. Koray nodded, asked a few questions, then bowed as the woman left.

He grabbed a crate. "The building on the left is the girls' rooms. At the back are the classrooms, and the building in front is the healing center and practice labs. We go right. Sorry, Nemerra, to house you with a bunch of unruly boys, but 'tis the only way to share with Ludik. Most of them are mere children and will not bother you with their attentions."

Nemerra chuckled as she grabbed her bag. "I survived Ludik's brothers. If they get too bothersome, I will shift to leopard and scare them off."

Koray blinked twice and opened and closed his mouth before walking away. Ludik loaded his arms, and they followed Koray through a small door at the end of the building instead of the prominent double doors at the front. The building was very plain, though absolutely clean, and a line of doors marched down both sides of the long hall.

"This was as close as we could get to giving you a private entrance." Koray's quiet voice echoed in the silent hall as he pushed open the first door on the left. "She's putting you in the room of one of the dorm monitors. He went home, and we have not replaced him yet. Put down your load, and I will show you around before you get the rest."

The room was small, just as clean as the hall, and well-lit by tall, narrow windows. The only furniture was one skinny bed and a stack of mats in one corner.

"We will get you another bed to push next to this one," Koray assured them.

Ludik and Nemerra piled their belongings on the floor and returned to the hall.

As they walked toward the other end, Koray pointed out the name markers next to each door. "I assume you cannot read Iskrit yet?"

Ludik shook his head.

"Then for now, just know a metal name plaque means a lower student, and wood means one close to certification. They do not teach their students trade tongue until near the end, so if you need help, go to one of the wood-marked rooms or the monitor at the far end of the hall."

"How long ago did you study here?" Nemerra asked.

Koray laughed. "I do not have magic. I studied elsewhere."

Nemerra shifted her arm in her sling. "Then how do you know all this?"

"Okechuku thought you might need help catching up in your classes and translating the texts and lectures. Though I do not have the magic, I do have the skills, and I'm not currently needed elsewhere. Unless you already have plans?" Koray raised his eyebrows.

"No." Ludik had assumed the class would be in trade tongue, which now seemed foolish.

What else had he overlooked? His stomach churned, and a headache tightened behind his eyes. He should have stayed home and learned from a Darrendrakar healer.

Nemerra nudged him with her good elbow, and he added, "Thank you."

Koray nodded. "They gave me quarters with the certified healers, but I will come each morning to accompany you to classes."

He pointed to a large door in the middle of the hall, just before a shorter hall that led to the front doors. "This is the cafeteria. All meals are provided, even for your wife."

"I have a question," Nemerra asked. "What will I do while Ludik is busy all day?"

Koray sighed. "The problem has never come up." He scanned her arm and neck and frowned. "I suspect they will have you see a healer first, then assign you chores or mentoring. Would you be willing to let students practice their trade tongue with you?"

"I would be pleased." Nemerra turned the full force of her smile on Koray.

The poor man blushed from collar to hair and swallowed twice. "That is the end of the tour."

He turned down the short hallway and held the door open for Nemerra. "While you unload the wagon, I will have another bed sent for you. Ludik, you have an appointment with Okechuku after lunch to assess your skills and assign classes." Koray glanced at Nemerra again and fled.

Ludik burst into laughter. "You did it again, sweetheart."

Nemerra shook her head. "All I did was smile at him."

"Exactly." He leaned in for a kiss from his beautiful wife.

2. SCHOOL
(TUKIKO DISTRICT, ISKRA)

The best Iskrin healers come from the Tukiko clan. The most talented earn the title of Shri. Legends claim they rescue patients from death itself.

Iskrin Culture and History, vol. 3

The grueling interview with Shri Okechuku in the healer's building exposed every gap in Ludik's medical education. He only learned parts of it when he traded places with his identical brother as a regular prank. He wanted to protest it wasn't his fault, but he saved his breath. It didn't matter why he was lacking, only that he was.

After the inquisition, Okechuku made a schedule of classes on a slate, staring at large slates on the wall as he wrote, erased, and wrote again. He paused and set his list on his knee.

Ludik fidgeted on the beautiful woven rug that served as his seat, then forced himself to be still. It was only the uncomfortable position that made him twitch, he lied to himself, and if Okechuku could sit cross-legged for so long at his age, then so could he.

"There are two ways to do this," Okechuku said. "Unlike the youngsters we usually teach, you do not need to take any of the basics except one advanced mathematics class, so that shortens your time here already. If you are not in a hurry, we can send you through most of the regular healing curriculum. Some of it will be review, but it is the easiest path. If you want to finish more quickly, we can let you study on your own for some of the classes you already know partially, then take the exams. But learning Iskrit, which alas, we do not have a class for, will already take much of your free time. The fast way will leave you with little time to spend with your wife."

"Time with my wife is important," Ludik said, "and it is difficult to learn a new language at my age."

Okechuku grinned. "Yes, your advanced age." Though the old man's hair was hidden by the usual Iskrin scarf, his eyebrows were gray instead of black, and his skin was developing the maze of fine wrinkles of the elderly. "Truly, though, you will find most of your classmates are much younger. We make an exception for healing talents and accept students before they pass their adulthood rite."

He made another note on the slate and handed it to Ludik. "Koray will be your tutor and translator. I trust this is acceptable, even though he is not Shri?"

Ludik nodded. "He told me. He is a good healer, and we are already somewhat friends."

Okechuku rose without difficulty. "Then we are finished here. Go help your wife unpack. Tomorrow, you start classes. If you run into difficulties we have not anticipated, please come see me."

After pounding his thighs to restore blood flow, Ludik struggled to his feet, hiding a sigh. Even sitting would be a challenge here. He grinned. If he came to class as a black jaguar, would it distract the other students from his inadequacies?

✦✦✦

The next morning, Koray arrived to eat the morning meal in the cafeteria with Ludik and Nemerra and the crowd of apprentices. Ludik found a table in the corner and put Nemerra against the wall while he took the seat next to her, facing the room.

"I thought it would save time if I went over your schedule while we eat," Koray said, "and I can translate if you want to talk to someone."

"So far, no one has even dared greet me," Ludik drawled. "And they can certainly tell who I am."

With their brown skin and colorful clothes, he and Nemerra stood out among the white Iskrin faces and tan robes like a parrot in snow. His gold hair and her russet were just as noticeable, even if the two of them hadn't towered over the younger Iskrins. Actually, Ludik was several inches taller than the tallest Iskrin here.

"They will get used to you." Koray stuffed food into his mouth and took Ludik's slate. "Hmm, mm-hmm, mmm." After he swallowed, he said, "You should catch up easily in these classes."

A bell rang somewhere outside, and Koray grabbed his tray. "'Tis the warning bell. Bright day, Nemerra. Hurry, Ludik."

After kissing Nemerra, Ludik hustled to the classroom building next door with Koray, who gave him a rapid lesson in written Iskrit numbers as they found the correct room. They settled in a back corner just before another bell rang and an Iskrin wearing a midnight-blue belt with the Tukiko crescent moon buckle stood at the front of the room.

Koray whispered a rapid translation from Iskrit to trade tongue, and Ludik took notes. This seemed to be a basic class, and most of it was familiar. The next class was also easy, but the one after that spawned two slates full of notes.

Then came a short class of hands-on procedures for first response treatments. Ludik knew the non-magical techniques perfectly, but wasn't familiar with the magical accompaniments. The other students snickered behind their hands, only to smooth their faces when the teacher looked up.

Koray refused to translate the whispers. "It does not matter. Ignore them."

So the little hyenas were being rude. Ludik took a deep breath to relax the knots in his belly. It wasn't his fault he was no good at this. The classes he'd stolen from his brother included no magic at all. In his brief lessons with Okechuku on his first adventure, he had learned only the most basic magical skills. His first lesson had been limited to "think about Ahjin healing well."

Since then, he'd learned to mentally feel damage as an incorrect texture in his patients' bodies. Touching the injured areas helped, when possible. He'd healed a friend's concussion by smoothing roughness inside his mind with his magic, and that was more complicated than this class.

Considering how old he had been when he discovered he *had* magic, he was doing well. No other foreigners had been invited to this elite school. He closed his eyes, reached for serenity, and tried again.

After class, he took Nemerra to the midday meal, where she again picked at the spiciest foods. Knowing she would eventually adjust and not wishing to draw attention to her, Ludik gave her his mildest dishes as he asked Koray questions about his notes. He didn't have time to finish before he hurried to his afternoon classes.

As in the morning, some of his classes were easy, some more difficult, and some completely beyond his skills. Most of the students ignored him, but some mocked and few made any attempt to help.

Ludik tried to think well of them. They were only children, as young as ten. Only a few of the almost-graduating students were his own age, and there was no common language to overcome the cultural and age differences. Still, when he met Nemerra for the evening meal, he was glad to be finished.

He and Koray spent two hours studying notes and language before Koray left and Ludik curled up with Nemerra to study by himself.

The next month kept him busy. From the morning meal to bedtime, if he wasn't in class, he was studying either healing or Iskrit. The more Iskrit he learned, the more he understood the whispers from the other students in the hallways and cafeteria. They mocked him for his poor language skills, race, and ignorance of healing. Why was a hunter in the best healing school in the world? Why admit a Darrendrakar who couldn't even speak properly? Though they didn't dare his wrath by harassing Nemerra, they whispered about her, too, and how odd for an apprentice to be married, and at such a young age. Who wanted a wife to distract them from their studies? Too old to be a healer, and too young to be married.

Ludik snorted. They might be right about his experience and qualifications, but they were very wrong about his wife. Nemerra was the best part of his life, sweet and encouraging and determined to find a place for herself in their new circumstances. She helped him review his notes and took care of their room so he had more time for his education. Even after she started falling asleep before he was ready for bed, her warmth next to him was comforting.

Once her neck and shoulder had been healed by the Shri and their most advanced students — and that was a huge relief for them both — she divided her time between her leather work, tutoring students in trade tongue, and general chores around the complex.

They both switched to Iskrin robes, and after Nemerra met the girls from across the square, she braided her russet hair like a proper Iskrin matron. But they kept their own shorter boots, and neither of them wore a scarf unless they went outside for a long period.

Every week, Okechuku asked Ludik to teach the full Shri how to make his healing ointment, including the magical part, which Ludik still had no idea how he added. The healers were surprisingly patient, though. After one of them asked permission to touch Ludik while he worked, they finally discovered what he was doing and could teach him how to do it on purpose. To his surprise, even after he could reliably add the magic, the Shri left the time in his schedule to make the salve.

Even more surprisingly, they brought in students from the advanced classes and had him try to teach them. Ludik felt peculiar tutoring the young men and women who were nearly at the end of their apprentice-ships, far ahead of him. Though he half-suspected this was meant as some sort of lesson for himself, he did as Okechuku requested. He expected the young healers to quickly learn how to make the salve, and it was obvious they thought the same. And yet, none of them seemed to have the knack, no matter how Ludik tried to explain. If he was supposed to be learning how to teach others, he was obviously failing. At least the herbs in the salve would still help their patients, even without magic.

After one session, he overheard some of them complain to the full healers that they couldn't possibly learn properly from someone who didn't speak adequate Iskrit. Those students didn't return to his lessons, and when he asked, he was told they had been sent back to practice their trade tongue. Ludik added another hour of practice in Iskrit to his own schedule.

The next students who complained made his nationality their excuse, and they disappeared altogether.

"They were sent home in disgrace," Koray explained over a meal. "After their clan elders think they have learned their lesson, they will have to appeal to return. It is one thing to whisper in class as a young student, but quite unacceptable for a near-graduate to refuse to learn from you because you are a foreigner. How do you think the Shri got so good?"

Ludik shrugged. "The magic."

Koray shook his head. "Sometimes they use their magic, and sometimes they do not. They always use their knowledge and skill. The Shri have the greatest reservoir of knowledge because they have been learning from everyone for hundreds of years. Their only weakness is their lesser knowledge of other races, and after Okechuku helped you with Ahjin last year, he has been working to add classes on foreigners to the curriculum. It will be a few years before the Shri can make the new classes standard for all students, though. In the meantime, they are learning from you."

Ludik blinked and leaned against the wall. "The Shri think I know something they don't?"

"They *know* you do," Koray said. "For now, they are learning your salve, but as you advance through the classes, I'm sure they will ask questions about the Darrendrakar. When I'm not helping you, they quiz me on anything I might know that would be useful for the other races, like bird bones or gills."

He leaned his chin on his hand. "Did you not wonder why they wanted you to come so badly? Why they let Nemerra come even though no other apprentices are married?"

Ludik inhaled to argue, could think of nothing to say, and let out his breath in a confused sigh. The best healers wanted to learn from *him*. His brothers would never believe it. He didn't believe it!

During his next salve-making class, Ludik tried harder to explain, and now that he understood Okechuku's goal, his patience lasted longer. He finally remembered how the older Shri had learned and suggested the younger ones do the same. Only one young woman was willing to touch him while he worked, but when she picked up the trick two classes later, more students tried, and his entire class soon learned.

He congratulated them on the way out, and they bowed and thanked him. The next week, he had a whole new group of students.

With Koray's help, Ludik did catch up in his classes, but he still felt overwhelmed. Sneaking into Gurryon's only-enough-healing-to-help-if-we-don't-have-a-healer classes was very different from the intensive lessons the Shri taught. The other students had been identified with healing magic as children and had trained since then. They ate, drank, and breathed healing, and couldn't understand why Ludik wasn't as dedicated.

Why, he even left the complex for the occasional hunt under the stars — with his wife, and as a panther! — when he could be practicing a new healing technique.

Ludik had no intention of giving up the midnight hunts, but despite his ointment, he did wonder if he was dedicated enough to healing. Or good enough. He frequently considered returning to Darrendra, but the healed scars on Nemerra's neck and shoulder reminded him of the good he could do when he finished.

After several more weeks, he finally caught up enough to have a little free time from his studies. The healing lessons were easier now that he understood the basics, and his Iskrit had improved enough for a casual chat with a cooperative partner. His teachers now found his practical work acceptable, and his understanding of theory should catch up soon. Though his entire education would still take a few years, the load was now manageable. He could become a good healer after all. Life was finally easy.

Whistling cheerily, he returned early from the library and found Nemerra lying in bed, eyes closed and holding her stomach. Ludik sat beside her and brushed her hair off her face. She groaned softly.

"Sweetheart, are you ill?"

"A little."

"Did you eat something that disagreed with you? I know you don't like all the spices here. Should I call for a healer, or is it something I can handle?"

"It's your fault," she whispered.

Ludik blinked. How could her stomachache possibly be his fault? "If it's my fault, can I fix it?"

"No."

"I'll get a healer." As he rose from the bed, Nemerra grabbed his hand.

"No." She opened her eyes and tried to smile. "It's improving and will only last a few more weeks. I didn't want to distract you from your studies."

"How long have you been ill? Why didn't the healers fix it when they fixed your neck?"

Nemerra laughed. "Oh, honey. When does your class schedule include a maternity unit?"

"Not until next year, but what does that—" He stopped and sank to the bed again. "Maternity?"

Fear wrestled joy in an equal match of tooth and claw.

"Yes," Nemerra said.

"Are you sure?" Ludik touched her shoulder, partly to comfort her and partly to steady his reeling head. He would be a father in a few months. Now *his* stomach hurt. So much for life getting easier.

Nemerra laughed, then groaned again.

If Ludik dropped out, he could devote all his time to his family. He didn't *have* to be a healer.

His conscience twinged. Koray and Okechuku and all the teachers had spent a lot of time and effort teaching him. Throwing their gifts at their feet like spoiled prey was ungrateful and impolite. But how could he leave Nemerra to care for their children alone through years of school?

Ludik jumped to his feet. "I have to see Okechuku."

"I don't need a healer," Nemerra whispered.

"No, I need to switch my schedule to the other track. If I'm going to be a father, I need to get out of here faster!"

CAPTURED

(TWO MONTHS AFTER SEED OF WAR)

CAPTURED
(NOKAILANA)

May your journey be pleasant and your companions cheerful, and may the currents shield you from adversity as they carry you to your desire.
Traditional Nokai farewell.

Humming an old lullaby in her slightly off-key alto, Kolina dragged the last net aboard and threw it on the deck. While their original crew and ship worked in the east, she and Alemana were fishing with the new workers at the northern end of their self-declared territory. If everything continued so well, they could expand their business again in another year or two. She might even consider having a baby next year.

"What are you smiling about?" Alemana asked, dropping a kiss on her neck, just behind her gills, before dumping his fish into the hold.

"Another good load, and we'll have enough for... something nice."

"I already have something nice." He winked at her and reached for her net.

She laughed and helped him empty the catch. The fish were almost volunteering to be caught, so it was good their new ship was bigger than their old one. Yes, everything was going very well. And after selling the fish tonight, she and Alemana would still have time for a leisurely swim and a great deal of kissing.

Thunder cracked, and she jerked to look upward. Oh, no. While they were busy pulling in the fish, a storm had blown in from nowhere.

"Hurry," Kolina bellowed, dragging the net toward the hatch.

Alemana and the other five crew dropped their nets or ran for the sails and anchor. With two masts, they might outrun the rain, unlike in their old single-masted boat. When all the fish were dumped in the hold, Alemana slammed and locked the hatches.

It was too late. The storm hit as they pulled up anchor. The fishermen and women furled all the green and yellow sails except the tiny storm jib and strapped themselves in to avoid being swept overboard.

Despite their efforts to sail south to home, the storm forced them farther north and east, away from Nokailana altogether. The fishing grounds ran for hundreds of miles between their islands and Darrendra. Surely they wouldn't be pushed all the way to the northern continent, would they?

Kolina wrapped her arms around the mast and kept Alemana company as he struggled with the tiller. Frigid rain poured over them, and thunder boomed while lightning cracked across the sky.

"I'm glad we hired only Nokai," she yelled above the wind. "At least nobody will drown if we sink."

Though even gills didn't make it easy to breathe in the chaotic tempest of wind and water.

He rolled his eyes and swiped water from his face, not that it did any good. "We won't sink. The storm will blow over soon enough, and then we'll sail home."

Above them, a spar snapped, shredding the rigging as it plummeted to the deck. The ship jerked sideways until Alemana regained control.

"Well," he shouted, leaning into the tiller, "we'll make a few repairs and then sail home."

As if the damage had been all the storm wanted, it belched a final round of lightning and eased to a mere sprinkle. Spouting curses, their crew surrounded the broken spar and started cleaning. The best climbers shimmied up the mast to repair rigging where possible and tear it down where not.

While Alemana directed repairs, Kolina grabbed a broom and swept up the broken wood to protect bare feet, concentrating on finding every splinter.

"Need any help?" someone shouted in trade tongue.

She looked up and discovered a larger ship sailing toward them. Fifteen or twenty sailors, mostly men from a motley collection of nationalities, leaned on the bulwark with sympathetic expressions.

Alemana laughed. "I think we can handle it."

"Oh, let them help," Kolina said. "We can get home sooner."

Alemana gave her a dubious look, but said, "All right, come on over."

He explained the help to the crew that spoke only Noki, then turned back to his repairs. It took only a few minutes for most of the new sailors to swing aboard and spread out. Kolina smiled and pointed out the spar to move.

A tall Darrendrakar barked an order in a foreign language. Instead of picking up tools, the sailors drew weapons and whirled on the fishing crew. At the tiller, Alemana was backed up with a sword pointed at his stomach. Kolina suddenly faced a serrated knife at her own throat, held by a scrawny Iskrin with a ferocious grin. She froze, even holding her breath until she ran out of air.

This was all her fault. She should never have told Alemana to let them aboard.

"Give us your cargo," the other ship's captain demanded.

Alemana silently pointed toward the hold. While the pirate captain stomped toward the trapdoor, Alemana watched Kolina, his lips clamped tightly and golden skin ashen.

Please, Makanavailea, Mystical Lady, help us escape. Kolina flicked her gaze between her sweetheart and the pirate who drew slowly closer and closer to her until his filthy robe pressed against her favorite ocean suit and his stark white face occupied her entire vision.

When she got home, she would burn this outfit.

The hold door slammed shut, and Kolina jumped. Her neck stung, and the scrawny pirate reached for the blood running down her neck.

"There's nothing here but fish," the pirate captain screamed.

What had he expected? They looked nothing like a merchant ship. Kolina dared say nothing, and two of the silent pirates exchanged speaking glances that made her think *they* knew a fishing boat when they saw one.

The captain took a deep breath and spoke in an ominously quiet voice. "But your ship will make a nice addition to our fleet."

Not their ship! Kolina squeezed back tears and glanced at Alemana, whose eyes and mouth gaped wide as he looked beyond her. Kolina's captor turned to watch with a grin.

"No," Alemana gasped, as a *snick* and a meaty thunk were punctuated with screams.

Too late, Kolina turned to check on the rest of their crew. Three of them now lay on the deck, and a nasty red stain crept over the sanded planks. The air gushed from her as if she had been stabbed herself.

The pirate raised his bloody sword again, and her last two crew members fell to their knees, crying.

Kolina reached toward them, throat too tight to speak. *Oh, Makana, help them.* But it was too late.

"Please," Alemana shouted. When the sword at his belly pressed forward, he lowered his voice. "Please spare us. We're just poor fishers. Have mercy."

The pirate captain leaned on his sword, watching the blood run across the deck. Kolina's captor touched the blood on her neck. His fingers were warm, too warm as they traced the trickle, and his chapped skin dragged on hers. She cringed from him, and he grinned.

One of the other pirates leaned toward the captain and whispered, motioning toward the hold.

The captain frowned, and the pirate whispered again.

"Oh, very well," the Darrendrakar said. "We've been a little short on food lately, and having expert fishermen at hand would be useful. If you agree to join us, we will spare your lives."

Alemana cast an anguished glance at Kolina, who nodded as much as she dared with the jagged blade against her skin. If they survived, there was hope to escape.

"We surrender." Each syllable sounded like it was dragged from Alemana's mouth. He repeated the phrase in Noki for their last two crew.

"No," Anela wailed.

The pirate captain cut her down without blinking an eye. "Does anyone else want to reject our hospitality?" he drawled.

The filthy Iskrin raised an eyebrow and grinned at Kolina. She closed her eyes and carefully shook her head.

The pirates spread out, binding the last three survivors and tossing the dead overboard. Kolina, Alemana, and Hoku were carried to the pirate ship and left in an untidy heap on deck.

With so many pirates available to help, they finished repairs the next day. The pirate ship swung north, followed by Kolina's beautiful little boat, now crewed by pirates. Kolina, Alemana, and Hoku made the trip lying on deck with their hands bound. Kolina shivered constantly with fear, but the sailors stepped around them as if they were nothing more than dead fish.

Her continued prayers to Makana remained unanswered.

This was all Kolina's fault. True, there had been no rumors of pirates in the area, but if she hadn't pushed Alemana into this trip, they would be safely at home. Now most of their crew was dead, and their ship was captured. He must hate her.

She tried to apologize, and a pirate rushed over to beat her into silence. Once they were left alone again, Alemana shook his head at her and mouthed "not your fault."

Kolina pressed her shoulder against his and closed her eyes to weep silently. He might forgive her, but how could she forgive herself?

Days later, or maybe weeks, after Kolina lost count of how long they'd been captives, they arrived at a haphazard dock at the edge of land. They couldn't possibly be far enough north for Darrendra, even if the pirates dared the wrath of Darravani by landing on her forbidden shores. The only land between Nokailana and Darrendra was the empty, mysterious Dragon Isles. Cursed, the legends said, and Kolina felt cursed.

All three Nokai were dragged to a ship that flew a red flag with a dragon emblem. Still under guard, they waited for an hour. The winter air was chilly, proof they had left Nokailana far behind, if she needed any more proof. Finally, someone emerged from the ship and stomped down to meet them, followed by an Iojif with nervously fluttering tan wings.

The first man had shiny black hair and the peachy skin of an Iojif, but no wings flowed from his back. Though he smiled, something in his face made Kolina cringe.

"N-new recruits, Crow," their Darrendrakar captor said in trade tongue, and his hands clenched on Kolina's arms. "We took their ship intact, and they're fishermen. They can catch enough fish to feed all of us."

Kolina nodded frantically, along with Alemana and Hoku.

Crow frowned. "I hate fish."

All three stopped nodding, and Kolina's blood curdled in her veins. With no value to the pirates, they would live as long as a bleeding seal in shark-infested waters.

The tan-winged Iojif pulled on Crow's elbow and whined something in presumably his native language.

Without changing his expression, Crow backhanded the Iojif to the dock. "I told you to never mention prison food to me again. And talk so everyone can understand."

"Sorry, Crow," the Iojif whimpered.

"Are they crew or captive?" Crow touched Kolina's cheek with the back of his hand, trailing his fingers across her chin.

Her skin crawled worse than swimming through a bed of eels, but she dared not turn away.

The hands on her arms tightened even more, and the Darrendrakar pirate shook her a little. "Crew, Captain."

Alemana choked off a protest when his captor slugged him. Kolina gasped for breath and sagged against the hands holding her upright.

Crow sighed and dropped his hand. "Too bad. We never have enough women captives. They don't last long enough."

Kolina shook like seaweed in a current. Beside her, Alemana mouthed a curse.

Crow waved his hand. "Take them to Aukai and have them trained."

"Yes, Captain."

When Crow turned his back, exposing the stumps of wings, the Darrendrakar pirate and his cronies dragged the three Nokai down the dock again and shoved them aboard a ship flying a mix of colorful Nokai and plain white sails. Big enough to be a merchant vessel, the craft was dirty and unkept, with uncoiled heaps of line on the brown-spotted deck and splinters around dings in the railing. As if the ship had survived a flight of arrows but some of the crew had not.

Kolina tried to stiffen her shaking knees. The only thing worse than being crew was being captive.

"Aukai," the Darrendrakar bellowed.

After a minute, a dirty Nokai emerged from below deck. His matted braids were a darker brown than his golden skin, like burnt sugar, and he carried a jug in one hand.

Kolina's hopes rose a little, and she glanced carefully at Alemana. One of their own people would surely be more sympathetic to their plight. Her sweetheart tipped his head slightly from side to side. Maybe, maybe not. He tilted his chin toward the Nokai who had helped capture their ship, and Kolina twitched a shoulder in understanding.

"Wha' now?" Aukai mumbled in Noki.

"New recruits," the Darrendrakar said in trade tongue.

"Wha'?" Aukai slurred.

"Crew," the Darrendrakar said slowly. "Train."

Aukai took a long swig. "Yes," he said in trade tongue.

In Noki, he streamed curses that made Kolina blush, but the other pirates merely looked bored. The Darrendrakar pushed Kolina forward, and Alemana and Hoku staggered along.

"Stay with Aukai," the pirate enunciated.

And then he was gone, though pirates bristling with weapons took up guard posts along the dock. Kolina grabbed Alemana's hand and tried to calm her pounding heartbeat.

"Sit and stop quaking," Aukai said in Noki. "I have a headache, and tomorrow will be soon enough. Just one word of advice — don't try to escape. Over half the pirates are Nokai and perfectly capable of catching you in the ocean. If you think Captain Crow is bad now — and you should — you don't want to see what he's like when he feels betrayed."

Aukai threw himself into a hammock on deck and drained his jug. "Tomorrow," he repeated, closing his eyes.

"We could jump overboard and swim away," Hoku whispered, peering over the railing to the lavender waves below.

Alemana led Kolina to a hammock. "We're being watched." He scrunched in beside her for a comforting embrace, then nodded warningly toward Aukai. "Tomorrow, we will learn everything we can so we don't disappoint Crow." He raised his eyebrows and pursed his lips.

Hoku grunted. "I understand." He threw an arm over his eyes and began snoring.

Kolina nodded. Learn what they needed to survive until they could escape.

☆⚓⚓◎
⌣⌣⌣⌣⌣

For the next two weeks, the three fishermen trained with Aukai and his men, mostly in the routine of the island and the idiosyncrasies of the larger ships. They also learned where to find food besides the ocean, which pirate captains had any mercy at all, and most importantly, how to make the crippled Crow happy.

Kolina and the two men pretended to comply and watched for their chance. Despite their sailing skills, their lack of weapons experience meant they were nearly always assigned to fish for the growing fleet. Once, they were forced to participate in the capture of another ship, and though they fought only in self-defense, the atrocities they saw the other pirates commit haunted Kolina.

"A quick end would have been more merciful," she whispered after she turned in her blood-stained harpoon.

Alemana said nothing, but his eyes were red-rimmed.

At night, they slept surrounded by pirates. Kolina learned to wake silently from her nightmares lest she rouse the horde. As she wept in the dark, her sweetheart pulled her close. She buried her face in his shoulder, and they shook together.

After a month, the three of them left on a fishing trip with only three other pirates, and for the first time, none of them were Nokai. This was their chance to escape. No foreigner could keep up with Nokai in the water. All they needed was a moment of inattention.

Or a nice distraction.

Kolina shoved her despair to the bottom of her heart and chatted gaily with the pirates. She kept up a steady stream of babble while they sailed out, then quieted when they anchored. After all, noise would ruin the fishing, and unusual behavior would ruin any chance of escape.

Despite her efforts to seem harmless, the pirates kept an eye on them the whole day. Kolina fought to keep her hands from shaking and her feet from tapping on the deck. She must not give away their plans by seeming nervous. How her companions stayed so calm, she didn't know. And were they really so confident or faking it as hard as she was?

While they pulled in the nets, she picked up her chatter again, smiling at the pirates as if they didn't turn her stomach and flirting harder than she had ever flirted before.

"This is a nice change," the taller Iskrin said. "I thought you would never decide to be friendly."

As he reached for her, Alemana smacked him across the back of the head with a weighted net. The Iskrin dropped like a dead fish, and all three Nokai turned on the other two pirates, fighting like krakens with everything they could reach.

Hoku got a net around the other Iskrin and snapped his neck, and Alemana pounded the Darrendrakar while Kolina knelt on his arm to keep him down.

Then Hoku staggered and fell bleeding across the deck. An arrow stuck out of his neck, and another hit Kolina in the shoulder like a bolt of fire. She fell back, screaming, and a third landed in Alemana's thigh. He collapsed, and the Darrendrakar rose and kicked him.

Kolina's shoulder hurt too much to move, even if she could. She cowered on the deck, covering her head with her good arm. More arrows fell from above, and then a blur of tan swept overhead. An Iojif landed on the boat and pointed his bow at them. Lapwing, that was his name.

Crow's whiny lackey frowned at the pirates. "Crow told you to watch them, he did. You should obey Crow. He's always right." He glanced at the Iskrin with the broken neck. "Now look what you did. Crow will be angry."

The Darrendrakar growled and kicked Alemana again, then started reviving the unconscious Iskrin.

Lapwing ordered, "Get up."

Kolina pressed her hands against the deck and whimpered as the pressure sent stabbing fire through her shoulder.

Lapwing smirked. "Get up." He drew back on his bowstring and pointed his arrow at Alemana.

"Come on, dear." Alemana pulled himself up using the mast, then leaned against it for support. Blood poured down his thigh, staining his ocean suit red.

Kolina rolled to her side and forced herself up with only one hand.

Lapwing pointed his bow at Hoku and laughed. "One for one is fair. Unless Crow decides two for one is more fair."

Hoku did not rise, and the red pool around him no longer spread. Kolina pressed her hand across her mouth and turned away.

The pirates threw Hoku overboard, and Kolina wept as hard for herself and her bleeding sweetheart as she did for her dead friend. He was back in the loving arms of Makanavailea, but she saw no end to her own misery.

Ignoring the injured Nokai, the three pirates clumsily sailed the boat back to the island. Once docked, they dragged Kolina and Alemana to Crow's ship and threw them at his feet. Kolina bowed her head and cradled her arm, too afraid to cry and too miserable to speak as Lapwing and the two sailors told a rather lopsided story about the attempted escape.

When they finished, Crow turned circles, the stubs of his amputated wings twitching. "I should kill you both," he snarled.

Aukai cleared his throat. "We didn't eat as well before," he offered. When Crow glared, the Nokai captain shrugged. "Whatever you decide, of course, but I do like fish." He stepped back into the crowd and slid behind a taller man.

"Give the girl to us," someone suggested. "We'll keep her company."

Alemana's bellow ended in a grunt when a pirate kicked his wounded leg.

No, no, no. Kolina fought for air, grateful only that her breathlessness meant she couldn't scream. If it came to that, she would rip the arrow from her arm and fight back until they killed her. At least then this nightmare would end.

"No," Crow said. "I have a better idea." He circled Kolina, eyes narrowed. "We will give our lovely lady the blessing of our hospitality and allow her mate the freedom to roam. If he disobeys again, *then* we will give her the pleasure of your company."

The pirates roared with approval, and Crow pumped his fists above his head.

Kolina's stomach tied itself in an even tighter knot. They meant they'd keep her as hostage to make Alemana follow orders. But what if her sweetheart *couldn't* obey? Crow didn't look like the sort of man who would accept excuses.

"Take them away," Crow ordered. "See to their wounds and find them a new home."

A new home. With *them*? Never, Kolina swore to herself while the pirates dragged them away.

When her sweetheart looked at her, fear and despair twisting his handsome face into a terrible mask, she straightened her good shoulder and smiled through her tears. She would stick with Alemana until they could find a better way.

If it took ten years, she would never give up hope of escape.

MARATHON

(ONE YEAR AFTER WIND OF CHOICE)

MARATHON
(EQUID TERRITORY, DARRENDRA)

In their annual cross-country race, the shape-shifting Horses cover 160 leagues. Some winners have run it in a mere four days.
A Brief Sketch of Mysterious Darrendra

"What do you mean, you aren't coming?" Rozali stopped packing her bag and gaped at her older brother. "Our family has run this race for decades. We're the best of the best. And you want to stop now because of some *girl?*"

Zinon flopped onto her bed, teeth bright against his brown skin in a dopey smile. He had braided his single white lock of hair separately from the brown, like a zebra stripe instead of the brown-and-white pinto he was in his other form.

"She isn't just some girl," he said. "She's the girl I'm going to marry."

Rozali tossed a pillow at him. "You barely started seeing her. You don't know if the two of you will marry."

Zinon shrugged. "I have time to convince her. We just turned seventeen, so we have a whole year to court, if we want. And she doesn't want to race for four days, so I'm not going."

"But we were going to win again," Rozali protested.

"Isn't four times enough for you?" Zinon asked. "Or you could wait a year or two. You're only sixteen, so it's not like you'll be too old. Or you could run at Mama and Papa's pace."

Rozali grabbed her hairbrush and yanked it through her pale hair. "No, no, and no. But if you don't want to go with me, I'll do it by myself."

Her brother snorted and rolled over, tucking the pillow under his chest. "You never remember the route. You'll get lost and disappear forever."

"I will *not*."

"Foreeeeeeever," Zinon moaned spookily.

"I've run it for ten years," Rozali protested. "How dumb do you think I am?"

Zinon shrugged with a grin.

Rozali glared. "They have stations all along the way."

Zinon buried his face in the pillow, shoulders trembling with laughter.

"You're an idiot." Rozali yanked her pillow away and hit him with it. "And how do you think you'll be happy with a girl who doesn't like to run?"

Zinon rolled to safety, laughing almost too hard to speak. "She likes to run, just not competitively."

Rozali threw the pillow right into his smirking face and returned to her packing. She didn't need *him* to win.

☆🎔⛰☺
〜〜〜〜

Two weeks later, she wondered if she'd even get to race. Everything had gone wrong on the trip west, including Papa spraining a leg, and she and her parents were running late. If they didn't reach the starting station at the northern lake by nightfall, they couldn't race in the morning.

"Come on, Papa. Keep moving." Rozali slowed to a trot and circled back, eyeing the afternoon sun in the apricot sky.

"I won't make it in time. You shouldn't miss the race for me." Papa's blue roan coat shone gray in the sunlight.

"And we won't." Mama stopped. "Rozali, turn around. I'll *carry* your papa."

Rozali spun on her rear hooves. Behind her, Papa's bag thumped to the ground as he shifted.

After a few more minutes of rustling, Papa said, "I'm dressed."

As Rozali turned, Papa pulled himself onto Mama's pale chestnut back and wrapped his hands in her flaxen mane.

"Let's go."

Mama and Rozali sped to a canter.

"I'm sorry, Rozali," Papa said. "I know you were hoping for an easier speed along the way."

Rozali shook her mane. "It can't be helped now. Let's just get there in time."

They ran silently after that, saving their breath.

As the sun crept below the horizon, they arrived at the home station. Two long bunkhouses formed opposite sides of a square, with a long wooden awning above tables and benches on a third side. The fourth side held only a small hut for the judges.

They checked in with the judges and found their bunks, Mama and Rozali in the women's dorm and Papa by himself in the men's. After shifting, Rozali pulled her tiny race bag from her travel pack and opened it to make sure she hadn't forgotten anything. To her surprise, four maps were folded on top of her dress and emergency kit.

She laid them out on her bunk and laughed. Each map covered the distance of one day's run, with Zinon's hand-written notes describing landmarks, watering spots, and pacing.

Mama glanced over. "What is so funny?"

Rozali waved at the maps. "Zinon is convinced I'll get lost without him."

Mama looked away, mouth twitching. "I seem to remember one of you is better at navigating than the other."

"Mama, I was *twelve*! It was the first time we left you behind, and we still won! I've run without you for four years now. I can do it."

Mama shrugged. "Who usually navigates, you or Zinon?"

Rozali grunted and shoved the maps into her race pack. "I'll be fine, Mama."

"I'm sure you will. And if you do get lost, I will be only a few hours behind you."

"Less, I'm sure," Rozali said. "Zinon and I get our speed from you and Papa."

Mama grinned. "Then why don't we win?"

Rozali took two steps away and whispered, "Because you're too old."

Then she raced for the evening meal, giggling as Mama chased her. They met Papa under the awning and stood in an endless line of brown faces and colorful clothing to collect their food. As they ate, Rozali examined her competition. Horses came from all over the territory to race, and hers wasn't the only family to make it a tradition. The children were no match for her and neither were most of her parents' generation. No, her biggest rivals were those around her own age.

Unfortunately, in their two-legger forms, it was even more difficult to judge how fast someone might be. She picked out a dozen she suspected might be her toughest competition and made mental notes of their hair color. Though color didn't always carry over, it frequently did and was her best chance of identifying her suspected rivals in the morning. Unfortunately for her own surprise factor, her hair was as pale as a two-legger as it was in her palomino form. If Zinon hid his white stripe, the rest of his hair was a generic liver chestnut that could belong to many of the herd.

As she scanned the room, a skinny strawberry blond caught her gaze and winked. He was cute but unlikely to be strong enough to challenge her, so she smiled back. He tilted his head toward the empty bench next to her. She smiled again and shook her head. She had plans for that bench.

When she thought she had identified her competition, she switched her attention to the children. With smiles and a little bribery from her plate of desserts, she lured a few likely young ones to her table and questioned them about their race strategy. Those who said they were just running because their parents did, she gave cheerful encouragement and sent back to their parents with a sweet. But three of them spoke of the joy of running and the thrill of competition, phrased with childish cuteness. Those children, she kept with her as she worked through three servings of food, giving them tips for pacing themselves and being well-rested. She promised to watch for them at the finish line and sent them off with dessert.

After a hug for Papa, she made one more check on her travel pack and went to bed with Mama.

In the morning, everyone woke early and showed up for a meal still in their night tunics. Some chattered nervously, while others stared silently at the wall. Rozali studied the first of Zinon's maps while she ate. When the warning bell rang, everyone turned in their dishes and returned to the dorms to shift to four legs. Mama and Rozali stretched while they waited for their turn.

Several race hosts stood by to assist with travel packs and opening doors, and within an hour, all the Horses had assembled at the starting line. The "track" was wide enough that the racers only had to form lines two deep, with the front line assigned to anyone who had raced before with a sufficiently fast time. Newcomers and the proven-slow got the back line, including her three little pupils. She smiled at them before turning forward.

Stretched out on either side of her, the front line contained nearly every Horse she had identified as rivals. Or maybe all of them, if their hair color hadn't carried through to their hide or mane.

Rozali pranced impatiently, tossing her mane and stretching her neck toward the distant finish line. Her travel pack was buckled securely but comfortably. The map was clear in her head. When would they start?

Beside her, Mama leaned in until her shoulders brushed Rozali's.

"Calm down and save your energy," Mama murmured.

Papa waved from the observer's line, smiling cheerfully despite not being able to race. Rozali forced her hooves still and took a deep breath.

One of the starting judges walked to the front. "Remember the rules. Run fairly and don't interfere with other racers. Drink at every watering station. Clock in at the waystation to get your start time for the morning. You all got a flag?"

Horses nodded mechanically.

"If you are injured or ill, run up your distress flag. If you get lost, *don't* wander. If you can't get your bearings, use your distress flag and we will find you."

Mama nudged Rozali, who kept her teeth firmly closed over her retort.

The judge scanned the lines of racers. "Any questions?"

Everyone shook their manes.

"Are you ready?"

Everyone nodded.

The judge walked to the side and raised a flag. After a few seconds, she dropped it.

With a thunder of hooves, the front line bolted.

Rozali shot off, leaving Mama within a furlong. Most of the Horses fell behind her, but three young stallions and a mare kept pace. She maintained the gallop until the others dropped back to a more reasonable, maintainable gait. They would catch her when she tired, or so they probably thought. They were wrong.

Once they were out of sight, she dropped back to a trot and alternated with a canter for the rest of the morning. At every watering station, she drank and stretched and checked for injuries before trotting again.

The plains were green with spring and scented with flowers. Though there would be no major waterways until she reached the river at the end, small streams crossed her path frequently, and when there were none, there was sure to be a well. Their territory was in the middle of Darrendra, and as far as she was concerned, it was the perfect location. Farther north was too cold, farther south was too close to the outside world. East and west were too forested for good running. This race was almost the epitome of an ideal run. Good weather, pleasant surroundings, and a sure win. If her family had been with her, it would have been perfect.

After a while, she noticed two of her rivals stayed on the horizon behind her. Their annoying proximity pushed her into a faster pace than she wished. No one was supposed to be that close except Zinon, and that lummox had abandoned her.

The first waystation could serve as an overnight stop for slower runners, but for her, it was merely a place to eat her noon meal. She settled for grain in her horse form to save time, and took off again quickly.

Contrary to Zinon's teasing, she recognized every landmark and had no difficulty finding her way. She was perfectly competent, even without her vexing big brother. If she could only shake the rivals on her tail, her win would be assured.

Rozali pulled into the second waystation in first place, well before sunset. After the station attendant recorded her time and removed her pack, she shifted and dressed in the little hut provided for modesty.

The evening meal was served outside, and she had gulped her second serving by the time the next contestants arrived. After eating a third plateful while smiling serenely at her out-of-breath rivals, she rolled up in the supplied blanket and fell asleep to the melodious hoof beats of the other racers arriving under the triple moonlight.

Rozali was almost the first one up in the morning, with plenty of time to eat and talk to Mama. One of her little pupils had made it to this station last night, and he looked over her shoulder while she studied Zinon's map for the day's route and pointed out important or interesting spots. She even had enough time to listen to the news about who dropped out from fatigue or injuries. About one-tenth of the racers had given up so far, which was fairly average.

As the first one to arrive the night before, she got a head start. At each station, the racers would have staggered start times based on yesterday's finish time. Gossip already listed her as the favorite to win, and rightfully so. She shifted and let Mama buckle on her travel pack, then pranced to the starting line.

When the race official dropped her flag, she cantered away, letting the other racers think she was overconfident and easily caught. Once out of sight, she sped to a gallop until she had a longer lead, then returned to alternating trot and canter for the rest of the day.

At midday, she glanced behind her as she stopped at a waystation. What was that speck on the horizon? She should have been too far ahead to see anyone. No! There were two red Horses approaching, too close for her to take a rest.

Rozali gulped down food and more water and galloped onward. She took off at a blistering pace and didn't slow until the spot on the horizon was gone. With more fatigue than she cared to admit, she dropped back to her alternating trot and canter.

Last year, her rivals didn't figure out that she spent most of the race running only as fast as they did, but with a substantial distance between her and the next closest runner. The trick, worked out with Zinon last year, was one of three key strategies to her win, and the second was merely her natural speed and trained endurance.

She had almost reached the day's finish line when she stepped on a rock. Pain shot up her leg, and she staggered. No, no, no. If she sprained her leg like Papa, she would never win. In fact, with half the race to go, she wouldn't even finish.

Rozali took a deep breath to battle the tears and stood still for a minute. When the pain settled, it was in her foot instead of her ankle or leg. Much better, until she took a step and the pain shot upward again. A mere bruise wouldn't hurt so much. No, she probably had a stone lodged in her hoof.

She glanced behind. No one was visible. No one was ahead of her, either, and the next station was just over the rise. What a fortunate conse-quence of her extensive lead. She hobbled behind the closest bush, to be safe, and shifted back to two legs. Without bothering with her dress, she quickly dug out the pebble stuck in her foot. Since she couldn't properly fasten her pack without hands, she hung it around her neck and shifted back.

Her first step hurt, but the second hurt a bit less. Galloping was out of the question, but even hobbling should get her through the day. She gathered her courage and took another step. By hopping every other time the injured foot should touch the ground, she managed with less pain than she anticipated.

When she reached the end, she was still in first place, but her closest rivals were clearly visible on the horizon as silhouettes instead of mere dots, gray and a pale red. The red was probably that dratted roan who had been too close the day before, though she was surprised to see the gray and not the blood bay stallion who had accompanied the roan earlier.

The judge marked her time and waved her immediately to the healer's tent. Rozali stayed as a horse so the healer could see the damage to her hoof, which was fortunately only bruised.

As soon as she was treated with a smelly ointment, she shifted back for the evening meal. This time, she was only halfway through her first plate when a dapple gray mare and the roan stallion arrived. The blood bay pounded in not long after, and after all three shifted, they sat together to eat.

To Rozali's surprise, the roan turned out to be the skinny strawberry blond who had flirted with her. So much for appearances. They smiled and waved at her, and she smiled back around gritted teeth but limped to bed instead of staying up to talk.

In the morning, she ate and studied Zinon's map for the third day, then shifted to let Mama and the healer smear her foot with salve again.

"This is the traditional salve," the healer said, "but this batch came north from a talented healer in the Felid kindred. Rumor says he has the healing gift. I would appreciate a report on your healing progress, if you don't mind."

Rozali nodded as they added a padded leather shoe on the injured foot, which already felt much better.

The judge asked if she wanted to stop, but she refused. The number who had dropped out had risen to a third of the original roster, and Rozali had no intention of being one of them.

"Be careful," Mama said. "Don't hurt yourself permanently. You can run again next year."

Rozali nodded. "Yes, Mama."

The dapple gray mare, already shifted for the day's race, approached tentatively. "Darravani bless you with speed and fortune," she said.

"Thank you," Rozali said. "How kind of you. Good speed to you, too."

The mare shrugged. "I saw your foot. You must need every help you can get, and I want to beat you fairly."

"Hmm. Thank you anyway. See you at the finish line." Rozali exaggerated her limp as she reported to the starting line. Her lead was less than it had been before, but she still had a chance, and if she could make her rivals overconfident, she had a better chance.

The gray mare and the two stallions watched her, heads together as they whispered. Then the judge dropped the flag, and Rozali trotted away slowly. She gradually lengthened her strides without increasing the cadence, which subtly increased her speed, invisibly to her rivals. Her foot hurt, but not too much to move. She breathed evenly and concentrated on her pace instead of the nagging ache.

Once out of sight, she again sped up, though she couldn't reach her top pace without her foot protesting. Instead, she settled into a steady canter for as long as she could maintain it, then alternated with a walk until midday.

At the waystation, she stopped for longer and let the station healer add more salve and tighten the leather pad while she ate. She reported on her pain levels so the healers could compare the Felid salve to the regular one, then drank again and ran while the red and gray shapes behind her were still merely colored blobs.

The salve was working marvelously, and despite the continued pounding, her foot felt no worse than it had in the morning and better than when she injured it. But altering her stride to be gentler on that foot was as wearying as the pain itself, and even though she ran slower, she was as tired as if she had raced at full speed.

Rozali tossed her mane and ran anyway. She would not give up. She would not lose.

With the afternoon's run a straight line from waystation to end, she concentrated on placing one foot after the other, thinking only of winning. After a while, her mind faded into the pleasant hum of running, and she thought of nothing at all.

Hours later, when the judge yelled at her, she staggered to a halt well past the finish line.

"Sorry," she croaked. "I wasn't paying attention."

The judge shook her head. "I will never understand you racers. Go eat before you fall down." She squinted at Rozali's leg. "And see the healer." She walked off, shaking her head again.

Rozali shifted and dressed and limped to the healer. After more salve and a long lecture she mostly ignored, she collected her meal. The strawberry blond had arrived while she was being treated and was already eating, and the gray mare and blood bay stallion arrived not long after.

Too tired to want conversation, Rozali propped her cheek on her fist and shoveled her food into her mouth between yawns. She waved off the concerned looks of the other runners and went to bed right after Mama arrived at the front of the first big wave of racers.

Rozali woke to Mama shaking her.

"Goway, Mama," she mumbled.

"Get up," Mama said. "The race starts in a few minutes. Here, I brought you food. Get up!"

Rozali jerked upright and rubbed her eyes. "Why didn't you wake me earlier?"

Mama shoved the bowl at her. "I tried! Hurry." She grabbed Rozali's foot and smeared it with more salve.

Rozali shoveled in the food but barely finished before the judge called her name. She shifted quickly and let Mama buckle on her pack and padded shoe.

"Did you check the map?" Mama asked.

"I don't have time," Rozali said. "Besides, I know the way. Leave it for the children when they arrive."

"Rozali," the judge called again. "Last call."

Rozali darted for the race line. "I'm here!"

The judge sighed and dropped the flag.

Rozali continued her dash straight across the line. It took her a moment to calm herself and concentrate on running. She galloped at full speed for a short time, then settled into a steadier pace. Her hoof was only a little sore today. Today was the last day, and she was still in first place. All she had to do was maintain her lead. Easy as eating hay.

Too bad Zinon hadn't come to share her triumph. This one would belong to her alone. She whinnied in joy in the sunshine.

Her morning run went smoothly, and she pulled into a waystation right when she planned. She ate a generous lunch and re-anointed her hoof, but she didn't dawdle because her three annoying shadows were on the horizon behind her.

As she set off again, she kept a steady pace, saving her energy for the last burst of speed at the end that was the third of her tactics. Even without it, she was far enough ahead to win easily, but she liked trouncing her rivals. And, of course, she normally had to pass Zinon at the end, and he was almost as fast as she was.

At the stream marked by a cairn, she turned right for the last stretch of the race. Her three rivals were not far behind, but she was almost to the end. She pounded across the grass, wind blowing in her mane and triumph fueling her muscles. Five-time winner. What a lovely phrase.

She ran over a small hill and down the other side and screeched to a halt. A chasm blocked her way, too wide to jump across and too deep to run down. This was not on the route last year!

Rozali retreated up the hill and looked both ways. To her left, a gray shadow ran beside two red ones. They reached the cairn and turned left.

Left! She had gone the wrong way.

Rozali galloped back toward the cairn, pounding across the grass. They weren't that far ahead. She could catch up. She had to catch up.

She reached the cairn and followed the red and gray. Behind her, more Horses ran, spread out in a glorious herd of flowing manes and pounding hooves.

Rozali ran harder, ignoring her bruised foot. Faster and faster, until the red and gray Horses were just ahead.

But so was the finish line.

Crowds of cheering Darrendrakar lined either side of the road, and judges waited to declare the winner.

Rozali forced a burst of speed and pulled ahead of the blood bay stallion.

The crowd roared.

Almost there. Rozali lowered her head and ran faster, past the dapple gray mare.

Only two more steps to the roan.

One step.

She sucked in a breath and... a judge swung down the flag.

The crowd cheered for the roan, swarming to pat him on the back or neck.

She had lost. How could she lose?

Rozali staggered to a stop, and a judge pulled her aside and hung the second-place wreath around her neck.

Zinon and his sweetheart wiggled through the crowd and grabbed Rozali's mane.

"Keep walking," Zinon said. "Don't let your muscles stiffen."

"But—" Rozali stared at the red roan, who nodded his head respectfully.

"Come on." Zinon nudged her down the road. "After you cool down, we can wait for Mama and Papa to arrive."

"Just Mama," Rozali said absently. "Papa sprained his leg and will travel back with the start judges." She craned her neck to stare at the roan again.

She had lost. How had she lost? She was the fastest runner, and her injury hadn't been that bad. Her strategy had been flawless. Even her unexpected detour hadn't taken her too far off course. She should have won.

Zinon patted her neck. "You did well, Rozali. Stop worrying about it."

Rozali hung her head. "I didn't win."

"Oh, you were beautiful," his sweetheart gushed. "A blur of gold and silver, flying down the road like a diving falcon. I can't believe you passed two of the leaders at the last minute. But why were you coming from the other direction?"

Zinon snorted. "She got lost," he whispered loudly. "I told you she would."

Rozali bumped him with her head. "I only got a little lost. At least I ran. You didn't even try."

Second wasn't bad, considering how far behind she had been. And next year, she wouldn't get lost.

"It's just a race," Zinon said. "The fate of the world doesn't depend on it."

Rozali rolled her eyes. "Fine. If the fate of the world ever depends on it, I expect you to run with me."

Zinon laughed. "Deal. Are you ready to go back to watch for Mama?"

"Oh, yes," Rozali said. "I have to show her my lovely wreath. I got second, and you got nothing."

She swung around and pranced back toward the finish line. Next year, she would be first, with or without her brother. But for now, she had a rival to congratulate and three children to cheer for when they crossed.

PIRATES

(DURING AND AFTER WIND OF CHOICE)

PIRATES
(DRAGON ISLES)

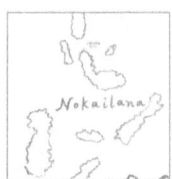

Wanted: Dead or Alive. "Crow" escaped prison with help of accomplice "Lapwing." Black wings, cut after conviction of multiple murders.

M onths had passed with no escape in sight. Despite his sweetheart's mysterious optimism, Alemana knew they had no hope. They would be trapped forever.

He kissed Kolina, one eye on her ever-present captor. "I'm on island patrol tonight, dear. I'll see you in the morning. Sleep well."

She smiled as cheerfully as if she didn't have an armed guard at her back. "I'll get your shirt mended before I go to bed. Try not to rip the one you're wearing."

When she hugged him tightly, he felt the tremors that never left her anymore. He smiled lightly, saluted the pirate in the kitchen, and closed the door to the shack quietly behind him. Most of the pirates slept on their ships due to the scarcity of buildings on the island. Though other pirates complained, Alemana would prefer that to the hut he lived in with Kolina, but they were no longer trusted on a ship without a full crew to keep them from escaping. Even their tumble-down shack, a mile from the ocean, was monitored if they were home.

Alemana headed inland with his Darrendrakar "partner" trailing him. In reality, anyone assigned to work with him was his guard. Ever since their attempted escape, they were always watched, as were any of the pirates who were pressed into the fleet. After their entire crew was killed, Alemana and Kolina dared not make new friends lest they provide the pirates with more hostages. The best they could do was obey orders and stay out of the way, and a quiet patrol around the lightly populated island was a blessing.

After their wounds healed, Alemana was allowed to continue his usual activities, but Kolina was kept as a hostage to encourage his good behavior. He volunteered for every unpleasant task on the island to reduce his pirating assignments, but he couldn't avoid all of them. Even when he was assigned to pillage the shipping and fishing lanes, he dared not disobey orders, from stealing cargo to killing or drafting the entire crew and stealing the ship. At least when he killed, he did so quickly and without torture, and he campaigned for impressment as often as he dared. Nonetheless, his nightmares multiplied. Worse even than the memories were his fears of becoming like his captors.

Many of the pirates were as cruel and insane as Captain Crow. Unfortunately, as the fleet increased, the number of heartless pirates grew while the kinder ones either became as cruel in self-defense or met with "accidents." At best, they turned a blind eye to what the others did.

How long before Alemana was no better? Even death would be no escape, for when they died, Makana would reject them from her paradise, exiling them to the waterless bounds of eternity.

Ignoring his guard as much as possible, Alemana walked slowly along his guard route. By the end of the night, he would walk several miles and his bare, webbed feet would ache. At least Kolina was spared this, though she might prefer it to an uneasy night with her least-favorite Iskrin pirate inside her home.

Suddenly, a loud noise rocked the island, and the sky lit up like dawn.

"What in Makana's playground was that?" he asked the Darrendrakar.

"I do not know." The pirate drew his sword and looked around.

"Let me see." Alemana shimmied up a tree.

The light came from the west, near the pirate's storehouse. He shouted down the information, then climbed a little higher. The light still glowed, though not as fiercely as before.

"The storehouse is on fire." Alemana dropped from the tree.

"Stupid," the pirate said, adding a list of insults. "Crow told them to be careful with the rum."

"Shouldn't we go help?" Even pirates didn't deserve to burn. Probably.

The Darrendrakar shrugged. "We cannot save any of the rum."

Alemana grimaced. "I thought we might see if any of the people need help."

"If they are foolish enough to set themselves on fire, they deserve their fate. We have a patrol to continue."

Alemana held his breath and fought the insane urge to punch his guard. "Look," he said, "what if we separate. You continue the patrol, and I'll go help with the fire."

The pirate scoffed. "You know I must stay with you."

"Don't you have any kindness left in you?" Alemana asked.

The pirate frowned and blinked. "No," he whispered, "I do not think I do."

Was there anything that would change his mind? Alemana couldn't take one more guilty nightmare, not when he could help.

"Kolina still has her guard," he said, "so you don't need to worry about me running off. I'm sure there will be plenty of your friends to watch me work."

He glanced at the smoke rising from the fire-lit sky. Would there even be survivors? "Think of it this way: maybe I'll get burned and die."

The Darrendrakar laughed creakily. "Go ahead, then; waste your time if you want. If I do not see you later, I will make sure Kolina has a new home." He mock-saluted and continued on the patrol route, taking the lantern with him.

Unsure whether kindness or cruelty had won the argument, Alemana ran for the fire. As he got closer, more pirates joined him. By the time he reached the remnants of the storehouse, it was too late to save the ramshackle building, despite the dirt the pirates frantically threw on it. Not only was the hut a sheer wall of heat, but the grass burned, and flames ran up the trunks of surrounding trees and burst into flower across the branches. The fire lit the night almost as brightly as day.

Screams and moans echoed through the crackle of the flames and the snaps of falling branches. Wounded pirates lay scattered on the ground, some ominously silent. A pirate crawled away from the fire, sobbing in pain. The pleasant smell of burning wood and grass was horribly laced with the smell of burnt meat and coppery blood. Alemana gulped and covered his nose.

"Forget the building," someone shouted. "Keep the fire from spreading."

With blankets and burlap sacks and whatever they could grab, the pirates beat at the grass. Those with shoes even stomped on it. The heat kept Alemana at the edge of the fire, endlessly fighting until sweat ran down his face into his eyes. Despite his care, sparks caught in his clothes and hair, leaving ash-pocked holes everywhere they touched.

Someone grabbed his arm, and Alemana jerked away.

"Be calm," Captain Aukai said, his burnt-sugar-brown hair turned gray with ash. "We need help with the wounded. Over there." He pointed, then ran for the next person.

Alemana struggled for a deep breath, then handed his sack to a pirate whose sack had half-burned. He limped the direction Aukai had pointed, passing a silent Nokai man whose skin bubbled through ashy holes in his clothes. Half his face had melted, and his shriveled hands clutched a blackened hole in his belly. The acrid reek of melted skin and scorched hair filled Alemana's nose with a mix of charcoal, sulfur, and the tang of branded leather. He swallowed hard to keep down the contents of his stomach.

Before long, he found himself in the middle of a different kind of chaos. Mildly injured pirates dragged the badly wounded to lie in rows to wait for treatment, while others carried bandaged victims to blankets or grass mats.

An Iskrin waved at Alemana, stumbling through trade tongue. "You know healing? Plants? Wash clothes?"

"No healing or wash," Alemana said. "I know only a little about plants." He shrugged.

The Iskrin, bare-headed instead of scarved, sighed. He examined Alemana from head to foot, frowning at his bare feet. "You cut—" He pointed at the bandages wrapped around a treated victim. "More."

When Alemana nodded, the Iskrin pointed again. "Wash is there." Then he turned to speak to the next pirate.

Alemana made his way to nearby tubs. A wet shirt slapped against him, and when he sputtered, a short Darrendrakar babbled something and mimed slicing the shirt into strips. Obediently, Alemana cut it up, passing each strip to eager hands. Then he moved on to an Iskrin scarf and a bright-patterned Darrendrakar tunic. Soon, the clothing blurred in front of his eyes, and he cut strips without even noticing what he sliced. When he ran out of clean laundry, he ripped up his own shirt.

After that, he carried buckets of water until the handles pressed lines into his fingers and his bare feet throbbed with cuts and burns. The pain blended into a chaotic ache, and his mind dimmed until all he saw was the bucket before him.

"Did you hear?" a pirate whispered to another. "He said there's a chance to leave. Would you take it?" He saw Alemana watching him and stopped talking.

A chance to leave? Not for Alemana. Not with Kolina still trapped with her sadistic guard.

But then he heard more pirates whispering in twos and threes. Supposedly, one of the Darrendrakar thought the Mouth of the Gods would forgive past crimes if the pirates fought now to free a group of marooned travelers at the docks. Could it be true? Did he dare hope?

As if any travelers would have survived the pirates. There was no such person as the Mouth of the Gods, anyway. And even if there were, how would he know of the pirates in their hidden lair? And then to offer a pardon for saving one group of travelers when the bandits had killed so many others. It was ridiculous. Even the home of the imaginary Mouth didn't exist. At least, Alemana had never heard of any place called "Arupa," though if pressed, he would admit he didn't pay much attention to the geography of other lands.

Still, if the other pirates believed the myth and acted together, there might be a chance to escape. Any hope, however slim, was more than Alemana had before. His heart ached, and he pressed a hand to his chest after passing off the bucket of water. Should he wait until he was back with Kolina? No, Alemana was unguarded, and Kolina's guard didn't know about the rebellion. Making his move in a group of others increased his chance of either success or anonymity. If he didn't at least try, Kolina would never forgive him.

The still-burning fire revealed the rows of untreated wounded were down to minor injuries, and as pirates slipped away in small groups, Alemana trailed after them.

One pirate scolded the others, waving his arms emphatically. "This is disloyalty to Captain Crow. If you leave, I will turn you all in for treason."

He put a hand on his sword hilt, and the crowd surged forward, drawing their knives. Under the attack, he went down and never rose again.

The other pirates watched each other, hands on weapons, and when no one else protested, trotted toward the shore in a loose crowd. Alemana followed at the back of the throng, and soon another light appeared in front of them. The pirates sped up, running to the docks where more fires raged and people shouted.

Every ship was aflame, including his own beautiful little fishing sloop. How would he tell Kolina?

The fire illuminated a fight at the shore. A handful of people at the top of the hill were fighting a horde of pirates who bellowed insults and threats. A makeshift catapult flung stones and debris downhill, while at the top, the battle was hand-to-hand with weapons and fire. Though most of the Iojif in the pirate fleet had old injuries that prevented flight, a white-winged stranger flew above Captain Crow, who swung his sword recklessly.

Alemana's crowd surrounded the hill. To his surprise, they seemed to be sincere, and instead of joining the battle, they grabbed at friends and allies and whispered urgently to them. Some of the pirates stopped fighting and joined them at the bottom of the hill, but a few turned viciously against the new arrivals. The pirates still on Crow's side looked just like those who were rebelling, and the confusion made Alemana's head swim.

Anything that got rid of pirates was a good idea, and he itched to kill a few unrepentant villains himself, but this battle was an excellent distraction and his best chance to save his sweetheart. He headed inland.

Before he got far, a sudden cry rose in the crowd. Alemana turned to stare, and Captain Crow fell to his knees, a harpoon stuck through the middle of his chest.

Praise Makana, the terrible Crow was dead! Hope flooded Alemana's chest until he could hardly breathe. His tiny chance of escape was suddenly expanding. Crow's whiny minion, Lapwing, was nowhere in sight, and none of the other captains stepped forward to take charge. Instead, the leaderless pirates gasped and scattered. Most of the Nokai ran to the dock and threw themselves into the ocean. The other men ran inland and vanished in all directions.

Alemana ran inland at full speed. He ignored the rocks and weeds stabbing his wounded feet and took the most direct path toward his sweetheart. If the news of Crow's death reached Kolina's captor before Alemana did, the pirate was sure to kill her, and maybe not quickly.

As the firelight fell behind him and darkness descended again, he prayed. *Please, Makanavailea, My Lady Omniscience, protect my darling. Help me defeat her captor. Please, Makana, I beg you.*

In the darkness, he heard an occasional fleeing pirate but saw no one. His frantic journey took no more than a quarter hour, but it felt like an eternity.

Just before he reached their little hut, he paused, gasping for breath, and drew his fish knife. Now would be a good time to have a harpoon or even a sword or net, but he was never allowed good weapons except on a raid. Why hadn't he grabbed a fallen weapon? Stupid, so stupid.

If he tried to warn Kolina, her guard would hear. He peeked in the window, squinting in the light of the single fish-oil lamp. The pirate sat cross-legged on the floor, watching the curtain across the bedroom doorway and caressing his sword. He turned his head, and Alemana dropped to the ground.

Had the pirate seen him? Heard him? Alemana waited, but the pirate didn't emerge or call out. Maybe the lamp had spoiled his night vision.

On hands and knees, Alemana crept around the tiny hut and crouched by the door. After one more big breath, he slammed the flimsy door open and threw himself onto the pirate, knocking the sword across the room.

The pirate bellowed and tried to roll, reaching for his sword. Alemana leaned harder on the pirate's chest to keep him still, clutching at arms and legs and stabbing wildly with his knife. But the Iskrin was bigger, and he slowly dragged them both across the dirt floor.

Suddenly, a blur of color rushed past, and someone grabbed the sword. Before he could turn to defend himself, the sword fell. Blood sprayed into his face. Alemana screamed and fell backward, holding his knife overhead and wiping his eyes with his other hand.

When had another pirate come? Was Kolina still alive or had Alemana doomed her with his failed attack?

The figure dropped the sword. "Shh," Kolina said. "Be quiet before someone else hears you."

The pirate's blood turned the dirt floor to mud. Alemana scrambled to his feet and reached for Kolina. She clutched him, trembling.

"I thought you were asleep," Alemana murmured.

She stroked his hair. "Who can sleep with a bad guest in the house?"

After a moment, they let go of each other, and Kolina headed for the bedroom.

"I assume you have a plan." She threw their few belongings into a bag. "How did you escape your guard?"

He gathered the last of the fruits and vegetables in the kitchen. "The storehouse blew up, and my patrol partner let me help. Some of the pirates decided to escape. Most of the other Nokai already swam away. I'm afraid our ship is gone, but we can swim, too."

Alemana picked up the sword, and hand in hand, they ran through the darkness, aiming for the closest ocean other than the docks. Surprisingly, they saw no one else along the way except in the distance, mere shadows against the coming dawn. When they reached the water's edge, Alemana discarded the sword. They tied their bundles onto their backs and dove into the ocean.

As the cool water washed over him, Alemana let himself hope for the first time in months. If they could avoid the other Nokai on the way home, they might make it home safely.

Home. It was a lovely word.

Alemana wanted to swim faster, but he paced himself. Home was weeks away, and they couldn't afford to exhaust themselves. Even at a starfish's pace, they would eventually get home, and they had no reason to go *that* slowly.

Except to give himself time to compose what to say to the families of his murdered crew. Time to forget the Dragon Isles. Was a lifetime long enough?

The first hint of dawn sparkled through the water, and Alemana checked for pursuit. Nothing.

Kolina interrupted his thoughts. "What made you think this escape would work?"

"Oh, the pirates were talking about a rumor." A southern current tickled his fingertips, and he moved to take advantage of its flow. "Someone told them if they helped save some marooned travelers, the Mouth of the Gods would pardon their crimes. I have my doubts it's even true, but the pirates believed it. I followed long enough to see if they would actually rebel, and I saw Crow die with my own eyes — may Makana feed his soul to krakens — and the island is in chaos."

"Were there really travelers?" she asked.

Alemana shrugged. "Someone burned the ships and fought the pirates."

"Burned our ship, too?" Kolina sighed. "What about the travelers? Shouldn't we help them?" She glanced over her shoulder, slowing her kicks.

He'd been trying not to think about the poor people they'd abandoned, though he didn't regret saving Kolina. She was his responsibility, not some strangers.

"The attack is broken," he explained. "They aren't Nokai to breathe underwater, and the ships are gone. I'm sorry for them, but with the pirates in disarray, they have a chance. One was an Iojif, so he can fly away."

They swam as quietly as the distant fish, but the memory of the strangers fighting the pirates brought back all the terrible raids, all the horrible things he witnessed. Alemana would never be the same again. His dreams were haunted by blood and terror and guilt. How could he go home to his carefree Nokai friends?

"Kolina," he started.

"Alemana," she said at the same time.

He waved for her to proceed.

Her lip quivered. "Home doesn't feel the same—" She choked to a stop.

Alemana nodded. "Fishing seems frivolous now, but what else can we do?"

Kolina rolled into a backstroke as smoothly as a dolphin. "We're killers, too, like the pirates."

Alemana copied her, staring at the dawn sunshine filtering through the waves. "Not by choice."

"No," she agreed. After a pause, she asked, "Is there really a Mouth of the Gods now?"

"Gods, plural? Working together? There never has been before."

"No. But if there was, where would he be?"

"They said Arupa, but I've never heard of it."

The light grew brighter and brighter. Raising his arm for another stroke, Alemana noticed the ocean had finally washed the blood off his skin. Now it stained only his soul.

"Do you think we could find Arupa?" he asked.

"We could try."

"It might take months of searching," Alemana said.

"True."

"He might say he doesn't need our help."

"He might," Kolina agreed.

Streams of sunshine lit the ocean, turning the shadowy kelp forests into cheerful gardens.

Alemana sped up a little. "Once we reach home, we still have one boat to carry us to Arupa."

"Well," Kolina said. "That only leaves one problem."

"Just one? What's that?"

She raised her eyebrows. "What happened to your shirt?"

Despite his worries, he burst out laughing. "I gave it to someone who needed it more."

He reached for her hand, and together they swam.

TOGETHER

(JUST BEFORE SPARK OF INTRIGUE)

TOGETHER

(EAST CORAL ISLAND, NOKAILANA)

The Nokai have no divorce, so few of them marry.

Everything You Ever Wanted to Know about the Nokailana Islands but Were Too Lazy to Ask

The early morning sun sparkled on the lavender water as Niamolenu-lanami leaned on the bulwark, yawning. She could swim to her old home from here. It might wake her enough to sort out her feelings about her parents getting married.

"Don't do it," someone said.

Nia whirled to stare at the captain of the small yacht. "But I could swim from here," she wheedled.

The Nokai captain shrugged. "You could, but you'd ruin your pretty dress. What would your mom think about you showing up at her wedding looking like a drowned kitten?"

Nia ran her hands over her gown. The heavy silk flowed over her curves in an emerald color exactly matching her eyes. Her long skirt swirled above her bare feet, revealing the different-colored paint on each nail of her webbed toes. She had braided her hair for half its length, then wrapped it around her head into a lavender crown while the remaining tresses waved down her back.

Nia yawned again. "I just wanted a little cool water on my gills, but it's too early to do anything."

The usual apricot sky was still streaked with the blue and purple of dawn. Mom must be crazy to want a morning wedding, and poor Nia had woken in the middle of the night to make the trip. She'd boarded in her ocean suit and slept for a couple of hours before dressing and doing her hair.

"We'll be there in a few minutes," the captain said. "By the time you get your bags, you'll barely need to wait at all."

Almost there, and she still hadn't decided how she felt. Oh, she was glad to have Kani — Alaneo, she reminded herself of the name he had returned to using — no, Dad — in her life. He had left on an exploration almost eighteen years earlier and was stranded until Nia rescued him eight months ago. Since then, he had tried hard to be the dad she always wanted, and everyone was happy. So why change when everything was already perfect?

Why they wanted to marry in a very un-Nokai fashion, Nia didn't know, but he had proposed to Mom the instant he walked off the ship. At least they had taken their time getting to the actual wedding in case one of them changed their mind.

Nia hadn't changed *her* mind about *not* marrying, even after several proposals from her favorite boy. Marriage was so *permanent.*

She yawned again and strolled to the small cabin. No swim for her. Not ruining her dress was the whole point of borrowing Ahjin's boat, even though he couldn't come with her. The bag with gifts was already packed, and it took only a minute to throw her hairbrush and ocean suit back into her personal bag.

She ran on deck and gawked as they approached East Coral Island. It was one of the smallest inhabited islands in Nokailana, and they got few visitors. But now, so many boats crowded the lone dock that some had beached themselves on the sand, and some had anchored in the ocean. Nia recognized banners from three different clans. Ahjin's yacht squeezed between two docked boats, just close enough to drop the boarding plank to the dock.

Nia ran off, waving thanks to the captain and sailors. "Pleasant journey. See you tomorrow."

Most Nokai weddings were held underwater in the town's festival arena, but not this one. Dad's encounter with pirates had marooned him with injuries that kept him from swimming home. His legs were well enough for the mild walking and swimming he did around the island, but his gills were permanently ruined. He could never live in the underwater village again. Under the circumstances, the clan allowed Mom and Dad to build themselves a house on land, next to the healer's hut to preserve the gardens covering most of the small island.

Nia followed the music and laughter through the orchard. An unbelievable number of people crowded into the healer's clearing and the orchard around it. Three clans, indeed! This wedding was the party of the season.

"There you are," Kalamoanana shouted. Nia's favorite near-sister ran through the crowd for a hug. Her dress was a pretty blue, and she wore blue and white flowers in her persimmon hair. She kissed Nia on both cheeks and spun her to see her dress. "You look beautiful. The boys will love this."

"I already have a boy," Nia reminded her.

Ahjin was a very nice boy, even if he was as obsessed with marriage as her parents. Her mom and dad's wedding, proving a few Nokai did indeed marry, had only increased his enthusiasm for the idea. As torn as Nia was about her parents marrying, she was sure *she* wasn't interested in joining the insanity. Despite missing him, Nia was glad for a break from his plaintive glances and repeated proposals.

"Pfft. He's not here, is he?" Kala dropped a flower wreath over Nia's braided coronet and beckoned to a boy standing under the trees.

The boy meandered their direction, flowers tucked into his orange hair.

Nia held her breath to avoid cursing her well-meaning sister. Most of her family couldn't seem to understand her relationship with Ahjin was permanent and solitary, nearly as un-Nokai as the current wedding. Since he had to prepare for a trip to Iskra, he couldn't come with her and prove they were still together. Sometimes it was annoying courting someone with so much responsibility. Why couldn't the gods behave themselves and release her sweet boyfriend from mediating among them?

"Where's Mom?" Nia glared at the boy and shook her head, and he turned and wandered another way, casting a wink at her over his shoulder.

"Aolani is dressing in the house. Alaneo is...right there, though." Kala pointed, then darted toward a green-haired boy.

Dad waved and meandered through the crowd. Nia dropped her bags behind a tree and headed his direction, greeting neighbors as she went.

When they met in the middle, she stretched up to kiss his cheeks. "Well met, Dad. You look nice."

Instead of the usual ocean suit, he wore an embroidered shirt and short lavender trousers. Even though Mom might be too old to worry about fertility, a garland of flowers topped his long, hibiscus pink braids that still showed traces of dark blue dye.

"Thank you," he murmured absently, craning his neck to peer behind her.

Nia turned with him. The new house looked very similar to her guest house on Arupa, which was built with the usual Nokai domed roof but without shark grates on the windows. She suspected the bedrooms were likewise on the top floor instead of the bottom, to accommodate land access to the public rooms.

The door opened, and someone shouted. Everyone hushed as Aolani exited, closing the door behind her. The crowd parted to let her reach Alaneo. Mom's dress had started as the traditional lavender, but it was so covered with embroidery that the original color was barely visible. Her pale blue hair streamed unbraided to her knees under a garland of flowers, and her golden skin was tinged with a pink blush. Best of all, her teal eyes shone with happiness over a beaming smile.

Nia's dad coughed and put a hand on his chest. Before Nia could ask him if he was well, he stepped forward, hands reaching for Mom. Tears shone in his amber eyes, and he cleared his throat several times.

Mom took his hands and turned to the clan. "Well met, everyone. Thank you for coming today. Would our witnesses please come forward?"

"We are here," Nia said.

As the only adult birth-child of Aolani or Alaneo, and the only birth-child of *both* of them, she was the primary witness. Despite her skepticism of marriage, she wouldn't ruin this for her parents. Nia's twin near-sisters, two far-brothers, and Kala also stepped forward. Of the seventeen children in the complicated family, they were the only adults.

Behind Nia, her younger sister and brother, born to Aolani while Alaneo was presumed dead, cheered until their dads hushed them.

Kala shoved a bucket at Nia, who stepped in front of Mom and Dad with it.

"We wash our hands to signify we come to the marriage with clean hearts," Mom said, suiting actions to words.

Dad copied her, hands trembling.

Nia put down the bucket, took a cup from her far-brother, and handed it to Dad.

"We share the same cup as we will share our lives," he said. After he sipped, he handed the cup to Mom.

She drank, watching Dad from under her eyelashes, then returned the cup and took his hands again. "Alancokawakani, for seventeen years, I thought you were dead. Now my heart is full again, and I take you as my husband."

Dad cleared his throat again. "Aolanikalia, I have loved you since we were children." He ignored the slightly shocked gasps and continued. "Thoughts of you kept me alive in the worst of circumstances. This day is the fulfillment of my dreams. I take you as my wife."

How could being trapped with one person fulfill his dreams? As they leaned in to kiss each other, Nia thought of Ahjin's sweet kisses. That was as much as she would ever get from him unless she agreed to marriage, curse his stuffy Iojif morals.

Dragging her mind back to the wedding, she cheered, and her siblings copied her, followed by the whole clan.

Someone whistled piercingly. Makanavailea, the Goddess of Water, made her way through the crowd, kissing cheeks as she went, until she reached the bride and groom.

"Congratulations." She kissed Mom's cheek. "Have a happy marriage." She kissed Dad full on the mouth and winked at him before disappearing into the crowd.

Dad blushed a pink that clashed with his hair, and Mom covered her smile. Nia rolled her eyes. Makana was a terrible tease but a lot of fun at a party.

The musicians struck up a cheerful dance tune, and Mom and Dad swung into motion. Everyone grabbed a partner, and the party exploded. Now would have been an excellent time for Ahjin to be here, both for her own enjoyment and to fend off the other boys. With no way to excuse herself any longer, Nia danced with boy after boy until she desperately stopped for a drink of water and a chance to catch her breath.

While she was busy, food had been set among the trees, and Nia filled a plate with fruit and fish and fresh baked bread. She didn't even finish eating before Kala showed up with more boys in tow.

Introductions took several minutes as the boys jostled for a position close to her.

Kala jiggled Nia's plate. "Hurry so you can dance again." She tilted her head toward the line of boys and winked blatantly.

"I'll dance," Nia said, "but I'm already in a committed relationship." And feather mites, she cursed, she could prove it if Ahjin had come with her.

Kala mouthed "committed" and shook her head. "You are so like your mom."

Nia choked on a mouthful of food. After swallowing, she blurted, "I'm not getting married!"

Staying with Ahjin was an easy decision, but marriage was an entirely different net of fish.

"Then what's the problem?" Kala asked. "Go dance."

She stole Nia's plate and stuffed a slice of pineapple into her mouth. The first boy grabbed Nia's hand, and she gave in. Even though she missed Ahjin, dancing was still fun, and he wouldn't mind.

Thanks to Kala, Nia never lacked a partner, and by noon, she told the boys she was too exhausted to continue dancing. She firmly turned down all offers to keep her company on the outskirts and sent them back to dance with other girls.

Nia filled another plate and wormed her way next to Mom and Dad to watch them open gifts. Almost everyone in the clan had given them something. Watching them, Nia thought all the gifts were expendable. Though Mom and Dad graciously thanked everyone, they kept forgetting to open the next gift because they were too busy gazing at each other.

Nia took a bite to hide a sigh. Ahjin wanted marriage, too, but she didn't think she was ready for that sort of permanence. What if Ahjin got tired of her in a few years? What if she got tired of him?

Kala flopped onto the ground beside Nia. "Why aren't you dancing? There are still boys waiting for you." She wiggled her eyebrows at Nia, then winked at her own boyfriend.

Nia put down her plate and held Kala by the shoulders. "Kala, I will say this one more time. I. Have. A. Boy. Already. I don't want another."

Kala waved her hand as if brushing off a fly. "He isn't even here to dance with you. Have some fun!"

Nia picked up her plate. "I was having fun, and now I'm having a rest. I want to spend some time with Mom and Dad. *You* go dance."

Kala jumped to her feet, frowning. "I don't understand why you've become so stodgy. You used to chase boys with me all the time. Your boy is a bad influence." She ran back to the dance.

Nia tucked her feet under her dress and wrapped her arms around her knees. Was she really so boring now?

A hand patted her knee, and she turned to look at Mom and Dad.

"She's wrong," Mom said. "You're acting like an adult and honoring your commitments."

"And I like Ahjin," Dad said.

Nia rolled her eyes. "You should, since he rescued you."

"I mean," Dad corrected, "I think he's a good influence on you. You seem happier with him."

Nia nodded, bumping her chin against her knees. "I am happy, and I do love him."

"If you don't want what Kala has," Mom said, "then ignore her advice. She doesn't have experience with real love." She beamed at Dad and leaned in for another kiss.

Kala was as carefree as Nia used to be, thinking only of the moment. She bounced from flirt to flirt with little heartache, which Nia missed, to be honest. But Kala also felt none of the deep joy that came from being with the same person day after day, growing closer all the time. What a steady relationship lacked in surprise, it gained in support and growth, like her parents. Like her with Ahjin. And if she wanted surprise, all she had to do was annoy him and watch out for his next prank!

Mom hugged her. "Now, will you sing for us?"

"Definitely!" Nia hopped up and consulted with the musicians, then sang a number of songs for Mom and Dad.

After that, the dance continued, though Nia sang a few more times when some of the musicians took breaks. Between her performances, Kala continued to pester her about boys.

By mid-afternoon, Nia was completely annoyed by her near-sister's nagging and constant match-making. She edged through the crowd and found her parents on the edge of the party.

"Pleasant journey, Mom and Dad," she said quietly enough to avoid eavesdropping. "I'm ready to go home."

Before today, this *was* home, but now it felt like a strange land.

Mom pursed her lips. "Home, hmm? Tell Ahjin we missed him."

Dad rumpled her hair. "We'll come visit."

"Anytime you like," she promised. "Keep my dress until I come again."

Mom nodded absentmindedly and turned back to Dad, who was already staring at her again.

Nia changed into her ocean suit in their house and snuck off to the beach. The wedding was over, and Mom and Dad didn't need her anymore. They would take care of each other for the rest of their lives. If ever Nokai were suited for marriage, those two were.

As for her, if she left now, she could swim back to Arupa by supper. Or at least before bedtime. The swim would be peaceful and quiet and boy-free. Best of all, she'd get back to Ahjin all the sooner. She missed him, and dancing or not, she wasn't interested in poor substitutes. She no longer cared for Kala's lifestyle.

Yes, Ahjin was better than a whole island of boys. She never wanted anyone else.

So, marrying like her parents might not be so bad. In a few years. When she was older.

She braided her hair to keep it out of her face, then dove into the ocean. Her heart longed for home and its other half.

SCORPIONS

(DURING SPARK OF INTRIGUE)

SCORPIONS
(HOTARU DESERT, ISKRA)

Iris: wisdom and valor. Kitten willow: bravery and compassion. Garlic: courage and strength.

Flowers and Their Meanings: A Guide for All Darrendrakar

Nemerra watched the sky, a hand shading her eyes from the midday sun. High above the tiny oasis, Kassian and Zefra fell, then disappeared, leaving a scream echoing in the air. Zefra had stolen a secret weapon from the enemy, and now they hoped to defeat the cult trying to kill the gods. Seconds later, they reappeared farther away and plummeted, only to disappear again. Nemerra shuddered.

"I can't stand to watch," she said in trade tongue so everyone in their mixed group could understand. "When Kassian brought me to Ludik that way, I thought I would die."

The eldest god's method of transportation was nauseating and terrifying in equal measure, and two years wasn't long enough to forget it.

Tarakh, the only adult Iskrin in their party, looked nearly green watching Zefra fall again, and the Horse siblings had already turned away. At least the seven children they had rescued from the murderous cult were napping.

"Zefra is a brave woman," Nemerra's husband, Ludik, said, cradling the sick little Iskrin boy. Ludik had traveled with Kassian, too, and a hint of gray showed in his brown skin as he watched the sky.

He was right about Zefra's courage, but Nemerra felt an unexpected pang of jealousy. All during their race across the desert, she had been afraid. Then she had been frightened when they found their cubs in the middle of the enemy army, and terrified when Ludik fought a duel to free them. She still shivered with fear. He would be so disappointed if he knew.

"Kassian's *jumping* is the only hope to save Ahjin and the gods in time," Tarakh said.

The pale Iskrin brushed his mare slowly with one arm wrapped gently around her neck. His other horse had died of exertion during their escape and had been left in the desert for scavengers.

Nemerra settled back against a tree trunk in the meager shade. Her four cubs lay tumbled together in a yellow, black, and white pile of fur, snuggled against the Iojif and Nokai babies, and she gently touched the closest fuzzy back.

"Not just for the gods." Rozali leaned against the next tree. "Zefra left for all of you, too. If she rode us, how would you get all the children home on only one horse?"

She also spoke in trade tongue. Even though the blonde young woman and her brown-haired brother were shapeshifting Darrendrakar and as brown-skinned as Nemerra's family, their Horse dialect differed from the Cat's.

Zinon nodded and put his arm around his sister. "Maybe you Cats can walk all day with your kittens, but Tarakh's horse can't carry him and three children forever."

They had carried Zefra across the desert to the lost city of Irad at a pace Nemerra wouldn't have believed if she hadn't seen the result for herself, and no normal horse could hope to match their speed or stamina.

He was right, but even with three horses, they had over one hundred leagues of desert to cross before Sardad. Other than the winter rains, the little spring in the oasis was the last source of water until they reached the river. For food, they would depend on what they could hunt or trap in the barren sands. Even under the best circumstances, it would be difficult, and they had seven infants, one of them sick. Nemerra chewed on her lip.

"At least Kassian's potion is helping this little one." Ludik rocked the black-haired infant. "By the time Tarakh's horse is rested, we should be ready to leave."

"What if the enemy at Irad finds us before then?" Nemerra forced her voice not to quake.

"If they haven't come by now, they probably won't," Ludik said. "They weren't looking for us by the time Zefra left, and she didn't think they knew she was there."

"They will eventually notice the children are gone," Nemerra said.

"We will run for it," Rozali said. "We will see them coming from far enough to give us a good head start, even if we must leave Tarakh's horse behind. Sorry, Tarakh."

The Iskrin grimaced. "We will do what we must. What about the better transportation Kassian mentioned?"

"We *are* better transportation." Rozali grinned. "We can make it back."

"Can we do anything else to help Zefra?" Tarakh asked. "Could we find the warring clans and stop them from fighting?"

"Which clans are fighting?" Ludik asked. "Do you know where to look?"

"No," Tarakh said, detangling his horse's mane, "but I could take Zinon and search while Rozali takes you to Sardad."

"Would Resef tell you where to go?" Nemerra wrinkled her forehead. Even her own goddess might not answer that sort of question, and she had no idea how cooperative the outkindred God of Fire might be. "How long would that take? Is there only one battle or several?"

Tarakh sighed. "Those are all good questions." He rubbed his forehead and winced.

"Which can wait until we are rested," Nemerra said. "We should sleep now and travel during the cooler evening."

Maybe she could find her courage in her dreams. She lay down and pulled a kitten close for comfort.

Rozali yawned. "An excellent idea."

She rolled up in her cloak under the spindly trees and was snoring even before her brother lay beside her.

"Which watch do you prefer?" Ludik asked Tarakh.

"You rest now." Tarakh kept his face turned toward his horse, but his voice sounded choked. "You have been healing, and I'm wide awake."

"I heard what Zefra said about your papa," Ludik said. "I'm sorry."

Nemerra blinked tears from her eyes. Zefra said the cult had killed anyone who dared speak for Ahjin. Tarakh said nothing, but his fingers tightened in his horse's mane.

Ludik squeezed Tarakh's shoulder. "Wake me in a couple of hours."

He lay next to Nemerra with the little boy in one arm and reached for her hand. Nemerra closed her eyes and rested her head on Ludik's shoulder.

Two years ago, if someone had told her he would trust a foreigner to watch while he slept, she would have laughed. But things were different now. With her trusted ally on guard, she let exhaustion pull her into oblivion.

☆✝⚕◎
♒♒♒♒♒

Nemerra woke to Tarakh's shout and the frightened whinny of the horse. Ludik dropped the baby on her and lunged to his feet with his long-handled ax. Staff in hand, Tarakh faced a cloud of sand approaching from the distance.

Nemerra pulled the babies closer to her and looked for the danger, heart racing. Had the army from Irad found them? Her heart sank. There were far too many to fight. They would have to run. She glanced at Tarakh's mare, who fought her tether though still drooping from exhaustion. Poor horse; Tarakh must abandon her. At least the enemy was more likely to steal her than kill her.

Tarakh would have to ride the siblings instead. Nemerra turned to tell the Horses to shift and stopped. From the other side of the oasis, more shapes scuttled across the desert toward them.

"We're surrounded," Nemerra gasped. "How did they get around us?"

"Perhaps 'tis the other clans," Tarakh said grimly. "We might be caught in the middle of a battle."

"We can't run." Zinon tugged at his tunic as if impatient to shift anyway.

Nemerra glanced at the branches above them. "Get the children up the trees."

She didn't know if it would do any good, but they couldn't just wait for their doom. Zinon boosted Rozali to a low branch, then his sister leaned down to take the sick baby from him.

Nemerra picked up her first cub and glanced back at the approaching enemy. As the shapes grew closer, she could see they were neither horses nor men, and they ran in a jerky, zigzag pattern.

"That is not the clans," she said. "What are those?"

"Scorpions," Ludik said grimly. "Giant scorpions."

There were dozens of them, as big as Nemerra was in her leopard form. They kept coming, and the bright sun reflected off their shells and monstrous stingers and claws.

"When I fought those before," Ludik said, stepping beside Tarakh, "a dozen almost killed the six of us."

Nemerra struggled for breath. Shivers ran down her neck, and her stomach twisted. She squeezed her son until he squalled. With Zefra gone, they had only two people with weapons against an army of monsters.

She clawed deep in her soul for even a bit of courage and shoved her son toward Rozali. At least the trees might be a better defense against dumb animals than against people. And scorpions didn't have bows or spears. Instead of taking the cub, Rozali stared at the monsters in shock.

"Hurry," Zinon said hoarsely, grabbing another baby. "I thought Kassian was our ally now?"

"Tell that to them," Rozali said.

The scorpions raced toward the oasis from all directions. Ludik and Tarakh braced themselves and raised their weapons, two men against an army of monsters.

Nemerra prayed to Darravani to protect her husband, while Zinon passed up another baby. To her surprise, the monstrous arachnids stopped at the edge of the sparse grass, their range of colors making a surprisingly pretty picture against the white sand. It didn't seem fair for death to come in beauty.

"Do we attack or wait?" Tarakh asked. Though his voice trembled, he stood his ground beside Ludik.

Ludik glanced behind and met Nemerra's gaze. "We can't stay in the trees forever. Attack. Push them away."

Rozali couldn't balance any more babies, so Nemerra pushed Zinon up another tree and shoved babies to him as fast as he could settle them.

Ludik and Tarakh yelled and ran forward onto the sand, charging the closest monster. The scorpions retreated, spreading into a large circle. Ludik and Tarakh halted and stood back to back.

All the babies were safe. Nemerra lunged for the lowest branch of Rozali's tree and climbed. As a leopard, she was very good at climbing, but even on two legs, she was faster than the others. She found a perch higher than the horse's back, grabbed the most precariously balanced infant, and wished for a bow or Ahjin's slingshot or even a pile of rocks. She was no warrior, but how could she watch her husband die without even helping him?

From the circle, a black scorpion approached the two warriors. Nemerra prayed fervently, but she was still surprised when it lowered its stinger and bowed over its front legs, bobbing up and down.

When Ludik stepped forward, ax raised, the black scorpion skidded backward and bowed again. Nemerra took a deep breath for the first time since the monsters had appeared. Ludik backed up and lowered his ax, and the scorpion took a step forward, still bowing.

"What sort of attack is that?" Tarakh asked.

Ludik waved his ax again, without stepping forward, and the scorpion flinched but didn't attack.

"This is not at all the way they acted the last time," Ludik said. "I don't understand."

Nemerra squinted at the monsters. Were they actually bowing, or was that a preparation for a lunge?

"Tarakh, I will try to lure them into an attack," Ludik said.

Nemerra whimpered as he laid his ax at his feet and raised his empty hands. Her beloved was definitely brave, but sometimes brave and foolish were the same.

Without approaching, the black scorpion raised both front pincers. Ludik took a step forward, but the scorpion didn't move. Ludik took another step, and the scorpion raised its pincers higher.

Nemerra sucked in her breath. The monsters wanted to talk, as crazy as that sounded. And crazy or not, talking meant a chance of survival, and maybe of peace.

"Ludik, they want to parley," Nemerra called.

He shot an incredulous glance at her.

She waved toward the scorpions. "Talk to them. They are Kassian's, aren't they? Why would He betray us now?"

"*Talk* to them?" Tarakh echoed. "They're monsters."

Another scorpion bowed and crept toward the first. When they were side by side, the second one, a brown-striped beast, patted the first on the back with a giant pincer, then waved at Ludik.

Ludik scratched his head, and the scorpion repeated the motions.

"I do not know what you want," Ludik called out in Iskrit, exaggerating a shrug.

Nemerra pressed her cub into a fork in the tree and climbed down, shaking so hard she almost fell.

The scorpions tried again, then one climbed on top of the other. After bouncing once, it climbed off and patted the other's back again. Then it beckoned Ludik, who only stared blankly.

Nemerra peeked around his back. "They want us to ride them." It was an insane idea, but at least Kassian hadn't sent them as assassins.

He whirled. "What are you doing out of the tree?"

"Ashes," Tarakh swore. "Please tell me I misunderstood you. We cannot ride those."

Nemerra gripped Ludik's arm and squinted at the giant scorpions. "I think Kassian sent them as his better transportation."

"Are you crazy?" Tarakh blurted. "How are they better than the Horses?"

Nemerra shrugged. "I don't know. Maybe they need less water."

"Those are monsters," Ludik said. "They almost killed Ahjin."

Nemerra gulped. Someone had to talk to them. Evading Ludik's grasp, she walked toward the scorpions, hands held open and high. Despite the hot sun, she shivered.

As she neared, the two scorpions bowed again, and one patted the other rapidly.

"Mongrel curs," Ludik cursed, grabbing his ax and following her slowly.

When Nemerra reached the scorpions, one backed up, and the other lowered itself almost flat. The rest of the scorpions blocked Ludik from approaching, though they bowed as they did so. Nemerra maneuvered around the scorpion's legs. She touched the hard shell with trembling fingers, and the monster tilted a little toward her.

Yes, it seemed they were offering a ride. But they looked like giant bugs. Giant bugs twice her current size, with poison in their tails. She wrapped her arms around herself to still her shaking. It didn't work. How could she get even closer? But if the men annoyed them, no one would survive.

"I will try it," Nemerra called, keeping her gaze on the arachnid.

Panting, skin crawling, she hiked her dress to her knees and climbed onto the scorpion's back. The shell was warm under her knees, and despite her fumbling, the monster held still.

Ludik cursed again.

"Stop, Ludik," she squeaked. "Speak nicely so you don't alarm them." The scorpion's tail shifted behind her, and she whimpered. "Please."

When she found a comfortable seat and stopped wiggling, the scorpion rose to its full height and tiptoed forward. The others parted their line, and Nemerra's mount came to a stop in front of Ludik, where it lowered itself again.

Nemerra slid off and hugged Ludik, trying to stop shaking. "There, you see. It will be fine."

"Ashes," Tarakh swore.

Nemerra patted his arm, too. "Don't you trust Kassian?"

Leaning around her to look at the scorpions, Tarakh raised his eyebrows. "But do I trust monsters?"

"I think we should take the ride." Nemerra somehow kept her voice from quaking.

"And what will you do if they decide to eat us in the middle of the trip?" Ludik asked.

Nemerra grinned. "Expect you to protect us."

Ludik growled. "You will be the death of me." He yelled at the siblings in the tree. "Bring down the children. We have a ride."

Nemerra stayed in his arms for a minute, trying to soak in his courage. Rozali and Zinon stayed in the trees.

"I will not go near those," Rozali insisted, tears rolling down her face. "I would rather run the whole way back by myself."

"You will not be alone," Zinon said. "I will stay with you."

"And I." Tarakh shrugged. "My horse cannot ride a scorpion, and I will not leave her behind. I can guide you back to Sardad and hunt for you. Hand me the children."

He took Zinon's three, who then helped Rozali with the other four.

"Are you sure?" Ludik asked. "What if Zefra has already moved on by the time you get back?"

"Then I will find her elsewhere." Tarakh grabbed Ludik's water pouches. "Rozali, please refill these. Zinon, give them the food from Irad. We can hunt on the way. I will write a note for Zefra, in case you see her."

Ludik and Nemerra turned their attention to the scorpions, who waited patiently, stingers down and pincers closed. By the time they figured out how to coil rope around two of the scorpions to hold the baby carriers and packs in place, Tarakh had a slate ready for Zefra.

Nemerra strapped the Iojif baby carrier to her chest while Tarakh and Zinon stuffed the cubs into their carriers. With Rozali's help at a safe distance from the scorpions, Ludik settled the Iskrin boy in a sling on his chest and fastened the little Nokai girl to his back with the net. All seven children in place, Nemerra and Ludik gingerly mounted the scorpions and grabbed the ropes.

"Keep well," Rozali said.

"Keep well," Zinon echoed.

"Warmth to you," Tarakh said. "Remember to give my note to Zefra."

"We will see you in Sardad in a few days." Nemerra smiled as if it was a certain conclusion rather than a dangerous risk for them all.

Ludik tapped the shell below him, and when the giant scorpion turned its head, he pointed northward. Both of their mounts shook themselves and rose, and all the scorpions skittered past the oasis. The giant arachnids wove back and forth like drunkards, but they made good speed, though slower than the Cats could run themselves.

Nemerra held the rope tightly to balance against the jittery walk. Had she doomed them?

Though Ludik had never told her the whole story of battling the monsters, she had pried some of it from Zefra. A scorpion like these had nearly cut Ahjin in half, and it was her fault their children were strapped to them now. The stinger behind her made her neck crawl, even held well above her head.

The scorpions ran for more than an hour, and her cubs cowered in the bottom of their carriers. Nemerra hummed to them, wishing she felt as unconcerned as Ludik looked. If he was scared, he hid it well.

Eventually, the scorpions stopped, wriggling until Ludik and Nemerra dismounted. The monsters picked at the ropes around each other and bobbed at the Darrendrakar until Ludik removed the children. When their mounts were free, they moved aside and two new scorpions, a blue and a gold, took their places. They left again almost immediately.

Every hour, the beasts made their riders switch mounts and allowed a few minutes for personal care, but that was all the concession they made to rest. When winter's afternoon rains came, Ludik collected fresh water in the bucket as they rode, letting everyone drink their fill and refilling the water pouches.

When the apricot sky darkened with streaks of blue sunset, the arachnids stopped again. After she and Ludik unloaded the scorpions, they opened a pack to grab the blanket, but a red and a tan scorpion walked in front of them and lowered themselves.

Ludik pursed his lips at Nemerra. "I guess we aren't stopping?"

Nemerra slowly approached the red scorpion with a rope, giving it time to escape, but it quietly stood while she reattached the baby carriers.

She climbed wearily onto its back and hooked her fingers under the rope. "I hope they know where they are going."

"So do I," Ludik muttered, wrapping the blanket around her.

He shrugged his shoulders to resettle the children he carried and climbed aboard his scorpion. Nemerra soothed the hungry children with a little food. Even the Iskrin baby woke and wanted to eat, smiling for the first time.

Night fell, and the scorpions continued. All seven children fell asleep, and Nemerra and Ludik tied themselves in place. Throughout the night, the giant arachnids zigzagged across the empty desert, tireless and unstoppable.

Every time Nemerra woke from bad dreams, Ludik smiled encouragingly. She wrapped her pitiful courage around her like a blanket and wished she were fearless.

☆♀♠◎
〜〜〜〜〜

In the morning, the scorpions stopped again to trade riders.

"At this rate, we should reach Sardad today or tomorrow," Nemerra said. "Do you think Zefra's plan succeeded?"

"I hope so." Ludik smiled. "If she can carry it off with sheer bravery, she will." He reached for a water pouch.

Nemerra sighed. "I wish I were brave," she whispered. "Like Zefra and you."

Ludik choked and spit out the water. "You think you aren't brave?"

Nemerra shrugged and shook her head.

"You crossed a barren desert with no map and no guide," Ludik said.

"You snuck into the enemy camp to rescue our children. You stole three extra babies from a cult powerful enough to fight the gods. You're riding a giant scorpion. How much braver can you be?"

"I just followed you." Nemerra reached toward him but was too far away to take his hand. "And I was scared the whole time."

"You approached a host of scorpions with no weapon!" Ludik shouted. When his mount reared, he tightened his grip and lowered his voice. "The rest of us didn't dare approach them. And if you want to go back farther, you stopped a war in Darrendra by letting a Wolf bite you."

He shook his head. "Fear is normal. Fear keeps you safe. I fear every time you go into danger. I swear, if you were any braver, my fur would go gray. Courage is doing what you must despite fear, not without it. A little more fear might do you good. Why do I have to be surrounded by brave women who are determined to get into trouble?"

He muttered to himself, and Nemerra decided she was better off not hearing the words.

She straightened on the scorpion. Courage was doing what was necessary despite fear. For her children, for her husband, for her friends, she could do that. She had done it before, after all.

She might be afraid, but she *was* brave.

Nemerra patted the daughter by her knee and looked northward with a smile.

LAPWING

(DURING AND AFTER SPARK OF INTRIGUE)

1. ROZALI
(ZEFRA'S OASIS, ISKRA)

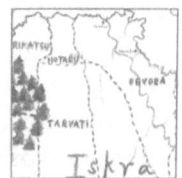

Adult Darrendrakar can shift from one form to the other in seconds.

A Brief Sketch of Mysterious Darrendra

Rozali shuddered. Finally, the monsters were gone. The colorful shells of the departing scorpions glimmered in the afternoon sun as they scuttled north across the endless white sand, leaving her, her brother, a strange man, and a horse behind.

Even though the giant arachnids were Kassian's pets, how could Ludik and Nemerra bear to ride them? She would rather face a thousand leagues of desert. She laughed. Fortunately, they only had to cross a *hundred* leagues of barren sand to get home, or a bit more.

When Zinon raised his eyebrows, she shook her head. Their situation wasn't really funny, but laughter was better than tears.

Rozali and her brother had come to Iskra for a little adventure, and they got more than enough. She was ready to sail back to Darrendra and return to normal life. All they had to do was cross this desert one more time. At least the hard part was over; after all, they had already crossed it in their horse shapes with Zefra, racing to find Irad, the lost city of the gods. No ordinary horse could have made the trip so quickly. In fact, few Darrendrakar could have done it, but Rozali and Zinon had run the annual Horse marathon since they were foals and had won in most of the last five years. But that was on the stream-crossed fields of Equid territory, not this barren desert with no landmarks.

If not for Zefra, they would have gotten lost and died of dehydration even before they starved. But now she was gone, carried back by Kassian to try to save the gods, and Rozali and her brother had only Tarakh, who was a farmer, not an experienced guide or hunter. They were still fortunate the desert native was staying with them to find food and water and navigate them back to civilization. This tiny oasis was the last green for days at racing speed or weeks for a caravan, and one false move or a bit of bad luck would kill them.

They were so close to going home, and Rozali didn't want to die now. Despite the burning heat, she shivered and hugged herself.

"Tarakh?" She bit her lip and tried to phrase her question in a non-insulting way. "You do know how to get back to Sardad?"

Zinon snickered, and Rozali jabbed her elbow into his ribs. Just because she got lost from time to time didn't mean he had to laugh at her. Especially if Tarakh might think the laughter was meant for him.

Tarakh stopped grooming his horse, and his mouth twitched a little. "I do."

"And feed us?" Zinon asked, his stomach grumbling loudly.

This time, Tarakh broke into a wide smile. "Of course, though my poor Grace will have more difficulties."

The Iskrin patted his mare, the only survivor of the three that had carried him to Irad. He had refused to ride the scorpions in order to bring her back, but only one bag of grain still plumped his saddlebags.

"We all need rest and time to collect food," he said, "but we must leave soon or the winter rains will end before we arrive. Indeed, they are already little more than a trickle."

Before her turn at watch the second night, Rozali shifted modestly behind a bush. Her bones reshaped in seconds, her hands and feet curling up and hardening into hooves. She stretched her equine muscles and tossed her pale mane before circling the grassy oasis. Whoever was sleeping got the blankets, and it was too cold at night to wander around in just her dress. And with everyone else asleep, it wouldn't matter that she couldn't speak trade tongue in this form.

Keeping watch was a little silly in the middle of nowhere, but it was a good habit. And there was still a slim possibility the enemy from Irad might return this way and find them.

To stay alert, she counted stars, searching for familiar constellations and finding only a few, all in the wrong spots. Iskra was much farther south than Darrendra, and even more than the stark desert, the stars reminded her she was far from home. Only the three moons were the same, and she watched the tiny lavender and blue twins chase each other around the large golden crescent.

Halfway through her watch, the golden moonlight caught the pale wings of a large bird in the sky. Though most birds slept at night, it flew closer and closer, straight for the oasis, the only green for days. Days of running, anyway. Flying was probably faster.

But she should watch for danger, not birds. The sand stretched empty to the horizon in every direction, silent and shadowed, but behind her, wings swooped down. If Tarakh said the bird was edible, maybe they could catch it for their morning meal, if they had time to cook it before they left. Not even on an adventure would she eat raw meat.

Something grabbed her mane, and someone whined, "Hold still, horsey. My wings are tired."

Nobody had *ever* seized her before, and the shock froze her for a critical second. In that time, the stranger jumped onto her back and kicked her sides.

Oh, no. She hadn't given permission to be ridden, and absolutely, under no circumstances, would she tolerate kicking. Rozali whinnied shrilly for help, then flung herself into motion. She jerked her head low, then smashed it into her rider's face. He screamed, and she immediately bucked and twisted. His grip slipped from her mane, and she reared, dumping him off her back.

"Bad horsey," he wailed.

Rozali planted her forelegs and kicked backwards, sending the horse thief flying. She whirled for another kick and found her assailant flat on the ground. Just in case, she moved closer and kept her weight on only three legs.

From across the small oasis, Zinon and Tarakh stumbled toward her as the kidnapper moaned weakly. His pale wings flopped on the grass, and a dirty hoofprint marked his stomach.

Tarakh rubbed his eyes with the hand not gripping his staff, then turned to scan the oasis.

"What happened?" Zinon asked.

"He tried to steal me," Rozali said.

After translating for Tarakh, Zinon nudged the Iojif with his foot. "I think you kicked him into next week."

Rozali sniffed. "I should have kicked him into next year."

"My sister, the warrior." Zinon laughed.

She feinted a kick at him, but he only laughed harder.

"Let me go," the thief whined. "Let me go."

"No, keep him here for a minute." Tarakh ran for his tiny lantern and examined the Iojif. "Black hair," he murmured. "Tan wings. And his voice." He turned to Rozali. "Do you realize who this is?"

"A horse thief," she said, and Zinon translated into trade tongue. When the Iojif tried to roll away, she stomped her hoof next to his head. "Almost a dead horse thief."

When Zinon repeated that, the man stilled, wingtips twitching.

"This is Lapwing, wanted for piracy at the Dragon Isles and neck-deep in the recent conspiracy." Tarakh scowled and clenched his fists. "He planned to murder babies to destroy the gods. His allies murdered my father."

"He could still be a dead horse thief," Rozali offered, lifting her hoof.

With their adventure so close to ending successfully, they didn't need a pirate complicating matters. Zinon translated again, and Tarakh puffed up his cheeks and ran a hand through his sleep-messy hair.

After a moment, he groaned. "No, Rozali. We should take him back to stand trial."

"No," Lapwing whined. "Let me go."

Rozali leaned over his face and bared her teeth. The pirate whimpered and pressed himself against the grass.

Zinon snickered. "Stop teasing him."

Tarakh bowed to Rozali. "He can ride Zinon, if I may ride you? We can put the lighter baggage on Grace."

After another nasty look at the pirate, Rozali bobbed her head at Tarakh.

"You want to drag him with us?" Zinon protested.

Her brother's shoulder-length hair stuck out even more than Tarakh's shorter crop, and both men were still barefoot.

Tarakh ran his hand through his hair again. "We cannot turn him loose or kill him in cold blood."

Rozali snorted. "We could let him *try* to escape. A dead pirate is easier to handle."

Zinon translated, shaking his head. "Wait until I tell Mama and Papa how bloodthirsty you are."

Rozali snorted again. "You aren't the one he tried to steal." And if he touched her again, she would stomp a hole in him.

"Never mind," Tarakh said. "Zinon, get the rope from my saddlebags."

"This isn't fair," Lapwing whined. "The Isles were Crow's fault. All Crow's fault. And in Iskra, I was following orders. I am only obedient, I am."

Obedient to bad orders. It didn't make him less evil, only less intelligent. Rozali leaned above his nose, and Lapwing fell silent.

Zinon returned, and the men tied the pirate's hands and feet while Rozali stood guard.

"We might as well leave now while 'tis still cool," Tarakh said, "since we're all awake."

Zinon groaned, but he and Tarakh packed their bags. Rozali threatened Lapwing with a hoof whenever he twitched. After refilling their water bags and loading the food, Tarakh loaded his tired mare with his saddlebags and the almost empty Darrendrakar packs. He threw a blanket onto Rozali's back, but Zinon, now shifted to his pinto form, wore Tarakh's saddle. Tarakh untied Lapwing's feet, bullied him onto the back of the kneeling pinto, and tied him to the saddle. Smoothly, Zinon rose to his feet with his reluctant rider.

"My rider is better than yours," Rozali taunted.

Zinon rolled his eyes. "If you don't behave, I'll make you take turns."

Oblivious to her brother's threat, Tarakh pulled himself onto Rozali's back and leaned toward the pirate. "Even if you free yourself, I would not try to jump off. Not only are you likely to break something in the fall, but I'm sure Rozali would love to stomp on you."

Rozali whinnied and snapped her teeth near Lapwing's feathers. She already dreaded the journey with the hateful pirate.

"Keep the crazy horse away from me," Lapwing whined as the three horses trotted from the oasis.

Rozali snorted in disgust and ignored the pirate, concentrating on getting used to a new rider. Tarakh wasn't bad, though not as good as Zefra, and they soon moved comfortably together. Zinon was having a much rougher time with Lapwing, who jerked and bobbled with each stride. Every time his flailing wings brushed Zinon's flank, the Horse flinched, which made Lapwing jerk even more.

While Tarakh attempted to show Lapwing how to ride, she apologized to Zinon. "When I said I had the better rider, I wasn't wishing this on you."

Her brother lurched to stay under Lapwing as the pirate leaned sideways. "I know, and I won't make you take a turn. You're faster, but I'm stronger, and this is harder than it looks."

Rozali brushed her nose comfortingly against his neck. Eventually, Lapwing's jerks calmed, and the journey continued in silence.

At the first rest break at sunrise, Tarakh unloaded everyone and held up the blanket for Zinon to shift behind. Once dressed, Zinon held the blanket for Rozali.

When she shifted back to two legs, Lapwing gasped. "She's a girl!"

Rozali wrapped the blanket close around her and glared at him. "Rozali is a girl's name."

"For a girl *horse*," Lapwing squeaked. "The other horse has a girl name, too."

"You watched *me* shift before." Zinon handed Rozali her share of fish leftover from the oasis. "Why assume I am the only Darrendrakar here?"

"She didn't change before." Lapwing stared at Grace. "Does that one turn into a girl, too?"

Rozali turned her back on the stupid man.

Tarakh led his mare to the thickest patch of sparse grass. "No, Grace is just a horse."

"Then there is only one girl?" Lapwing narrowed his eyes. "I want to ride her next time. The brown and white one bounces too much. Besides, I like girls better."

Rozali whirled, mouth dropping open. How dare he!

Zinon clenched his fists and lunged for the pirate. Tarakh barely caught him, wrestling him to the sand.

"No," he ordered. "You cannot hit a bound man. Stop it!"

Lapwing leered at Rozali, ignoring the fighting men. Rozali stuffed the rest of the fish into her mouth and swallowed quickly, then shifted back to horse, letting the blanket fall as her hands changed to hooves. Without a word, since he wouldn't understand anyway, she stomped over to the pirate and set her hoof on his leg, pressing gently at first. As she increased the pressure, the sneer dropped off Lapwing's face, replaced by a wince and then a yelp.

Behind her, the shuffle in the sand quieted.

"You are right," Zinon said calmly. "I do not need to hit him. My sister can take care of herself."

Rozali stepped off the pirate. Her brother and Tarakh picked themselves up and brushed off the sand.

At a nearby cactus, Tarakh cut a small piece for each person to chew, tucking a little extra inside his saddlebags. Rozali stared at it, nose wrinkled, until the Iskrin explained the waning afternoon rains would not give enough water for all day. Zinon shrugged and chomped into the cactus, and Rozali nibbled. The taste was mostly mild, a bit sour, and not too distant from other green vegetables.

Though they drank during the afternoon sprinkle and refilled the water bags, the water never lasted through the day, especially for Grace, who could not eat the cactus without dripping most of the moisture from her mouth.

At the midday rest break, Rozali went behind a nearby dune to change and eat, rejoining the others only when she was back in her horse form. To avoid walking in the heat, they took a much longer break and slept for hours.

Bad dreams plagued Rozali, and she roused several times. Whoever was on guard waved, and she went back to sleep. When she woke yet again, tan shadows drifted over the white sand by her brother and Tarakh.

She blinked sleep from her eyes. No, the tan was the pirate's wings. He crawled away from the men on hands and knees, then sprang into the air.

Without thinking, Rozali lunged upward, clamping her teeth on his wing.

2. TARAKH
(ISKRA)

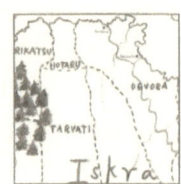

Guide for Desert Survival: Never start a desert trip without adequate provisions and maps. Carry at least a gallon of water per day. Stay on the road.
Iskrin Culture and History, appendix 1

T arakh watched Zefra's red hair gleam in the sunshine as fire danced on her fingertips. His breath caught in his throat when she smiled at him in a way she seldom did, a blush creeping across her cheeks.

Ah, he was dreaming, then. He had admired her from the first, but she was not interested in anything but friendship. For now. Tarakh was patient, and the talented fire mage was the greatest adventure he could imagine. Someday she would look at him like that in real life, and the spark in his heart would flare like the desert sun. While he dreamed, he might as well enjoy her admiration.

And then her mouth opened in a scream.

Tarakh jolted awake and discovered the howl was real. He scrambled to his feet and tangled with the scarf strung from his staff to a rock to provide shade. Trying to free himself, he bumped into Zinon, who staggered sleepily and muttered nonsense. Not far away, Rozali in her horse form pulled something large and thrashing across the sand. She shook it, and the screams rose even higher. Zinon blurted in his own language and threw himself onto... Lapwing.

This was *Tarakh's* fault for falling asleep on watch like an incompetent fool. He grabbed the ropes abandoned on the sand and lunged to help Zinon tie Lapwing's hands and ankles again.

"She broke my wing," the pirate wailed. "The crazy horse bit me!"

Rozali whinnied something, and Zinon shook his head. "Yes, feathers taste bad."

His sister snorted and dunked her muzzle into the water bucket.

"The damage is slight," Tarakh said after examining the wing. "The bleeding has almost stopped, and nothing seems out of alignment."

Lapwing continued sniveling while the other three packed up and ate. "Where's my food?"

Tarakh scowled at him. "At the next meal, if you behave until then."

He pursed his lips in thought for a minute, then spread his cloak on the sand and cut a slit in each side at elbow height. With Zinon's help, he untied the pirate's arms, slid them through the new holes in the cloak, then wrapped it tightly around his wings and pinned it shut in the back with several rows of long cactus spines.

"It's too hot," Lapwing complained. "You'll bend my feathers."

Ignoring him, they retied his hands, and the Darrendrakar shifted. After saddling Zinon and tying Lapwing into place, Tarakh took Grace's lead and swung up on Rozali to continue their journey.

With the rhythmic motion, Tarakh soon let his mind wander. Now that Father was dead, murdered by those in the conspiracy, Mother would lead the family business, as well as the clan until the next election, and she needed his help. As for Zefra, she might still be dealing with the secret cult, or she might have found new employment as a caravan guide already. Unfortunately, he could not track her down until he knew Mother was well.

His impatience chafed like saddle sores. The longer it took to find Zefra, the longer it would take to convince her — Resef willing — they should be more than friends.

Perhaps capturing Lapwing would impress her. He certainly had no other way to dazzle the fire mage, now so famous she had earned the name Kezhekori. Tarakh had first seen her a year and a half ago, and after watching her stand up to several clans at once, he had listened to all the stories and gathered every bit of gossip. Zefra was a trained cartographer, an amazing explorer, an expert horsewoman, and a competent warrior, besides calling Resef's holy flame.

Tarakh had been infatuated for two years before he actually got a chance to talk to her, and spending weeks with her on their recent adventure had made the seeds of his interest sprout full-grown. She was intelligent, generous, always prepared, a dedicated friend, and single-minded in chasing her goals. Even before reaching adulthood, she had discovered a new oasis. With her friends, she had saved the gods twice, assuming her plan with Kassian had succeeded.

Nausea churned his stomach into compost. Why would she be interested in a mere farmer?

Perhaps he needed Rozali to kick some sense into *him* so he would stop daydreaming. Tarakh looked for a patch of halfway decent grass for Grace.

After the next rest stop during the afternoon drizzle, Lapwing's complaints returned, just louder than the crunch of hooves on sand. "Now we can't get messages through to Irajahan, so who do they send to talk to him in person? Me. I do everything I'm told, and what thanks do I get? None. Find the potions, Lapwing. Get a baby, Lapwing. Crow was bossy enough, but Irajahan and his nasty priests are even worse."

Then he started naming everyone who had picked on him, an apparently endless list. But everyone was *from the conspiracy!* Tarakh pulled a slate from his belt pouch and took notes. Zefra had hopefully overthrown the head of the cult, but this might help the Iskrin guard clean up the rank and file. Perhaps that would impress her. If she smiled at him with more than friendship lighting her beautiful brown eyes... His stomach dissolved into butterflies at the mere thought.

Tarakh shook his head to clear it. Like irrigation in the summer, he needed to focus on the important points. Impressing Zefra was not important — yet; weeding out the cult was vital.

But it would be nice to do both, his disobedient heart whispered. He thumped his head and concentrated on his notes for the next several hours.

At midnight, the group stopped for a meal and a nap. Long before dawn, Tarakh roused everyone to walk in the cool night air. Lapwing kept whining, and either he thought he could not be overheard or he did not realize how much information he revealed, because his complaints listed people, dates, and cities involved. Tarakh took notes until the pirate started repeating himself.

For over a week, they walked late afternoon through late morning, sleeping in the heat of the day. Their food ran short despite Tarakh's snares, especially with an extra mouth to feed. The waning rains gave just enough water for Grace while the people sucked on cactus flesh, but Lapwing complained strenuously about being starved until Rozali offered to kick his stomach smaller.

As a farmer, Tarakh had been well fed, and though he did not care for the pain in his growling belly, he and Zinon silently conspired to give Rozali an extra mouthful from their shares. Poor Grace got hungrier and hungrier, despite the sparse winter grass, and Tarakh reluctantly rationed the shrinking store of grain, hoping to reach Sardad before it gave out entirely.

One afternoon, Tarakh stood on Rozali's back for a better look at a cloud in the distance. More rain would be welcome, but that was no rain.

"Sandstorm coming," he said, pulling his mare to her knees behind the biggest rock. "Lie down without shifting, and if you think Darravani can help, pray to your goddess!"

While the Darrendrakar lay head-to-head with Grace, Tarakh dragged Lapwing from Zinon's back and pulled the cloak over the pirate's head before pressing him flat on the ground by the others. After winding his scarf across his own face and around his neck, he knelt, arched over the horses' heads, and buried his face in his arms, clamping both sets of eyelids shut tightly.

Taking his own advice, he fervently prayed to Resef to protect them. Without his god's blessing, he would not live to find Zefra again. His mother would never know where his body lay.

The wind howled, blowing grains of sand up his sleeves and down his collar, scratching him like a million cactus thorns. Despite his shielding arms and scarf, the sand crept into his nose and inside his mouth. The horses fidgeted, and Lapwing squirmed, and Tarakh patted each of them to remind them to be calm.

And still the wind blew. Tarakh would *never* pray to Irajahan, the great betraying God of Air, but he awkwardly pled for Darravani, Goddess of Earth, to settle the desert sands, though the prayer of a stranger would probably count for less than the entreaties of her own children.

After an eternity, or half an hour, the wind slowed to a gentle breeze, and the desert drifted in ripples. Tarakh stirred cautiously, wincing as his clothing rubbed sand against his abrasions. At least they were alive and unburied.

"Stay down," he croaked, wiping his face enough to open his eyes.

The sky was cheerfully apricot, as if nothing had happened. A small drift of sand marked the progression of the dying storm, and as he watched, the last puffs fell still.

"You can get up." Tarakh brushed dirt from Grace's nose and eyes, then did the same for the siblings. When he hauled Lapwing to his feet, he refastened the cloak snugly around his wings.

"I want to wash my face," Lapwing complained.

Tarakh coughed to clear sand from his throat. "Cannot waste water."

He poured water in the bucket for Grace, then turned to discover Lapwing guzzling from the last bag, letting it overflow down his face and onto the desert.

"You fool," Tarakh croaked.

As he looked up from the damp sand, he thought he saw a smirk on the pirate's face, but it instantly dissolved into a wail.

"Oh, the water is gone," Lapwing whined. "Now we will all die. I don't want to die. Let me go, and I will fly to Sardad and send back help. I don't deserve to die for your mistakes. Let me go."

"Be quiet," Tarakh roared, then coughed when his dry throat scratched. He swallowed as best he could and continued in a softer voice. "You deserve to die for your own mistakes, and if you do not obey, I will leave you here for the jackals and vultures. I suggest you shut your mouth to preserve water."

Lapwing subsided into a pout, and Tarakh packed the bucket and water bags and nudged Rozali into a stroll instead of their usual brisk walk. He zigzagged their route from one widely spaced cactus to another, returning to their northwest path whenever no cacti were in view.

If Zefra could find an unknown oasis, he could make it back alive. His mother still needed him, and he still hoped to persuade Zefra that she wanted him. He needed to live for both.

The rains, already light, tapered to a soft mist and disappeared. Rozali and Zinon shifted to two legs to take advantage of the sheltering Iskrin clothing, and Tarakh shoved Lapwing ahead of him while leading Grace. Their pace slowed, and they cut their rest stop at midnight, sleeping longer at midday instead. Their lips cracked, and their skin dried to sandpaper, and still they staggered one foot after another. Lapwing did not talk but hummed a constant whine.

Grace died two days later. After shoving part of a dune downhill to cover her body, Tarakh held a short funeral for his beloved mare, leaving the saddle to mark her grave. All three of his favorite horses were now dead, but he lacked even enough moisture for tears.

With despair and determination quarreling in his heart, he turned northwest and walked again. He must make it back. Left foot. *Mother.* Right foot. *Zefra.* Prod Lapwing. *Mother.* Check on the siblings. *Zefra.* Walk. *Mother.* Look for a cactus. *Zefra.*

Three miserable days later, the stone buildings of Sardad whispered on the horizon as they staggered across the uneven sand. Rozali and Zinon shifted and let the others ride, but even at a trot, the last leg of the journey took all day, and the setting sun turned the white stones blue as they entered the city.

"The guard station is around the corner and three streets down," Tarakh told Zinon, nudging Rozali with his heel. Just a few minutes before he could look for his favorite women. "There is a well on the way."

Lapwing looked around at the Iskrins walking along the streets and grinned. Before Tarakh could wonder what was so amusing, the pirate held up his bound hands in a pleading gesture.

"Help me," he screamed in trade tongue. "They kidnapped me. Save me!" He flailed on Zinon's back until the Horse had to prance to keep him mounted. "Help, help, help!"

With each cry, Lapwing's voice rose shriller and louder until Rozali flinched and Tarakh covered his ears. The bystanders pointed and shouted.

"We did not kidnap him," Tarakh shouted. "He's a criminal we are bringing to justice."

"I'm innocent," Lapwing screamed.

"He's a pirate from the conspiracy," Tarakh called.

"Someone is lying," the crowd argued. "Summon the guard and let them judge."

Tarakh sat back on Rozali, and she lurched to a halt. When Zinon stopped, Tarakh grabbed Lapwing's arm before he could dismount.

"Go ahead," Tarakh said. "We will wait here."

A youngster raced around the corner in the direction of the jail.

"Let him go," a woman in the crowd shouted.

"Yes," Lapwing whined, "set me free." He turned his weeping eyes and quivering lip toward Tarakh. "Mercy."

Tarakh rolled his eyes. "We are waiting for the guard." When someone reached for Zinon, he lost patience. "Do not touch the Horses! They are Darrendrakar and will consider it an international offense. We will wait for the guard, *with* this pirate."

The crowd grumbled and surrounded them loosely.

Soon, city guards ran down the street. "Back up," they shouted. "Go home!"

Some people left, but others pulled back against the buildings to watch. Lapwing increased his protests until Zinon bounced him hard. Tarakh dismounted, and when one of the guards reached for the horses, he repeated his warning. While the guards stared at Rozali standing untethered, he approached Zinon, who lowered himself.

Tarakh yanked down Lapwing, who fell to his knees and begged for mercy. "Stand up, you sniveling coward."

Despite the pirate's continued wails of innocence, Tarakh dragged him to the guards. "This is Lapwing, a known pirate and conspirator from Irad."

"I'm not Lapwing," Lapwing whined. "You've mistaken me for someone else."

"How do you know?" a guard asked.

"Kezhekori recognized him in my presence." Tarakh took a hopeful breath. "Is she still here?"

"She left a week ago, not long after the Mouth of the Gods."

Tarakh sighed. Of course she had. But before he could look for Zefra, he still had a job to finish.

He dug into his pouch for his slate. "He also talks to himself, and I took notes. I imagine Kassian and Resef will want to clear out Irad, and you can give them this information about the conspiracy. The Horses will confirm my word if you let them shift and dress. Perhaps at the jail?"

Though the guards kept Lapwing confined, they also surrounded Tarakh and the Horses during the trip. While a healer saw to Lapwing, the captain gave food and water to the other three, questioning them and searching the lists of known criminals. Then he questioned the pirate, and his stern face grew even grimmer. At the end of the interrogation, he proclaimed Lapwing suspect and ordered him into a cell to wait for trial, not far from the old jailer, a white-haired Darrendrakar, and various other suspicious characters.

When Tarakh left, relief to be free of the high-pitched complaining poured over him like cool water. He walked the siblings to their inn and ordered the bill sent to him as an inadequate thanks. Zinon promised to visit if they were ever in the country again, but Rozali snorted, clasping Tarakh's arm in farewell.

After filling his water bag and buying a large snack, Tarakh headed to his father's agent in the city to see if Mother or Zefra had left a note for him. Mother almost certainly had. Zefra... perhaps. If not, it did not matter. Once he was sure Mother was as well as possible without Father, he would find his red-haired girl and convince her they could have a worthy adventure together.

HOME

(SHORTLY AFTER SPARK OF INTRIGUE)

1. LOST
(ISKRA)

Though most of the world is civilized and beautiful, monsters roam the deep wilds.

A Comprehensive History of the Gods, vol. 2

Dinner would be lizards again, but at least it wasn't rats. The trick was to stretch the two hand-length reptiles into a meal for a dozen people.

Tucker shrugged his wings to ease the ache from a day of aerial scouting and pulled out battered pans. He chopped the meat and the vegetables from caravan stores into small pieces in the frying pan and soaked grains in the large pot, then laid out a tiny fire and lit it with flint and steel. Though used to the smell of the kiziak fires, he still missed the odor of burning wood instead of dried dung-and-desert-grasses. Out here, in the middle of the barren desert, there wasn't so much as a twig. Tucker sometimes dreamed of watching a real wood fire burn to ashes.

More disturbingly, he still dreamed of home. It was a dangerous weakness, when he never knew if someone might be listening to his dreams.

When he came to Iskra, he'd worked his way across hundreds of leagues of desert before reaching the fertile south, learning both Iskrit and trade tongue as he went. After two dozen years, he was comfortable in his new life, but despite his best efforts, he missed home so badly his wings cramped.

For the last ten years, he'd irresistibly — foolishly — crept north again. Tucker touched the bit of wood tied to his belt with a frayed ribbon, polished by decades of his touch. The Iskrins thought he'd paid too much for an expensive name tag instead of settling for metal or even ceramic, if he needed one at all. They didn't realize the simple wood, cheaper than metal where he grew up, was infused with precious memories, the last touch of home he'd ever have.

And if he didn't stop brooding and start cooking, he'd waste the fuel. As Tucker stirred the food, the children of the caravan mistress ran to sit beside him, nearly identical in bright green robes. Kazuki adults wore their clan brown with only touches of the blinding green, but children wore the brighter of the two clan colors so they could be found quickly. Tucker still wore the tan robe with auburn trim from his last job, and the steel-blue belt from the job before that. His aerial scouting was such an advantage for caravans that he had nearly always found one willing to risk hiring an out-dweller.

Now the children's tilted brown eyes stretched wide under their black eyebrows, and their cheeks were flushed pink instead of the usual stark white.

"Did you hear, Tucker?" The boy bubbled with excitement.

"I want to tell him," the girl protested, bouncing on her toes.

The siblings frequently argued but obviously loved each other. Tucker tried so hard to avoid them and the memories they stirred up that he hadn't even learned their names yet, despite being in the caravan for a month now.

"Both of you can tell me." Tucker turned the pot of grains to avoid scorching.

"Another scout crossed paths with a scout from up north," the boy said.

"That scout said the clan war is over," the girl said.

"Good." Tucker stirred the meat and added a bit more oil. It was good, but they hadn't been near the war, anyway.

"Resef himself made them stop fighting," the boy said.

"Can you imagine seeing that?" the girl asked. "Resef, the Most Holy Flame, himself?"

Tucker tried not to wince. He didn't want to see *any* god in person. Gods were nothing but trouble.

Her brother pushed her shoulder. "'Tis not even the best part. The gods fought again, and Irajahan lost and was sent away."

Tucker stopped stirring. Irajahan the Omnipotent had lost? The god of Ioj was gone? He squeezed the wooden tag at his belt, trying to take a deep breath, but his lungs wouldn't expand.

"You're right," the girl said. "That is more exciting."

"I heard it was all because of His Holiness," the boy said. "Ahjin Machol, the Mouth of All the Gods."

Tucker pushed away the twinge of pain at the familiar last name. The Mouth of the Gods would be some old man, irrelevant to him and inconsequential compared to the news.

"Where did Irajahan go?" he asked, redirecting the gossip to the part he desperately needed to know.

The boy leaned forward, hands on his knees. "The other gods stuffed him into a comet and shot him around the sun!"

The girl nodded vigorously. "Now Kassian will be the god of Ioj until Irajahan comes back in a hundred years or a thousand or ten thousand—"

"Stop." Tucker held up both hands, still holding the spoon. "Irajahan is gone, and Kassian is taking over Ioj?" The spoon shook in his fingers, and he dropped it into the pan.

Both children nodded. "Yes," the girl said. "We will hear the story after dinner."

Tucker shook himself and checked his pans. "You may go collect everyone."

The children cheered and darted off, and Tucker put out the fire. If Irajahan was gone, were Tucker's dreams finally safe? Could he even go home?

After dinner, the caravan members leaned against their saddles and gossiped about the new rumor. It seemed to be true, since the northern scout had passed a note from Kassian himself.

The caravan mistress read the scroll. "Though I will divide my time between Ioj and the Dragon Isles, I intend to move all my creatures to a new home in the Isles. From Iskra, I will gather my giant scorpions. I've already sent messages to them. Please do not be alarmed if you see them moving north to Sardad, where they will go by ship to their new home. Leave them alone and they will not harm you. If there is anyone willing to travel with them through the desert or on the ships, please let Resef know."

She put down the scroll and showed everyone a rune stone. "If anyone wants the job, this is a sign for the scorpions to follow the bearer."

Everyone erupted in discussion.

"Giant scorpions? They eat people! Who would be foolish enough to go near them?"

"Yes, let Kassian lead them himself."

"What if they get lost and eat everything in their path?"

"I agree," their leader said. "Guards, you need to keep a careful watch. If we see any scorpions, we will let them pass, or take another way."

Tucker wrapped his arms around his knees and relaxed his wings against the sand. Irajahan was gone. He clutched the wooden tag and nearly choked on hope. He needed an excuse to get closer and ask questions. And that scroll held the answer.

Tucker raised his hand. "I will guide the scorpions. I know the way."

The caravan mistress frowned at him. "You just started your contract with us. Would you abandon us before we even reach our destination?"

"The gods are asking for our help." Tucker winced. Him, helping a god...

She waved her hand. "Someone else can help."

Tucker tried again. "Someone else might be in danger, but the monsters can't touch me when I fly."

"The desert is large, and we are unlikely to cross paths with the scorpions. You will stay." She rolled up the scroll and put it in her saddle bag.

The others stayed up gossiping, but Tucker went to his tent and stared at the ceiling, searching for an argument to persuade the caravan to let him go. The Dragon Isles were fairly close to Ioj, and Sardad was even closer. From either place, he could easily take a ship home.

Home. He could barely remember what it was like. If he went home — if he dared — would anyone remember him?

He dreamed of home even before he fell asleep.

☆🜚🜛◎
〰〰〰〰

For three weeks, the caravan traveled northward without seeing any monsters, to everyone's relief except Tucker's. Late one afternoon, Tucker spotted a group of shadows on the white sand. They were almost as big as horses, but they moved very differently. He waved at the caravan mistress below, then pointed toward the shadows. When he signaled "wait," the caravan pulled into defensive formation.

Tucker flew toward the mysterious shapes, swooping lower but still out of arrow range. As he approached, the black shadows grew more colorful, and soon he could see details.

Dozens of pony-sized scorpions meandered across the desert. Besides the black shells he had expected, there were myriad colors, from brown and cream through blue and red, plain or spotted or striped. And all of them headed on an intersecting course to the caravan.

At top speed, Tucker flew back to the caravan, landing near the leader. "The scorpions are here," he said, "and they're coming this way."

She rubbed her face. "Do we wait for them to pass or try to outrun them?"

Tucker grimaced. "They're pretty fast, and your horses are heavily loaded. If you allow me to leave my contract, I can try to redirect them."

He pressed his elbow against the tag on his belt and wished for a higher power he could trust with his prayers.

She sighed. "Yes, perhaps that would be best. I will hire someone else in the next town. I'm afraid I will not have your pay until after we sell our cargo, though."

Tucker shook his head. "May I send word when I stop?"

"I have an agent in Sardad. That will do." She gave Tucker the rune stone for the scorpions.

Tucker collected the narrow pack that fit between his wings. He'd already thinned his belongings, and the caravan would keep the remnants he left in his saddlebags. Besides the cloak he wore that would double as a blanket, only his knives and staff, a single change of clothes, a fire kit, a small ceramic pot, a waterskin, and a bit of food would go with him. His lone extra was the name tag on the frayed ribbon at his belt.

"Thank you for your service," the caravan mistress said, "and good luck in your future endeavors."

Tucker bowed in his best Iskrin manner, and the entire caravan bowed back.

"Don't get eaten," the young boy said, and his sister elbowed him.

With a laugh, Tucker sprang into the air. Assuming the scorpions didn't eat him — and that seemed unlikely if Kassian said it was safe — he'd see if the new god of Ioj had different views than the old one, or if He was willing to forget the past. And if not, perhaps guiding Kassian's pets home would buy him forgiveness.

Tucker blinked rapidly. He wasn't crying; it was the wind blowing in his eyes.

Within minutes, he reached the swarm of scorpions and landed a short distance away. As the scorpions spread out to face him, he pulled the rune stone from his pocket and tossed it on the sand in front of the closest monster.

While several other arachnids watched Tucker, a red one scuttled to the rune and turned it over with a pincer. It chittered something to its companions, and all of them lowered their venomous tails and looked at Tucker. The red leader slowly approached, stopping each time Tucker flinched, until they were face to face.

The nearly waist-high scorpion bent his legs and bobbed a little, and the arachnids behind him copied the motion. Tucker tilted his head to the side, and the scorpions bobbed again.

Ah, yes. Tucker bowed, extending his wings from beneath his cloak.

At that, the scorpions all chittered and ran closer. Tucker ran several steps backwards and cupped his wings to take off. The red scorpion jerked sideways between him and his companions, and the monsters skidded to a halt.

The red scorpion turned slowly back to Tucker and held out one claw.

No way. Tucker took a deep breath. He would guide the monsters, but there was no way he was touching one. He shook his head and took another step backward but folded his wings to indicate he wouldn't take off.

Big Red waited another minute, then dropped its claw. It took a step west and looked at Tucker, then took a step east and looked again.

Tucker pointed north.

Big Red turned around and chittered loudly, pointing north. A brown-spotted scorpion cowered to the sand and clicked softly. All the monsters turned back to Tucker and bobbed again.

Apparently, it was time to go.

Tucker pointed north again, then spread his wings and launched into the air. After gaining a little height, he circled the group and headed north. Below him, the giant scorpions followed.

To his surprise, though the scorpions walked much slower than he flew, they could keep going all day long, and his stamina became the determining factor. Eventually, they figured out the best way to travel was to let him fly ahead at an easy pace. When he tired, he stopped for a rest and a meal. After flying high enough for them to see him again and make sure they were still going the right direction, he took a second easy flight, then landed and made camp, mounting a flag on his staff for them to find when they got closer.

Hours later, the scorpions would catch up and camp nearby, frequently leaving a gift of dead rabbits or lizards for Tucker's breakfast. Whenever they woke, Tucker turned down the never-ending requests to touch his wings and flew again, happy to be farther from the creepy arachnids.

It took weeks to cross Kazuki territory, and the swarm kept growing as local nests joined Tucker's group. By the time they reached Devora, he had hundreds of giant monsters trailing him. It took nearly as long to cross the shorter farmlands because they had to travel at night to avoid panicking the local populace, but every day, they moved farther north.

North toward the scorpion's new home. North toward Tucker's old home.

He touched the wooden tag. North toward hope.

2. FOUND
(DRAGON ISLES)

Though most people stay in their own country, a few adventurous souls work in foreign lands.
The Visitor's Guide to Ioj, 5th edition.

When Tucker and his hundreds of scorpions arrived at Sardad, they nearly caused riots in the streets despite Kassian's warning. The citizens and visitors ran screaming, and the city guard lowered spears and raised bows in shaking hands.

"They mean you no harm," Tucker shouted. He landed and laid his staff on the ground. First in Iskrit and then in trade tongue, he said, "These are Kassian's creatures, here at his request. We are merely passing through to the docks, from which we will leave for the Dragon Isles. Please do not startle them or try to touch them. You may watch or retreat behind closed doors. They mean you no harm."

He kept repeating it, alternating languages, until the guards put away their weapons and the streets cleared. People hung out windows and through doors, watching and whispering as Tucker led the scorpions along the dusty road.

One guard fell in beside Tucker. "I will show you the way to the docks, and I can assure people they will not be attacked. I think." The young man made a face and straightened his shoulders. "Do you know which ship—"

He glanced behind at the hundreds of giant monsters skittering after them. "Ships, I mean, which ships will transport your, er, group?"

Tucker laughed. "I have no way to talk to them and very few instructions. Here we are in Sardad, and that's all I know."

"Oh." The young guard looked at the scorpions again, then touched his knives before clasping his hands behind his back.

When they reached the docks, he left Tucker with the scorpions and went from ship to ship, talking to captains. While he waited, Tucker removed his pack and shuffled through it for something to eat.

"Here," a girl's voice said, and a delicious-smelling sandwich appeared in front of his nose.

Tucker reached for it before thinking, then remembered his manners. "Thank you, miss," he started in Iskrit, then looked up and discovered a pretty, lavender-haired Nokai holding the sandwich. "Thank you," he repeated in trade tongue, hoping she would understand. His long-practiced Iskrin manners forced his gaze politely away from the white scar that sliced down her cheek past one green eye.

"So, you're with the scorpions," she said, using his native language as she had before without him noticing.

When he stared in shock, she pressed the sandwich into his hands.

"Eat," said. "You won't be ready to leave for a while yet."

He took a bite, and the spicy meat tasted even better than it smelled. After swallowing, he asked, "Are you one of the sailors? How do you speak Iojo?" He didn't ask what sort of shipboard accident had caused her wound.

She laughed. "I know how to sail, but I'm here for you."

His cheeks grew hot.

She laughed again. "You have pretty eyes, but you're old enough to be my dad. I'm here to help you with *them*." She waved at the scorpions.

He took another bite while he searched for a diplomatic way to question her expertise. Finally, he gave up. "And what do you know about scorpions?"

She shrugged. "More than you think and less than I need. But I have one advantage."

She patted his shoulder, and before he could stop her, she walked toward the monsters with a remarkable lack of concern. Tucker winced but couldn't look away. She didn't even draw her knife, and when she reached Big Red, she reached out one hand and waited for it to touch her. Tucker shuddered, folding his wings so tightly they hurt. To his further surprise, she pretended to talk to it in a poor imitation of the clicking that now haunted Tucker's nightmares.

The scorpion made its bouncing bow and chittered at high speed. The two held an apparent conversation for some time, while Tucker tried to decide what sort of scam she was pulling. Perhaps she would ask him for money for her to take over escorting the scorpions. He was inclined to go along with it so he could find a ship to Ioj.

The girl patted Big Red's ugly head and returned to Tucker. "He says you led them well."

Tucker grunted. Since he had no way of verifying what she said, he suspected the compliment was the lead into the scam.

She grinned. "He also says they wouldn't have hurt your wings."

"What—" He gaped at her. How could she have guessed the scorpions' obsession? "You can actually talk to them?"

"Makana gave me the gift of all languages. Have you finished eating?"

Tucker crammed the last bite into his mouth and forced himself to swallow. She clicked at the scorpions and led all of them down the docks. After greeting the captains of four ships next to each other, she divided the monsters and directed each onto one of the ships.

She pointed. "You'll travel with that one, and I'll be there." She pointed again. "I'll swim over from time to time to translate for you, but I've got to help everyone on all four ships." She reached out for a proper Iojif hand-shake. "I'm Nia, by the way. And you are?"

"I'm — Tucker." He fingered the name tag on his belt.

She raised her eyebrows but didn't comment. "Fair winds, Tucker. Go settle in, and I'll see you later. Hurry; the captains want to catch this tide."

Her bare feet pattered on the worn planks as she ran onto her assigned ship behind the last of the scorpions. She hadn't even asked if he planned to continue with the scorpions. But he could get to Ioj from the Dragon Isles almost as easily as from here, and then Kassian would owe him an even bigger favor.

Tucker boarded the ship. He could use all the favors he could get.

As they sailed, Nia swam over every day to interpret for the scorpions. She seemed to spend the minimum time on the other three ships and most of the day on Tucker's, babbling incessantly and staring into his eyes. Nia asked about his family and where he grew up, and of course, he refused to answer. She asked how long he'd been in Iskra and when he was going home. She never stopped asking nosy questions, no matter how many times he ignored her or gave her ridiculous lies for answers. Despite the frustration, he found he couldn't give up the chance to talk in his native language.

Finally, he grew tired of her infatuation. "Look, Nia," he said gently, "please stop flirting with me. You're a young woman, and like you said, I'm old enough to be your father. Be smart; find someone else."

She stared at him, round eyes growing even wider and face scrunching up.

Oh, no, she was going to cry. Tucker winced but held firm.

Then she laughed. Nia leaned against the bulwark for support and laughed until she couldn't breathe. When she slid down to the deck, gasping for air, Tucker walked away.

He wasn't *that* old.

Nia found him an hour later, sitting on the other side of the ship with Big Red.

"I'm sorry," she said. "I thought you knew I already have a beloved. We'll be married as soon as we settle negotiations."

"You do?" Tucker asked. "You will? Isn't marriage a little unusual for a Nokai?"

Nia pursed her lips. "You really don't know? I'm going to marry Ahjin Machol, the Mouth of the Gods."

Tucker ignored the jolt the name gave him again. There was no way an Iojif would marry a Nokai, and if an elderly Mouth of the Gods were actually interested in her, she wouldn't be so happy about it. The real problem was now obvious. Nia wasn't brainless; she was delusional.

"That's nice," he said.

"Yes, isn't it?" She grinned at him and sat on Big Red's shell. "And he has pretty eyes just like yours. He's from Vasi, you know. Have you been to Vasi?"

"A few times."

"Hmm. Not your home town? Ahjin used to be an aerobat, you know, before the whole Mouth of the Gods thing came up. Do you like aerobatics?"

"Sure." Tucker stared at the horizon as painful memories flooded him. He wrapped his wings around himself and pressed a fist to his chest.

"I could introduce you," Nia wheedled.

Tucker turned his head to hide his expression. She was *so* delusional. "That won't be necessary, but thank you for the offer."

Nia sighed. "If you change your mind, let me know."

S ometime in the middle of the third week, the Dragon Isles came into view. Soon, the small fleet pulled up to one of the southern islands and threw down gangplanks. From her ship, Nia led scorpions onto the barren island. Well, it wasn't barren compared to Iskra, but Tucker's heart was beginning to remember his home. He shoved the yearning back behind his ribs and led his contingent of monsters off the ship. Both he and Nia made another trip with the scorpions from the other two ships, then walked inland with the arachnids.

"The colonists will take the middle and northern islands," Nia said. "The spiders are getting the other small island on the other side."

Tucker rubbed his chin. "How does a young girl like you know so much about all this?"

He thought he saw her roll her eyes as she looked away, but when she looked back, the empty-headed look was on her face again.

She smiled. "Oh, I ask a lot of questions. And most people like talking to me. I'm very nice, you know. My beloved would tell you."

Tucker clasped his hands behind his back. "Mmm. I'm sure."

The scorpions needed little help settling in besides a firm discussion about boundaries, which Nia handled. Well before evening, Tucker and Nia were back on board, headed north. This time, she dumped her belongings on his ship and declared, with her witless look, they would be shipmates till the end.

"Why are we going north?" Tucker asked. "I wanted to see if someone will pass near Ioj."

"I already talked to the captain," Nia said, "and he'll be happy to do that next week, if you still want. But first, Kassian arranged a special treat for everyone involved in the relocation of his friends. And since you said you like aerobatics, and you certainly helped with the relocation, you're going with me." She smiled and batted her eyelashes. "If you want, I can introduce you to Kassian himself."

Tucker laughed. Delusional though she was, she was also quite charming.

B y morning, they anchored at one of the northern islands, and Nia dragged Tucker inland, chattering all the while. All day, she led him from one spot to another, telling him improbable stories of shipwreck and fighting pirates with fire mages and famous healers and, of course, the Mouth of All the Gods. Tucker bit his lip and listened to the sweet, ditzy girl babble her lies.

As they walked, she talked to sailors from all over the world in their own languages, and all of them smiled and kissed her cheeks Nokai-style. They listened to her stories with every sign of enjoyment, and after a while, Tucker forgot she believed her crazy tales and merely enjoyed the entertainment.

At dinner, she loaded his plate until it overflowed and pulled him onto a grass mat by the docks.

"Kassian scheduled the best aerobatic troupe in Ioj," she cooed. "I can introduce you after." She batted her eyelashes again.

Tucker laughed. What else could he do in the face of her outrageous claims? "Sure," he said.

She clapped her hands and turned her face upward as the winged troupe sprang into the air.

Tucker couldn't bring himself to watch. For more than twenty-five years, he had avoided reminders of his old life, not daring to even remember in case Irajahan might notice his thoughts and find him. Despite his hope in the face of Irajahan's unexpected departure, Tucker wouldn't have the strength to return to Iskra if he let memories overwhelm him now.

Tomorrow, he must start for Ioj. The trip would take him two weeks by ship, but there weren't enough resting places between here and there to make a flight.

Tucker closed his eyes and tried to ignore the gasps and cheers of the crowd around him. After twenty-five years, it should be easy to wait two more weeks, but it felt like an eternity.

"Oooh," Nia said. "Did you see? They were almost close enough to touch. Aren't they marvelous?"

"Mmm," Tucker said.

"Oh, there you are," Nia said. "Come sit by me and meet my new friend."

She elbowed Tucker, and he reluctantly opened his eyes. On the other side of Nia, he caught a glimpse of curly white hair. A white wing wrapped around her shoulders.

She really did have an Iojif friend. White hair on an Iojif didn't necessarily mean old age; in fact he knew someone — Tucker squelched another bout of homesickness — but he also saw wrinkles. His age might explain Nia's fascination with older men.

"Ahjin, this is my new friend, Tucker. Tucker, Ahjin Machol, the Mouth of All the Gods."

Tucker flinched. Which was worse, meeting Nia's delusion or a distant relative of his former best friend?

On Nia's far side, Ahjin, or whatever his real name was, groaned. "Nia, do you have to do that?"

Nia stuck out her lip and folded her arms. "He didn't believe me. And Ahjin, you should introduce him to your parents. I really think you should."

Ahjin leaned around Nia and, still watching the aerialists, held out his hand. "Just call me Ahjin. Please. Fair winds, Tucker."

Tucker shook his hand numbly. Those weren't wrinkles on his face but scars. Ahjin was definitely young enough to be Nia's friend, though the story of getting married was still unrealistic. Even more shocking, the embroidered crest on the young man's shirt showed the emblems of all five gods. Could Nia have told the truth? Not likely, but her friend might work for the Mouth of the Gods.

This was Tucker's chance to find out if he could go home.

He gathered his courage. "If you don't mind me asking, can you tell me anything about this news of Kassian replacing Irajahan? Is it true?"

Ahjin wrapped his arm and wing around Nia. "Yes. Irajahan is gone, at least for a hundred years. Kassian is taking care of Ioj in his place."

"Is Kassian much like Irajahan?" Would he punish Tucker if he went home?

"Not a bit," Ahjin drawled. "Fortunately. Is there something you are specifically worried about?"

"What about the Presentations?"

Ahjin lowered his wing and looked sideways at Tucker. "Aren't you a little old to worry about that?"

Tucker shrugged and gripped his fingers together until his knuckles turned white. Irajahan never forgot and never forgave.

"Presentation assignments are now merely counseling and suggestions," Ahjin said. "You don't have to take the priests' advice if you don't want to." He flicked a glance at Tucker. "Even for old assignments. One of my cousins quit being a priest, and there's nothing tougher."

Tucker sucked in a breath and buried his head against his knees. He could go home.

Over two decades of loneliness, never daring to make friends in case they talked about him, never mentioning his family, never even safe to *think* about home. Now he could go back. Would anyone still be waiting for him, or had they forgotten him long ago?

A hand patted his shoulder, and when he stopped trembling, he looked up. Nia and Ahjin both watched the show, but Nia still absent-mindedly patted Tucker.

"I have to go." Tucker jumped to his feet. "I have to catch a ship."

"Oh, no." Nia bounced up and pulled on his elbow. "You need to meet Ahjin's parents. Tell him, Ahjin."

"Nia," Ahjin groaned, "let the poor man go." He stood and reached for Nia.

Nia grabbed Ahjin with one hand and Tucker with the other and yanked them around to face each other.

"Ahjin," she ground out between clenched teeth, "introduce him to your parents."

Tucker looked into Ahjin's eyes and gasped. Those were the plum-colored eyes that reflected back at him from every quiet pond. The eyes he shared with his sister — but set in a face that, other than the branching scars, matched his memories of his best friend as much as the curly white hair did.

Tucker couldn't breathe. He pressed a hand to his chest and wavered on his feet.

Nia cursed and dropped Ahjin's arm to wrap both arms around Tucker. "Ahjin!"

Ahjin slipped under Tucker's arm to support him and bellowed, "Lyell!"

In a few seconds, a brown-skinned man with a bouncing black dog at his heels ran to them.

Without giving him a chance to speak, Ahjin barked, "Get my parents. And a healer."

With a startled glance at Tucker, the Darrendrakar darted through the crowd, calling orders. Ahjin and Nia lowered Tucker to the ground and pushed his head between his knees. Still breathless, Tucker grasped for the wooden tag on his belt, trying to pull it free.

"Let me help," Nia said softly. "I'm sorry I didn't tell you earlier. When you thought I was stupid and wouldn't answer my questions, I thought this would be more fun. I didn't think about how you'd feel."

Her small fingers worked the knot loose and pressed the tag and ribbon into his numb hand. Hands touched his back, and healing energy flowed into his lungs. Tucker finally managed a breath, squeezing the tag.

"What's wrong, Ahjin?" a soft voice asked. Tucker almost recognized it.

"What happened?" The gruffer voice was also familiar.

Tucker forced his head up. In front of him, Nia and Ahjin knelt, identical looks of concern on their faces. Behind them were four legs and two pairs of wings, white and pale gold.

Tucker looked higher and higher until he could see their faces. They were different, but not so different he couldn't see the people he remembered in their features. The past whirled back, suffocating him in memories.

"Stand up," Nia urged, and she and Ahjin slid under his arms again and hauled him up.

Ahjin's mother no longer wore pigtails tied with ribbons. Her pale hair was pinned back, but their flying routine had pulled free strands that drifted around her face. Ahjin's father had cropped his white hair so short his curls no longer showed.

Tucker probably didn't match their memories, either, so much older and dressed as an Iskrin with tanned and dry skin. Wordlessly, he held out the wooden name tag to the blonde woman. The frayed plum ribbon dangled limply across his fingers.

"I don't understand," Aria said, though she took the tag. "Tucker," she read.

"Is that your name?" Jayan asked, then lunged for his wife when she staggered.

"Tucker," Aria repeated. "Tucker." She clenched her fist on the tag from his old toy dog and lurched forward to rip his scarf off his hair and stare into his eyes. "Keelin," she sobbed.

Tucker — Keelin once again — somehow raised his arms and tightened them around his sister as his best friend encircled them both with arms and wings.

Aria's tears soaked through Keelin's robe. "Come home, brother."

"I am home," Keelin whispered.

WEDDING

(AFTER SPARK OF INTRIGUE)

1. NIA

(ARUPA)

He who is not impatient is not in love.

Nokai Proverb

As dawn crept through the window in the temple's inner office, Nia danced with impatience. This was the biggest party of the century, but for once, she didn't care. She would rather have skipped the fanfare and gotten married months ago. And considering how long she'd been against marriage altogether, that was a strange thought.

She held up her arms and let Mom pull her dress down over her head, blocking her view of all the ladies who had come to help her prepare for her wedding. The room was full enough that she decided Mom had been right about making the rest of her sisters and Ahjin's cousin, Sufa, wait with the guests.

While Mom laced the low-cut back, Nia's sister, Kala, fussed with the many layers of the annoying skirt.

"I'm so glad they let you wear lavender," Kala said. "Imagine getting married in *orange*."

Her dress, like Mom's, was the typical Nokai bright colors, but the pattern was Mom's latest feather print to honor Ahjin.

Nia sighed. "I know. So many arguments over which Iojif customs to follow and which Nokai, and what to change altogether for the other gods. It's torture." And the torture wouldn't end for a while yet.

Aria closed the fan she'd been examining and furrowed her brows. "Are you unhappy, dear? I know Ahjin tried to compromise."

Her pale blonde hair was already escaping its pins, and her orange dress ended at her knees over cream leggings. The simple cut showed off her athletic build and beautiful wings.

Nia wiggled away from Kala to hug Ahjin's sweet mother. "He did, and I'm not. I don't care about the details. I just want to marry your son, but the stupid details took too long."

"Then hold still while I finish lacing you," Mom ordered.

"We still need to do your hair," Zefra said gently, "and we're running out of time."

Instead of her usual tan robe, she wore cheerful yellow with turquoise accents, and no scarf covered her beautiful red hair. Her sword belt held only a long knife today, but her staff rested in the corner of the office, so, she had solemnly informed Nia, it would be nearby in case of trouble.

Nia forced herself to hold still, though eagerness pulled at her like a cresting wave. Despite the traditional Nokai wedding color, the design was mostly Iojif, with a high bodice that tied in a ribbon around her neck. Fortunately for the nerves of the modest Iojif, the plunging back to accommodate wings she didn't have was covered by her hair. Considering her new scars, she was happy to skip a low bodice, but she had argued with the seamstress until the poor lady agreed to shorten the sleeves to a length considered shocking for a proper church wedding. As if Nokai got married in a church. Nokai rarely married at all! Wasn't that enough of a compromise? Couldn't they just get married and forget everything else?

Kala let go of the skirt's final layer. "Finished."

The fluffy monstrosity was supposed to represent clouds or wind or some such nonsense. It would probably look amazing flying through the air in a normal Iojif wedding, but Nia was stuck on two feet, and all the layers tangled in her legs. If she tried swimming in it, she'd drown. Ahjin had voted with her to let her wear the green silk dress her mother had made two years ago, but they'd both lost.

While Zefra and Mom brushed Nia's hair and braided it in some intricate Iskrin pattern, Nia let herself remember, trying to relax in the middle of the chaos.

After the disaster with the cult seven months ago, she and Ahjin had tried to get married quickly, but it hadn't worked. No one would even talk about the wedding until after the trials of all the conspirators, including Lapwing and the captain who had tortured Ahjin. Winter had ended, the executions and jail sentences had been arranged. Then Kassian insisted his pets needed to be moved to their new home, so Nia had helped with that to speed it up. Ahjin's eighteenth birthday had come and gone, all the giant scorpions and spiders had been relocated, and now summer was almost over. Bad enough to have the first intercultural marriage in living memory and have to work out all the compromises between traditions, but add in Ahjin's status as Mouth of All the Gods and they had a diplomatic nightmare.

Even his proposal showed the first of the cultural clashes. Ahjin had shown up at East Coral Island, dressed his best and with his hair neatly combed and tied back, and asked Nia's Mom and Dad for their permission to marry her. They stared blankly at him, then looked at Nia, who merely shrugged.

"I already said yes," Nia explained.

Mom cleared her throat. "Why are you asking us?"

"Be— because it's customary?" Ahjin stammered. He yanked the tie from his hair and ran his fingers through it until the curls stood on end.

Dad laughed. "Not in Nokailana. If she said yes, that's all you need."

"If it's that important, why didn't you ask them the first time?" Nia asked.

Ahjin rolled his eyes. "We were stranded on an island and didn't know how to get free."

She pursed her lips. "And the second time? Or the third? Or—"

"You said no." He pulled her in for a kiss to stop her from talking, and Mom and Dad laughed.

The real problem hadn't been the casualness of the proposal, which was fine with her, but the time Nia had wasted by not accepting the first — or second, or third, or any earlier time he'd asked. Even after she figured out she loved him, she'd been stuck in the Nokai attitude of dismissing marriage. She'd regretted that for months, starting with Irajahan's terrible suggestion to make the Mouth of the Gods a hereditary position and lasting all through their most recent horrid adventure. When Ahjin had been framed for murder, the situation only got worse.

Nia rubbed the scar running from her shoulder to hip. For a while, she'd been sure they would never have a chance to marry. So she ought to be more forgiving of the complications of arranging the wedding, but by now, she couldn't bear the wait.

"Stop wiggling," Kala said, tugging on her hair, and Nia forced herself still again.

The proposal hadn't been the worst mess. The Houses of both of Ahjin's parents, as well as Nia's clan, all wanted to have a say in the wedding contract the Iojif insisted they make. According to Iojif custom, Ahjin should have provided a dower for Nia, but as Mouth of the Gods, he couldn't own property. Nia said Ahjin was enough for her, and the gods suggested a monetary sum instead of land. Of course, the gods also had demands, including that one of Ahjin and Nia's children must inherit his position, and all of their descendants forevermore would be potential heirs.

It took months, and Nia was ready to kill someone. And then Iojif tradition was for the Houses to negotiate the preliminary contract and have the bride and groom ratify it during the wedding ceremony. Nia threw a fit and said they could sign by themselves, and Ahjin pointed out that no one but the gods had authority over him anymore.

Ahjin and Nia wanted to skip the public announcement, but they woke up one morning and discovered the gods had done it themselves. The whole world knew, and only holding the wedding on the tiny island of Arupa kept their audience manageable. A fleet of international ships had been patrolling the ocean for the last two weeks, keeping out anyone without an invitation.

And that brought them to today, and her current irritation. Nia still didn't know why she and Ahjin couldn't have gotten ready together. The Iojif custom forbidding Ahjin from seeing her on their wedding day before they met in church was stupid, since they'd see each other every day for the rest of their lives.

Now she was stuck dressing in Ahjin's office while guests lined up in the main room of the temple, and Ahjin and his attendants would have to trek through the mud to get here from his house next door. She'd offered to dress in the house, but he pointed out fancy gowns were harder to keep out of the mud, while the men wore boots and trousers, or at least shorter tunics.

"Almost finished," Zefra said, winding two narrow braids in a coronet around Nia's head.

The rest of Nia's hair waved to her hips in the new rainbow stripes that were Ahjin's wedding present to her.

"I wish you hadn't cut it," Kala fretted. "Or dyed it. Imagine your ankle-length lavender blending in with the skirt."

"Hush," Mom said. "She can color it if she wants. I'm sure Makana is flattered at Nia copying her."

Nia was grateful Mom didn't discuss the haircut. After some of Nia's hair had been hacked off in the same attack that scarred her, it had made sense to cut the rest the same length, but she missed the swirl around her ankles. And the new colors might honor Makanavailea by accident, but Nia had chosen them just to have a rainbow in her hair. Ahjin, sweet boy, knew what she liked.

For his gift, she'd replaced his worn-out flying jacket with one he could wear on light duty. She kept the fabric a more neutral pale blue and embroidered his new badge on it in the gods' traditional colors. When he needed to be very formal, he'd still have to wear his ugly regalia, but the jacket was appropriate for casual wear when he was acting as His Holiness. His old one, besides being too damaged for further wear, had been decorated with waves and dolphins and implied favoritism for Makana. He'd been substituting a boring cloak, but it didn't keep him warm when he flew.

Someone knocked on the inner door, and when Zefra opened it a crack, a curly blonde head poked through. Ahjin's little sister waved at her mother and spoke in her native Iojo.

"Neo says almost time. Ready?" Maili looked at Nia and covered her gasp with her tiny hands. "Pretty dress."

"We're almost ready." Aria waved a pale golden wing at Maili. "Is your brother here yet?"

"Nope, just Kee." Maili started through the door, revealing an orange dress even poofier than Nia's. Before she took a second step, webbed hands swooped her back, and the door closed.

"Oh, no, little one," Dad said in trade tongue. "We wait out here."

"Wait," Tala squeaked in Darrendran on the other side of the door.

At least she wasn't playing in her wolf-shape today. Ahjin's father and his chief of staff would be helping him get ready, so it made sense for someone else to watch their little ones before the ceremony.

Nemerra stepped up, quite pregnant and dressed as colorfully as the Nokai but in Darrendran geometric patterns, and set the garland of flowers over Nia's braids. Nia had won the argument over the traditional Iojif veil when she pointed out the customary Nokai flowers would also honor Darravani. The only advantage to the veil would have been hiding her scars, and that would have only lasted a few minutes before she had to unveil. She'd rather have the flowers.

Mom pinned the wreath in place with the gorgeous combs Ahjin had given Nia last year, decorated with flowers made of dozens of tiny, painted seashells.

"You look beautiful." Mom blinked back tears. "Are you ready?"

All the ladies stood, and Aria held out the white feathered fan.

Nia took a deep breath and touched the scar on her cheek. Ludik had spent a long time working on it over the past few months, and it was fainter than it had been, but it wasn't gone. It would never disappear entirely, and she didn't want to shock the crowd. At least it had missed her eye.

"Remember," Nemerra said, "you're not the only one with scars." She tilted her head to reveal her own scars, tooth marks marching down her neck to her shoulder.

Nia took another breath. Ahjin had scars, too, both obvious and hidden, and people stared at him every day. If he could do it, so could she.

She took the fan and gathered her skirt. "I'm ready."

Finally, it was time. Eagerness flushed her skin like cool ocean waves. Just a little longer, and she and Ahjin could be together forever.

Zefra opened the door. A murmur rose and fell, and Dad stepped forward with Maili. His own multi-colored outfit matched Mom's, who took Maili's other hand and started forward, pale blue hair contrasting with his hibiscus-pink. That was one blessing, at least, having Dad at her wedding after he was lost for so long. Nia rubbed her eyes with the back of her hand until Aria handed her a handkerchief.

Kala brushed her persimmon braids behind her shoulders and walked with Zefra and Nemerra on either side. Nia winced a little at the pinkish-orange hair between the red and russet. If nothing else, this wedding was colorful. Aria pushed her gently into the dim room and closed the door behind her obnoxious skirt.

Lyell slipped through the ornate front doors, picked up Tala, who wore a green dress as fluffy as Maili's, and swung the doors wide. Silhouetted in the light of dawn, figures walked through, ending with a familiar shape with slightly flared wings.

Nia's heart took flight, soaring as high as the remembered sight of her beloved in the bright apricot sky. She pressed her shaking hands into her skirt and stepped forward a little faster. Her heartbeats counted off the long seconds still left before she reached him.

As Nia walked toward the middle of the room, candles lit above her. She ignored the crowd of friends and family pressed against the walls and the rest of the wedding party lining up at the far end.

The only person she cared to watch was the young man with white curls and plum-colored eyes who met her in the middle and escorted her toward the gods who would marry them. Every time he blushed, the lightning scars on his face showed white against the pink. Though under strict orders not to speak or touch each other, her hand reached for his before they both forced their unruly fingers to their sides and walked on.

2. AHJIN

(ARUPA)

And thus was changed the policy of the gods from privacy to cooperation with the help of His Holiness.
A Comprehensive History of the Gods, vol. 7

Ahjin glanced sideways at Nia again. She looked even more beautiful than usual, despite the awful dress. Of course, his outfit was no better. The white shirt had only a bit of orange trim, but the pants were bright orange, and so was his fan. The Iojif tradition to honor Irajahan was completely ridiculous under the circumstances, but since the only alternative Ahjin had been offered was wearing his official regalia, he submitted to the orange. Today, he wasn't serving as anyone's priest. Today, he'd be on the other side of the altar.

His hand stretched for Nia's again before he remembered they weren't allowed to touch yet. Bah!

The temple was decorated with streamers — Iojif tradition — and flowers for the Nokai. Resef, the Iskrin god of fire, lit candles as Ahjin and Nia strolled forward. At least Resef could be trusted to keep the flames under control so they didn't catch in the other frills.

If Ahjin had his way, this wedding would have already taken place months ago, with no decorations and no fancy dress. Not for the first time, he regretted his lofty position.

To keep from grabbing Nia's hand, he forced himself to look around. Along the walls, he spotted Nia's large family; the bright yellow wings of his favorite cousin; several representatives from his parents' Houses, including his long-lost uncle; Irajahan's old Typhoon, now Kassian's new chief priest and assistant; and Tarakh and Izo holding the hands of Ludik and Nemerra's children.

At the end of the room, just before the gods, Nia's escorts lined up on one side and Ahjin's on the other. He'd kept his to only four, gently refusing even Tarakh and Izo, who were good friends. This morning, only his father, one friend, his chief of staff, and his unshakeable servant had helped him get ready. Father was now behind him, as Mother flanked Nia. Lyell, Ludik, and Kaito had reached their final positions. Lyell and Kaito looked suitably solemn, but Ludik was winking at Nemerra across the room.

Ahjin glanced at Nia and noticed a bare foot under her skirt. He swallowed a grin. Shoes had definitely been on the list. Three more steps took them right in front of the gods. His parents joined the others along the walls, and Ahjin and Nia faced Kassian.

The eldest god was flanked by Darravani, Resef, and Makanavailea, the gods of the other lands and elements. Irajahan, of course, was absent, and Ahjin tried not to gloat. He much preferred Kassian as the temporary god of Ioj, even though he wasn't their traditional God of Air. And "temporary" would last at least a hundred years, longer than Ahjin would live.

"Welcome, everyone." Kassian's voice echoed off the marble walls. "We are pleased to meet today to marry Niamolenulanami of the East Coral clan and Ahjin Machol of the Machol and Faron Houses." He looked at Ahjin and Nia. "Please face each other."

Ahjin turned and met Nia's brilliant emerald gaze. A smile curved her tempting lips, and pink tinted her perfect golden skin. She never looked more beautiful than when she smiled at him. Heat rushed through his body, as strong as an updraft, and his wings quivered with joy. After more than three years as best friends, they would finally be husband and wife. If he could keep breathing for a few more minutes.

"I will admit this is an odd wedding," Kassian said. "We seldom have marriages between the races, but this one has our personal approval." He waved his hand to include his siblings behind him. "We've done our best to combine traditions and add new elements to reflect this historic occasion. To accommodate Nia's physical abilities, we removed the Iojif sky dance with fans. The bride and groom requested the simplest possible ceremony, so we also moved the Nokai dance and music to after breakfast, as part of the celebration only."

Various sighs of relief or disappointment passed through the crowd. Ahjin was only sorry they hadn't let them out of *carrying* the fans, too. At least they wouldn't be torturing everyone by making them listen to him sing. Nia had promised to sing for him privately, so that was fine.

Kassian smiled and continued. "First, the bride and groom will wash their hands to signify they come to the marriage with clean hearts."

Resef presented a basin of steaming water, and Ahjin and Nia took turns washing.

"Next comes the Iojif contract." Kassian handed a pen to Nia. "Normally, we'd read the entire thing, but that's pretty boring, so we won't bother."

Not just boring, but private. Ahjin didn't think the gods wanted the general public to know some of the terms. Even his parents' House representatives hadn't seen all of it. He took the pen from Nia and signed below her name as Darravani held the contract. The goddess rolled the old-fashioned scroll and tied it with a pretty ribbon, then presented it to Ahjin's father for safe-keeping.

Makana presented Nia with a goblet of water.

As Nia drank, Kassian explained, "Another Nokai tradition says the bride and groom share the same cup, as they will share their lives."

Nia handed the cup to Ahjin, who drank and handed it back to Makana.

Kassian spoke again. "The Iojif wear marriage rings and have an elaborate ceremony that names the winds and honors Irajahan as they put them on for the first time while they pledge themselves. Ahjin and Nia have chosen to recite their own vows as the Nokai do."

Ahjin tugged on his collar. Because Nia had badly wanted them to write their own vows, his awkward thoughts would be exposed to everyone. At least they had timed the cup to wet their throats first.

Nia took a plain gold band from Zefra and reached for Ahjin's hand.

Finally, they could touch. He held her fingers lightly, though he wanted to squeeze them forever.

"Ahjin," Nia said, emerald eyes gleaming, "you are stubborn and contrary, and you play the meanest pranks in the world."

Ahjin raised an eyebrow, and Nia's mouth twitched.

"You are also brave and determined," she continued. "Your boldness brings me adventure; your kindness brings me joy. You are the other half of my orange, completing me in every way and encouraging me to be a better person. I love you. You are my best friend, and I can't bear to live without you."

She held his gaze as she slid the ring onto his finger. "Since marriage is a sacred expression of love, I take you as my husband and give myself to be your wife only, forever and ever."

Ahjin's vision blurred, and he blinked hard. After a minute, a hand tapped his elbow, and Ludik's fingers opened, revealing Nia's ring. On the rare occasions Nokai wed, they didn't mark the union with jewelry or anything else. Nia had agreed to wear an Iojif ring, so Ahjin picked out a circlet of colored gems for her.

He fumbled the ring into his own hand and cleared his throat twice. "Nia, your intelligence and optimism bring color to my life and keep me from being boring. You make everything worthwhile. You are my happiness, my reason for existence. Your love is the warm updraft that lets me fly high enough to reach my dreams. I can hardly believe I get to spend the rest of my life with you. You, my dear best friend, are the only lady for me."

Ahjin slid the ring onto her finger and then surrounded her hand with both of his. "I take you as my wife and give myself to be your husband forever."

Nia smiled at him, and his heart swelled so much he thought his ribs would crack.

All four gods stepped forward and put their hands over Ahjin's and Nia's joined hands. "We, the gods, protect the ones we love," they said. "We honor our creations as Nia and Ahjin pledge their hearts and lives together. May earth support their marriage as it grows stronger through the seasons. May fire warm the love in their hearts. May wind carry them through life safely. May water clean and soothe their relationship, that it may never thirst for love. May the universe give them harmony as they enlarge their souls together. Amen."

The gods let go and stepped back. Ahjin exhaled. It was done. He smiled at Nia and squeezed her hands.

"Now you kiss," Makana prompted.

Nia winked, and Ahjin felt his cheeks heat. Kissing in public hadn't been his idea, but when Nia pulled him forward, he wrapped his arms around her. Her lips were soft under his, and her arms around his neck held him close. He slid his hands under her hair and, to his shock, found skin. When she'd said she was wearing an Iojif dress, he'd assumed they were altering it since she didn't have wings, but her bare back was warm and tantalizing under his hands.

A cheer filled the temple, rattling the stained-glass windows. Ahjin ignored it and pulled Nia a little closer. After a minute, Nia grinned in the middle of the kiss and tapped his shoulder until he let go.

"Later," she whispered, taking his hands and turning to face the crowd.

Ahjin felt himself blush harder.

Kassian's mouth twitched with laughter. "I present Ahjin and Niamo-lenulanami Machol of the East Coral Clan."

At least no one had argued about that. Nokai didn't have family names, so there was no reason she couldn't take Ahjin's, and it was only fair to adopt him into her clan.

Lyell handed Tala to Father and stepped forward. After bowing to the gods, he turned to the guests and motioned toward the front doors. "All of you are invited to a feast in the town square. The bride and groom will stay long enough for everyone to wish them well before they leave."

It was over. Ahjin's grin threatened to split his face. He squeezed Nia's hand — his wife's hand — and let his wings relax. Nia winked at him, smiling just as broadly.

The crowd surged out the double doors, followed by the wedding party. Ahjin and Nia thanked the gods and headed for the doors. When they exited, birds flew from suddenly opened cages, turning the sky into a rainbow of feathers, and the crowd cheered again.

Ahjin had no chance to escape with Nia. She had no wings, and their guests surrounded them with congratulations and compliments. Kaito directed them to chairs at the head table with their parents, then he and Lyell brought them plates stacked with their favorite foods. Ahjin thanked them, then grasped Nia's hand under the table as musicians played in the background and a host of servants catered to the guests and took care of the gifts.

As awkward as it was to eat breakfast with everyone staring at them, it was more embarrassing to deal with the gifts. Some were offered wrapped, to be opened in private, and Ahjin and Nia merely had to thank the giver. Some were presented openly, and then they had to find something praiseworthy to say. The Machol and Faron Houses, for instance, jointly gave them a new crest for their family that included Nokai elements.

The first gift table filled, and a new one had to be brought out. Ahjin swallowed his embarrassment and continued to say thank you. Nia somehow always sounded gracious and flattered instead of awkward, but she was always enthusiastic about everything. It was one of her delightful personality traits. He ran a finger over her hand until she twitched and grasped his hand firmly.

Since Ahjin and Nia had firmly declined the traditional Iojif chivaree, the party dwindled as people ate and spoke to the guests of honor. The more-distantly related guests left first, then the friends and family that had small children or farther to travel.

"You will love marriage," Nemerra promised, hugging Ahjin and then Nia.

Ludik said nothing, but instead of his typical arm clasp, he also embraced them. His eyes shone as he wrapped an arm around Nemerra before letting go to bolt after their four rambunctious cubs and Tala and Maili, whose parents couldn't leave yet.

The next to leave were the young people, who had their own party planned. Kala and most of Nia's siblings swarmed them, teasing and laughing and sharing kisses indiscriminately. Ahjin tried to ignore their shocking comments as he thanked them for coming.

After the Nokai bounced away, Tarakh bowed exquisitely. His eyes twinkled as he congratulated them and asked to visit later.

"Come with Zefra," Nia suggested mischievously.

Tarakh laughed and agreed.

"Do I get a choice in this?" Zefra asked, bowing to Ahjin and Nia and then hugging them.

"No," Izo said. "I will help Tarakh bring you." Her brother pushed her out of the way and bowed to Ahjin, then leaned to kiss Nia's cheeks in Nokai-fashion. "Be happy, Nia."

Nia kissed him back. "You, too, Izo. Remember, invite me to your wedding." With a soft smile, she touched his cheek.

Wordlessly, Ahjin patted his old rival and older friend on the shoulder. How could he even be jealous when he had Nia but Izo had no one? He, too, hoped to attend Izo's wedding someday.

"Hurry," Kala yelled from down the road.

Izo and Tarakh took Zefra's arms and marched her toward the laughing Nokai.

None too soon for Ahjin's tastes, though Nia seemed to be enjoying herself, the other guests departed. Lyell and Kaito piled the gifts into a wagon, and only their parents and a few unobtrusive guards were left.

Alaneo squeezed his long-lost daughter until she squeaked. "Congratulations." He kissed Ahjin on the cheeks in the typical Nokai way, then ruffled his hair.

Aolani kissed both of them. "It seems marriage runs in our family," she teased. "Do you suppose Kala will be next?"

Nia laughed. "I doubt it."

"Come visit us when you can," Aolani said.

She and Alaneo headed for the dock, holding hands, and Ahjin's parents and uncle took their place.

"Since you can't leave without guards, we thought we'd give you as much privacy as possible," Father said. "We're borrowing your yacht and taking Lyell and the girls on a cruise. We'll take Ludik's family with us to connect to their ship home. Lyell already sent most of the workers on vacation. Kaito will leave meals at your door and keep your guards out of the way. The island is yours for a week. Enjoy." He hugged Ahjin and kissed Nia's cheeks.

"We love you both," Mother said, copying Father.

"Congratulations," was all Keelin said, but he embraced both of them and tweaked Nia's nose.

All three of them headed for their house, next to Ahjin's — Ahjin's and Nia's, he reminded himself joyfully. No longer would she have to stay in the Nokai guesthouse down the road.

Ahjin turned to Nia. "Shall we go home?"

She picked up her skirt with both hands. "An excellent idea. I'm dying to get out of this thing."

Ahjin's face burned. "Also an excellent idea."

He put his hand carefully on her back and led her toward home. She talked lightly about the party and their guests, but any replies he tried to make spun from his reach in a whirlwind of happiness.

Their guards followed silently at a distance, and Ahjin pretended they weren't there. When they reached the house, he opened the door for Nia. She led the way to his — their — bedroom and looked at the new additions.

"I like the bigger bed. I see Kaito moved my things over." She opened the closet door to see her clothes, closed it again, then pulled the curtains shut. "Now, will you help me with my laces?"

Nia turned her back to him. She pulled her hair aside and smiled over her shoulder. Golden skin showed to her waist.

Ahjin swallowed hard. "I love you."

He fumbled with the laces at her neck and waist. His fingers tingled as they brushed against her skin, and the scent of flowers wafted to his nose. She smelled as nice as she looked, making his knees weak.

"I love you, too." Nia turned, biting her lip as she held her bodice against her shoulders. "Are you sure you're ready to see all my scars?"

"I bet mine are worse," Ahjin whispered. "Should we compare?"

He unbuttoned his collar and reached for the next button with shaking fingers. He would do anything to make her feel better, even for something so unimportant as a few physical scars. It was the memories he minded, and together, they could replace the nightmares with good dreams.

"Mmm. Never mind. I have a better idea." Nia stood on her toes, lips a mere inch away from his.

A *much* better idea. Ahjin pulled his bride closer for a kiss.

PATIENCE

(AFTER SPARK OF INTRIGUE)

1. HOMECOMING
(DEVORA DISTRICT, ISKRA)

Rarely, an infant is born with red hair, chosen of Resef and able to call fire. Distant legends tell of even fewer adults becoming fire-touched.
Iskrin Culture and History, vol. 3

The afternoon was hot and clear, as always, and even sitting quietly, sweat trickled down her back. Zefra fanned her hem to cool her legs and looked east as if she could see the desert through the tent wall. The winter rains had ended almost a month ago, and Tarakh still had not returned. *Please, Resef, keep him safe.*

But Tarakh not only had to cross hundreds of leagues of desert to take the Darrendrakar siblings back to Sardad, he then had to return home to Chisato. He had probably stayed in Sardad for his horse to recover. If he still did not arrive in another month, then she would look for him. And Rozali and Zinon, of course.

Or perhaps she would go in two weeks.

Like her, Hariskandra Ekorov looked east before turning back to her slate. Though she and her son — and previously her husband — considered themselves farmers, the word was too simplistic for their extensive farmlands and comprehensive delivery networks.

"So," Tarakh's mother said, "that is the current crop situation. Next, we must decide which caravans will fulfill which contracts."

A shout outside cut off the conversation. "Mother! Mother, are you here?"

Hariskandra bolted to her feet so fast she tripped on her embroidered skirt. By the time Zefra helped her get untangled, the shouts were right outside the tent. Sobbing, Hariskandra ran outside like a young girl instead of a stately matron and threw her arms around a dirty fellow in a tattered robe.

After a quick peek to confirm Tarakh had really returned, Zefra ducked back into the tent. Blood buzzing in her ears, she sank to the soft mats and rested her head on her knees, one hand brushing the filigree pin of Irad on her shoulder. *Thank you, Most Holy Flame.*

Outside the tent, a noisy crowd gathered to greet the returning hero. Tarakh's long absence was well known, and though the community had cared for his mother unobtrusively as she took over clan leadership after the recent murder of her esteemed husband, nothing would heal her heart but the presence of her only son. Tarakh's laughing voice wound hoarsely through the greetings.

Against her knees, Zefra smiled. Then she poured a tall glass of water, filled a plate with the pastries Hariskandra had made every week in case Tarakh arrived, and piled the softest mats by the table. When all was prepared, Zefra returned to contemplating her knees.

Perhaps Hariskandra would prefer to finish their work tomorrow and spend the rest of the day with her son. Zefra could sneak out of the tent and leave them alone. She could welcome him back later. This afternoon, perhaps. She wiped her sweaty hands on her robe, and her dowry bracelets jingled. Stupid bracelets. If she did not wear them, the merchants and caravan masters dismissed her scrawny self as a child, but they put ideas into Tarakh's head.

Zefra crammed the bracelets into her pouch. Tomorrow was a better idea. She scribbled a note for Hariskandra, then hid behind the door flap, looking for an opportunity to slip away unseen. Unfortunately, most of the crowd had already dispersed, and the few left provided no cover for her. And then Tarakh slapped the last two on the shoulder and headed for the tent, and her chance was truly gone.

"Mother," Tarakh said, "I want to be back on the road within a week. Unless Zefra left a message with you? Do you know where she went?"

Hariskandra laughed and pulled him close. "Come inside and talk."

Zefra flattened herself against the wall and took a deep breath. This was ridiculous. She was a grown woman. She had faced gods and pirates, hurricanes and deserts, monsters and a deadly maze. How could a pair of dark bronze eyes and a warm smile be more intimidating? Because monsters and murderers could only kill her, but distractions could slay her dreams. With no escape, she straightened her shoulders and clasped her hands behind her back, bracing herself to focus on a job with a caravan.

Just in time, for Hariskandra led Tarakh through the doorway. Zefra's heart pounded at the sight of him, dirty and thin but all in one piece as far as she could see. His mother urged him to sit on the pile of mats, handing him the full cup. Tarakh's gaze fell on Zefra standing in the shadows. He gulped the water and jumped to his feet.

"Zefra! Mother, why did you not tell me?" He dashed around the table and stopped in front of Zefra, eyes wide.

Smiling, Hariskandra popped a spiced treat into her mouth and shrugged.

"I was afraid I must hunt you all across Iskra." Tarakh held out his hands, and after a minute, Zefra put her hands in his. "What are you doing here?" he asked. A grin spread across his very dirty face. "Were you waiting for me?"

Zefra snatched back her hands. "I work for your mother."

Still grinning, Tarakh sat at the table and selected the biggest pastry. "So you will always be around?" He stuffed half the dessert into his mouth and wiggled his eyebrows.

Hariskandra swatted his hand. "Do not flirt with the employees."

He shrugged. "That might be a problem."

Sitting on Hariskandra's side of the table, Zefra retrieved her slate. Steadfastly reading instead of watching Tarakh, she asked, "So, we were discussing the distribution of goods among caravans?"

Hariskandra picked up her own slate. Tarakh sighed and took another pastry, but he offered good advice and grabbed a slate to make his own notes.

After an hour or two of half-hearted analysis, they began to cook dinner.

"Where did you put your horses?" Hariskandra asked while chopping onions.

Tarakh rubbed his hands across his face. "Faith died on the way to Irad. Joy collapsed when I arrived, drawing the attention of the enemy and leading to my capture. Grace...made it over halfway home." His voice cracked, and his mother pulled him into another hug.

Zefra blinked hard, blaming the sting in her eyes on the onions. Poor horses. They had done more than their share and deserved a better fate.

"What about Rozali and Zinon?" she asked, fearing the answer.

The Darrendrakar siblings had carried her faster than she could have imagined, and she could not have saved the gods without their help.

Jaw still tight, Tarakh said, "They're fine. I left them in Sardad to sail home. They asked me to give you their regards. And we caught Lapwing on the way back. He's currently residing in Sardad's fine jail."

"How did you manage that?" Based on his actions in the Dragon Isles, Zefra had expected Lapwing to hide in a dark corner of the world.

"I will tell you the whole story if you tell me why you decided to work for my mother." He picked up the knife and continued slicing the meat.

Besides wanting to know what happened to him, the opportunity to remind him of her plans was timely.

"You know your father offered me a job," Zefra began, "and when I got back from Irad, I took it until I can find something with a caravan."

Tarakh contemplated her with serious eyes. "Is it so bad here?"

Zefra lifted her chin. "No. I'm learning a lot."

Tarakh grinned. "I'm happy to teach you anything you want. We will see a lot of each other."

She nodded, but her stomach clenched. Spending time with him was distracting, and she needed to concentrate on her goals.

At breakfast, Tarakh announced, "I need a new horse." He winked at Zefra. "Want to come with me?"

"I'm sure you do not need my help," she said.

Laying a hand on his heart, Tarakh bowed. "But I enjoy the company."

She frowned at the flirtation but agreed to go. They quickly washed the dishes and headed for the horse corrals on the edge of the market. Zefra trailed Tarakh from one corral to another, looking at every horse before returning to the corral she had marked as the best.

After greeting the merchant, they entered for a closer look. The horses all seemed healthy, even under Zefra's detailed examinations. Tarakh wandered through the herd, stopping by a flashy buckskin.

"Hey, pretty one," he crooned.

The gelding pinned his ears and turned his hindquarters toward Tarakh.

Zefra immediately abandoned a chestnut mare and pulled Tarakh away from the buckskin.

"You do not want this horse," she said.

The merchant, hovering in the background until now, hurried forward with an empty bridle. "No, no, he is an excellent horse. Strong and fast and beautiful, yes?"

Zefra scowled at him. The horse should not be available for purchase until his bad habits were fixed.

"Strong," she agreed, "and ready to kick his new owner through the fence."

"Really?" Tarakh turned away. "Which do you recommend?"

"That one." Zefra pointed at the chestnut mare.

Tarakh looked from one horse to the other. "I would be foolish to ignore your advice."

"But no," the merchant wailed. "The gelding is perfect for you. He matches your clan colors. Think how magnificent you will look together."

"Beauty is nothing but pleasure for the eyes," Tarakh said, watching Zefra instead of the merchant. "I have higher standards."

Remembering when Tarakh suggested beauty was less important than pleasing the heart, Zefra blushed and turned to pet the chestnut. Flirting was only a distraction from her career.

Tarakh untied his purse from his belt. "I will take the mare."

The merchant pulled the gelding forward. "Your friend is too young to know a good horse. This is the one you should buy."

Tarakh walked to the chestnut. "Are you suggesting an Ashvakosha is a poor judge of horses?"

Sputtering, the merchant waved the bridle at Zefra. "Her? But she does not wear Achira colors."

"I'm from the Hotaru branch," Zefra explained, slipping the bridle over the mare's head. "Do you want to sell this horse, or should we buy the excellent sorrel in the next corral?"

"I will sell." Though he still scowled, the merchant held out his hand for payment.

Horse trailing behind, Tarakh and Zefra stopped to buy a saddle and tack.

"I will call her Hope," Tarakh abruptly said, throwing the saddle over his shoulder.

Zefra took the rest of the purchases. "Do you name all your horses after virtues?"

Tarakh grinned. "So far. This one will remind me I still have hope of gaining favor in your eyes."

To her great annoyance, Zefra blushed again. She quickly changed the subject to business.

Each day, Tarakh and Zefra spent hours together. With his mother, they dealt with clan affairs and the Ekorovs' own farming and trading business. After work, they often rode horses or walked through the market. She encouraged him to make more plans, while he tried to distract her with gentle flirting and humorous comments on the merchants or customers or even the cactus in the desert. Eventually, they reached an agreement. For every hour he taught her something useful, she spent an hour with him at a local entertainment or talking about the latest tale from the storytellers.

As she walked through the market with Tarakh a month after his return, someone trimmed in the plum and olive of the Soreka clan squinted at Zefra's shoulder, then grabbed her arm and pulled her to a halt.

Zefra tried to shake him off, but the man held on.

"What is that pin?" the pinch-faced man demanded. "Were you in Irajahan's cult? Guards!"

Tarakh whistled shrilly and waved at someone, who ran through the crowd.

Zefra yanked her arm free and took a two-handed grip on her staff. "I fought against the conspiracy."

She was satisfied for her efforts to pass unknown, not adding to the burden of her legend, but accusing her of being the enemy was unfair.

"Then why do you wear the emblem of Irad?" The man reached for her again, and she blocked him with the staff.

Tarakh stepped sideways out of her fighting space and raised his own staff.

"'Tis Kassian's emblem, not Irajahan's," Zefra insisted. "Leave me alone."

The crowd gathered around them, blocking their escape. If she called flame, how many innocent bystanders might be injured?

"Let us go before the guards arrive," Tarakh said, "and we will not tell them you accosted us."

But already, the Chisato guards were working through the crowd, and Zefra recognized the one in front from the time she called flame on a No-kai to defend herself. Now she had no chance to escape subtly. The guards spread out, encouraging the crowd to disperse while the familiar constable edged between Zefra and her accuser.

"You again." The guard sighed. "What now?"

"This — person — is a conspirator from Irad," the pinch-faced Sorekan shouted. "Arrest her!"

The guard flicked a glance at Zefra's pin, then turned to face the Sorekan. "I see you are a stranger here. Let me give you some advice. Do not accuse our legendary heroes of being conspirators."

"Hero—" the Sorekan spluttered.

Zefra groaned but lowered her staff. "The cult is gone, and Kassian would not care for you insulting his home."

The guard took the man by the arm. "Let me explain. Kezhekori, thank you for your restraint. Warmth to you both." He nodded at Tarakh and Zefra.

As the pinch-faced man was marched toward the city limits, he looked over his shoulder, eyes wide. "Kezhekori?"

"Let us go home," Zefra begged Tarakh, ducking her head to hide from the stares. Every time someone reminded the neighbors who she was, they stared for days before returning to normal.

Tarakh took her arm and chattered loudly about nothing in particular. When they were out of hearing, he lowered his voice. "I'm sorry. I know you hate being a legend." Despite his sincere words, the corner of his mouth twitched with amusement. "I rather like being with a legend."

Zefra pinched his arm, but he did not even twitch.

"Why do you still wear the pin," Tarakh asked, "when it brings you attention you dislike? Do you want to remember your last adventure so badly?"

Blushing furiously, Zefra covered the pin. Wearing the pin was a mistake, but she had gotten in the habit while Tarakh was gone, to remind her she might need to go find him.

Tarakh narrowed his eyes. "No, with that face, 'tis not about the adventure."

"Never mind," she said quickly.

"Not the adventure," he mused. "Not Kassian, surely? No, you're still loyal to Resef."

While he tapped his chin, Zefra frantically asked questions about his mother and his horse and whether his new boots were comfortable. Tarakh ignored them all.

Then his eyes widened. "Is that the pin I found in the street or a different one? Did you keep it because I gave it to you?"

Zefra's face turned to fire, and she pulled the pin from her robe and tossed it at him. "Here, you can have it back."

Even after his return, she kept wearing it for friendship, but she could stop. She turned to stomp away, and he grabbed her hand.

"I think you should keep it," he murmured. One hand still holding hers, he opened her fingers and held the pin above her palm while his dark bronze eyes gazed into hers. "Unless you want me to buy you something you like more?"

Impossibly, she blushed even hotter. Grabbing the pin, she shoved it into her pouch and turned her back.

"I like the person better than the legend." Tarakh patted her shoulder. "My boots are very comfortable, thank you for asking. Hope is also doing well. I mean my horse, of course."

He took her arm again and resumed walking, answering every question she had asked while trying to distract him.

He said nothing more about the pin, even when she tentatively wore it again a week later.

2. WEDDING

(ISKRA AND ARUPA ISLAND)

He who has hope, has everything.
Iskrin Proverb

Three months later, Zefra woke to the realization she was now seventeen years old. As the morning sunlight filtered through the ceiling of her little tent, lighting dust specks like stars, she thought of her family, so far away. Alone, she would have no celebration. No one in Chisato even knew it was her birth anniversary. She dressed slowly and left to eat breakfast with the Ekorovs before starting work like every other day.

When she entered the big tent, Hariskandra and Tarakh were waiting, dressed in their festival clothes. An elaborate breakfast filled the low table, which was decorated with scarlet candles and fresh flowers.

Before dropping the tent flap, Zefra looked outside, but the area was nearly empty. "Are you expecting someone?"

Hariskandra motioned her to a pile of soft mats in front of the table. "It seemed a good day for a feast."

"Last year, I asked Izo when you were born," Tarakh admitted, ears turning pink.

Zefra stopped serving herself delicacies and examined the table. All her favorites were spread in front of her, even the ones she had never mentioned she preferred. Flowers, expensive candles, a special breakfast. All for her.

"Your family sent messages early, and I saved them for you." Tarakh reached behind the large clay water jug and pulled out several slates.

Looking through them, she found letters from everyone in her family. Little Haru had scribbled a note under Usri's letter, her crooked runes wandering all the way to the edge. Even Izo, currently working on a blacksmithing commission on the western edge of Iskra, had a letter in the pile. Tarakh must have requested them months ago.

"Thank you." Zefra took a bite and chewed rapidly to hide the quiver in her lip.

Though she could not be with her family, the letters were the next best option. Happiness filled the cracks sorrow and loneliness had carved in her heart.

After patting her shoulder, Hariskandra filled her own plate. Tarakh reached behind the water jug again and retrieved a stack of packages. Sitting across the table, he handed the first package to Zefra, then grabbed a plate.

"From your parents," he said, wiggling his eyebrows.

The cloth wrapping unfolded to a practical tan scarf, and inside was a new pair of boots, just in time to replace her worn-out pair.

"From your brother." Hariskandra handed her a wooden box the length of her forearm.

Inside were two dozen arrows with razor-sharp heads in various styles. The package from her three little sisters held a leather map case.

"Perfect." Tarakh passed her a smaller package. "This is from me."

Inside was a beautiful map of all the major trade routes, as nice as she could chart but in full color and illustrated with tiny pictures.

"Oh, Tarakh," she breathed. "'Tis beautiful."

He grinned at her, and when she slid the map into the case, Hariskandra handed her a package wrapped in a beautiful turquoise and yellow silk scarf. Inside was an actual book, printed on expensive Iojif paper using their new printing press.

"Iskrin Culture and History." Zefra caressed the smooth leather cover. "I cannot possibly accept this, Hariskandra. It must have cost a fortune."

"Nonsense," Hariskandra said. "Even a great explorer has room for one book, and this will be useful when you travel."

"Now," Tarakh said, "hurry and eat. We're all taking the day off work. You need a little fun in your life."

And from horseback riding to entertainments in the market, they did it all, ending at sundown near a display of fire-juggling. Before falling into bed in happy exhaustion, Zefra wrote a return letter to her family, telling them all about her special day with friends.

☆🐦🐾◉
~~~~~

Near the end of summer, Zefra and Tarakh reunited with her brother and caught a ship to Arupa, the island of the gods, for the wedding of old friends, Ahjin and Nia. Ludik and Nemerra were already there, all the way from Darrendra despite their wiggly children and Nemerra's advanced pregnancy. When the Iskrins disembarked, they were pressed into service in the chaos.

The next morning, everyone rose before dawn. While Tarakh and Izo kept track of four mischievous shape-changing kittens, Zefra helped Nia dress. At sunrise, Ahjin entered the temple, and the wedding began in the presence of the four remaining gods.

Zefra smiled at both her friends, but neither of them spared her a glance. Their attention was completely on each other, so much that Ahjin almost forgot the ring.

What would it be like to have someone love her that much? But despite her colorful new robe of yellow with turquoise trim, she was not beautiful or cheerful like Nia, and she had plans for her life. Mother had been a cartography apprentice with *her* parents until she married, but gave it all up for Father. That might be fine for Mother, but Zefra wanted more.

The gods blessed the happy couple, who leaned in for a kiss. Though most of the guests cheered, Zefra looked politely away, catching the gaze of Tarakh, who bounced one of Ludik's two-year-old daughters on his hip while grasping her brother's hand. After a flirtatious wink, the farmer turned his attention back to the children, holding them tightly as the crowd dispersed.

During the wedding breakfast, Zefra sat between her brother and Tarakh, who competed to see who could fill her plate first from the platters servants offered. After a while, the guests trickled away, and soon there were few left but family. Once the noisy horde of young Nokai bounced down the road, Zefra and her companions made their way to the head table.

After their farewells, Izo and Tarakh dragged her to yet another party, this one thrown by the frivolous Nokai for no reason at all. Worse, they made her dance.

Breathless and exhausted, she finally slipped away for a quiet lunch by herself. Before she truly relaxed, the men were back with news of the turning tide, and they packed and ran for their ride home.

Throwing his bag into a corner of the deck, Izo tossed his sweaty hair from his face. "What a party!"

"I'm so happy for Ahjin and Nia," Zefra said, carefully watching her brother's face. At one time, he had courted Nia himself.

A slight twinge of pain narrowed his eyes, but he kept smiling. "Indeed, so am I. They are a perfect match." He wrapped his arm around her shoulders. "Do not worry about me, sister. Someday I will find an equally perfect woman for me."

Zefra leaned her head on his shoulder. "Someday, if Resef wills. You deserve happiness."

Tarakh leaned on the railing and thoughtfully stared at the lavender waves. In a while, Izo went below deck, and Tarakh turned to face Zefra.

"Everyone deserves happiness. What about yours? Or mine? I think we could be very happy together." He took her hand and smiled so charmingly she could not help smiling back.

"Tarakh," she said, gently pulling back her hand, "I am happy. I have a fine job — for now — and someday, I will fulfill my dreams of exploration. I do not have time to stay home with a family."

He rubbed his chin. "We could compromise."

"You stay home with the children while I travel?" Zefra smiled lightly, though marrying him was unexpectedly more appealing than it had ever been. "What kind of life would that be?"

"Would you consider it?" His smile grew. "I had a different option in mind, though. What if I learned enough to come with you?"

Zefra raised her eyebrows. "With me? You have a business to run and a mother who needs your help."

His plans were impractical, nothing more than wishful thinking. She hardened her resolve and turned partway to watch the ocean swells.

Tarakh ran his hand along the railing, stopping not far from her hand. "Mother can hire someone to help her, and I will visit often."

"I think you underestimate the difficulties," Zefra said.

"I'm no more afraid of hard work than you are."

"I know. But... what if it does not work? I do not want to disappoint you." She did not want to disappoint herself, either. She had worked so hard and waited so long to reach her goals.

Tarakh shrugged. "You would not disappoint me. But until you see that, all I need is a little patience."

And then he changed the subject, but Zefra could almost see his thoughts whirling the entire way home. What would it take to discourage him?

For the next six months, Tarakh spent every spare hour studying maps or taking weapons classes or practicing camp cooking. No matter how hard Zefra made the lessons, he merely took a deep breath, said he only needed a little patience, and tried harder. If she did not have time to teach him or lacked the skill — like cooking — he hired other teachers. Though she had been preparing herself for exploring and caravan work for years, he soon approached her competency in many areas and passed her in camp chores and staff fighting.

The first anniversary of Irajahan's exile passed quietly in Iskra, though Ahjin and Nia's letters told of the extensive celebrations planned across Ioj. Zefra felt a long-forgotten pang, remembering how she had missed her best job offer in order to save the gods and her friends. Despite continuing to search, nothing better than the Ekorovs' employ had turned up since then.

One day, a messenger delivered a letter from her brother. Anticipating a nice chat about his current commission, Zefra opened it with a smile. A few minutes later, she lowered the slate to her knees, eyes wide. Though welcome, the news was equally surprising.

"Is your family well?" Tarakh asked.

She shook her head in wonder. "Izo is getting married. Next month, when the rains are over. I will barely have time to get there." She bowed her head to Hariskandra. "If I may go?"

Tarakh's mother smiled. "Certainly. Whom is he marrying?"

Zefra checked the slate again. "Her name is Kiziah, and she's a Rikatsu. They're getting married on the border."

Tarakh rubbed his chin. "One of our shipping contracts is about to expire, and we need one or two new ones. We could combine business with your family celebration. Would you mind me traveling with you? We will bring another woman for propriety."

"Who am I to stand in the way of your business?" Zefra hoped he meant the shipping contracts. Telling him no over and over was beginning to hurt.

"Accompanying you is a pleasure." He bowed as much as possible from his cross-legged position.

As she returned to her mail, Hariskandra discreetly covered her mouth with her hand, but her eyes crinkled. Face heating, Zefra bowed back.

Her brother was getting married! At least his heart had finally recovered.

"What will you wear?" Hariskandra asked.

"I will buy you a dress," Tarakh offered eagerly.

"You will *not*," Zefra and Hariskandra chorused.

Zefra covered her burning cheeks with her hands.

Hariskandra glared at Tarakh. "I did not raise my son to make improper advances to ladies."

Red crept across Tarakh's face. "I just meant—"

"Stop," Zefra blurted. "I can get my own dress."

Grabbing her staff, she ducked through the doorway and stood outside until her face cooled, reconsidering the entire ridiculous conversation. Behind her, voices argued in whispers.

As she stepped forward, Hariskandra emerged. "May I come with you?" the stately woman asked.

Zefra glanced at the tent, but Tarakh fortunately did not appear. "I do not really need a dress."

Hariskandra hooked her arm through Zefra's elbow and started walking. "I enjoy shopping and pretty dresses," she said. "Tarakh will watch the shop."

Her own dress was Devoran saffron, embroidered at hem, sleeves, and neckline with brown flowers and waving wheat. Though appropriate for a matron, it was flattering and much too expensive for Zefra to copy.

"I can wear my yellow robe," Zefra said. "What would I do with a nice dress *after* the wedding?"

Hariskandra muttered something, then dragged her to the clothing section of the market. "You can consider it a uniform for important meetings." She rifled through the options. "Ah, here we go."

The dress she held up was a softer turquoise than the bright Hotaru shade. After a quick word with the merchant, she hurried Zefra into the tent to try on the dress. Though the long sleeves and high neckline were modest enough, the bodice fit closely, and the skirt hugged her waist and hips before flowing to her ankles.

"You look lovely, dear," Hariskandra said. "So mature."

Zefra felt her face heating again. Though still slender, the last year of good food had made a difference. She now looked like a woman instead of a little girl, and the dress did not mask her figure like her usual robe. 'Twas embarrassing. She looked like a doll instead of an explorer and warrior. How would she even ride a horse in this?

"Never mind," she started, but Hariskandra was already paying the merchant.

Another customer desired to try on clothing, and Hariskandra waved her in over Zefra's protests about changing back into her robe.

"Come along, dear." Hariskandra folded the old robe into a bag and pulled Zefra from the tent. "You can change later."

As they approached home, Tarakh waved. Mid-gesture, his hand froze and his mouth dropped open.

"This was a bad idea," Zefra blurted. She must look even worse than she thought.

She grabbed the bag and turned back. Before she took the third step, Tarakh was by her side.

"You look—"

"I know," Zefra said. "I'm returning it." She never should have let Hariskandra buy the dress.

"No!" He reached for her, then drew back and bowed. "You are beautiful, my lady." He rose, dark bronze eyes shining in the sunlight. "You will outshine your brother's bride."

"That is not the plan," Zefra muttered, but she let Hariskandra lead her home.

His admiration was pleasant, despite her intent to concentrate on work. But the wedding would only last a day, and then everything would go back to normal.

3. IZO

(DEVORA AND HOTARU DISTRICTS, ISKRA)

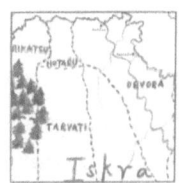

Do not be in a hurry to tie what you cannot untie.

Iskrin Proverb

W ithin three days, Zefra and Tarakh rode west toward her home, with a stableboy and a female clerk. Though Zefra had protested she could take care of the horses and scribe, too, Tarakh wanted her free to learn negotiating and contract-writing. As they rode, Tarakh on Hope and Zefra on a hired gelding, he explained their current business situation and a few vital points for the contract. As usual, though he taught her well, he spent half his time flirting.

Since all four of them were good riders on strong horses, they arrived three days before the wedding instead of just one. Her thirteen-year-old sister Risa spotted them riding in and roused the clan for a noisy welcome. Zefra slipped from her horse into Father's arms, then passed from person to person until her head spun. Her scarf fell off and her sword banged her knees, but she was home. She finally relaxed in Mother's embrace, watching Tarakh laugh as he and their companions were also cheerfully welcomed.

Izo wormed through the crowd, dragging someone behind him with a huge smile. "This is Kiziah," he said, wrapping his arms around her.

She was a pretty young lady, a little taller than Zefra, and she smiled at Izo as if he made the desert sprout trees. Better yet, he looked at her with none of the old heartache, and only happiness beamed from his brown eyes.

"I'm so pleased to meet you." Zefra bowed deeply.

Kiziah pushed at Izo's arms, her dowry bracelets chiming musically. "Let me greet your sister."

Izo only laughed and leaned down to kiss her cheeks. "Zefra does not care."

"She's Kezhekori," Kiziah wailed in a tiny voice.

Izo laughed harder, and so did Tarakh.

Zefra sniffed. "Rude as they are, these lummoxes are correct. I'm not Kezhekori with family." Kiziah still plucked at Izo's hands, so Zefra patted her exposed hair to give the poor lady a chance to escape. "Do you mind showing me where to pitch my tent? I want to wash my face and rebraid my hair."

"Right this way." Kiziah pulled free and led the way to a spot behind Zefra's family tent. "You missed the contract ceremony when we were betrothed," she said, "but my dowry arrived today, and you're welcome to help Izo sort it."

"I will help with anything you like," Zefra promised, anxious for a chance to get to know her new sister despite her still-missing scarf. "Have you already sewn your tents together?"

"Your sisters are working on that with my siblings." Kiziah chattered about the rest of the preparations as they pitched Zefra's tent.

By the time they finished, Izo and Tarakh had set up Tarakh's tent on the other side of the big tent. Her ten-year-old sister Usri brought Zefra's scarf and called them all for dinner.

The next few days passed quickly in the rush of preparations, and the all-important day dawned bright and clear. Zefra dressed in her new turquoise dress and braided her hair in a gleaming coronet. For the wedding, no one wore a scarf, and though she could do nothing about the color, she wanted to look respectable for her brother.

Both clans waited for the bride and groom to emerge from their ceremonial washing and seclusion. Despite the bright holiday colors everyone wore, among the sea of black hair she easily found old friends who had arrived that morning. After greeting those among the guard she recognized, including Kolina and Alemana, Zefra sat cross-legged on the beautiful mats around the wedding canopy to talk to Ahjin and Nia. Ludik was missing.

Unsurprisingly, he had not dragged his family across the ocean for the wedding. Their first litter of four had been joined by three more kittens, and his last letter said Nemerra was pregnant again.

"I'm sorry I have not visited since your wedding," Zefra said.

Ahjin shrugged. "We've all been busy. We got your letters every month, though."

Since he was not officiating today, he wore the casual version of his priestly uniform, with only the embroidered crest on his shirt and the silver star around his neck marking him as the Mouth of All the Gods. The sunlight glowed on his white hair and wings and highlighted the branching lightning scars on his face. Despite his youth, his position made everyone but Zefra's family watch him nervously.

Nia patted Zefra's knee. "You can come whenever you have time." Her lavender hair was caught in combs decorated with flowers made of tiny seashells, then flowed past the gills on her neck and over her green silk dress, puddling around her bare feet. She leaned forward and whispered, "You should at least come for the baby's blessing."

"Ludik's baby?" Zefra asked.

Nia put a hand on her flat stomach and winked at Zefra. She and Ahjin had been married half a year, but it was only the blessing of the gods that allowed an Iojif and a Nokai to have children together at all.

Zefra bent her head in a discreet bow. "Congratulations." Her friends deserved all the happiness in the world.

Ahjin groaned. "I thought we weren't telling anyone yet."

Nia shrugged. "Well, I already wrote to Ludik about attending me in a few months." Rolling her eyes, she held a finger to her lips. "It's a secret, Zefra. Don't tell anyone until Ahjin decides he's ready."

"Nia," Ahjin groaned, pulling on his white curls until they slipped free of the tie at the back of his neck.

His beautiful wife pulled him over for a kiss, and Zefra politely looked away. Across from her, Tarakh caught her gaze and smiled.

"They're coming," someone squealed, and the crowd jumped to their feet.

Hand in hand, Izo and Kiziah approached the canopy. Both wore scarlet robes with black embroidery and beading, but Izo's belt was yellow and turquoise, while Kiziah's was the Rikatsu bronze and lavender. Izo had grown out his hair for the occasion, and their unbraided hair streamed over their shoulders, gleaming blue-black in the sunlight. Their hands and faces were painted with delicate red-brown designs, and an entire row of gold dowry bracelets jingled on each of Kiziah's arms.

Behind them, their parents carried torches lit from each family fire. The procession walked solemnly through the middle of the watching crowd, ending under the canopy. Izo and Kiziah stood on the brocade mat in front of Isvah, the Hotaru priest, and their parents flanked them.

Across from Zefra, her younger sisters squirmed in excitement. Tarakh put a gentle hand on Haru's shoulder until the seven-year-old stood still.

"In Resef's name, I welcome you," Isvah said. "We gather today to celebrate the love of this man and this woman."

Izo and Kiziah bowed to each other and to the priest.

Zefra glanced at her sisters again, and Tarakh caught her eye. His intent gaze was fixed on her instead of the bride and groom.

"Izo Ashvakosha and Kiziah Wataru," Isvah said, "Resef is pleased to bless your union today."

Tarakh continued to watch Zefra. Her heart pounded, and fireflies swarmed in her stomach. She tried to pay attention to her brother's wedding, but she could not look away from the handsome Devoran. A flare of light sparked at the corner of her eye, and the smell of incense rose into the summer sky. Isvah's words faded into a background hum under the weight of Tarakh's gaze.

Izo and Kiziah took turns kneeling to let the other braid their hair and tie it with ribbons in the other's clan colors. Zefra stiffened her quaking knees and stared down Tarakh, feeling like a rabbit in a coyote's gaze.

Izo said his vows in a strong voice, and next to Zefra, Nia sniffled. Kiziah went second, voice sweet and low, and Zefra made a mental note to ask Izo how they decided Kiziah would take his family name instead of the other way around.

All four parents witnessed the vows, and as Isvah started the blessing, Tarakh smiled, gaze still fastened on Zefra. He pressed a hand to his chest and winked. Finally, she managed to look away, straight at Nia, whose lips pressed together with amusement. Ahjin raised an eyebrow, and Zefra focused on her brother, face hot.

To her surprise, the ceremony was already over, and Izo and Kiziah leaned in for their first married kiss. The crowd cheered, and the couple took the torches from their parents and led the way to their new tent site.

The families pitched the new joint tent, and hand in hand, the couple lit their new fire with the old family flames.

On the way to the wedding feast, Tarakh caught up to Zefra. "They are a lovely couple," he said.

"They look very happy," Zefra agreed.

Ahead of them, Ahjin and Nia greeted the bride and groom, and Nia pulled Izo down for a resounding kiss. Ahjin patted Kiziah's shoulder and whispered in her ear, and the lovely woman smoothed her frown, though she took Izo's hand and pulled him onward.

Platters of traditional, symbolic wedding food waited, and Izo had made a tiny steel firefly for each guest. Zefra hung hers around her neck temporarily. Her family beckoned her over, and Risa invited Tarakh to join them, giggling and patting her hair. Ahjin and Nia and their guards soon joined them, and pleasant conversation swirled between bites.

After the younger girls dissected the ceremony, Risa turned to Tarakh. "When are you and Zefra getting married?"

Zefra glared at her, mouth too full to chide her for her rudeness.

Tarakh choked on his drink and barely covered his mouth in time to prevent spraying everyone. He shrugged, still coughing, and Zefra transferred her glare to him.

"Patience," he mumbled.

While he spluttered, Zefra swallowed her mouthful. "We are not."

Her family should know that already. In every letter home, she detailed her progress toward her goals and her frustration at obstacles.

"She didn't mean any harm," Nia said soothingly, "and it's a perfectly normal question."

Hands shaking, Zefra clambered to her feet. "Mind your own affairs. All of you."

She took her plate to the dishwashers, wished Izo and Kiziah well, and found her borrowed gelding in the corral. Hiking her pretty dress to her knees regardless of witnesses, she threw herself into the saddle and pounded across the desert sand. The sounds of the cheerful celebration still carried faintly on the wind, but she dismounted when the tents were out of sight.

Under the hot sun, she reached up to adjust her scarf and found only hair, now curling free of her careful braids. How foolish could she be? No scarf, staff, or sword because of the wedding. Not even any water or a sheltering cloak or a proper robe. *Ashes.* She must go back soon.

Zefra sank to the ground and dropped her head into her hands. But not yet. Not until she could face everyone calmly. She buried her shaking hands in her pretty, useless skirt and took one deep breath after another, staring into the clear apricot sky. How could her family and friends expect her to give up her dreams so easily?

But what about Tarakh's idea of going with her?

Finding a caravan with openings for both of them would be difficult. And what caravan master would hire a guide with children to feed and guard on the way? Her loyalties would be split and untrustworthy. No, her best chance for a career was on her own.

And what if having a family weakened her own resolve? Would she eventually surrender her dreams?

White and blue streaked across the sky, too big for a bird. No, it was Ahjin, circling above her. A few minutes later, another horse trotted into view, with a rider in a brown robe with saffron trim. Zefra pulled her skirt firmly over her knees to her ankles.

Tarakh slowed to a walk, then dismounted Hope to sit nearby. He handed over her scarf and waited for her to wind it around her hair.

"We should not be out here alone," she finally said.

He nodded upward. "Who would disbelieve the word of our chaperone?"

Shading her eyes, Zefra looked up at the white wings turning lazy circles above them. She waved, and Ahjin flipped into a somersault.

When she said nothing more, Tarakh sighed. "I'm sorry I hurt your feelings. I have never hidden my heart from you."

Zefra stared at her turquoise knees. "I cannot do this anymore."

Without speaking, he traced a picture in the sand and rubbed it out. After a moment, he handed her a water pouch. "Do what?"

"The — the flirting, the looks. The marriage proposals. You do not fit into my plans."

"I could adapt," he said softly.

Blinking back tears, she shook her head. Her voice trembled as she explained her reasoning, but she pushed through. From the corner of her eye, she watched sorrow change the landscape of his face into a barren desert and the light die from his eyes. Thankfully, he did not interrupt. As miserable as it was to burn his hopes to ash, it would have been twice as hard to start over. At the end, she hid her shaking hands under her knees, crumpling the beautiful dress so tightly it creased.

After a long moment, he stood. "I understand. We should return before our horses overheat."

He mounted his horse and waited, back turned, while she hiked her skirt to her knees and mounted. Once she kicked her horse into a walk, he moved off, staying always just far enough in front to preserve her modesty.

Neither said anything more the whole way back to camp.

4. HOPE

(DEVORA DISTRICT, ISKRA)

We never know the worth of water till the well is dry.
Iskrin Proverb

After Izo's wedding, Zefra and Tarakh went a little farther west to negotiate the new contracts with the Rikatsu clan. Though courteous as always, he kept his conversations with her to business and practical matters, and he never smiled or flirted.

He started calling his chestnut mare Home instead of Hope, and when the stableboy asked why, Tarakh said only, "Home will have to do."

Zefra said nothing, though she blinked back tears. If she was getting what she wanted, why did her heart ache and her stomach churn?

The longer trip back to Chisato from Rikatsu felt like an eternity instead of six weeks. Tarakh said little beyond the necessary, and Zefra found herself with too much time to think. She had few good friends, and most of them lived far away. For the past year, she had spent more time with Tarakh than anyone else, and now she missed their daily conversations.

Surely he would return to normal in a few weeks, and they could be friends again without the pesky romance.

But they arrived in Chisato still not speaking freely, and Tarakh promptly arranged to handle all the distant business he could find, leaving

Zefra to help Hariskandra. They saw him at meals and on days he had nowhere to go, but those were rare. Zefra could finally concentrate on her job without his constant distractions. He had given her exactly what she asked for, as always.

She should have been pleased. Yet, somehow, she often turned around to tell him something and was still surprised he was gone. She scribbled lists of things to tell him, then hid them in her tent.

Soon, she would find her equilibrium and focus on her tasks and goals.

When she got used to him being gone.

Two months after returning, Zefra got an unexpected message from the caravan master who had offered her employment in Sardad. Though she had canceled at the last minute to race to Irad, it seemed he was willing to give her another chance.

"His caravan is returning north in a couple of months," she read to Hariskandra, "depending on travel. His current guide is getting married and does not want to travel anymore," — exactly why she wanted to avoid entanglements herself — "and he still likes my qualifications. He says he understands why I could not make it last time but hopes circumstances are more favorable now."

"Does he give other details?" Hariskandra asked.

"His caravan travels across many districts," Zefra said, "taking two years per circuit. He planned to talk to me when he returned, but had to send a message to someone else earlier, so he included this note to me. Rather than write back, I should wait to talk to him when he arrives. If I'm otherwise committed, he understands, but he hopes I will be available." She lowered the slate. "It sounds perfect."

"Yes," Tarakh's mother agreed. "All your practice here will be put to good use."

Zefra read through the letter again. "Only two or three months to wait, after a lifetime of preparation."

"I'm so happy for you," Hariskandra said, yet she frowned slightly, and her eyes looked sad. "Do you want to tell Tarakh or should I?"

Oh. Zefra took a deep breath. It would not matter; he barely saw her anymore, anyway. And it would be cowardly to shift the task to his mother.

Still, she had to swallow twice before she could answer. "I will tell him myself."

That night, she waited outside the tent until he came home.

"Bright stars, Zefra," Tarakh said courteously enough, but he sounded weary.

She stepped closer, close enough to catch the way he smelled of the desert wind. "I — I have some news." Zefra bit her lip. This was harder than she expected.

"Not good news, then?" Tarakh asked.

"Oh, no," she hurried. "Great news." And yet her voice dropped nearly to a whisper as she told him of the caravan.

After a moment of silence, Tarakh quietly said, "May Resef make all your dreams come true." He lifted one hand, then dropped it and retreated to his tent.

Zefra watched the distant stars for an hour before she went to bed.

In the following weeks, Tarakh disappeared before breakfast and came back after dark, and Zefra only spotted him occasionally in the distance.

Not long after the message from the caravan master, on the eighteenth anniversary of Zefra's birth, she was not surprised to find a feast spread in the main tent when she arrived for breakfast. Tarakh, however, was absent, and his empty mat taunted her.

After the meal, Hariskandra passed her gifts from her family and a dozen pairs of good stockings from herself. Finally, she handed her a small package, which turned out to be a hand-sized book of Iojif paper, but the pages were blank. The package also included a new pen and a tiny bottle of ink, tightly capped.

"I do not understand," Zefra said. "Did the bookbinder make a mistake?"

Hariskandra smiled sadly. "Tarakh thought you might like to record your travels when you leave us."

But he had not come to give it to her himself. Her stomach clenched and her eyes stung. She would never see him again.

She turned to the first page and discovered a note. "Zefra, Write your own story as you follow your dreams. Do not let the legends define you. Have hope and patience for yourself. Tarakh."

Slowly, she closed the book, squeezing it in both hands before slipping it into her pouch.

Hariskandra cleared her throat. "Well, you are ready. We — I will miss you. Do write to me, please." She rose, patted Zefra on the shoulder, and cleared the dishes from the table.

As they worked on their business for the day, Zefra found herself tracing the outline of the little book in her pouch. "Follow your dreams." She had always dreamed of being an explorer and guide. Everything she wanted was now within her grasp, but somehow, the accomplishment felt hollow. What was wrong with her?

After struggling with the mysterious disappointment all day, she took her place for dinner and turned to ask Tarakh what he thought, but the rug across the table was empty. Despite Hariskandra's expert cooking, the food tasted like ashes in Zefra's mouth.

After washing the dishes and promising Hariskandra she would return before dark, she hired a horse and went for a ride in the desert. Tucking her cloak under her knees, she hunched over the horse's head and set him into a gallop. With her second eyelids closed against the wind streaming through her hair, she tried to clear her mind. For a decade, she had set certain goals and worked to reach them. She had learned every skill she needed and risked her life to prove her capabilities. Her single-minded determination had finally paid off.

She should be ecstatic, and yet, she was not. Why not?

A funny-shaped cactus appeared on the horizon, and Zefra turned with a smile to point it out to Tarakh.

The empty sand at her side echoed her empty heart.

Her smile died. What good were her dreams if she had no one with whom to celebrate?

But how could she give them up?

Before, she had admired Ahjin for accepting the position as Mouth of All the Gods, but she had not considered what it meant for him personally. He had sacrificed not only his own goals, but his privacy, his future choices, and almost his life and love. In the end, he had even promised the service of his descendants for eternity.

Nia had surrendered her cultural norms to be with Ahjin, as well as her own privacy and free time. The giddy girl had steadied into a mature woman despite — or because of — the unwanted responsibility. Ludik had exchanged an occupation he liked for one that carried a high personal cost. Nemerra had nearly forfeited her life to prevent war. Even Tarakh had offered to change his life to follow Zefra.

How had they all been so willing to pay the price? Was Zefra merely too selfish?

The thought stung like sand in a whirlwind.

What made the difference?

She remembered the light shining in her brother's eyes as he looked at his new bride. The same light was in her friends and in the priests who taught of Resef's care for his people. Love was the answer. Either for an individual or a people, all her friends were full of love, and that gave them the strength to make painful choices in order to spare others pain.

The bee stings increased into a whirlwind until Zefra had to dismount to ease her heaving stomach. She *was* selfish, thinking only of what she wanted. Selfish and unloving and unworthy of Tarakh's devotion, who wanted to change his dreams because he loved her. Why he did so was incomprehensible, though she knew it was not because of her non-existent beauty or wealth. Nor was it for her ambition, though he accepted that. Somehow, he saw something in her she could not see in herself.

The funny cactus mocked her on the horizon. Zefra flopped onto the sand, reins clenched in her shaking hands, and laid her head on her knees. As the setting sun bled blue across the apricot sky, she flayed open her heart for a savage examination of herself. What kind of person was she? Who did she want to be, and how could she avoid hurting people? Were her plans so inflexible that they had no room for others?

Tarakh, for whatever reason, loved her enough to honor her choices, laying his happiness at her feet to accept or trod into the sand. What would spare him the most pain? Certainly not marrying him from duty or resignation. If she could not offer her whole heart in return, she should stick to her original goals and leave him alone to heal and love another, like Izo had.

Did she love him enough to marry him? Could she picture a life with him? *Without* him? The thought of him smiling at another woman, bronze eyes lit with love, stabbed at her like cactus spines.

For a long time she wept, until approaching darkness pushed her home before Hariskandra would worry.

After pondering for days, Zefra thought she knew the path that would cause the least pain over a lifetime. She wrote a letter to her father and sent it with her dowry bracelets by the fastest courier she could afford. Each evening after finishing her work, she mended her tent to perfection or wrote letters to her family or sorted through her belongings to determine which would serve best in the coming years.

Her reply from Father arrived six weeks later with the same messenger, faster than she expected. Father had sent a beautiful mare, just old enough to be sold, whose neck arched proudly as she tossed her dark mane and pranced lightly despite her long, hurried journey. Father's letter listed her bloodlines and training and assured Zefra of her suitability and mild temperament. He had even changed the horse's name in the official records to match Zefra's choice. Perhaps by coincidence, though she suspected Father's sense of humor to be at fault, the mare was a gorgeous blood bay, almost the same red as Zefra's own hair.

After thanking the messenger, Zefra brushed the mare until her coat shone and her mane and tail flowed without snarls. The beauty nuzzled her affectionately as she worked. Truly, Father had made an excellent choice. She could only hope her own choice would end as well.

And since Tarakh was home as he so rarely was now, 'twas time. Zefra wiped her sweaty hands on her robe, then thought twice and changed to a clean robe. She polished her boots and oiled her sword and rebraided her hair carefully into a smooth coronet before covering it with her scarf. Once she looked professional, she led the mare to where Tarakh sat under a canopy working on business matters.

"Bright day, Tarakh." She gripped the bridle until her fingers ached, trying to smile and failing.

"Bright day, Zefra." He glanced up from his account ledgers and paused, chalk raised, to examine her from boots to sword to solemn face. After a moment, he swallowed visibly and put down the chalk. "Is this the horse you're taking in the caravan? Is it time already?"

Zefra twisted the lead around her hand, searching for the right words. "Father sent her to me."

"She looks lovely." His jaw tightened. "When do you leave?"

"I—" That had obviously been a poor explanation. She gulped and tried again. "I have always wanted to be an explorer."

Tarakh rubbed his forehead. "I will not keep you from your dream, Zefra."

"I bought this horse with my dowry bracelets."

He sighed. "'Tis sensible to trade something you do not need for something you do."

Zefra patted the mare to give herself time to think. This was not working.

"Are you leaving today?" Tarakh asked.

"I—" Zefra took a deep breath and blurted, "I traded my bracelets for a different dowry. Her name is Patience." Her skin burned so hot she checked her hands to make sure she had not accidentally called flame. "If you want me," she mumbled.

Tarakh stared at her with his mouth hanging open and eyes wide. His body stilled, even his breath. His eyes met hers, but he said nothing.

After what seemed a thousand heartbeats of silence, Zefra buried her face against Patience's glossy hide, her heart broken into pieces smaller than grains of sand. "Never mind."

Tears burned the back of her eyes, and humiliation churned in her stomach. Since Tarakh wanted to travel with her, she thought she could include him in her plans and have more, not less, but it seemed he had already changed his mind.

She cleared her throat twice. "I will tell the caravan master I will take the job."

Turning to go, she bumped into Tarakh, who stood too close for her to move. The sunlight angling under the canopy lit up his dark bronze eyes, and his desert-wind scent flooded her nose. The crumbled grains of her heart spun in a windstorm of misery and loss.

"Let me see if I understand," he said slowly. "This horse is now your dowry?"

Zefra shrugged and blinked away the tears. "I can ride her in the caravan."

Tarakh put one hand on her elbow. "But that was not your first plan?"

She shrugged again.

A slow smile crept across his face. "Because all I needed was Patience? Did you just make a joke?"

She had thought nothing could hurt worse than him not wanting her, but his mockery turned the ashes of her heart into an angry fire. Zefra punched him in the stomach, and he doubled over with a groan. As she stepped past him, he grabbed the arm not leading Patience.

"Stay," he gasped.

She tugged on her sleeve, but he did not let go. Inch by inch, he straightened up.

"Please do not burn me," he whispered, slowly closing his hands on her arms.

Zefra turned her face away, but he pulled her closer and closer until her cheek brushed his chest. His arms crept around her, and when she did not move, they tightened into a firm embrace.

"To make sure I understand," Tarakh said, "did you just ask me to marry you?"

"No," Zefra lied, but her free arm snuck around his back.

Under her ear, his chest shook with silent laughter.

"I accept," he said. "I like the horse." He ran a finger along the mare's bright red shoulder. "Such a nice color."

She pinched his side, and he laughed aloud.

"You do not have to give up the job," he said. "I could come with you. If you want."

Zefra shrugged. "We can talk about it."

He leaned down to whisper in her ear. "If I try to kiss you, will you set me on fire?"

She stepped back and covered her burning cheeks. "Perhaps."

His mouth twitched as he stepped forward and leaned down, caressing one curl escaping over her ear. "I have loved you for years."

Zefra tilted her face toward his. "I love you now."

Tarakh grinned. "Good enough for me."

When their lips met, fire ran through her veins.

THIS IS CLEARLY THE HAPPY ENDING AT
LONG LAST. YAY!

You don't want any more, dear reader?

OF COURSE I DO. BUT WHAT ELSE IS
THERE?

So glad you asked.

I've written another collection of short stories, set in Kaiatan's past. Turn the page for info about **Legends of Kaiatan,** wherein we see what fairy tales would be like on this fantasy world.

LEGENDS OF KAIATAN

You think you know the stories...

12 Dancing Princesses, Snow White, Red Riding Hood, The Frog, The Stonecutter, & more... But what if they didn't happen that way? What if they really occurred on another world and the true tales were lost in the mists of time?

From the world of **Unexpected Heroes**, read the true **Legends of Kaiatan**.

Timeless fairytales have been twisted to seamlessly balance adventure and emotion in this sixth book in the **Unexpected Heroes** *series of clean YA secondary world fantasy. These stories can be read in any order without spoilers.*

Check my website MCLeeBooks for links to buy the next story or get the entire series at once.

Still want more? Get free stories by joining my newsletter. Every two weeks, I chat about my current writing or my life and offer book news and deals. And did I mention free stories? Sign up at MCLeeBooks.com

Free Story: The Cat's Fortune

On another world, so long ago that truth faded into legend, a cat and a boy seek their fortune together.

Orphaned and homeless, young Aktar travels to the city of Rapata for a better life. But it seems the rumors of gold-paved streets are false. Can he find a home and a job before he starves? Maybe with the help of a foundling kitten.

A retelling of Puss in Boots and Dick Whittington, with timeless themes of belonging, courage, and self-

*discovery, set on the fantasy world of Kaiatan, home of the **Unexpected Heroes**.*

Please leave an honest review on any retailer or reader site. Seriously, it would really help me. :)

If you found a typo, you're welcome to report it at mcleebooks.com/report-a-typo/

CHARACTER LIST AND PRONUNCIATION GUIDE

IF YOU ARE INTERESTED IN THE
MEANINGS OF THE NAMES,
PLEASE SEE MCLEEBOOKS.COM

Name (Pronunciation) Identity

<u>People</u>

Agu (AH-goo) Darrendrakar, Maon hunter
Ahjin Machol (AH-jzin MACK-ole) Iojif, Mouth of All the Gods
Alaneokawakani (Alaneo/Kani) (AH-la-NAY-oh-KAH-wah-KAH-nee) No-kai, Nia's dad
Alemana (Ah-leh-MAHN-uh) Nokai, fisherman, later Ahjin's guard
Amrafel (AHM-rah-fell) Iojif, priest in Vasi
Anela (Uh-NEH-luh) Nokai, Alemana and Kolina's crew member
Aolanikalia (Aolani/Lani) (AY-oh-LAHN-ee-kah-LEE-uh) Nokai, Nia's mom
Aria Faron (AH-ree-ah FARE-un) Iojif, Ahjin's mother
Askari (Uh-SCAR-ee) Iskrin, Hotaru clan, guard
Aukai (AWK-eye) Nokai, pirate captain
Chitra (CHIT-ruh) Iskrin, Hotaru clan, Sayaka's older daughter
Crow (CROE) Nickname of Iojif serial killer/pirate captain
Darravani the Omnifarious (DAR-uh-VAHN-ee) Darrendrakar Goddess of Earth
Gurryon Moriko (GURR-yon) Darrendrakar, Ludik's brother
Haider Moriko (HIE-der) Darrendrakar, Ludik's brother

Hariskandra Ekorov (Hahr-is-CAN-druh) Iskrin, Devora clan, Tarakh's mother

Haru Ashvakosha (HAHR-oo) Iskrin, Hotaru clan, Zefra's younger sister

Hesketh Ashvakosha (HESK-eth) Iskrin, Achira clan, horseman, Zefra's father

Heti (HET-ee) Iskrin, Hotaru clan, healer

Hiranya Moriko (Her-AHN-yuh) Darrendrakar, Ludik's younger sister

Hoku (HOE-koo) Nokai, Alemana and Kolina's crew member

Irajahan the Omnipotent (Ear-AH-jzuh-han) Iojif God of Air

Isaura (ISS-ah-ruh) Iojif, Jirish's wife

Isvah (ISS-vuh) Iskrin, Hotaru clan, chief priest

Izo Ashvakosha (EE-zoe) Iskrin, Hotaru clan, Zefra's older brother

Jayan Machol (JZHAY-an) Iojif, Ahjin's father

Jirish (JZHIR-ish) Iojif, priest in Vasi

Kaimana (KAY-mah-nuh) Nokai, Lani's childhood friend

Kaito (KAY-toe) Darrendrakar, seal

Kalalamoanani (Kah-LA-la-moe-uh-NAHN-ee or KAH-la) Nokai, Nia's older near-sister

Kassian (KASS-ee-an) Eldest god, architect of world

Keahi (Kee-AH-hee) Iskrin, Hotaru clan, Sayaka's younger daughter

Keelin Faron (KEE-lin) Iojif, Aria's brother

Kiziah Wataru (KIZZ-ee-uh What-ARE-oo) Iskrin, Rikatsu clan, Izo's bride

Kolina (Koe-LEEN-uh) Nokai, fisher, later Ahjin's guard

Koray (CORE-ay) Iskrin, Rikatsu clan, healer

Krevan (KREV-un) Darrendrakar, Fox from Kairri

Lapwing (LAP-wing) Nickname of Crow's former first mate

Lelei (Leh-LAY) Nokai, healer

Ludik Moriko (LUD-ick) Darrendrakar, hunter

Lyell Ulriksin (LIE-el UL-rick-sin) Darrendrakar wolf, Ahjin's chief of staff

Madden (MAD-dun) Darrendrakar, forester Fox

Madigan (MAD-uh-gun) Darrendrakar, Dingo from Kairri

Maili Machol (MAY-lee) Iojif, Ahjin's younger sister

Makanavailea the Omniscient (Mah-KAHN-uh-vie-LEE-uh) Nokai Goddess of Water

Manuai (MAHN-oo-aye) Nokai, Lani's friend

Nemerra (Neh-MERR-uh) Darrendrakar, Ludik's wife

Niamolenulanami (NEE-ah-moe-LEN-noo-la-NAHM-ee) Nokai, singer
Okechuku (OH-keh-CHOO-koo) Iskrin, Tukiko clan, healer
Pillan (PILL-un) Tempest priest in Ioj
Prathap (PRATH-up) Iskrin, Hotaru clan, chieftain
Rada (RAH-duh) Iskrin, Soreka clan, priest applicant
Razi Ruchi (RAH-zee) Iskrin, Hotaru clan, Sayaka's son
Resef the Omnificent (RES-eff) Iskrin God of Fire
Risa Ashvakosha (REE-suh) Iskrin, Hotaru clan, Zefra's younger sister
Rozali (Roe-ZALL-ee) Darrendrakar, Horse spy
Sayaka Ruchi (Sae-YAHK-uh RUE-chee) Iskrin, Hotaru clan, guard
Sefu (SEFF-oo) Iojif, priest in Mura
Shankhi (SHAHN-kee) Darrendrakar in Kairri
Shara Kaniyar (SHAR-uh CAN-ih-yar) Iskrin, Hotaru clan, mapmaker's
apprentice, Zefra's mother
Sparrow (SPARE-roe) Iojif, Amrafel's nickname for a priest
Sufa Faron (SUE-fuh) Iojif, released priestess, Ahjin's distant cousin on
mother's side
Surahava (SUHR-uh-HAH-uh) Iojif, daughter of Jirish and Isaura, Ahjin's
grandmother
Tala Lyelldin (TALL-uh LIE-ul-din) Darrendrakar, Lyell's daughter
Tarakh Ekorov (Tah-ROCK ECK-uh-rov) Iskrin, Devora clan, farmer
Tucker (TUCK-ur) Iojif, exile in Iskra
Usri Ashvakosha (OOS-ree) Iskrin, Hotaru clan, Zefra's younger sister
Varin (VAHR-un) Darrendrakar in Kairri
Vasu Ruchi (VAH-soo) Iskrin, Hotaru clan, Sayaka's husband
Zefra Ashvakosha Kezhekori (ZEF-ruh ASH-vah-KOASH-uh KEZ-eh-
KORE-ee) Iskrin, Hotaru clan, guide
Zerach (ZEH-rack) Iskrin, Chiharu clan, priest applicant
Zinon (ZINE-un) Darrendrakar, Horse spy

Groups, Locations, Languages

Achira (Uh-CHEER-uh) Iskrin clan, specialty: horses
Alekona (Al-eh-KONE-uh) Capital city of Nokailana
Arupa (Uh-ROOP-uh) Isle of the Gods
Chisato (Chih-SAT-oe) Largest city in Devora, Iskra
Darrendra (Duh-RREND-druh) Northern country

Darrendrakar (Duh-RREND-druh-car) People of Darrendra, shapeshifters
Darrendran (Duh-RREND-drun) Darrendrakar language
Devora (Dev-OH-ruh) Iskrin clan, specialty: grain
Dragon Isles Islands between Nokailana and Darrendra
Durriel (DUHRR-ee-ell) Canid village
East Coral Island Farthest occupied island in Nokailana
Heresa (Herr-ESS-uh) Iskrin clan, speciality: gems, precious metals
Hotaru (Hoe-TARE-oo) Iskrin tribe, specialty: maps
Ioj (EYE-ojze) Eastern country
Iojif (Eye-OH-jziff) People of Ioj, avians
Iojo (Eye-OH-jzo) Iojif language
Irad (EYE-rad) Lost city of gods
Iskra(ISK-ruh) Southern country
Iskrin (ISK-ree)People of Iskra, desert-dwellers
Iskrit (ISK-rit) Iskrin language
Kairri (KERR-ree) Village in Canid tribe
Kazuki (Kuh-ZOO-kee) Iskran clan, speciality: spices
Mura (MURR-uh) Tiny northern village in Ioj
Nokai (NO-kie) People of Nokailana, aquastrians
Nokailana (NO-kie-LAHN-uh) Western islands
Noki (NO-kee) Nokai language
Rikatsu (Rick-AT-soo) Iskrin clan, speciality: ships
Sardad (SAHR-dad) Medium-sized city in Devora, Iskra
Saverio (Suh-VERR-ee-oh) Smallish city in southern Ioj
Shark Island Nokailana, one island west of East Coral Island
Soreka (Sore-AKE-uh) Iskrin clan, speciality: fruits, wine
Tarvati (Tar-VAHT-ee) Iskrin clan, speciality: glass
Tetsuya (Tet-SOO-yuh) Iskrin clan, specialty: weapons & metalwork
Tukiko (Too-KEE-koe) Iskrin clan, speciality: healing
Vasi (VAHS-ee) Capital of Ioj

ACKNOWLEDGMENTS

Special thanks to my Day Group: Carol Malone, Donna Gonzales, and Gail Porter, for their excellent advice,

and to my extraordinary alpha and beta readers who read almost every story: Becky James, Laura Drake, Lea Carter, Matt Peel, Molly Morrison, Naomi Miller, Robin Cranney, and Virginia Cummings.

Thanks also to my beta readers who gave me feedback on least one story: Alex Albulbanat, Amanda Iverson, Bill Feline, Brenna Jardine, Carrie Snider, Cheree Myatt, Chris Cornetto, Chris Weston, Christen Faulkenberry, Daniel Cerga, Jennifer Cote, Joanna Fischer, Leisl Roberts, Liz Nix, Maria Farb, Nikki Rush, Parul Sha, Rachel Perez, Rebecca Lommers, Ruth Morley, Samantha Mueller, Shoshana Edwards, Sue McKerns, Sumbul Shahin, and Trisha Conlin.

ABOUT THE AUTHOR

Marty C. Lee told stories for most of her life, but never took them seriously until her daughter asked her to write this one. Between writing and spending time with her family, she reads, embroiders, paints-by-number, and gardens.

She has lived in five states, seven cities, and ten houses so far. She currently lives in the West, but not in a tropical paradise. She doesn't like flying, even in an airplane. She wishes she could produce her own fire to warm her hands. She's glad she didn't have to wait a year to marry her sweetheart, who also wishes she could warm her hands.

You can find her at
MCLeeBooks.com and on Facebook and book sites